Dear Cathe,

Thanks for your interest in poker... You're one of the nicest poker people I've ever met. It's been a joy knowing you. I'm glad we didn't play at the same limits— I wouldn't have wanted to win all your money (ha.)

Sincerely
"BB" 424) 241 3717

THE
FREE LUNCH
BUNCH

THERE'S NO SUCH THING AS A FREE LUNCH

BRUCE BROWN

BookBaby Publishing

BookBaby Publishing Bookshop at store.bookbaby.com

DEDICATION

Cameron and McLane Brown

Sons' order determined neither alphabetically nor chronologically but by their coin flip.

INTRO

Publishing standards impelled me to prune around fifty thousand words concerning interesting anecdotes, observations, and characters; moreover, my anecdotal masterpiece is long enough that I did not want to detail my corporate world or home game experiences. Brevity won out over giving more details. This book is really about the poker milieu and any lessons gleaned. I ever so humbly profess that I was a rare, poker, success story. Although my last name is Brown, some of book is blue.

ACKNOWLEDGMENTS

The late Dr. JBahr for fifty years of friendship and support and researching a cool tool to facilitate my writing. (Lamentably, he passed before writing a blurb which would have been hilarious.)

Peter Rumsey, a Houdini of hardware and a Sherlock Holmes of solving infuriating computer glitches, malware mysteries and other problems. For keeping my computer humming and running and happier than puppies at a dog park.

Sears for many educational discussions and his generous friendship.

Chris "Tozzi" Pierantozzi for his first-rate marketing ideas and flyer.

Monet Stalle-Davis for oenophilic taste.

Daniele, "Betty Boop" Meadows for perspectives from the distant, strange land of the female mind, and hilarious verbal jousts and arguments.

Curtis Brown, Ltd. for permission to use Ogden Nash's "The Wasp."

Finally, editor A.E. Williams for his editing, creativity, invaluable ideas and gracious pre-publication aid.

TABLE OF CONTENTS

The Free Lunch Bunch

A Parable

There once was a young king who wanted to know the meaning of life. He assembled wise men and women from the realm and charged them to study all knowledge and compile it for him to read. After years, they produced a magnificent set of fifty volumes and presented this to him with great pomp and celebration. Though somewhat pleased, the king saw that he would never have time, patience, or memory to absorb it all. He instructed them to reduce the number of books.

After five years, the academics and philosophers culled their findings to ten volumes. They offered these with less ceremony. Once again, the king realized this was too much. He sent them back to work boiling down the knowledge. Three more years passed, and the researchers were proud to present him with one volume. Still unsatisfied, he commanded them to reduce this even more. After arguments and struggles among themselves, the scholars condensed their work to one page. With great hope and trepidation, they presented the king their work.

But the sovereign shook his head, and back to the grind they sullenly went. Months later they presented him with one paragraph.

"No, no," the king said. "It must be reduced to just the essence. Bring me the bare essential lesson of life."

Wearily, they returned with one sentence: *There ain't no free lunch.*

Today the Free Lunch Bunch and I need to learn this.

1
Gambling Called Collect

I'm JM.

Gambling called me as a young man, and I answered. I recall my early playing days encountering a smorgasbord of Runyonesque poker characters in Southern California. One was "Old Man" Carroll, who claimed to be 104, hustled at poker, and held court on the rail—an elevated waiting area encircling the playing floor. He'd regale his audience, like *El Presidente*, waving a Cohiba Espléndidos cigar about the diameter of a fungo, "Well, boys, I remember back in Chicago when I was running numbers for Alphonse Capone ..."

One time he sat on his unlit see-gar and broke it in half. Undeterred, he asked a chip runner to get him some tape, and he tried, unsuccessfully, to smoke the bandaged, hand-rolled leaves. As he told us with a toothless grin, "They are made best when rolled on a virgin's thigh."

Another time he screamed, "Ow! My balls. My balls are on fire!" after he spilled a pot of scalding water onto his lap.

Everyone who heard his yelps turned to see what the commotion was about, and then laughed. Because of his age and demeanor, Old Man Carroll got away with a great deal of unacceptable behavior; consequently, he had no qualms taking his wool slacks off, revealing a pair of spindly, very white, bowed-legs, and his knee-length, magenta skivvies. It was only natural that he wanted to let his slacks dry, so he gave them to the porter to dry. What a sight! Players were coughing liquids from their noses, choking on, or expelling food, slapping neighbors on the back, and roaring. Staff standing nearby doubled over, gasping for air. At least none of the gentile, I mean genteel, women fainted. When things returned to order, the Floor man asked him to put his pants back on. Old Man Carroll gleefully, but defiantly, refused. So, there he sat with a gold-colored napkin tucked into his shorts, the colors reflecting an emerging nation's flag. Since everyone was having such a great time, the Floor man wisely compromised that Carroll could play so long as he continued wearing the napkin. Most astounding? No one complained. For you see, as Michael Weisenberg notes in *Card Player Magazine* (10.18.1996), "... Players like complaining better than almost any other aspect of the game."

Another memorable habitué was Nicky "The Greek" from ... you know. He had a bulbous, vein-thatched nose (visualize W. C. Fields) with a small cleft in the tip. He wore his thinning gray hair combed straight around a balding landing strip. He had a deep, raspy voice and always wore a suit. His family supposedly owned a hotel in a small fishing village on the Aegean Sea.

A Floor man, Charlie Sepulveda, told me about the notoriously frugal Nicky. Charlie said, "In all the years I've known him, he's never toked me. So, I was shocked one night when I passed his table, and he handed me a $5 check [*chip*]. Here, Charlie, take this."

I said, "That's okay, Nicky."

"No, take it!" he insisted.

Then I hear someone at the table shout, "Put that chip back in the pot!"

Another Floor man told me that The Greek once gave him a toke wrapped in tin foil. The Floor person made a fist, a universal, poker thanks sign. Opening the wrapper later, he found a check-sized Melba cracker in it.

The Greek had a delightful sense of humor. "Yeah, da las time I gava this much action was back in 1936. I'd only been America two weeks and didn't know any betta. I played like I hadda million in da bank. Now I gotta

job and get paid weekly—very weakly." "This game is
some chips is like tryna to pulla tooth from a hillbill
pay more than $2,000 a month in collections *Never.* (
pre-paid sum to play for the next thirty minutes. $2000 w
impossible amount for the limits we played)

How would he handle adversity?

"I can't believe Imma stuck in this game with seven idiots." He once folded a hand that would have been the winner of a $200 pot. We could tell that he was steaming, as anyone would. When he returned from a ten-minute walk, he said, "That's okay. I tooka nice long walk. I gotta plenny of fresh air. Wassa good for me."

His pearls were almost on par with the master of poker epigrams, "Amarillo Slim" Preston who won $80,000 in the 1972 World Series of Poker (WSOP). Amarillo Slim had a lot to say about a lot of things.

Looks: "You're as pretty as a spotted pup in a red wagon on Christmas mom," and "I'm so skinny I look like the advance man for famine."

People's traits: "There're more horses' arses than horses," and "That boy is as light as June frost in Texas," and "He can't track an elephant in four feet of snow," and "Warmer than a widow's love."

Losers, underdogs, suckers: "You can shear a sheep many a time, but you can skin 'em only once," and "Very seldom do the lambs slaughter the butcher."

And his signature poker aphorism: "Not all trappers wear fur hats." At the risk of stating the obvious, these last two pertain to setting up an opponent to believe they have the best hand, and, thus, allowing the opponent to lose a lot, if not all, their money when the trapdoor is opened.

This is anonymous, but it certainly seems like "Slim": "He wins (eats) like a chicken but loses (sh*ts) like an elephant."

2

All In!

THESE PLEASANT, HUMOROUS MEMORIES flashed for a second after I say in a firm voice, "All in!" My fate is sealed. I can't change my mind.

The dealer repeats, "All in."

I carefully slide my stacks forward, trying not to topple them like a pile of tiny plates. I am deathly afraid that if I look clumsy and unconfident, my opponent will perceive it as a tell. My mouth is as dry as Albert Brooks' humor and feels stuffed with sawdust. I'm positive my opponent can hear my heart lub-dubbing.

After shoving, time stands still! How'd I get here? How did I reach this point where my adversary's calling or folding decision affects the rest of my life? I didn't start my life planning to end here in a casino, with my future dependent on another person's decision.

← (We're going back in time)

job and get paid weekly—very weakly." "This game is so tight, tryna to win some chips is like tryna to pulla tooth from a hillbilly's mouth." "I never pay more than $2,000 a month in collections *Never.*" (Collections were a pre-paid sum to play for the next thirty minutes. $2000 would be an almost impossible amount for the limits we played)

How would he handle adversity?

"I can't believe Imma stuck in this game with seven idiots." He once folded a hand that would have been the winner of a $200 pot. We could tell that he was steaming, as anyone would. When he returned from a ten-minute walk, he said, "That's okay. I tooka nice long walk. I gotta plenny of fresh air. Wassa good for me."

His pearls were almost on par with the master of poker epigrams, "Amarillo Slim" Preston who won $80,000 in the 1972 World Series of Poker (WSOP). Amarillo Slim had a lot to say about a lot of things.

Looks: "You're as pretty as a spotted pup in a red wagon on Christmas mom," and "I'm so skinny I look like the advance man for famine."

People's traits: "There're more horses' arses than horses," and "That boy is as light as June frost in Texas," and "He can't track an elephant in four feet of snow," and "Warmer than a widow's love."

Losers, underdogs, suckers: "You can shear a sheep many a time, but you can skin 'em only once," and "Very seldom do the lambs slaughter the butcher."

And his signature poker aphorism: "Not all trappers wear fur hats." At the risk of stating the obvious, these last two pertain to setting up an opponent to believe they have the best hand, and, thus, allowing the opponent to lose a lot, if not all, their money when the trapdoor is opened.

This is anonymous, but it certainly seems like "Slim": "He wins (eats) like a chicken but loses (sh*ts) like an elephant."

2
All In!

THESE PLEASANT, HUMOROUS MEMORIES flashed for a second after I say in a firm voice, "All in!" My fate is sealed. I can't change my mind.

The dealer repeats, "All in."

I carefully slide my stacks forward, trying not to topple them like a pile of tiny plates. I am deathly afraid that if I look clumsy and unconfident, my opponent will perceive it as a tell. My mouth is as dry as Albert Brooks' humor and feels stuffed with sawdust. I'm positive my opponent can hear my heart lub-dubbing.

After shoving, time stands still! How'd I get here? How did I reach this point where my adversary's calling or folding decision affects the rest of my life? I didn't start my life planning to end here in a casino, with my future dependent on another person's decision.

← (We're going back in time)

3

A Gambler's Youth

I HAD A SINGLE mom who had to put me in temporary foster care for much of my youth, because she worked nights. I got to live with her during weekends and parts of summers. We were as poor as cross-eyed pickpockets. So poor that we couldn't afford to use a word like *penurious*. A slight exaggeration, perhaps, but the Dickens kids in *Oliver Twist* would have been my rich cousins.

I remember when mom had to buy an iron on layaway. For God's sake, we're talking about an iron! Now we put things on a credit card and pay the devil later. Back then, a dime was a treasure, and it was worth bending over to pick up a penny. In the years since, I've had a revelation: You can take the child out of poverty, but you cannot take the poverty out of the adult. Look at "The Great" Gatsby. I might have had an abnormal childhood, but does anyone really consider their growing up normal? Mussolini probably was the mozzarella of his mother's eye.

In junior high school, Jer, my best friend, and I gambled for small stakes. However, after he had some painful losses to me—up to $1.50—we stopped gambling with each other. I guess we were mature enough, even in our preteens, to understand that if one gambles, one must accept the consequences. There are some adults who haven't learned this. Or they cannot take it to heart. One must pay the piper, so to speak, and any Pied Piper might be one who lures youth to a land of dark chance.

Continuing our *hegira*, I dropped out of college and joined the service. My food, lodging, clothing, travel, and education were provided by the government. What could be sweeter than having all of one's necessities paid for? Having by now read and absorbed a book that a steady winner in college recommended, Herbert Yardley's *The Education of a Poker Player*, I was a huge favorite and winner in poker games. Free money. So sweet!

$$$

After the service, I re-enrolled in college. Before I landed a job after college, as luck would have it, I found the card clubs of Southern California. One of my college friends suggested, "Let's go to Gardena."

I gravitated toward these casinos like a homing ... nocturnal pigeon. Oh, I suppose a bat. Also, it was like a black hole pulling me with a dark, unseen force. For a naive, almost farm-bred boy, I entered a bright, plush, dazzling festive environment, and gambling there was like being in high school and going to an exciting, glitzy carnival on a first date. At least it seemed that way in the beginning.

I even bought and read a book by Frank R. Wallace, PhD, called *POKER, A Guaranteed Income for Life by using the ADVANCED CONCEPTS OF POKER*. Opposite the title page the author put this inscription by Eric Flame, the main character in one of Wallace's novels:

Rational selfishness—man's greatest virtue.

Through it, greed grows beautiful; life becomes joyful.

Serve only the highest cause—man the individual—you.

While Wallace's concepts mostly apply to home—not casino—games, the winning strategies and manipulative concepts are applicable to casinos. But his message is so venal and craven like Libertarian Ayn Rand's. And Ol' Gordon Gecko's "Greed is good" mantra couldn't have spewed it better.

I befriended a kindly older man, a Normandie regular it turned out, named Jack. He took a liking to me, and me to him. He became my cicerone and mentor. One night, months later, he shocked me when he said, "I hope you lose your ass." This caught me so off guard, was such an incongruity that I felt sucker punched in the gut.

"Jack, why on earth are you saying that? I thought we were friends."

"Son, if you lose your ass in the beginning, maybe you won't come back."

"Why don't you want me to come back?"

"I've seen so many things. So many waste their time and money here. There's no upside, only down. I've lost my business, my sailboat, *Jack's or Better*, my home and wife among other things."

It turned out he lost his health, too, but that was mostly from smoking.

"This is no life. It's a dead-end," he ruefully concluded.

How true. It became apparent that new players who won in the beginning came back for more. Moreover, if the novice—despite his or her lack of knowledge, skill, or who utilized normally unprofitable play—went on a winning streak, that just encouraged them to continue with that ultimately ruinous style. A winning streak was like a gateway drug to playing higher stakes and taking more risks. Getting lucky also discouraged study, discipline, and good money management. Years later I bumped into Jack leaving the lowest limit game, and he was cadaverous, unshaven, grizzled and hunched over almost like Quasimodo. I asked about him, wished him well, and I thanked him for his earlier concern. I heard that he died later that year.

$$$

As Bertrand Russell wrote, "We have in fact, two kinds of morality, side by side: one that we preach, but do not practice, and another that we practice, but seldom preach."

Navel gazing, I struggled with the deep gut feeling that we should better society, our environment, and the world. This was my mantra, an instrument of thought. At least that's how I was raised. Mom's and church preachings must have percolated into my subconscious. I don't know about other poker players, but that is the nagging feeling I had when I reflected upon my life and the way I earned money. I discussed this with my bud, Shah Kwah. With his ever smiling, cherubic face he said, "I know, JM. I think about that too. But the clubs create jobs, and we help support this casino's employees, especially the chip runners and food servers and Floor men. And you know how I tip. Big. And then the casino pays taxes."

I felt this was a stretch and a begging the question logic flaw. "Sure, Shah, that may be true, but I wonder. Does gambling better society or add anything of value?"

Sometimes when Shah was ebullient, he'd puckishly smile and bounce in his chair as if he were trampolining on his butt. Pogoing he said, "We help players have fun."

"I agree with you there. Gambling is entertainment and viewed that way it does create some value. Players use their own discretionary income, pocket money. But do games of chance and the gambling industry better people and the world?"

Like a driver of a jacked-up low rider doing Diamond Lifts, he launched in his seat and said, "Who told you that you had to better the world? That's not my problem or my job. That's beyond my pay grade."

Later I resolved that people in the casinos playing poker against me were adults who entered voluntarily. No one put an RPG to their head and made them drive to the joint. Mostly, at the limits I played, they weren't playing with the rent money. If poker decreased their drug spending that would be a *good* thing. There I go again, putting moral value, on others' behavior. If an adult, being of sound mind and body, wanted to compete against others in a game of skill and chance (notice skill's ahead of chance), in a legal pursuit, who am I to second guess them? Moreover, should I win, and mostly I did over the years, I'd invest that money. Surely that would contribute to society or at least the economy.

$$$

In the beginning it *seemed* one could get something for nothing. To a poor kid, poker money was very alluring and so very cool. But *Mira*, there's a dark side, invisible like dark matter, to gambling, and more specifically, poker. It casts an old siren song of seeming to give something for nothing. Nothing is free; everything has a price. There ain't no free lunch warns you that cannot get something for *nothing*, and anything one receives for *free* will be paid for in another way.

Decades later I'm older and wiser? Okay, at least more seasoned, fledged, and worldly. Sure, I now know that nothing is free. There are prodigious costs. If, as Will Durant wrote, "Latitude is morals," for me the artic zone of poverty was formative. Dah. Sometimes I feel so dumb that I say *dah* instead of the King's English accepted *duh* for self-deprecating humor. Also, spelling's subtlety is just beyond my grasp.

4

A City in a Valley, not on a Hill

THE CALIFORNIA LEGISLATURE, IN its infinite wisdom, or perhaps finite utilitarianism, wanted to protect the citizenry from corruption and sticky moral turpentine. Thus, they passed laws against gambling; however, a city could offer games of *skill*, unlike games of chance. Since these municipalities couldn't provide games of chance, there were no slots, roulette, craps, blackjack, chuck-a-luck, keno, etc.; consequently, card clubs weren't casinos. And, oh, unquestionably there were many club license application procedures that were ... above reproach.

There were advantages worth paying to play in a card club. Unlike a home game, one could come and go as one pleased without worrying about leaving a game a big winner and ruffling friends' feathers. Or scrambling their nest egg. Since gamblers usually must play for sums that hurt—had strong emotional impact—one could find a suitable limit. Unlike home games, the checks were redeemable for real money—a personal check from a home game might bounce higher than 400-pound, bungee jumper's recoil. Different from a private game, too, one could usually find a game in progress without the hassle of trying to assemble a wheel barrel full of frogs to show up at a certain time, date, and place. Put another way, sometimes trying to arrange a home game was like trying to get the constipated House and Senate to compromise and pass legislation. There is a lot of wind and gas, but nothing will pass.

$$$

With purity of purpose and magnanimity in their enormous, altruistic hearts, Gardena legalized card clubs, and they dictated that the clubs close every day at 7:00 a.m. They couldn't reopen until 9:00 a.m. Cynics speculated about the reasons.

Shah Kwah said, "I wonder why they make us jam at 7?"

Me, "It's probably so the degenerates are forced to go to work."

"You're right. They have enough time to shower, change clothes, and commute to work. That way they won't lose their job. They'll have more money to gamble with."

"Yes, sometimes I see the guy the next night."

"Yeah, it's what's referred to as a symbiotic relationship. The parasite doesn't want to kill the host. It wants to suck the life out of the host."

"Shah, that's really harsh!"

To protect its constituency further, the casinos had to close every day at 7:00 a.m. Alcohol could not be served on the premises. Cleverly, each club had a bar within a two-minute walk. The six were spread around the city on major boulevards. However, there was a pair of casinos located next to each other and separated only by two driveways, two for egress and two for entry, to the parking lot. Deplorably, there was a narrow bar situated on the median. Cute, but yo, business is business.

Before I landed a job after college, or between jobs, I gravitated toward these casinos like a homing ... nocturnal pigeon. Early on gambling at the poker casinos was like being in high school and going to an exciting, glitzy carnival on a first date.

5

Biplanes and Other Games

SOMETIMES AFTER THE CASINO closed at 7:00 a.m., we'd go to breakfast at the nearby Chinese restaurant, Wok This Whey. Depending on our mood we might wait two hours and return to the club when it re-opened at 9.

"JM, you Pyongyang half-breed. How'd you do?" Shah Kwah asked.

"I won about $50. How 'bout you?"

"I lost $110. I guess you're buying breakfast."

"Sure." I sympathized and asked, "So what went wrong?"

Shah made a disgusted face and said, "Man, I just couldn't hit a hand. It was a blood bath. Toward the end, I made a six, but the guy had a pat six better than mine. That hand'd have gotten me even."

"Sorry, bud ... What'd see that looks good?"

"I like the war wonton with spicy noodles. What're you getting?"

"I love to make a scrambled egg sandwich." This was before I started eating more healthily. I reminisced, "Yeah, it takes me back to my military days. One of my buddies taught me this cholesterol busting recipe. You get scrambled eggs hard, four to five crispy bacon strips, and toast slathered with butter. Boy, that's *de-licious*. And I always get my eggs scrambled, because in one foster home, the parents' future son-in-law teased me saying, 'Do you know what eggs are? They're chicken guts!' For decades, even now, I get queasy thinking about eggs sunny side up. Those yokes as guts. Yuck."

Shah grimaced and said, "Oh, thanks for spoiling my appetite. But what kinda Korean are you? For breakfast ya gotta have bulgogi and kimchee." He'd smile with his cherubic, baby face, and he would bounce slightly on his buttocks in the booth. Many other degenerates and *rounders* (hustlers) who'd played all night, would also come over.

Shah pointed out, "Look over there. See that babe? Talk about *de-licious*. She was at my table, and she played so bad. She constantly was drawing two, trying to bluff, calling with trashy hands. She'd have to be hit in the face with the deck to win."

"I wonder how she gets her money?"

"With a body like that, she can get money any time." Bounce-bounce.

"Well, yeah. But you don't mean sell her body?"

"No. I mean with her body she can get any man, even a rich one, and get him to finance her."

"I ought to go over and see if I can get her number, but, man, I'm just too beat. Plus, I don't wanna get egg on my face."

"Yeah, but your chance of picking her up is slim and none. And Slim left town. Yeah, she'd shoot you down like I do in Biplanes. Hey, let's go play while we wait for our breakfast?"

"Sure. It's always fun to kick your butt. Dollar a game?"

"Of course."

In the 1970s, video games didn't have the sophistication or spectacular graphics like now, but the game was so much fun. Using a joystick to control your small biplane, you would take off and try to shoot down the other's plane. The programmers did a wonderful job by having biplane motor sounds that changed in pitch if one were climbing (lower pitch) or dive (higher pitch)—Döppler. The firing of the machine guns was primitive, but cartoonishly realistic. They created a magazine of maybe 20 shots.

Also, the slow-moving bullets were affected by gravity; hence, you'd have to lead the target. In other words, one could not just hold down the fire button and have bullets shoot out like lasers. Since you didn't have unlimited bullets, but one had to reload by touching down on the runway. If one killed one's adversary, that player's plane reappeared on the landing strip but had to slowly take off. A smart strategy was to buzz over and shoot the slow-moving plane as it tried to take off. "Bastard!" that player would yell. No matter how dismally we might've done over the green baize gambling, we would smile and laugh after a session of Biplanes. I contest that we had more fun playing this than hours of poker.

"Did you see that they installed a Western Union, cash advance machine in the club lobby? That's sick," Shah chortled.

"Yeah, so if you're running bad, you can get more money to lose. That's sick all right. Sick as cigarette shaped candy for kids."

"And you have to pay an exorbitant fee to get the money to the cage. Maybe $27 on $100. Really twisted," Shah continued. "But I don't know if it's as perverted as Vegas. I saw a $1,000 slot machine. Who plays that?"

"Cuckoos. You playing tomorrow?"

A biochemistry PhD. Candidate, he replied, "I don't know. I've got to do some research."

"Well, I'm *bailing*, get it, and I'll see you if you come."

$$$

I was playing the next night, and I asked Nicky for a piece of his Milky Way, but he roughly pushed away my outstretched hand. He was destroying the game, and I was being slaughtered. I pointed to his mountain of chips, and said, "Why don't you give the chip girl a dollar and buy me one?"

He whispered something to the chip runner, and she left. After about thirty minutes, when she hadn't returned with a candy bar, I asked

The Greek what happened to my candy bar. So, he slid over an obviously opened Milky Way wrapper that appeared empty.

Forewarned by Floor man, Charlie Sepulveda, I didn't want to fall for the trap as he had, so I responded, "Are you kidding? I know it's empty."

"No, here, take it."

When I pushed it back with a knife, he stood up as if offended and gruffly said, "No, here take it!" He poked it toward me with his finger.

Wanting to avoid being the fool, I carefully examined it without feeling it. I didn't want to look a gift horse in the mouth, and I wanted to Beware of strangers [Greeks] bearing gifts. [Now politically incorrect. Henceforth abbreviated PI.] These two sayings derive from Virgil's *Aeneid*. But why wouldn't you want to look in its mouth? If the people of Troy examined the wooden horse left as a gift by the Greeks, they may have found Greek soldiers inside and prevented losing Troy and the Trojan War. However, this proverb means Don't question the value of a gift.

To my amazement, there's a chip inside. "You're all right, Nicky. Thanks." Later, when I was hungry, I opened it to use the check to buy a Snickers. Not only would it be sweeter if he, rather than I, bought it, but a bar would soothe the bitter taste in my mouth from getting beaten up— no annihilated. I was trying to get a free yum-yum, so sue me. Instead of the card club chip, there was a hard cracker inside. He'd pulled the Melba cracker trick again, and he snicker-ed uproariously. "Youa not gonna be a good gambler if youa worried about one dollar!" True that.

"Nicky, what are you eating?"

"Not eatin'. Chewin' gum."

"Where'd you get it? They don't sell it in the gift shop."

"Nah. I bring it from home."

This is how he beat the gum embargo. I read that the act of chewing reduces cortisol levels and so relieves stress. This somewhat explains comfort eating. Poker is nothing if not stressful; hence, some sessions I want it.

Interestingly, card and casino shops don't sell gum, for they realize if they sell it, some of their low-life, inconsiderate customers will fasten depleted wads under furniture like the card table itself. Did these people grow up in a barn or juvie? Or some rude turd will spit a glob out onto the carpet. Sm-ack, sm-ack, ptui. Then we'd hear op-lop, op-log, op-lop as patrons would walk around with gum on the bottom of their shoes.

$$\$\$\$$$

This Nicky The Greek wasn't the legendary Nick "The Greek" who gambled mostly on the East coast, but this other Greek who visited Gardena once. I don't know if the following story is true, but it encapsulates some of the flavor of Gardena. It demonstrates the strategies of High Draw, the game within the game, and the art of deception. It was a battle between two legends: One from the East by way of Las Vegas, the other a local woman known as "Sitting Bull." A notorious rock, one of the tightest players around, she supplemented her pension by playing Draw during the day. She sat like Gibraltar wrapped in a shawl with a withering stare. When she opened the pot, strong men sadly threw away two queens. Taking an excursion from Vegas, Nick The Greek found his way to one of the Gardena card clubs.

Sitting Bull opened the pot, and with three aces (A's), Nick naturally raised her. Unaware that someone had raised her, she told the dealer, "Give me two." Someone pointed out that she had been raised. She feistily inquired, "Who raise Sitting Bull?" Players pointed to The Greek. "Well, then I reraise!" Some of the day regulars knowingly nodded to each other and tried to suppress smiles. Since Nick had three A's, the best three of a kind, he raised her again. She reraised. After about five or six raises, Nick felt something was fishy, so he just called. Once the betting was complete, the dealer asked her how many cards she wanted. "Sitting Bull pat." Nick had to shake his head and drew two. She bet, and Nick, not improving his hand, sadly hurled away his beautiful three aces. Always a gentleman, he said, "Madam, I don't know who you are, but I applaud your play."

$$$

"Fingers" acquired a Runyonesque nickname from his pickpocket, magic, or deck manipulation proclivities. His friends wouldn't reveal the source. Because of his light brunette fro, he could've been called "Curley." He and his buds were indigenous to Gardena, and although he was just twenty, he snuck into the card clubs. A few years after I met him, he went over to Australia as a roadie for a band. When he returned to playing cards, he had an Aussie accent. Interesting.

Writing of colorful nicknames, there were many that, like most handles, fit like a slightly soiled glove. "Clam" was very conservative, expressionless, and tight. "One-eyed" Earl, "Tall" Paul, "Laughing" Bob. To relieve stress, "Toothpick" Dick always had a well-chewed, soggy toothpick planted in his mouth. "Stumpy's" Ring Lardner-ish nickname arose not for missing a limb, but because he was about 4' 11". In Gardena if he wanted to borrow a stake, he'd solicit with, "Can you put me a game? I'm a little short." (Wee bit of Toulouse-Lautrec humor.)

$$$

Someone who's tight with money is known by terms on a sliding scale such as frugal, cheap, penny pincher, parsimonious, skin flint, stingy, miserly, money grubber. As you might imagine, there were other derogatory synonyms: Rock(y), solid, snug, tightwad, tight fisted and tight ass. I cite this because I was known as a tight player, and I want tightness in myself and looseness in opponents. Sure, I talked as if loose or lax but played tight, snug—laxnug. This game within a game was foiled by observant opponents who could tell I was conservative by the hands I showed and my speculative action.

One night, I entered a Low game consisting of the greatest assembly in the poker world of mean needlers, baiters, taunters and teasers. They loved to needle and nettle to test your mettle. "Suitcase" Stu said, "JM is so tight he lectures at Gamblers' Anonymous," implying I no longer gave action, gambled or took chances.

I weakly defended myself saying, "Th-that's not true. Since Barlowe has come to the game, I've lost three stacks."

Barlowe joined the hilarity, "That's hard to believe since you only put in the minimum blinds per round. You're such a rock." (A blind is required amount put into the pot to build a pot and encourage action.)

"Oh, but I can be a wild man, not rock-ous."

Peter Princely, after careful reflection, added, "No, JM's okay for the game."

I thought that was kind until he twisted the shiv, saying, "Yeah, he's worth about $40 more to the table than an empty seat. We should nickname him 'Dead Money.'"

"Suitcase" Stu laughing, added, "If I played like Dead Money here, I'd have to get a job."

"Go on, laugh at poor Dead Money, I mean JM." As revealed in the beginning, my mom and I were dirt poor, and this greatly impacted me. Johnny Moss, "The Grand Old Man of Poker," reputedly said, "What's the use of money if you can't gamble with it." I didn't subscribe to this; on the contrary, I was a very frugal and a saver (tight), for I wanted savings for security and freedom.

Their talking smack may seem like good natured ribbing, but it wasn't. It was mettlesome and mean spirited. And their goal was either to get me to leave the game or to put me on tilt.

I saw a connection in one's attitude. Overcoming short term bad luck in poker determined how successful a player would be in the long run. Luck surely was a big element in periods of hours or weeks; however, the cards and good hands' distribution would even out in the long run. Likewise, a person who was dealt a bad hand in his or her youth could surmount that and be successful later in life. I was betting on it. Princely taunted, "By the way, nice perm."

"Yeah, it's new wave."

6

First Tectonic Shift and Economics

CAPITALISM VS. MONOPOLIES OR oligarchies. Throughout modern history, variations of these systems have waged gargantuan battles for supremacy. Since poker was legalized in Southern California, c. 1936, Gardena, a city in southern California, had a quasi-monopoly by offering the only legal poker gambling to a target market of about six million people. The people who ran card rooms were well-aware of the power of this monopoly and were very dismissive and cavalier regarding customers' needs and desires. Each card room was like a fiefdom within Gardena. The city council was like the House of Medici running the clubs. Club's motto seemed to be, "Hey, if you don't like our way of doing business, start your own card club. If you don't like our menu, tough. You don't like our collection rates, too bad. You're unhappy that we are raising these time rates (rent), go to another card club." However, like an oligopoly, each of the six card emporiums in Gardena acted in unison.

Soon, however, the first of three cataclysmic, tectonic shifts occurred in the poker landscape when other cities introduced ballot measures to open a card club, and some were approved; namely, City of Bell—The California Bell Club (8.1980); Commerce—California Commerce Casino (3. 1983); Bell Gardens—Bicycle Club (The Bike, 11.84); Huntington Park—Huntington Park Casino (3.1984). These new casinos compelled Gardena to evolve. But just to round out the cities following suit: Inglewood—Hollywood Park Casino (5.1994); Hawaiian

Gardens—Hawaiian Gardens Casino (1997); Gardena—Hustler Casino (1998) resurrected on the old site of the Embassy, later the El Dorado Card Club.

As these other casinos opened, one could see the salutary effects of competition. Gardena had to be more willing to meet the wishes of its patrons. Hence, heretofore banned TVs were installed. Food improved in quality and variety, and its cost stabilized. Promotions and giveaways increased. In other words, Gardena's once dictatorial, high-handed treatment of customers became a thing of the past. Since the new card establishments instituted professional dealers at each table, Gardena had to follow suit. This dramatically cut down cheating. It was a double-edged sword, though, for toking dealers increased the cost of playing.

$$$

Backtracking to pre-professional dealers, there were suspicious guys in Gardena called "mechanics" who had a rep for dealing seconds—cards under the top one or the bottom one. Skilled cheaters usually played at the highest stakes while I played near the lowest end. Apparently, it wasn't worth a double dealer's turn to troll the small stakes, Lowball games. However, when I graduated, a dubious term to higher limits, I encountered Tan, a putatively ex-professional dealer who could manipulate a deck like Houdini during foreplay.

In those days I guess about one in maybe every three to five thousand players were mechanics. Although mechanic usually refers to auto mechanics who fix and or tinker with cars, in the poker milieu a card mechanic adjusts cards. A cheater like Tan could peek at cards and shuffle to place cards in known positions: First, second, fifty-second, etc. Next, he could deal the desirable card(s) to whomever he wanted. Put it another way. He could deal the second card from the top (dealing seconds) or bottom. He could save the top card for himself or a confederate if need be.

To accomplish this double dealing, a mechanic employs the mechanic's grip. A right-handed mechanic tightly holds the cards like this: In his left hand; the thumb along the left edge; the forefinger at the front, and the other three fingers curled around the right edge. He holds the cards in a manner that looks as though it would feel awkward, like tightly holding a detonating trigger; moreover, it just looks weird. If the reader thinks this is natural or comfortable, try it. I get a hand cramp thinking about dealing like this. Players who hold a deck like this are unique, and even the run-of-the-mill card player notices him. Mental alarms scream like a coked-up banshee. Players in the know— heck, even those weren't, were very cautious when he dealt and gave such a prestidigitator a wide berth.

Ever wanting to evolve our language, I believe that, due to his card manipulating dexterity, calling a mechanic a "surgeon" is more apropos. I don't know if you are old enough to remember Frank Sinatra in The Man with the Golden Arm. Sinatra was a card surgeon.

So far as I know, unscrupulous card surgeons were male. In roughly ten years, I saw one woman hold the deck with this revealing grip. I speculate she might have grown up in her dad's casino or some backwater town, the desert, or a roadside bar where there'd be a local game in the back room. Who am I to talk about a misspent youth, but what kind of parent teaches their princess to double deal? It'd be like raising a girl to be a madame in a bordello. And that's being disrespectful to the working girls.

A "pasteboard chiropractor," an even better analogy than surgeon, had a secondary means of cheating. Since the player to the next dealer's right had the option to either cut the cards (supposedly to ensure a square deal) or riffle the deck before returning it for dealing, Tan always gave the cards a shuffle. Tan had a unique ability to casually, and seemingly innocently, pull the deck for the next deal toward him in such a way that he quickly could scan up to five of the bottom cards, shuffle them into his desired order, and then precisely cut that slug to the top of the deck. A slug is a packet or clump of cards.

In Lowball, the rank of hands is the inverse of high hand's rank. Thus, having no pair is bad in High, but desirable in Low. So, 5, 4, 3, 2, A (A = ace = one) was the best. Straights and flushes weren't counted against a low hand—only the hands' high numbers are compared. Since he knew the sequence and numbers of the top cards, Tan could deal a face card to an opponent crippling its value. Phenomenal skill. This gave him a small advantage. What? No, it massively could tilt the fairness scales like a butcher's thumb.

$$\$\$\$$$

Another well-known scam is employing teams whose m.o. (*modus operandi*) involves, as team implies, at least two accomplices acting in concert. This is somewhat like having a plant at an auction to bid up the price. Card teams differ from an auction plant in that there's usually two, not one. Via subtle signals (I rarely saw any, and believe me I scrutinized my opponents), teammates know when the other has a very strong hand. If there're other opponents competing for the pot before the draw, these two would raise, and reraise each other to the max. An innocent victim of this ploy is being whipsawed or trapped. There was a universal casino rule that any hand that was live, still playing, at the showdown, had to be shown at a player's request. Teams could counter this by having the weak, *supposedly* other strong, raising hand, draw a card, and then fold before the showdown. Apparently, there was honor among thieves, for I'm told that they split the session's profits later. Players who suspected collusion would say, "You two gonna split the money in the parking lot." I always was leery when I saw two regulars speaking in hushed tones in the shadows in the bathroom or especially the parking lot. Oops, is this being superstitious?

$$$

I made a friend with whom I played once or twice a twice a week. Raymond was as amicable and pleasant as a Golden Retriever, and he was a live one, loose, loved to gamble, and didn't mind taking the worst of it, odds-wise. But his most endearing quality is that he had this great, warm laugh which he did often. I think God Him—or Herself—couldn't have created a more happy, sincere, join-the-party laugh than his. It was perfect. He would roll in after work or on a day off.

We'd been playing about an hour when Raymond suggested, "Come on, JM. Let's take a break. Have some Dewars with me," he said with his usual chuckle.

"You know I don't drink while I play, but I'll buy you one."

At the bar, we discussed teams. Raymond's idea of playing against teams was against the grain and unique. "You know what they say. Cheaters never prosper, but at least they're their own boss. I don't mind playing against a team; if I beat them in a hand, I get double my money."

"There seems to be a flaw in your idea," I offered. "You might think you win twice the money, but more often you'll lose twice the money. Most of the time you'll miss your draw, and you won't even be able to call a bet after the draw. Also, the odds are you're up against an extremely strong hand; consequently, you might make your best hand, but already be up against a better pat hand. I speculate that you'll win twice the money 20 percent of the time but lose twice the money 80 percent of the time."

"I don't care. I'm here to gamble," he chuckled.

Pros and good players profit from many who play loosely and adhere to this motto who are called live ones, fish, or appropriately, *producers*. (Concomitantly, in any gambling, fish is very derogatory.) The pros and pro wannabees welcome this attitude, and with Machiavellian friendliness, encourage it. They even feign playing too loose, like Lautrec. They employ a talk loose, play tight strategy. This lets gamble spirit keeps the little world of card clubs spinning like a roulette wheel.

"You know, JM. I've always wondered what JM stands for."

"'Junior Mafia,'" I joked.

"No, really. Tell me."

"John. John Maynard. Of course, don't tell anyone else. There are some who know it, but they don't call me by my real name."

"You got it."

While we were away from his table, I wondered if others thought we were a team? Nah. Not the way he played—too loose. The person wanting him as a partner would have to hate money.

$$$

Of course, there are more mundane methods of gaining an edge, an unfair advantage. These were more prevalent in Draw games, either self or dealer dealt. One is supposed to protect and conceal one's own hand, but sometimes an unethical neighbor cranes their head sideways to see an opponent's cards. In Lowball, seeing one card can be critical in evaluating a hand. Or another type of player in this menagerie, pretending to look for a chip runner or food server, would swivel the head around, but not as far as the 270° of spotted owls. Some would mark the cards with daubs of ink or use their fingernail to indent the card. Some would crimp the corner of a card to know what someone received or to deal it to him or herself.

The casinos' staff were cognizant of people trying to mark cards, and they employed counter measures. In Gardena the card of choice was manufactured by Kem Playing Cards. They were exceptionally durable and just stiff and slick enough to shuffle and deal easily. About every four hours, the old packs of cards were removed from play throughout the club, and new—freshly inspected and cleaned—cards were put in. Usually, two women in a well-lit room would examine each card, clean them on towels with a strong smelling, cleaning solution, and confirm the deck was a full deck. One might say that they were Kem-istry majors. Another advantage of Kem cards was that if the inspectors found a bent, marked or otherwise defective card, they could replace it with the right suit and number. The club could order replacement cards from the factory, and, thus, not have to throw away a complete deck because of one bad card. In the Lowball era, the Joker (Jo) was often a target for marking or crimping. Hence, the club could keep an extra supply of these.

$$\$\$\$$$

Ma Nature uses natural selection, a kind of extraordinary trial and error experiment over eons, to aid the survival of the fittest. The process of Darwinian natural selection helped mankind survive on the Pleistocene plains of Africa and eventually land in the jungles of Gardena. I've likened Gardena's poker lairs as a jungle or eco-system for competition. As an arena, like the Roman Forum, there were the triumphant and the vanquished. Cheaters and mechanics, by natural selection tendencies, had manual dexterity, quickness, visual acuity, and didn't have night blindness. Nor did they have high morals. And surely, they were predatory; however, I believe another part of Darwinism was missing. They didn't emerge from the survival of the fittest kiln. Consequently, they didn't employ honest, winning strategies and discipline, but relied on devious, lazy methods to win. By lazy I don't mean they weren't industrious, but they'd wasted so much time honing their skill that they developed neither winning strategies, nor spent hours and hours learning and reading. They cut corners which in any job resembles wanting something for *nada*. Rest assured that they also lacked discipline, a crucial trait. They took the easy way. They wanted something for nothing. They relied on cheating to carry or save them; hence, it isn't counterintuitive to note that most of them lost. Summarizing, they usually were not *good* players. And taking the easy way bad. Discipline good.

$$$

The previous discussion deals with the intentional cheaters. There also existed some normally honest players who broke the covenant with a card emporium—to refrain from cheating—and engaged in crimes of opportunity. For instance, Saul Offenbach was a nice Jewish boy, late twenties, and usually smiling. Imagine a clean cut, younger, Sephardic Joe Cocker, and you will capture his raspy tone. I presuppose since he knew I liked him, he relished telling me this story in his unique hoarse voice.

"I was playing last week, and this hand seemed to be going on forever. There were a lot of older guys in the game, so already the action was very slow. So, I says, 'Hey, guys. How about speeding up the game.' 'Mom' was in the game too, and she says, 'Saul, quit your *noodging*.' Now the discards were in front of me, so out of boredom, I started going through the discards putting a hand together. I made a 6-4 [the second strongest hand in Low]. So 'Mom' sees me with a hand and asks, '*Bubele*, what do you do?' 'Me?' I say, 'I raise it.' Well, they were none the wiser, and I took down about $80." He chuckled and *kvelled* as if he had committed The Great Brinks Robbery.

I didn't know what to say, so I just slightly smiled. After the conclusion of our hand, I said, "But Saul, that wasn't *kosher*."

He joked, "But I'm a Reformed Jew" Still, I was stunned and revolted that someone would brag about cheating. Apparently, he wasn't that reformed.

$$$

Eventually all casinos and card emporiums, employed dealers. The unwashed heathen believers in dealer witchcraft now had a vast, new minefield to worry about. They were like the *Millennium Falcon* crew attempting a jump to hyperspace through an asteroid field. Countless players suffering heebie-jeebies lamented: "She hasn't dealt me a winner in years." Naturally Moustafa Goldwing was exaggerating. Or I'd heard this when a new dealer rotated to the table. Tyche, "I sit out until Yellowbird leaves. She kills me every time." As Tralfamadorians say about death, "So it goes." [Death, i.e., L̶i̶f̶e̶, will be symbolized by 💀.] When players started bitching about how deadly a specific dealer was to them, it could become a real fatalism fest.

Obviously, a *dealer avoider* is suffering, and perhaps unknowingly using, memory bias. Moreover, the phenomenon of false memory has been well documented: In many court cases, defendants have been found guilty based on testimony from witnesses and victims who were sure of their recollections. Later DNA evidence helped overturn some convictions. Consequently, the believer in *witch* dealers would rather sit out for thirty to forty minutes, wasting considerable time.

On this bad luck topic, the host of players saying, "If I didn't have bad luck, I wouldn't have any luck at all," were as numerous as lumps of coal filling a barge.

$$$

This is as good a place as any to discuss poker profitability, economics. A standard axiom is that only about 5 percent of players can make money playing poker. This mythical elite included professionals, and some commonly called props, or stake players, in California.

Technically props aren't house players who're also titled shills. A prop's duties include helping start a new game or entering a short game. Parenthetically, many think that to prop up—brace a game from collapsing—a game was the etymology of prop. However, prop refers to being a proposition player—someone who plays conditionally. Incidentally, to class up the profession, job description, eventually prop morphed into Host circa the 1990s. These employees' title really got elevated (like a self-employed person who puts President on his or her business card) in the 2000s when they often were referred to as Player Relations Representatives. Well, la-de-da, title inflation.

If we assume that a ballpark 5 percent of all poker players were winning players, who would be in this elite clique? Disclaimer, a winning player on one end of the bell curve could, by definition, win $1 for the year; however, I'm discussing the run-of-the-mill, everyday player who treated poker as a full-time job, and earned enough to live. This winner also would've played long enough for statistical significance. Let's arbitrarily stipulate greater than ten years. Mentioning statistics, I'll exclude the new breed of players, tournament specialists, who make up 0.3 percent of them (to Math Drew, 3 SD—Standard deviations—out). In the era when I started, there weren't tourneys, and thus, no tourney specialists who now can earn millions in one tourney.

7

Dealers, Superstition I and *Jaboneys*

IN LOWBALL, AKA LOW, house dealers lessened the chance of mis-deals, fouled hands, many customers' self-dealing problems. Unlike the superstitious, I admit disliking certain card chuckers, but only if they were rude, incompetent, and or caused me to lose a pot by their mistake. An incompetent, inattentive, or a hard-of-hearing dealer has given me more or fewer cards than I requested; thus, my hand was fouled or dead. This has happened to everyone. I eventually learned to spread the cards before inserting them into my hand, and, therefore, undoing the mistake—making a correction. Furthermore, I was more alert when a poor dealer was pitching the pasteboards.

In addition, having professional card pitchers usually sped up the game and gave rise to bantering. We played with a Jewish woman, a regular named Sarah who was about sixty. She'd moved with her family from Hell's Kitchen as a child, and at around forty-five discovered poker and Gardena. About 4' 11", she had big hair, a compact case full of makeup, ropes of jewelry, and big, gold-framed glasses with a safety chain. Phillip kept dealing winning hands to Sarah. Finally, someone who was getting hammered asked Phillip in exasperation, "Are you two related?"

She continued stacking her new chips, and with a shoulder shrug said, "*Meh*. Don't get all *meshugenah*."

After winning yet another pot, she toked him even more. Without missing a beat, Phillip said, "Thanks, 'Mom.'" (Actually, she could've been his mother-in-law, a *shviger.*) You can bet that Mom went into the lexicon and became her nickname. It was normal to call elderly Asian women, "Mama-*san*," or in Sarah's case, she more accurately should've been called, *Bubbie*, grandmother.

$$\$\$\$$$

While honest, professional dealers decreased cheating from self-dealing players, it dramatically increased the cost of doing business for the card clubs and players.

Since the clubs could pass through the additional staffing expenses, the customer inevitably bore it. It was another cost that depleted potential wins. Obviously, it would add to losses, too. In addition, customarily the winner of a hand toked the dealer. Seemingly insignificant, this tip, plus tips to food servers, chip runners, floor staff, cashiers, and house collections, would add up to a fair amount over time.

Having honest dealers is another topic. While almost all card pitchers were honest, from time to time in Gardena, we'd hear of some dealer-player grift wherein the dealer, or Floor person would slip in a *cold deck* into a game. Deriving its name supposedly from the Mississippi River boat days, a cold deck had prearranged cards, and a Confederate brought it into a game from elsewhere. Having been outside it'd be cold to the touch. A dealer in collusion would false shuffle. The resulting hand(s) would bust the sucker(s). This etymology could be apocryphal, but surely it sounds real and is certainly colorful. With modern AC, maybe a crooked deck coming out of an accomplice's pocket should be renamed a hot deck.

Depending upon the Gardena table's limit, this crooked hand could result in thousands of dollars going to the schemers. Other skullduggeries could be employed, but I'm not privy to them. In fairness, cheating is universal. I'm positive there've been almost infinite attempts, ploys and devices created to game the system in Nevada, Europe and now the rest of the world. There was a true story of a man who bought 1,000 blue $1 casino chips, bleached out the color with acetone, meticulously repainted them by hand, and then tried to cash some of the doctored chips as $25 and $100 chips. Easily discovered, he was arrested outside the men's room after trying to flush some of the evidence down the toilet. One man built a small computer to fit in his shoe. He counted blackjack cards by learning to type with his toes. Security noticed he was always fiddling with his shoe and peering down. Space doesn't allow all the myriads of casino scams. Why work legitimately? Rationalizing, it'll be more fun to beat them at their own game. They won't miss the money. They can afford it. The Free Lunch Bunch's motto, Something for nothing. (Strangely, and I suppose hypocritically, I don't think cheating against a Vegas casino is as reprehensible as against other businesses. Still, I'd never do it.)

$$$

Floor men and women made good money but having foibles and weaknesses like the rest of us, often gambled. Losing one's gambling bankroll through ill-advised activities is referred to as having a hole or leak in one's game. It's a destructive financial drain, a bad habit, or can be a serious defect in one's play. I don't mean that some Floor people just gamble with poker, but they travel to play Las Vegas casino games (with immutable odds against them), bet sports, and of course, play the ponies. It may be difficult for the younger reader to understand this fascination, but back in the day, horse betting was quite attractive and addictive. We'll see later that another hole in one's game, probably the biggest, involved using drugs. Using was like dealing with problem tenants: You can learn law, exercise creativity; however, it's stressful and eventually can be extraordinarily expensive.

$$$

Luck and superstition, what a cornucopia of material. Players keep all manners of lucky charms and paraphernalia on the table. There were pyramids during the pyramid power craze—a type of pyramid scheme? Crystals of all shapes and sizes during the crystal power boom. Superheroes of all ilk. Lucky coins from every country. Even mundane talismans like rabbit's feet, plastic encased four-leaf clovers, horseshoe key chains, and, for extra insurance, key chain fobs or coins depicting a four-leaf clover etched inside a horseshoe. Keep a genuine badger's tooth in your left-hand trouser pocket. One cannot cover enough bases or take any chances; one must be sure. One needs to summon all possible sources of good fortune. It was as if they couldn't take the sulfurous heat of bad luck. These gamblers remind me of the exceptionally superstitious boys in Twain's *The Adventures of Tom Sawyer*. Players will do anything but fully take responsibility for their own results. Luck can deliver that elusive something for *nada* product.

$$$

Dale Dimcock was a retired US Army Sergeant Major who'd served in WWII. He revealed, "I loved it. I was on the front lines, where the sparks fly, where the axe meets the stone. When I enlisted, I came out of a holler in Appalachia, West Virginia. It was the first time I had three squares a day, good shoes, and regular pay."

He must have been getting a substantial pension, for he played high limit Lowball. He wore a big gold chain, fashionable at the time, but the medallion was too big. He may have bought it from "Frenchie" whom you'll meet later. Dale really was quite dapper with nicely cut grey hair and an exemplary moustache waxed ramrod straight. He habitually called an opponent who beat him in a big pot, or someone he wanted to tease, *jaboney*. He'd never tell us its meaning. "The only way you'll ever find out is if you ask an Italian from the Abruzzi region of Italy." Years later "Gatsby" Tommy—another Italian American who got his nickname because he always dressed sharply in sport coat and tie—said it meant jerk or clown.

Sergeant Major once asked, "Hey, Saul. Do you know why poker chips are round? They have no home and like to roll around."

Saul answered in his Joe Cocker timbre, "And there're like blood. They gotta circulate."

"Saul, you *jaboney*."

"Dale, do you know when a woman is coming?"

"No, how?"

"Who cares? I'm a guy."

A very patient woman at the table wryly commented, "Yeah, a very lonely guy."

Nowadays, Saul wasn't PC (Politically Correct), so his facetious, who-cares statement would be PI (Politically Incorrect). But back in the early 1970s, Feminism was emerging. The terms sexism and PC hadn't entered the lexicon or collective mind set yet.

%%%

I played against a tough opponent, Drew, aka "Math" Drew. His heavy stubble somewhat accentuated his slight overbite. He was one of the roughly 5 percent who won—he'd describe it as two standard deviations, 2SD, out from the mean. Reputedly a math whiz, he said, "I was born with this ability; it was a Godsend. I can figure odds, probabilities, stuff like that in my head." Then he ruefully added, "But I've always regretted not doing more with this gift." He laughed, "I feel like I have high IQ but no clue." He had too many academic talents in high school through college. This multipotentiality stymied and frustrated his finding a challenging field and direction. He was like brilliant kids in elementary school who were bored out of their minds with the level that subjects are taught. In high school someone mega-gifted like Drew could become intellectual bullies, snobs, or truants. He didn't.

Once an opponent was bragging that he was a math maven who claimed that he knew all the odds or could figure them out. Drew took up the challenge. "I think I'm pretty good at math. I'll tell you what. Let's make a bet who's better."

"How'd we do that?" the interloper asked …

"Let's go to USC and find a math professor. We can have him give us some problems about Modolos, Zero Dimensions, Transcendental Numbers. Whoever solves the most wins." This semi-bar bet was far too complicated and time consuming to consummate. Moreover, Math Drew violated a cardinal rule of making sucker bets. He appeared too self-assured. He needed to utilize the ol' broken wing act. This weak-is-strong act will be covered subsequently, and it used to be very effective in poker.

Thinking of his wounded bird act, I said, "Drew, baby. I saw this drawing by B. Kliban. It shows a man in a carny booth holding a duck on a string. A woman at the head of the line is kissing the duck's bill. The caption is 'Superstition—Kiss a duck to change your luck.'"

He replied, "How about Kiss an ibex to grow your checks?"

I shook my head, "Good one."

He asked, "Did the duck look sickly?"

"No, why?"

"It might've had some kind of mallard-y."

Turn arounds fair, for usually people groan at my stuff.

$$\$\$\$$$

I played with an affable, pleasant Southeast Asian woman who was no *jaboney* but very superstitious. Sookie was around thirty and always dressed immaculately and coiffed. Svelte, petit, with flawless skin, and a beautifully contoured jaw, she was beautiful. I feel she could have been a model in her homeland. She had a lilting, high-pitched voice. Unlike Chinese's four tones, Vietnamese has six tones. I stupendously admire people who come to a foreign country and assimilate foreign language and customs. I salute them, so I mean no disrespect for the following. Try as hard as we could, it was difficult to understand her. It was trying to follow a Doestoevsky novel with hundreds of characters whom he refers to by title, physical descriptions, nickname or first, middle, or last Russian name that are unfamiliar to most non-Russians. To wit, "You bet melike arum" translates to "You're beating me like a drum." Maybe like a Taito Drum Master. Meaning, "You guys are killing me tonight." She unnecessarily apologized, "My Englick not too good." Another night, pointing to a pack of matches, she asked the porter, "Gib me dat-one."

Do you think the following ritual of Sookie's was black magic, hocus pocus? If she really were getting beat like arum, she lit a match and set one of her chips on fire hoping alchemy might change her luck. Crazily, casino checks were flammable. This voodoo-like ceremony invoking dark magic would grab our attention like a krait bite. If one didn't see her torching the bad chips, one couldn't miss the carcinogenic stench. This caused pollution like a steel-belted, truck-tire bonfire. Pollution on a Beijing scale. Yao! Yao Ming! Permit me to borrow from P. J. O'Rourke who, in *Holidays in Hell*, wrote about horrendous air quality: "A dense brown haze from dump fires and car exhaust covers the city [Beirut]. Air pollution probably approaches a million parts per million." Being health conscious, I detested her polluting habit; creating her foul incense incensed me. I warned, "You can't burn up the chips."

"I didn' know dat rool."

If I were sitting near her, I'd blow out the flame. "Don poot out my fire." I was fighting the fire of her voodoo with the whammy of the wind of cold rational science. (That sentence is like a perfectly cut diamond facet. Not.) This accomplished two results; namely, it decreased the very toxic, disgusting, smelly pollution and broke the spell she cast to exorcize bad luck from her chips. Hopefully she might be further thrown off her game and go further atilt and off axis. At least in her mind the spell was broken.

I loved her—her sense of humor, grit, malapropisms <M> and Spoonerisms <S>—there is a difference. The malapropism comes from the fictional character Mrs. Malaprop in a 1775 Restoration play by Sheridan. It is "the mistaken use of a word in place of a similar sounding one, often with often humorous effect." Synonyms are wrong word, solecism, misuse, misapplication, infelicity, Freudian slip, blunder. For example, "He's a wolf in cheap clothing"

Spoonerisms, as opposed to malapropisms, are "words or phrases in which letters or syllables get swapped. A person accidentally, or intentionally for humor, transposes the initial sounds or letters of two or more words. It, too, is often accidentally made like slips of the tongue (or tips of the slongue as Spoonerisms are lovingly called)." For instance, "You have hissed the mystery lectures (You have missed the history lectures)."

So, Sookie might Spooner-istically say, "I blon't duff (I don't bluff)." After one pot, she complimented her opponent, "I lye the way you play dat one. You play it good. You poot on a poker expedition <M>." Her adversary said, "Sorry, Sookie. I'll let you win the next hand." She sadly shook her head and said, "Dat point is mute <M>. I losing too muh. I not toopid. I go home now."

$$$

Like superstition when mindless behavior becomes rote, it's time for self-examination. Personal evolution is one of my main points:

> When a ritual becomes habitual,
>
> Not productive or spiritual,
>
> It's time to reexamine
>
> Your futile regimens.

When a ritual becomes habitual,

Not productive or spiritual,

Forget status quo

And set a new goal.

Some of the "Stupidstition" Faith would ask to exchange one of his or her chips for a chip from someone who seemed lucky. Maybe the luck will rub off. Look over there. There is a guy swinging his shades by one ear frame like a helicopter propeller. "What are you doing?"

"Oh, I'm exorcizing the bad spirits in these shades. They're bad luck tonight."

"Why not throw them away then?" I suggested.

"No, mannn. They cost me eighty bucks!"

That player might be losing $4,000. Look in another direction and one might see someone doing squats, jumping jacks, or running in place. Strangely and insightfully, I never saw yoga practiced. A veritable circus sometimes. Look, that guy is changing his chair with one from an empty table! What a surreal zoo, too.

Other believers in unseen forces, *aficionados* of stupidstition, would pronounce, "When I take a horrible bad beat like this, I walk around the table." (An opponent, perhaps playing poorly, defies the horrendous odds against them, and gets lucky to win the hand. This isn't the same as a jack-pot bad beat where one *wants* a qualifying hand beat.) Or "After a bad beat, I take a walk around the casino to cool off." The idea of cooling off is valuable. However, since I want to increase my earnings per hour, needless or very long breaks are time consuming.

I regularly take breaks to rejuvenate, but *not* because of a bad beat.

$$$

"Change the deck! Floor man, *change* the fucking deck, now!!"

This is another, very common strategy to change one's luck. Being a man of science and logic, non-stupidstitious, or perhaps being sub-stitious, I never subscribe to the theory that the deck—if unmarked and non-sticky to ensure random shuffling—has anything to do with my results. It seems to me that the stupidstitious' logic is as confused as the tenses of lay and lie. Still, if one of the players feels that this deck is unlucky, then I try to block that deck change. This might increase that opponent's tilt—increase her or his poor play. Still, I eventually learned that while stymying an opponent's wishes and throwing her or him off somewhat, I earned astonishing enmity from them. Granted, being disliked at the table probably is counter-productive—the costs of objecting far outweighed the possible benefits of playing on the requestor's superstitions. This is JM's Law #3.

8

JM's Ten Commandments and Religion

I DEVELOPED A BODY of principles and rules, a canon, over years of experience. Listed in descending order of value pertaining to me, JM's Laws or *Mitzvahs*:

#1. If one's up an inordinate amount, perhaps four-five times one's average win, strongly consider Quitting At Peak (QAP). Put another way, avoid the chance of a big Negative Turn Around; i.e., you could have left with a good win, but instead played on and lost *that* money (profit) and more (your session's stake). Although the future, a high point, is unknown, you want to minimize NTAs and strive for optimal quitting.

#2. Suppose one was down about 80 percent of one's budget, implying a long session. If one has broken even, eject out of your seat like James Bond from an Aston-Martin, and land running. Skirr, baby.

#3. *Laissez-faire*: Stay out of arguments, rule disputes, opponents' taunting bait, and requests for deck changes.

#4. The quieter one is the better; unless, one has a need or strategy to be the center of attention and action or join in the table's party mood.

#5. If there are greater than two players at a table wearing sunglasses, avoid table if possible.

#6. If there are many players drinking, it can be a spirited game and very profitable.

#7. If there's one drunk at the table, it can be profitable, depending. An inebriate may be lucrative for the game; yet, a mean drunk, who slows the game to a glacial pace and irritates and or insults patrons, may be bad. (This is like Ferengi Rule of Acquisition 163—A thirsty customer is good for profit, a drunk one isn't.)

#8. Obviously, be courteous and nice to live ones.

#9. Make poker work an exercise in patience, clear thinking, will power, and flow playing.

#10. Long poker sessions and a good night's sleep *do not* mix.

It would have been easy to add more, like "Tip staff well," but I had to stop—encountering the Law of Diminishing Returns.

$$$

Re deck changes and JM's Law #3: Requesting a deck change to alter one's luck is a common habit. Gardena management foresaw that constantly switching decks would slow the game down and, thus, slightly decrease club revenues. However, there was a scheduled time to give tables brand new decks, and the Floor men made quite a ceremony of cracking open the cellophane wrapper. The players customarily took a dollar per hand from subsequent pots to toke this Floor man. It's possible that constantly changing the decks, especially with a new deck on some player's whim to change one's luck, wouldn't only be expensive but invalidate the specialness; consequently, tokes might evaporate.

Invariably, though, rules existed to prevent deck change abuse. Players devised counter measures, as cyber criminals do, like surreptitiously bending or breaking a card to force a deck change. Usually someone would see or feel this marked card, and, therefore, the card bender got their way.

Inevitably, one night a player running badly broke a card. Being summoned by the dealer, the Floor man asked the dealer, "Who broke the card?"

The dealer, who knew the culprit, but whose livelihood depended upon tips, facetiously replied, "I did."

Trying to defuse a ticklish situation, the Floor man, tongue-in-cheek said, "Then deal yourself out."

I weighed in, "He's already dealing himself out. The real penalty would be for you to make him deal himself in and play his own money."

The Floor man saw a chance for a graceful exit and said, "Gentlemen, please don't break the cards or I *will* have to penalize you."

Aside from attempting to throw opponents off, shatter their comfort zone, and decrease their luck-based hopes, I also objected to useless setup changes; it slowed down the game—perhaps wasting one to two minutes, about one hand. Bottom line, this slightly reduces the time available for making profits, my main concern. Conversely, if I'm losing, stuck, I'm naturally out of sorts. I don't want to sit around and watch the above exorcism of cards procedures. I want to play, try, get even, and go home! I want to apply JM's Law #2, the Holy Grail in these situations: Get *even* and eject homeward!

Before embracing JM's Law #3's, that it wasn't worth creating ill will by objecting to a deck change, the following happened: An Asian with whom I wasn't acquainted, asked for a new setup. Losing substantially, he thought changing the cards would change his luck. Although he was good for the game, out of habit, I objected. Speaking before I thought, the words involuntarily seemed to shoot out like vomitus. Anyway, he looked at me with hate in his eyes, and he said, "You a penie!"

By chance, he combined penis and weenie. I knew what he meant—*you're a dick*—and I, along with everyone else, laughed. He assumed they were laughing at me. That defused his anger, and I pretended to be offended, saying, "Floor woman. Oh, Floor woman. This gentleman in seat 3 is calling me a penie."

"A what? A peanut?"

The Floor woman couldn't understand why everyone was now laughing harder and reaching a red-faced, tear-streaming apoplexy.

During another session, I objected Raj's request to change the deck. Raj was a feared opponent, because he had a very aggressive m.o. All in all, he was, or wanted to be, his table's alpha male. He raised his voice, "Oh, bite me. If I want a deck change, I can ask. It's in the rules," he whined. "You *are* a real penie."

I retorted, "Well, yeah. But you're a *Pithecanthropus erectus*. And a smooth-brained one at that."

Raj ignored my barbs and asked, "Why do you always object to a change?" I was asked this hundreds of times.

My answer, "I want more hands per hour." I left it unsaid, but thought, *Let's face it, my time is way more valuable than yours. Ironically, I'm patient, but not regarding deck switches.*

I, who didn't believe in this mumbo jumbo of improving one's luck by getting new cards, finally concluded that objecting to a deck switch and incurring the wrath of opponent(s) wasn't worth it. I learned to tolerate these deck changes. Most of the time I'd catch myself and neither object nor satirically expound, "It can't be my play that's causing my misfortune; it *has* to be the cards. So naturally we have to change them." Instead, I said, more to myself than the requestor, "Change the decko; kiss a gecko." While on the topic of mumbo-jumbo, let me to take my cue from George Carlin. He claimed that he was confused whether a jumbo shrimp was a large shrimp or a tiny jumbo. Similarly, is a mumbo jumbo a mumbling, unintelligible jumbo, or a large mumbler? Granted, not Carlin's caliber. Dah.

But in retrospect, what a penie I was. Still, if a change was during an approved time, I'd read, eat, take bathroom breaks, meditate, or study my player profiles to make good use of this downtime.

$$$

My *modus vivendi* before playing, working was to meditate, and I reviewed my oft updated "60 Second Commercial to Me" wherein I mention the Holy Grail and "God likes me." But without opening a murder hornet's nest or stirring up Pandora's box, some might deem religion as an old wives' tale. Freud expounded this in *The Future of an Illusion.* John Mellencamp sang of religion in trying to get something for nothing in his 1991 "Nothing's for Free" saying, "'Cause nothin' worth nothin's for free." Whether one agrees or not, do you know the difference between prayers in church and prayers in a casino? In a casino, the people praying *really* mean it.

Guilty myself of this profane, self-serving praying, I cannot count the number of times I (and most really) vowed out loud, "God, *please* let me get even" or "I swear to God, if I get even, I'll do this or that." Occasionally I dug myself out of a huge hole, got even, and having made a deal with myself, went to church without being caught and branded as a heretic.

Other times, depending upon the amount I'd recouped, when I reached even, I'd gaze skyward and shout, "Thank you, Jesus!"

Contingent upon the amount of coffee I'd had and sleep I didn't, if I got even, I'd bolt from the top section. Like a British colonist *bwana* suffering jungle fever running amok in a 1950s, African jungle movie, I'd yell "Bwaa-ha-ha-ha. The rums! The rums! They're driving me *mad*! Deal me out! I'm even!" Relieving a mountain of stress, I didn't care what people thought although everyone could relate.

9

Optimal Quitting and Sour Grapes

THE MONTEREY CLUB HAD about four props, and one was named Dan, known as "Cowboy." He was unique, for he always wore a Western shirt, cowboy hat, and boots. He was resplendent when he took his wife dancing in some of those gol-darn, shit-kicker bars on the weekends. He didn't fit my image of a riverboat gambler, but more of an old West, saloon type habitué. Taciturn at the tables, when he spoke, it was softly. Invariably polite, he reminded me more of a Civil War officer or jazz musician with his moustache and goatee. He smoked through a cigarette holder. "It has a filter in it," he rationalized. When he was unneeded to prop a game, he'd sit along the rail awaiting a Floor man's shouting, "Player," the prop's call to arms. At these times I'd try to pick his brain, and he'd relate his time in the casino industry. He'd seen many poker pro wannabees who'd failed: "Oh, I've seen 'em come and go." He wisely devised a personal system by which he'd leave, whether up or down, when his shift was over. He reasoned, "The game'll be here tomorrow."

I also had the privilege of playing with an amusing fellow named Mike Caro who nicknamed himself, "Crazy" Mike, a composite of him. He usually dressed nicely in a sports coat and gave the impression of being goofy, if not downright crazy. His hair down the middle was vanishing at a gallop, and, fittingly, it looked as though someone took an eggbeater to the long hair that remained. He had an interesting way of moving, too, as if his joints were working at cross purposes. I suppose when he started writing books, he transformed from Crazy Mike Caro and anointed himself "The Mad Genius of Poker."

"Cowboy" Dan and Caro were of a similar mind. The Mad Genius of Poker espouses that good players beat bad players. He views poker as one, long, continuous game. If one's losing today, there's no necessity to try and get even for the day. Caro reasons out what makes this day any different, or more valuable, than any other 24-hour period. He assuredly concedes that one year is important. And he defers that a month is a reasonable time to be meaningful. But as an object question, like an Einsteinian thought problem, mind experiment, should one mount time periods on a sliding scale and further narrow the pathology report for two or three days, to one day, or to one hour? By this logic, one conceivably could distill the time horizon to the length of one hand. It seems illogical to him to worry about one day's outcome.

Cowboy Dan revealed, "So when my shift is over, I go home. But if I can break even playing in the games, I'll be able to save my paycheck. That paycheck is steady. And, of course, winning at the tables is a bonus."

I responded, "Very wise. I have a different mindset like a lot of the players. It seems that if I'm losing, I do everything in my power, legally of course, to try and get even, including playing marathons manically. I just feel rotten when I go home broke."

"Sure, JM. You're like most of the players. Even some, or most of the props I work with, have the same mentality. When I swing by the tables as I'm leaving, I often see one or two of my compadres still playing. We call it OT, overtime, and I don't like doing unpaid OT. Our OT is unlike other businesses in that the employee, the prop, doesn't get paid for OT. He's working for the club for free."

"Oh, I bet the club loves that," I said. "Because the club gets off-the-clock prop's services for free, this may violate my dictum that there ain't no free lunch. It gets an extra body to help keep a game going, collecting from a table that may've broke, and gets his collections, too."

Cowboy Dan went on. "Sometimes an off-duty dealer will sit in our game. Some are really bad. The other day, Clay was walking by, and all the players yelled, 'Hey, Clay! Come on over and play a little.' He said, 'Oh, no. I learned my lesson yesterday. I'm probably the worst player in the city. No make that the state.' Lou, 'The Lip' Lipsicky teased, 'Probably in the universe.' That was just cruel."

$$$

Samuel Butler scribed in *The Way of All Flesh*: "It is not as a general rule the eating of sour grapes that causes the children's teeth to be set on edge. Well-to-do parents seldom eat many sour grapes; the danger to the children lies in the parents eating too many sweet ones."

Some regulars came in late at night. I always saw Gordon arrive after sunset and leave prior to sunrise. I speculated that he either was a photophobe or a vampire. He was very pale—no tan, the sun's souvenir. In time I saw he was a pro. We often chatted. He was a highly successful *hombre* on the poker field and worked these hours to optimize his win rate. Opponents at that hour he arrived were tired, impaired by losing or drinking alcohol, or both, etc. He, on the other hand, was alert and fresh.

In one of our sidebar discussions he pondered, "Shiko tells me, 'Man, the game the other night was awesome—it was on coke. But I couldn't make a hand. If I'd have had the cards I got the next night, I wouldn't have gone broke.' And one time he actually said, 'If I was getting these cards in this game, instead of winning a thousand, I could've won two.' What could I say? It's like he always wants the best of it, and felt he missed out winning a ton in the prior game. JM, do think that's sour grapes?"

I said, "Yes. You can't order great cards in a great game. We can't predict how loose or good the lineup will be—doesn't work like that." Shiko's like someone who wishes he ordered a dish that you got. Sour grapes is somewhat like FOMO—Fear Of Missing Out—and seems a little like saying the grass is always greener on the other side of the fence. But I think that The grass is always greener saying just means that your neighbor waters or fertilizes their lawn better.

Gordon nodded and with a wry smile said, "But you could say the grass is always greener on the other side of the fence; unless it's blue."

"Blue?"

"You know, bluegrass," Gordon quipped.

"Love it. For sure Shiko saying those things means he has sour grapes and greediness." I postulate that the following three traits are like relatives you're ashamed of: Wanting something for nothing, incorporating a sour grapes mentality, and having your cake and eating it too. The latter means you can't have it both ways or have the best of both worlds.

"You're right," I concurred. "It's also like wishing we were born on a different date or era. The superstitious might want a different sign. That's out of our control. All we can do is control our reactions and decisions. Hence, if there's only bad games going, we can choose *not* to play."

"You sound like an Existentialist, JM."

"I can't spell it, but I am. I take full responsibility for my actions. I have free will in the limited Catholic sense of choosing right or wrong, too. But in the poker cosmos, players owning their results often is as implausible as having a winning streak of thirty days."

Poker habits, behaviors, and attitudes seep from our poker solar system into the everyday world, like beaming this sour grapes attitude into one's outside personal and business life, carrying over bluffing is a somewhat distasteful habit—some might call it lying. Of course, from the fog shrouded days during the invention of poker, bluffing was an acceptable strategy of poker. Whatever one says about one's hand is taken with a grain of salt. Lying about one's hand's okay; fibbing to family, friends, clients, or business associates not so okay. If you tell a lie, don't believe it deceives only the other person.

$$$

I broached the fact that The Mad Genius of Poker, Mike Caro, wrote books. He also lectured at the card clubs. To visualize Mike Caro lecturing, imagine Christopher Lloyd, "Doc," in *Back to the Future*. Take Doc out of his lab coat and put him into a rumpled, dark sport coat; tone down Lloyd's wide-eyed crazed look a little; and have him gesticulate with up-facing hands. At one of these pow-wows, attended by about seventy, someone asked, "Mike, how do you know when to leave a game?"

He grinned and quipped, "If you hum a few bars, I'll sing it." Then, getting serious, with his typical asymmetrical grin and professorial manner, he'd put both hands out as if he were pleading his case in front of SCOTUS and replied, "This is an age-old question. Should I go home with this win or stay and try to win more? Or, even though I'm stuck, should I leave a very tight game, *although* I could go on a huge rush and get even? My advice is that if you're playing well, and the game is good, stay. If the game is really juicy, but I've been playing a long time and I'm exhausted, I'd do anything I could to keep playing. I even might prop my eyelids open with toothpicks. *But*, if I'm playing poorly, I'm aggravated at myself or angry at someone at the table. If I have a pressing engagement in the morning, then I might leave, no matter how good the game is. Leaving is an art, not a science. You hear or read about a stop-loss system whereby you set a percentage of that day's winnings that you're willing to lose back before quitting. Naturally, like stocks, you let your profits run up. But again, it depends on my alertness, mood, and discipline. There's no ironclad rule. Now, the leaving ahead habit has a snowballing effect. It can be a self-perpetuating, good habit.

"On the other hand, there's another method regarding quitting. Although, to me, it seems like a fool's errand to set a goal, before you walk in, to win $500. *But* if you hit $500, and you're very happy with it, then leave."

With his characteristic stiffness in his upper body, altruistic demeanor, and pleading facial expression, he concluded, "I hope this answers your question."

To reiterate, the stop-loss plan advises that when ahead, one sets an amount that one's willing to accept losing prior to retiring. Like stocks. I'm ahead $1000, but I'm okay with selling if my profit drops to $800. From another view, one leaves when they reach a set point—the amount of chips in front of them. I've tried this system with varying success. Mostly I'd estimate that it only worked for me about 10-20 percent of the time. Suppose I was up a satisfactory or great amount, I'd think, *When and if I lose back 10-15 percent, I'll play to my blind and go.* Or I tried using a nominal amount like $100-150 as my supposed quitting trigger. Be that as it may, to be up a hefty amount meant that: 1. The game was great, 2. I was very fortunate in receiving an inordinate amount, a statistically skewed group, of favorable starting hands, 3. I was making winning hands by completing draws in either draw or Hold 'em; thus, I'd feel invincible, blessed, and far superior to my opponents. This latter feeling is common among players on a rush, heater, or *sizz*—a sizzling streak of disproportionately good hands. (BTW, marketing's mantra, Sell the sizzle not the steak.)

When I didn't adhere to the cutoff point (supposedly triggering my hoisting my ass up), I was as distressed as a parent missing a child and really mad at myself for losing back more than the predetermined amount. I tried to keep my vow to quit at that cut off, stop-loss point by swearing on my life or on my mother's soul. Being human, and not a totally logical, unemotional computer, my implementation of a stop-loss had flaws. Emotions entered the equation rather like extraneous, wrong path data in a formula or hypotheses. No, what it really takes to utilize any system successfully was discipline. Recall JM's Law #9 (Make poker work an exercise in patience, clear thinking, will power and flow playing). It was a *sine qua non.* Sear that into your noodle, JM.

Recall that losing the potential winnings plus what I took for that session, is an NTA, Negative Turn Around. Let's say I was up $1,000. Instead of leaving when I was *still* up $850, I might lose that $850 *and* $1,000, my day's budget. I'd be down $1,000 net, resulting in an $1850 NTA Furthermore, this doesn't help subsequent play, work. It's an NTA hangover, a gift that keeps on giving (taking). These NTAs were my *bête noires*—from French, literally meaning a black beast—a person or thing strongly detested or avoided, synonymous with a bugbear. This bugbear was the *gigantic* hole in my game.

10

The Melting Collage

ONE MEETS ALL KINDS of people from all over the world in the card clubs. As the great American project, some describe the United States as a mosaic rather than a melting pot. I, however, see the casino world as a melting pot, a metaphor that has *pot* in it. While any table might represent a microcosm of the local population, so a card club might be a microcosm of the social, economic, and political world.

Occasionally, walking through the card clubs is like strolling in Morocco through a bizarre bazaar.

"*Bon jour, monsieur.* Look at zis gold bracelet. Zee finest gold and finest workmansheep. *Mon ami*, don't you like eet?" "Hey. Look, I've got this TV out in my van that fell off a truck. I'll give it to you for $100." "Sir, I've got some men's cologne or woman's perfume I'll sell you cheap. They slipped off the delivery truck. Get some for yourself. Your girlfriend or wife or both. Make me an offer." These guys must have followed trucks around like blood hounds. I know one thing: Someone better fix those trucks' backdoors. Of course, fell off the truck meant the merch was boosted.

"My friend. Here, have a piece of chocolate. I have some Yves St. Laurent, velvet jackets out in the back. They fell off the camel. I'm sure I have your size. Only $100."

"JM, let me tell you about Korean brides. I'm a marriage broker, and I'll give you $1,000 to marry a young Korean woman from a rich family who wants their daughter to become an American citizen. I've helped lots of women. It's all legal. Here, look at some pictures. After meeting all the citizenship rules and being married for a year, you can divorce her. But many of the men fall in love and don't want to divorce." I guess I had a dazed and confused look on my face, because she gently put her hand on my arm to calm me like a lost child. She soothingly cooed, "Sh-sh. Have a piece of ginseng."

$$$

Whatever one's background, people basically were civil, and they kept their mouths shut about political differences. If you want to gamble, you have to abide by the rules and common courtesies or be banned. Leave your prejudices and racial animosities at the entrance, or at least control them. In fact, we're alike with atoms from the stars, from when the universe formed. Mostly everyone got along. I swear Judaic and Islamic tolerated each other. The same for Muslims, Sikhs, Hindus. Pakistanis and Indians. After all, since we're in The Big Enchilada, Los Angeles, even Mexicans and Texans were amicable (LOL). On a lighter note, fans of sports teams like Oklahoma-Texas peacefully coexisted. Putting aside their rivalries and differences also were supporters of the following: Alabama-Auburn, Lakers-Celtics, USC (Fight On!)-Notre Dame, even Navy (Go Navy. Beat Army!)-Army. Trying to be facetious, not offensive.

I suppose a gambler's need for action is greater than his or her need for political grudges and retribution. Put another way, gambling is apolitical. In some small way it's Utopian, and I hope this never changes. Of course, tempers occasionally explode like a solar flare five times the size of Earth, but for the most part things run smoothly. Furthermore, as inconceivable as it seems today, since 1936 when the Embassy Palace (using Palace is sick) opened in Gardena, gambling sites don't have metal detectors.

I always felt if this spirit of mutual acceptance and or tolerance could be adopted by the world, there'd be so much less conflict. Realistically, this is blue sky, for a card palace has a security force that can eject and or banish offending people. This seems impossible worldwide. If you suggest using a United Nations' peace keeping army, Pu-lease.

Backtracking. Here's my dream and wish if I were Ruler of the World. Whatever a divinity's name, it seems that the world's religious accept on faith that there's a Supreme Being. It seems so logical, simple, and desirable for each faith to advocate this: We believe in our God; you believe in yours. We live in our country and practice our way and you do the same in your country. That's natural and acceptable. We don't need to change your mind and vice versa. Virtually all religions preach that killing is always forbidden, so follow that teaching. Can we all live by the Golden Rule? No, not the one that proclaims that he who has the gold rules but treat others as one would want to be treated. Isn't there enough suffering and pain caused by nature without adding to this for religious and political reasons? Let us live together in peace.

In *The Journals* Søren Kierkegaard propounds:

The most terrible fight is not when there is one opinion against another, the most terrible is when two men say the same thing—and fight about the interpretation...

* * * * * * * * * * *

A man is inclined to want to support himself by killing people. Now he sees from God's Word [any religion's Prophet's Word] that this is not permissible, that God's will is, "Thou shalt not kill."

"All right," thinks he, "but that sort of worship doesn't suit me, neither would I be an ungodly man." What does he do then? He gets hold of a priest [any spiritual guide] who in God's name blesses the dagger. Yes, that's something different.

This addresses the people of faith, the devout who have arrived at similar philosophic views by different routes. What about a credo for the nonreligious who suspect there isn't a Supreme Being? (Die you heretics!) Is it so difficult to live and let live? Apparently, it is.

Do terrorists, extremists, religious fanatics, so called faithful, rationally dream they'll achieve any of their goals, or change people's minds, by killing and maiming noncombatants and innocents? Does their God condone murder? (Deny the Sword Verses and embrace the Peace Verses of the *Quran*.) What purpose does it serve to vandalize, destroy, and desecrate ancient artifacts, museums, and places of worship except to sow hatred and discord? Do extremists rationally foresee that Israel, or the Western world—its values and religions—will disappear? Is it righteous to kill innocent women, children? Do they not have mothers and loved ones? Incidentally, it's incomprehensible that a country's government would suppress girls and women and keep them uneducated. Religion aside, it seems stupid to waste one half of its population's intellectual capital and their fresh POV; problem solving; creativity, etc.

Agreed—enough pontificating already.

$$$

As kumbaya as I've been above, often one ran into real assholes. I thought Collison was the biggest penie in the world who relished tormenting me and others (small comfort). One might say the reptilian part of his venal brain was over developed. A South African immigrant, he probably playfully tortured golden moles and tenrecs when he was a kid on the veldt. There was a rumor that he was a *ganef* who embezzled a synagogue's money, had a standing warrant for his arrest and can never go back.

We all view others through our own prisms of experience, upbringing, country's culture and so on. Therefore, perceptions of others sometimes are totally opposite mine. I might think so and so is a total jerk, but another player might think that s/he is a saint. Take for instance, Frenchie, who for decades made his living buying gold jewelry wholesale, and then selling it in casinos. I usually worked higher limits than Frenchie, but when our paths crossed, in a lower limit game, I deduced that he wasn't a good player—too conservative. By too conservative I mean he was too timid, and money was too dear. He didn't treat checks as tokens or counters but translated the check's face value into US currency. One can't successfully compete like that. I heard the Frenchman say of Collison and his wife, Dee, "I zink zair Ingleesh. Zair good people, an' I lahk zem."

Talk about cognitive dissonance. I almost barfed. Yet, Frenchie obviously had a good experience with them. It was a puzzle, a perfect example of a parallax view.

Another instance of a parallax occurred when Frenchie chatted with me on the rail. "JM, yew zee ze guy over at zat table? Ze guy in seat 5 witz ze Nik-ee 'at? 'e eez a real ahss 'ole. 'Ee slow rolls me an' other bullsheet."

"Frenchie," I said. "I've never had a problem with Bobby Boudreaux. He's always been a gentleman with me."

"Frenchie" replied, "*Jamais deux sans trois.*" [Never two without three. Things happen in multiples.] "Joost wait."

Here are two different, conflicting experiences and interactions. Like life. Moreover, regarding revenge, I felt *esprit d'escalier*—something one wishes s/he had said or thinks of a good retort later. Hence, when Frenchie wanted me to exact revenge for him, I wished I'd said, "Confucius say, when you start on a journey for revenge, dig two graves." Brilliant Confucian lesson.

Being meticulous, a rule-invoking nit sometimes, I'm sure I rubbed many players against the grain. But I accepted people at face value; I respected another unless s/he dissed me. My credos of live and let live, *laissez-faire*, and a good guy until proven otherwise, were invaluable in the rough and tumble card jungle.

After many clashes with him, altercations that really exasperated me, I thought I'd try and be mature about our friction. One night while we were on the sidelines waiting, I said, "Hi, Collison. Look, can we bury the hatchet? Just not in my back? When we first met, I treated you with respect, but it seems since then you don't treat me equally. I know we've had our differences, but can you treat me with respect, and I'll do the same to you?"

"Sure. Let's see."

The detente didn't last long, maybe two sessions, when he needled me by asking to see my losing hand. There's more chance of a leopard turning into a jaguar than Collison changing his abrasive attitude. He still wanted to plant those *bandilleras* in my neck. Also, I realized by adding an *i* to his name I got a description of our interface—collision.

$$$

Let's see if I can delve into Collison's nefarious, scrofulous mind. I felt that he had venom in his veins. No disrespect (to snakes, not him). This is speculation, of course, but my working theory is this: Perchance he must have been raised as a rich kid, a favorite, probably spoiled. In the poker clubs he had a gigantic sense of entitlement and superiority. As Twain, Mark not Shania, wrote in *Tom Sawyer*, he had "the calm certainty of a Christian with four aces."

At first blush, because of his near-English accent, he seemed classy, but he had no class the way he treated some, including dealers. Again, the reason was unfathomable. He'd often needle or insult me, or others, by asking the dealer to show a losing hand. "Let me see that hand!" Chortle-snort. Smirking's what he did best, and he got a perverse pleasure from his digs. While within the letter of the cardroom laws, this is an extreme breach of etiquette and colossally rude. As the reader might surmise, the player who'd just lost the hand would be crestfallen or mad enough already without someone skewering them with a 7-gauge needle. Oddly perverse, he didn't give a damn. Since the casino natives weren't supposed to abuse this rule, he couldn't ask at every opportunity. Thus, he'd often craftily wait for me to lose a big pot, and then, he'd gleefully pounce like a smirking hyena, "Dealer, show his hand!" Enchanting.

Believe me, there were thousands of times I was dying to see an opponent's losing hand to learn four things: 1. If I had the best hand all the way or sucked out. 2. If I'd deduced my opponent's hand correctly (to test and improve my hand reading skills). 3. Maybe I folded in a multiway pot. By requesting the losing hand showing, the winner'd have to show. Would I have beat the *winning* hand? 4. especially, if I might have played the hand differently to maximize my profit. My minimax goal is to minimize my losses and maximize my profits compared to another player with those cards. However, I'm courteous. Knowing how I feel when I'm needled, I'm a gentleman and refrain from asking to see losing hands.

$$$

Naturally, players not only meet people from all over the world, but they also rub elbows with people from all US regions. When I first met Donny, I knew neither his nickname nor origin. Then I heard him talk and knew where he was from. Nicknamed "Boston"—he never let it be said that poker players weren't creative—he was stocky, with a fair Irish face and freckles. I said, "To me your accent hints of New England boarding schools or English private schools."

Boston said, "Thanks, pa-l."

"Yeah, pa-l in the elite sense, not the Bowery or gangster sense," I observed.

"A-yeh."

Over the months we'd clash in a friendly way. He was very skilled, tough, and conservative. He was likeable—players liked his wry sense of humor—and his game was respected.

One night he joined our table, and he haled me, "Hi-yah, pa-l."

I replied, "Hi, Boston. If I won't be imposing—"

"I'm ah ustah being imposed on. Wha's the youse o' being Ahrish if yah don't know that lifer will break yawr haht?"

"I see you're wearing your Boston Red Sox hat as always. Is it your lucky hat?"

"It wahkts fah me wicked good. But aftah basebahl seasohn, and when basketbahl seasohn comes, I hafta wearh my Celtics jersay."

Even though I liked Boston, that didn't mean I wanted to be in his game. Since he was so tough, he considerably tightened up the game, and he made it much less profitable. Once a man who was buried—losing big— saw that Boston was coming to his game. He said, "Oh, great. I'm at a table with a bunch of vipers, and here comes the king mongoose."

$$$

Part of the casino (by now clubs outside Gardena were known as casinos) rules allow a change of tables. Sometimes another game is so juicy—filled with live ones—compared to the game you're in that switching to it will be more profitable, potentially. This is a meta-game wherein one jockeys to be first on the so-called change list. To use a college lesson, I habitually wish to keep my options open, but I sheepishly admit that for poker, FOMO plays a part. Thus, I always discreetly request a table change before I sit down. I could decline the change. The smart, savvy floor staff knew my idiosyncrasy, and s/he would automatically put up my initials when I sat in.

For most poker players, the bromide that the grass is always greener on the other side of the fence couldn't have more truth and clarity. For me, wanting on the change list had nothing to do with superstition, but rather dealt with profit potential. Likewise, grazing herbivores also seem to believe that the grass is always better on the other side. Since even cows know there ain't no free lunch, they should pay, perhaps with moolah, to cross over to the other side.

11

Penies and Records

"HEY, JM. COME SIT with me," Tony said. He was a very amiable, *Nisei* gentleman, with a flat top. Always pleasant, I don't remember ever seeing him in an argument, almost unheard of in the card clubs.

"Nice to see you, Tony. How long have you been waiting for a game?"

"Not long. I got here about fifteen minutes ago. The Rams are here."

"The football team?"

"Nah. The Raggedy Assed Masses. You know, the overfed, undereducated and under washed."

True. With three-day weekends like this, there was so much nervous energy and excitement that the synaptic discharging current could have powered Mombasa for a month. "Yeah, the joint is jumping. There'll be a lot of new blood. Tourists, out-of-towners, and local, non-regulars."

"There could be some juicy games tonight," Tony said, grinning.

"Hope so. So, Tony, I see that you usually come after work. What do you do?"

"I work in aerospace. I'm an electrical engineer. How about you?"

I pretended to be worried and said, "On the advice of counsel, I'd like to assert my right against self-incrimination, as guaranteed by the Fifth Amendment to the US Constitution, and respectfully decline to answer."

"Oh, you're a tricky one."

"You know I'm really private about my business. It seems that the more players and the riffraff know about you, the more ammunition they have to use against you. Lest you think I'm being paranoid, you know Shiko? Japanese guy … Pudgy. About five-eight. He has a baby face with pudgy cheeks like a devious chipmunk about to steal your nuts. Pretends to be an action player."

My heart rate was rising with a white coat effect even as I thought about Shiko. No, my systolic was pounding higher not from not seeing a doctor, but more from a tight, white, institutional, funny suit effect.

Tony asked, "What's he do?"

Clenching my teeth, I answered, "I'm not sure, but I'm sure he's a jerk of all trades. No, seriously, I think he's in sales, for he's usually wearing a suit and tie." In my opinion if he worked for free, he'd still be overpaid.

"Oh, yeah. Has kind of pursed out lips?"

"Yeah. He knows I want to be called by my initials. You and most everyone honors that. But if he's losing or trying to throw me off my game, he'll call me by my first name. He knows that gets a rise out of me. Plus, he'll tell everyone at the table, 'Hey, everybody, this is John.'" I didn't confide to the general population that Shiko's jibes and taunts echoed throughout my next days like a rifle shot in a canyon. "Oh, but wait. If he wants something, or needs something, it's 'Hey, JM, did you make your hand?' Or 'JM, are gonna change seats 'cause I want it if you don't.'" Perhaps I detested his hypocritical manipulation, for I have a smidgen of hypocrisy, too. Frequently we dislike a feature in others that we ourselves have.

"You know, I've been meaning to ask you. Why don't you want to be called by your real name?"

"It's a long story. Do you really want to hear it?"

"Sure. I got nothing better to do," and he shrugged and nodded toward the long wait list.

"When I first started playing, I was just out of college. I was interviewing. I went to the Normandie Club in Gardenia—"

Tony caught what he thought was my mispronouncing the city. "Don't you mean Garden*a*?"

I explained why I sarcastically call it Gardenia. I learned from experience that Gardenia was the antithesis of a beautiful, soft, bright, sweet-smelling flower. With all due respect, it's like calling New Jersey the Garden State. First, evidence.

I asked him, "I don't know if you heard about the heavy drug user, Chris? 'The Ace of Space' who committed suicide?"

While Plato advised moderation in all things, Chris' credo might have been: Nothing in moderation, including moderation. Obviously, he and his credo were confused. Chris chose the ultimate relief from pain, death. 💀. Now, if there ain't no free lunch, there most assuredly ain't no free drugs. Rad.

"The Gardenia police entrapped him, and he was sentenced to jail. He couldn't face jail, so he jumped to his death. The city's *own* police entrapped one of their card club patrons!"

Switching me even further off track, he asked, "Hey, JM. You ever been arrested?"

"Seven arrests. No convictions. I didn't heed the warning signs. Don't touch the strippers!

"Second reason for calling it Gardenia. I opened an account for check cashing. Would you believe my credit limit was $10? I had a college friend, Allan, who knew my full name and where I played. Apparently, needing the money to gamble, he filled out and cashed a $10 counter check on my account." Proving the rule, he did get something for zilch, but at what a gigantic risk. In retrospect, he seemed to be spiraling downward, for he took a huge chance writing a fraudulent check, committing a felony and was on the path to becoming a degenerate gambler.

I took a deep breath and continued. "The cancelled check showed his and my signatures weren't even close. His signature scratching resembled the dirt floor at a chicken fight. My signature was much more refined like hieroglyphs. Obviously, the cashier didn't verify his ID, nor put a driver's license number on the back of the counter check, nor compare Allan's signature to mine on file. Since this was their error, I thought they'd refund my money. No dice." This example of Gardenia ethos also is why I call it Gardenia.

After this long digression, I finally answered Tony's question, "So, I was out $10, and so that's why I don't want people to know or use my name. I told you it was long."

I didn't divulge to Tony that I had other reasons for not using my first name. It is, however, solipsistic. To be inconspicuous isn't paranoia, in my opinion, but a meta strategy. First, if opponents want to compare notes about me, I want to be less identifiable and more camouflaged. Second, it also created a kind of litmus test, i.e., players would reveal their true colors toward me if they called me John.

Tony smiled, "Now I understand. So, when people ask me about you, I'll say, JM's real name is John. But he wants to only be called JM. That's because he's paranoid."

"What! I'm not paranoid. Wait! *Who* said I was?"

"Relax, JM, I'm joking. And see! I already know your real name."

"Yikes, ya got me." We laughed. "You know, when Shiko and I first became acquainted, he was friendly and jovial. We discussed where we had each lived. Later, when we were almost mortal enemies, out of the blue he asked, 'John, I mean JM. Do you still live over by Japonica Boulevard? I'm curious about the home prices.' Since he wanted something, he used my initials rather than my name. He was extraordinarily manipulative. I thought about answering, but I thought better of it. I thought, *You've got a lot of* chutzpah. *Why on earth would I tell you? You'll eventually want to use this info against me.* Tony, have you ever been in a no-win situation? Interacting with him was lose-lose."

"Oh, sure. We've all been there."

"You know," I went on, "Although rare, especially in poker, I was once in a win-win spot. A college friend introduced me to his boss, Ray. I became a regular at their home game and became friends with Ray and his wife. They always paid for dinner when we went out. Always. He was like an older brother, and they were making good money, while I still was interviewing. I was on a double date with them, and I decided that I wanted to pay once. He wouldn't hear of it. I tried to grab the check, but he was faster. I didn't want to create a scene, so I proposed this. Let's gamble. How about we flip a coin, and the loser pays. He agreed. I so badly wanted to buy them dinner that I truly wanted to lose the flip. Even if he lost and bought, I'd be ahead some money. It was an unusual situation where I couldn't lose—a win-win."

Tony acutely noted, "Kind of like when you volunteer. Both sides benefit. So, JM, who paid?"

"I'm not sure."

Lest the reader bust me for getting something for *nada*, I often house sat for them and took care of their pets. Ray said, "I view paying for your dinners as home insurance and pet sitting costs."

Tony and I stopped to listen to initials being called, but he didn't hear his. City ordinances limited the card rooms to 35 tables, so if all the tables were in use, they couldn't spread another game.

Having stewed about Shiko's insults, I still had an ax to grind. "Once I was leaving the game we were in to change tables. Being ever courteous, I waited my turn to act, and then I tossed my cards toward the discards. As I moved my chips and trays toward my new table, I hear him indignantly sneer, 'Hey, *John*! You almost killed my hand.'

"I thought, *You asshole. Why do you insult me? I'd never intentionally throw my cards and foul someone's hand.* Naturally, I didn't say that." Since Shiko's claim was a total lie, I just ignored my malefactor. I didn't take the bait. He couldn't get the satisfaction of irritating me if he was unaware that I heard him. I probably should've ignored him more, but often we were butting heads at the same table within earshot. I concluded to Tony, "In this instance, I wasn't going to be at his table. So why on earth would he try to rile me? He had no reason to try and throw off my game except spite and maliciousness. What a penie."

"What's that? A penis?"

"Yeah, a dick. Humorously in Yiddish, *petsele* or small penis."

"I noticed, too," Tony agreed, "that when he's losing, he can really be a jerk. Shiko-Shiko and I are heads-up. He checks. Since I've paired, I try to bluff. When he calls, I say, 'Pair.' He laughs, and needles me with, I have a peach. Get it fixed. Hey, I've been meaning to ask, what do you do for work?"

"Since you're a decent guy, I'm in the video games industry. This is under the strictest confidence. I have a company installing video games in places like bars, restaurants, convenience stores, and pizza places. This gives me a lot of free time ... time to play poker. As we speak, my games are out there working their processors and hearts out making money for me. Sweet."

"That's interesting and explains that when I'm here you're here. I thought you played every day. I thought you were a professional player or at least a regular."

"Nah-ah. The way I play, no way." I'm sure he could see through this self-deprecating statement, for he should've discerned that I was a winning player. As much as I tried to downplay my skill and winning results, I'm sure most denizens of the poker underworld knew or guessed I was a winner. Probably most didn't care.

Like a mom hearing an almost inaudible, newborn's cry, Tony heard his initials called over the fray. "Okay, JM, I gotta go. See you later. Good luck."

$$$

I studied others' game, motivation and skillfulness like a lion stalking on the Serengeti. I also ruminated on my worthy opponents' tells. (This topic would require a book, and in fact there are books about reading one's opponent.) The expert poker smith is aware they should attempt to get inside the opponent's head. Keynes put it succinctly: "Successful investing is anticipating the anticipations of others." However, it's very challenging trying to see through another's lens and or prism. It's akin to trying to understand what's going through the mind of a high-speed-chase driver. Also, seeing yourself from another's point of view is like Einstein's relativity—their perception depends on where they are.

Would it be overly egocentric that whereas, I dissected them, did they study me? It's debatable, and certainly dependent upon the individual. The more serious player and or the professional would. Yet, as mentioned above, I think most didn't care.

I had varying success delving into an opponent's mind. I could impute these motivations: A need for excitement and action; winning money; comradery; abusing others; being the boss, top dog, etc. It's costly to over or underestimate one's antagonists. Is this not true in most competitions? Still, I couldn't bank on my reads. Oh, to be clairvoyant. But then again, if I were a mind reader, a mass herd reader, then I'd use those skills making billions in financial markets, not in *relatively* penny ante poker. Later I even clocked the hand-playing frequency of an adversary with whom I was unfamiliar or forgotten.

Retreating way back to my nascent, neophyte Gardenia playing days, there was a friendly, bookish, professional player named Quentin known as "The Book." He went on the board by the initials Q.E.D. (*quod erat demonstrandum*). Unlike me, who feigned indignation at being addressed by my name rather than initials, he didn't get irritated if someone called him Quentin—he too was unflappable.

Uniquely, he made notetaking on opponents an art form. Periodically he'd record something on an 8 ½" x 11" page of dead tree. He alphabetically inserted these observations in a huge notebook. "What are you recording?" I once asked. I was a wide-eyed rookie, and I wanted to learn from this reputedly very successful player.

"Oh, it's just numerology," he dissembled.

I'm thinking, *Like, the Kabala?*

His book's size couldn't be concealed, so he made no attempt to hide that he was noting players' patterns, style, bluffing tendencies, etc. Surprisingly, he'd graciously let people look in it. Of course, one wanted to see notes on oneself. "Oh, thanks, Q.E.D. Ah-ha, here I am. JM. No, wait! It's coded."

When The Book first entered a Draw High game, or when a new player entered his game, he'd open the binder, find the person's page, and see prior notes for strategic use during the current session, or update whatever new pearl he'd gleaned. If he was sure he hadn't met the adversary before or no notes existed, he'd create a new page on the spot. What about someone he intuited he'd played against, but couldn't recall? Quentin just said with a smile, "I remember playing against you, but I've forgotten your name." It was amusing to see the opposition tell The Book his or her name, and then see The Book flipping through his notes searching for that player.

In contrast, when I adopted Quentin's technique, I secretly made notes into a small booklet in my lap under the table. I entered my observations by categories; i.e., tells, m.o., action scale, bluffing tendencies, etc. Later this note updating evolved to putting the notebook on top a small tray, covering it with newspaper's stock quotes section, and rolling a larger tray over everything to prevent observation and theft of my stuff.

Apparently, I fooled most, for many asked for my stock picks; however, I didn't fool the more observant players who often teased about my note taking. Tyche once asked me, "What're you gonna do with all this info"

Collison's wife asked, "What's your book say about my husband?"

Being very cerebral (or maybe anal), I recorded extensive notes. Due to my makeup, I'd also feel lazy if I didn't work at this. My notes usually weren't as extensive as those on Kelly (below). When I competed with someone for whom I'd created a card, I reviewed it as soon as possible. Knowing their tendencies was advantageous. As I mentioned earlier, I considered playing poker working. Hence, I adjusted Pasteur's quote: "In the fields of observations, chance [poker] favours only the prepared mind."

$$$

I speculate the amount of time and effort over the years to accumulate this intel will prove that my prepared mind will be profitable. I kept this precious intelligence inside a photojournalist's, sleeveless vest from Banana Republic that I called my work jacket. It's fabulously designed in an ergonomic sense and is an excellent utilitarian garment—it has a pocket for everything. Form follows function. Fishers like it, for it has a-lure.

With the player profile cards, one of the most important items in it was my records' sheet. I recorded the date, the casino, limit(s) played, start and end times, rank of game, working capital (WC) brought, and crucially, the net results. Whereas most don't keep records, and, thereby, fool themselves whether they're winning players, I knew my results to the dollar. Each session's outcome goes into a master accounting allowing me to study later and find areas to improve. Unlike notes on players, I made results data away from the table, hopefully at the cashier.

Shah Kwah also showed me a way of counting in blackjack using two chips, and I adopted this to track the number of hands won-lost per ten.

Okay, maybe I overdid record keeping and have a twinge of CDO. Most know this as obsessive-compulsive disorder, OCD, but I insist that we call it CDO—the letters *must* be in alphabetical order.

Re WC taken and or check(s) written, from years of experience I concluded that it was expedient only to take a fixed amount of WC, enough ammo, to compete at my game's limit. Mainly, though, this was to limit *big* losses. Re start-end time, I wore a chronograph with stopwatch and alarm functions that permitted me to take periodic breaks and return before my next blind arrived in 10 – 14 minutes.

$$\$\$\$$$

After decades playing against The Book, Q.E.D., one night I found some of his notes on a scrap of paper he'd discarded after he left the game. It showed opponents' initials, and since I'd been in his game, I knew each player either by their initials or seat number. By each person were various numbers and letters. For the life of me I couldn't make sense of the cryptic notes, especially on me. I put this evidence into my all-purpose jacket. The next time I saw him, I asked, "What do these letters and numbers mean? I can't make heads nor tails of them."

"If you understand them, what kind of code would they be?"

Years later, I bumped into him. We both had metamorphosed from High Draw in Gardenia to Lowball. But when Low died, he traversed to Seven Card Stud. I, on the other hand, now was well versed in Hold 'em. We chatted, and we compared notes on old people we used to play: Stumpy, Fingers, Aussie Pat, One-Eyed Earl, Nicky The Greek. Toothpick Dick was tall, lean, perfectly quaffed, and, in short, he looked stately except he always played with a toothpick in his mouth. "Gatsby" Tommy's name paraded by like a Tommy Hilfiger model on a catwalk. Tommy had a square face and frame, stood about 5' 9", was always immaculately attired—resplendent like Jay Gatsby—and there wasn't a stray hair to be found. The Book nodded and said, "Gatsby Tommy. That's a blast from the past. Well, you know I keep records. It's interesting. In 20 years, he didn't bluff me once. So, when I played him, I never had to worry about that. What an advantage. When he bet, I folded my weak hands or bluff catchers with a clear conscience."

I added, "I know a friend of his, Jamie, who has known him forever. My friend said Tommy never worked a day in his life. He just played poker." But by dressing to the nines, Gatsby burnished his image to non-regulars as a successful businessman. His Chinese girlfriend, Nina, was also a poker pro. What an interesting pair. She played the highest limits, and she was one of the best.

"Good seeing you, JM. I've got to go back to my game."

"Great seeing you, Q.E.D. Good luck."

I had an ah-ha moment. From his own admission, probably one of the letters on The Book's cheat sheet, the scrap of paper he left behind, assigned the chances that an opponent bluffed. I also believed I cracked an obvious category whether someone was strong, good, or live—loosey-goosey. Nevertheless, with this additional bit of intel that bluffing was one of his categories, I still wasn't confident of my deciphering. I desired to break his code into some uniform-cuneiform, but I'm neither George Smiley nor Richard Feynman. Put another way, I needed an Enigma machine like the WWII Allies used to break the German codes. I desperately wanted to find a *Rosetta Stone*. Alas, The Book's little piece of papyrus wouldn't be my key. I might have to hunt him down some day and ask him point blank.

12

The Fine ART of Tells

"TELLS" IS SHORT FOR "telegraphs" or behaviors revealing the strength of someone's hand. On the green, baize battleground, most often a person is trying to hide their hand's real strength, but that's difficult to conceal. Like lying, there's a kernel of truth present. The challenging trick is *detecting* the body language clues and *deciphering* their true meaning. It's more art than science—it is a gestalt process; i.e., this method is more than the sum, integration, of its individual parts. In conjunction, since a tell is very brief and involuntary, it's hard to fake. In the poker cosmos, is my opponent subconsciously revealing a sincere, true tell or a false tell? False tells sell, or try to promote, a story of one's hand. But false ones must be subtle, for as a Minimalist might say, Less is more. I suppose divining a tell with certainty would encompass telepathic ability to read someone's mind.

Caro wrote the definitive poker book on body language clues, *Book of Tells: The Body Language of Poker*. (Dr. David Hayano also contributed to this code cracking in *Poker Faces*.) The gist: If a player's hand is weak—bluffing for example—s/he acts strong. If the opponent is strong and really wants you to call, often s/he acts weak. Using the aforementioned broken wing act. This Hollywood-ing can be subtle or obvious. The opponent might even forlornly sigh!

Simple examples. In Lowball: A player looks at the card drawn, but if s/he looks back at the other four, it might mean the card paired her or him; thus, s/he virtually had a losing hand. In Hold 'em: Rechecking their hole cards for suits might be similar. Sometimes the indicators are subtler. The adversary might take a sip of water, stare you down, or bet clumsily. Once you think you have read an opponent's tell, however, the observer must consider that the opponent might be aware of tells theory, being almost microscopically scrutinized and consequently intentionally emit a false tell(s).

To demonstrate the wide range of tells, not all tells are acts. A non-poker-playing girlfriend once told me that her dad said having shirt cuffs monogrammed was classier than having one's shirt pocket monogrammed. It was rare to see a monogrammed shirt in the card palace; however, it is indicative that this player probably was precise, conservative in betting, and unlikely to bluff. So, it was not only a fashion statement, but a fashion tell. Poker is fascinating, *n'est-ce pas*?

Another term for tells is micro-expression, a quick, involuntary, facial expression happening during stressful, fiscally, or emotionally important situations. Micro-expressions were described in Paul Ekman and Wallace Friesen's *Unmasking the Face* and in Malcolm Gladwell's *Blink*. By the way, Caro's *Book of Tells* predated these other two books, but Caro didn't coin micro-expression.

Micro-expressions express the seven universal emotions: Disgust, anger, fear, sadness, happiness, surprise, and contempt. With that in mind, in the 1990s, Paul Ekman expanded his list of basic emotions to include a range of positive and negative emotions—not all of which are encoded in facial muscles. Naturally, there's some overlap. These emotions are amusement, embarrassment, excitement, guilt, pride, relief, satisfaction, pleasure, and shame. They are very brief, lasting only 1/15 to 1/25 of a second. Jill Taylor wrote of Ekman in *Time Magazine*: "Thanks to Paul Ekman and his work on facial expression, emotion and deception, we have a better understanding of how the expression and gestures we display on the surface are a direct reflection of what is going on in the neurocircuitry deep inside our brains."

$$$

Another theoretical camp for translating facial, body expressions is Neuro Linguistic Programming. Remember, the prime reason a poker player wanted to find tells was for profit, not to advance research. Dah. Richard Bandler and John Grinder, in their book *Frogs into Princes: Neuro Linguistic Programming,* hypothesize that the direction a person's eyes look can reveal whether they are making a truthful statement; for instance, a right-handed person will look up and to the right after lying. Sorta. But it isn't as simple as some recent television shows or movies portray. (I, and I, believe most poker players loved the series 'Lie to Me' and 'Bull.') In these shows, a Sherlock deduces if a person is being untruthful simply because the person looked left or right while making a statement. In reality, it's foolish to make such a snap judgment without further investigation, but scientists feel this technique does have some merit.

$$$

In the real world, this ability to read is invaluable; for example, in business, child rearing, police work, and counter terrorism to name a few. Is it true when a loved one informs me, with a slightly askew smile, that they aren't cheating? Is it true when a seller says their used car is a great deal, but they have a slight stutter or a catch in their voice?

Across the land of innumerable bars, honky-tonks and juke joints, how many broken hearts could be avoided if people knew how to pick up tells on those using pickup lines? (Nowadays, though, the pickup artiste may be hetero—or homo—sexual, so I shouldn't say just women could dodge a broken heart wreck.) How much more sports can men watch if they can read their spouses? How much happier could my audience be if I could see their reactions while reading this? I cannot *tell* ya.

13

A Koan for Arniss

ARNISS CAUGHT ME AND said, "Hi, JM. Can I talk to you a minute?" Arniss, pushing forty hard, was a kindhearted woman. A small winner at best, she was always in the card club. Arniss' home life must've been tenuous, for if she had a husband, he probably never saw her. With her aquiline face, hawkish nose and always wearing a tightly wrapped bandana on her head trying to keep the club's smoky, wretched smell out of her hair, she reminded me of a Hieronymus Bosch. Don't get me wrong. Shah Kwah and I loved her. She was far more experienced than us who were in our early twenties. She took a liking to us, and she gave us free poker lessons. She voluntarily schooled us in what I called the Arniss Lowball Poker Academy.

"Sure, Arniss. What's up?"

"First, sorry to bother you. Where're you headed?"

"I'm done for the night. I'm heading home. Hallelujah."

"I'm glad, JM. I have this problem at work. I'd like your advice." She told me a detailed story of volunteering as treasurer for a committee at work chaired by an Andy. Essentially, "Do you think I should attempt to sue them for slandering me?"

I couldn't read the committee's mind. Also, I didn't want to get my fingerprints on this mess, be embroiled in an internecine war. "As I said, I'm not a lawyer." Dundun. "But as I understand it, it's extraordinarily hard to win this type of suit. You have to prove that they meant malice, and that it caused you losses. Don't get me wrong. I don't want to come across as holier than thou ... I know I'd feel as you in your situation, and I'm sure I'd be gnashing my teeth and maybe losing sleep. But the meds help," I laughed. "But my best advice is to let it go. The time and energy and money that you'll spend won't be worth it. You may spend a lot of money by suing, but you may never get anything back. And I guarantee that the aggravation isn't worth it."

"Well, so far, I haven't lost any sleep nor spent any money. Just my time."

"Yeah, but your time is worth something. I mean, it's yours to do with what you want but think of all the annoyance." Then I put my hand on her shoulder and joked, "Not just your aggravation, but you're dragging me in."

"Sorry about that, JM. I didn't mean to waste your time."

"No, no. Honestly? Not a problem. Listen, I don't know if you ever heard this koan?"

"*Scone*, like pastry?"

I spelled out, "K-o-a-n. Co *ahn*. Koans're like Zen parables on which one meditates. As a result, you derive life lessons and insights." The classic ones are What sound does one hand clapping make? and If you meet The Buddha on the road, kill him. "Maybe you read this koan John Vorhees wrote about in *Card Player Magazine*. There're two disciples of a Chinese religious order walking along. When they get to a deep stream, they encounter a finely dressed lady who is obviously very distraught. She says, 'I must get across this stream, but I don't want to ruin my wedding gown. Can you help me?' One of the monks carries her across, and she thanks him profusely. Later, after the two men have walked about a mile, one turns to the other, and says, 'Our vows prohibit us from touching a woman. You have broken your vow.' The other replies, 'I put the woman down long ago. You are still carrying her.' I loved that. It's valuable to me ... when I remember to apply it. Arniss, let her, it, go."

"I get it. But there's also other things involved—"

I cut in. "What are the possible benefits of pursuing this? Breathe in ... breathe out, Let her go ..."

"Yeah. The world doesn't want to hear about your sore toe. It wants to show you its sore toe. Tell you its troubles."

"Or not show you its toe but smash yours." I begged off by saying, "I've got to go. Goodnight, Arniss, and good luck with this."

She slouched off. I thought of the despondent Romeo telling the apothecary, whence he has gone for poison: "The world is not thy friend, nor the world's law, The world affords no law to make thee rich"

People, life, the universe aren't always fair. Are you listening, JM?

$$$

I bumped into Arniss a couple of weeks later. She'd been playing at another club. "Hi, Arniss. How're you doing?"

"Fine, JM."

"Hey, how're you doing with that mess at work?"

"Oh, I'm at peace. I just figured, if they don't want professional auditing, and want to rip off the petty cash, more power to them. Let them stew in their own corruption."

I was happy for her. "Good for you! Some of the board guys sound like poker players or rounders who want freebies, comps and twofers. You've certainly heard this bad to the bone koan. When the student is ready, the teacher will appear. Allow me to flatter myself saying I'm your teacher."

I saw her about a month later, "Oh, hi, Arniss. I read another koan that I think perfectly applies to your situation. 'The mountain doesn't care about the clouds. It isn't touched, it isn't moved, and it isn't changed at all'. So, it lets all the turmoil, hub bub and troubles pass over it."

"Yes. Now I exhale the past and inhale the future."

$$$

Six months later, I was playing with a semi-regular who played well. He looked respectable, meaning he was attired in business casual, had the friendly demeanor of an insurance salesman, and never raised his voice. He pointed out Arniss to me and told me he worked with her. Then I realized that he was the committee member, Andy, whom Arniss had problems with. Usually, I'd ask someone how the subject played. Yet, in this case, since I'd listened to her stories about the volunteer committee, I was curious about his perceptions, so I asked, "I kinda know her. Tell me about her at work."

"Sure, but in the strictest confidence. She's in the accounting department but was on this committee that I'm on too. She just made so much trouble and strife. She got onto tangents that weren't our concern."

"Like what?"

"I don't want to go into the particulars, but finally the group decided to phase her out at the first chance. We phrased it that we wanted to rotate the members and get new people with new ideas. She went ballistic and said, 'You can't do that.' She took it like we were kicking her off, and I guess in a way we were."

It's *always* intriguing hearing both sides of a story, seeing each party's perceptions, their sometimes diametrically opposed take on facts and events. Judges' heads must throb to the point of developing an aneurysm. I didn't disclose that I'd heard her side. As I've bragged, I'm very discreet, so I didn't inform either one of my discussions.

Like Frenchie who really liked Collison whom I abhorred, these diametrically opposed viewpoints were a minor mystery, not gigantic ones. When I faced major puzzlers, I was like a Neanderthal trying to grasp an echo. Where are Amelia Earhart, Jimmy Hoffa, MH370 and O. J.'s knife? On what date does a new decade start—January 1 of year 00, 10, 20, 30, etc. or 01, 11, 21, 31, etc.? Who are first generation in US: The immigrant parents born outside the US, or their kids who're born in the US? Why do Russians, Chinese or others in dictatorships vote? Why do people love to pop bubble wrap? How do you properly pronounce Qatar in English? Why would a person be a transgender (trans), transvestite, cross dresser and homo-, bi-, abro-, or demi- sexual? Whaa?

14

Table Talk of the Town

ONE NIGHT, PLAYERS SAT around an empty table waiting for a new game to start. Math Drew was gossiping about Floor men. "You know 'Tonopah' Tony? As incredibly negative as he is, he could be on the perpetual honor roll for negativism. Don't get me wrong, I like Tony, but, man, he has pessimism coming out the wazoo." Like most Floor arbiters, Tonopah Tony had a reputation for not playing favorites and adjudicating player disputes in a fair, consistent way. We players liked fair and consistent rulings. Everyone liked him. He was lithe, handsome, well-manicured, had perfectly coiffed, glossy, black hair, and he spoke with a hoarse baritone. All in all, he was very patrician. Envision Richard Cory, except Tonopah wasn't suicidal. Just then, he cruised nearby, and Drew said to us, "Watch this. Hey, Tonopah, how's it going?"

"I'm still sucking air. Barely though."

"Has the casino's water heater exploded?"

Without missing a beat, "Well, Drew, not yet." He continued on his rounds.

"See?" Drew was as proud of his proof as a geometry student. Tonopah Tony not only adhered to Murphy's Law (If anything can go wrong, it will), but he also subscribed to O'Toole's Commentary on Murphy's Law (Murphy was an optimist). Interestingly, the English call this jaundiced outlook, Sod's Law that has an added twist of fate mocking you. To ward off this mocking, Camus, ever jocular, wrote "There is no fate that cannot be surmounted by scorn."

It was fun to know about the staff's outside peccadillos and quirks. Young players like me were like high school students looking up to the teachers—but in this setting it was the Floor men who held a great deal of power on the floor. They could rule favorably on an altercation over a pot that might be $200 or more, and for the stakes I played then, this pot could make or break my session's results. They could cut a player some slack for bad behavior, and they had a further power. Within reason, they could issue collection refunds for the pre-paid thirty minutes. If one'd lost their last dollar, this might ease the sting somewhat, and it was good PR. If one were smart, s/he tried to get on a Floor person's good side by toking.

$$$

"I'm in sales and import and export manufactured goods," a player known as "Bangkok" explained. A self-employed salesman who often traveled to Bangkok, he went on the waiting list as BK. One can visualize a stranger's confusion when other players called this Anglo, hulking, gregarious, smoker Bangkok. Someone at our table heard, "Bb on table 14." Seat 3 asked, "Who is BB?" Without missing a step, Bangkok replied, "Oh, it's Burt Burrito. Or his cousin Benvenuto Bizzarrini."

Not realizing that Bangkok was teasing and making an alliterative riff, another player, Steadley, tried to correct Bangkok. "No, a bb is a blow back. A collection refund."

Ignoring that, Bangkok continued, "Or it could be Burrito Bandito. Or Bigbird Botticelli."

Holding his head, Steadley moaned, "Make it stop!"

After a few more hands, Math Drew ignored Bangkok's interrupting his gossip and continued. "It's sad. You know the Floor man, 'Round' John. He's got this cherry, 1957 Continental Mark II he restored. It's a beaut."

"Yeah," I agreed. "I've seen it. What about him?"

"He isn't much older than us and got this great job, but he's making good money, *but* too much. It's all going up his nose. Apparently, he'll party hard overnight, then call in sick. Management got fed up and fired him."

"Really sad. Maybe you've heard this epigram, Cocaine is God's way of showing that you make too much money."

Drew concurred, "So true in his case." As reported earlier, drugs can be an enormous hole in one's game and life. In his case, it was an open pit, copper mine-sized hole that was debilitating. "And did you hear about 'Sulu?'" Sulu, at the Normandie Club. This was the mid-70s, so there were a lot of *Trekkers* in the poker universe. He couldn't have had a more appropriate nickname. His girlfriend and he had a huge fight. One night she comes in and shoots him. He may wish differently, but she didn't kill him. Just paralyzed him from the waist down. Yikes.

I now pictured him. "Oh, is that the good-looking Asian guy in a wheelchair?"

"Yup. Poor guy."

15

Clichés Game and Evolution

ONE EVENING I SWUNG by the Commerce Casino. I bumped into Math Drew in the parking lot, and we walked into the casino.

"Hey, Drew. Listen. You liked the epigram Change your luck—kiss a duck. You seem to like wordplay, so I wanna tell you about this game I invented. One substitutes dildo for the noun or verb in clichés, and you create a funny, new adage. This seems to work for all clichés. Case in point. One of my favorites is Strike while the iron is hot perfectly alters to Strike while the dildo is hot. Where there's a will there's a way transforms into Where there's a dildo there's a way. Another is A fool and his dildo, money, are soon parted. Very apt in poker. But I admit that there seems to be at least one exception. I can't make this work. Waste not, want not. Altering it to Dildo not, want not is senseless."

But Math Drew, having patiently listened, answered, "How about Waste dildo, want dildo?"

"Drew, you saved it. Yay!" I literally cheered. "My dildo substitution game survives without exception." Encouraged, I added, "The dildo is mightier than the sword. True in some circles. And I never met a dildo, man, I didn't like."

Drew pretended to choke himself and said, "Now you're just being silly."

Undaunted, I resumed, "An ounce of prevention is worth a pound of dildo, cure."

Drew made a time out sign. "Please, give it a rest," he pleaded.

"Last thought, I promise. Waiter, what's this dildo doing in my soup? I don't know, sir. It looks like it's either spawning or making cream soup. See. This can go on forever."

He pretended [barf]. "That's what I'm afraid of."

$$$

I hadn't seen Shah Kwah playing for maybe six to eight years. After spying him the week before, I now always looked for him when I came in and before getting into action. Sometimes I'd spot him bobbing like a red-white, round buoy float. Mysteriously, he never came over to where I played, and I never asked him why. Perhaps he didn't want to be tempted to play higher. This Friday we discussed the old days while he was dealt out to eat. Being philosophic, I propounded that poker, like all organisms, had to evolve: "Remember when Lowball was invented? It became all the rage, and it killed high, Jacks or Better to Open."

Bouncing like a tenant's bad check, Shah responded, "Yes, half-breed. It had way more action, so people felt they could win more. And it was way more exciting. You know me, I like action!" He laughed. Boing-boing.

"Oh, yeah, I remember. Anyway, when the state legalized Hold 'em in 1987, it's the game of the times—the game in vogue—where all the action is. Most casinos don't even offer Low anymore." Hold 'em had killed Lowball, 💀, as Lowball killed High Draw. Now Lowball too had become a dead mineshaft, passé, *démodé*.

He was incredulous. "They don't spread Lowball anymore?"

"I haven't seen it spread anywhere else except here at Commerce," I observed. The old Low *mavens*, now fossilized players, impatiently tapping their canes for chips or service. I heard a food server once asking, "Is anything okay here?" They complain and noodge about the heat or cold. "If I'm here overnight, when I'm stuck, I walk by their morning game, and I hear someone gumming, *Feh. I raise you, you alter kaker.*

"What's *alter kaker* mean?"

"Oh, Yiddish for old fart, geezer. And you remember Sarah or Mom? I see her in the game from time to time. She's still her old feisty self, giving the guys hell."

I posed, "Hey, what do you think the average age of a Lowball player is?"

Shah stopped bouncing, looked down and to the right, doing the math, and he guessed, "I'd say seventy."

"No. It's deceased. Ooo, that's cruel. But you know, Shah, you probably aren't that far off guessing seventy, but that'd be the average of those currently playing here. Remember. I said average age. There's one guy who's a hundred. They call him 'Wimpy,' for he looks like the cartoon character in Popeye who's always begging for a hamburger. And I see old Let's gambol 'Doc.' Morty Morgonmoth. But we'll all be there some day. This guy Richard Farnsworth was in a movie, *The Straight Story.* He said, 'The worst thing about being old is remembering when you was young.' Hey, you remember Q.E.D.?"

He paused, thinking, "Wait. Oh, yeah. 'The Book.' Yeah, what about him?"

"He tried Hold 'em, but he told me, I just don't get it. I don't do well at it. So, I stick to Low and 7 Stud. No disrespect, but he's like the Lowball senior citizens still only playing Lowball—they're like dinosaurs not adapting."

After we caught up, he told me an arresting, though disturbing story. While he played up in San Jose, he met some players—grifters really—who formed a team to come down to LA to play big limit Lowball and fleece the locals. I mentioned teams when I discussed cheating methods alleged in Gardenia, but I maybe only saw it once, and suspected it five or ten times.

Proof was hard to come by, but now Shah was giving evidence. This team would get into the same game, usually the biggest game in the poker club. Then they'd use hand signals to inform their teammate(s) what they had. He didn't know all the signals, but their fingers' position, the way they held their cards, would indicate their hand strength, drawing or pat, etc. In any case, the idea was only *one* of the team got involved in any given hand; hence, the team always had its strongest hand vying for the pot. It'd be like two or more picking the best combined hand to play against the field. Shah didn't know how this reprehensible card-tel fared, so I neither learned the upshot, nor tried to corroborate these allegations. Soon the Board lady called me, I said goodbye to Shah, and I bounced.

$$$

Like Lowball players, some industries didn't change with the times. The classic examples are makers of horse drawn gigs, drays, carriages, and buggy whips. Incidentally, the best buggy whip company was the last buggy whip maker. Also mostly gone, the ordinary, lowly clothespin. Yet, we still need flyswatters and mouse traps. A late nineteenth century saying attributed to Emerson, "Invent a better mouse trap, and the world will beat a path to your door" probably is no longer true. One unusual case of an industry that couldn't evolve was weekly diaper services that picked up your soiled diapers and left lean ones. They were environmentally better than the replacement, disposable diapers, which overload landfills. Convenience won out.

Probably more lamentable are once successful companies or industries that suffered from hubris. Hubris on the ginormous scale of O. J. (*If I Did It*) and Gary Hart. He essentially said to the press, "Catch me cheating, if you can." They did—with his mistress on the aptly named boat, *Monkey Business*!

Smug corporate thinking predicted there was no need to adapt to changing market conditions, and, consequently, either folded or massively shrunk, *viz,* titans like Kodak, Sears, GE and Xerox; Blockbuster, Napster, Myspace, AOL, and Netscape, and the auto industry during OPEC's embargo during 1970s. Believe me, I've blown it sometimes, everyone has, but not on the monumental scale that those corporations did.

$$$

Way back to the dawn of my card playing, I played for decades with most of the previously mentioned remnants of the Low cadre. Though I joked about them, I liked them. They're now retired businesspeople, lawyers, dentists, and doctors. They weren't, however, ex-professional poker players; therefore, they didn't play for remuneration. Playing for social reasons now, the atmosphere felt like what you'd expect at a senior's center or retirement home. They were lucky in still having the health, mental acuity, ability to drive safely, and financial means to play regularly. Yes, they were lucky old dogs.

Just as I didn't see Shah regularly because he stayed at a lower limit than I, there were other people that I liked but rarely saw. One night after I put my initials on the board, I heard this perfect laugh, and I saw Raymond, whom I hadn't seen in years, getting up from a table and walking toward the bar. I called out, but he didn't respond. So, I chased him down. "Hey, Raymond. I called you out on the floor, but you ignored me."

"Oh, hey, JM. I must've thought you were going to ask to borrow money. Great to see you." He asked me to join him, and I agreed to after I told the Board woman to locate, page me in the bar. Soon we joined the lovable, lounge lizards. "JM, what'll you have?"

"Just a Coke, thanks."

Raymond decided that rather than having his usual Dewar's, he'd try some skunky beer. He chuckled and asked the bartender, "Do you have DuClaw Repent?"

Once back at his table, he was sloshing his ever-present drink and having a grand old time like Peter O'Toole on a bender. He seemed bordering on dipsomania, but I didn't know if he refrained from drinking when he was not gambling. He said, "Yeah. I think I like drinking more than playing cards. But you know that."

"Great to see you," I said. "You know drink is the curse of the working class."

"Yeah, but *work* is the curse of the drinking class," he quipped. Spoken like someone living on the shores of dipsomania. I didn't know if he abstained when he wasn't gambling.

"Funny. I'm in the boob-eoisie class," I replied. Out of common courtesy, I asked the other players, "Do you mind if I sit behind Ray?"

He was so darn likeable, no one objected. He snickered at himself and said, "JM, pull up a chair. You're welcome to watch me if you don't think you'll develop any bad habits. Of course, watching me that's bound to happen." Most players had lives outside of the poker arena, but movie and TV ad campaigns cracked our insular world. *Sudden Impact* contained Det. Harry Callahan's famous tagline, "Go ahead make my day." Shaking his head, Raymond cautioned me by sneering in that Clint Eastwood hoarse voice, "Go ahead, play my way. Donkey see, donkey do."

The players at the table smiled in agreement, for they'd played with him for months and knew his loose style. He neither worried if he lost a little, nor cared if he was the yo-yo bozo. As I squeezed in, someone was telling a story. "Much to my regret, I found Gardena when I was twenty-two. I played $1-$2 Lowball, and I won. Worst thing that could've happened— learning to gamble *and* winning in the beginning by sheer luck. Now I have two ex-wives because of cards."

Some wag interjected, "Yeah, but your card playing's improved. Right?"

The game continued apace, and being genuinely interested, I asked Raymond, "How's work?"

"Good. I got a promotion more into management, and that should keep me in enough money to gamble." He chuckled from his heart. "Hey, I think I know the answer, but can I buy you a drink?

"I just came in, and I haven't played yet. But if I win, and I quit, and you're still here, you're on," I said. As I've mentioned, I didn't drink while playing, for I didn't want my judgment, logic, decision making, and especially my discipline, compromised. However, in the outside world fortunately, I was a happy drunk. There were some in the poker galaxy, as in regular life, who were mean drunks, and those types were very unpleasant. JM's Law #7: If there is one drunk at the table, it can be profitable, depending on who it is. An inebriated visitor may be lucrative for the game; yet, a mean drunk, who slows the game to a glacial pace and irritates and or insults patrons, may be bad for the game. I can't claim to understand those people's need for chemical, grape-or-grain courage.

Raymond asked me, "By the way, have you been back to Gardena lately?"

"Yeah, I went by about a month ago to see what the games looked like. Very grim. I hadn't noticed before, but the couches and chairs along the rail were dumpy. I'm sure when they were new, they looked nice, but now they were like furniture in some sordid massage parlor waiting room—or so I imagine. How about you? Have you been back?"

He chuckled and replied, "I went back to the Monterey Club last weekend. The place was dead. But something funny happened when I went over to the Elbow Room. I'm sitting at the bar enjoying the high-class ambience. This woman walks in. Hard looking and displaying a lot of ink. She sat down next to the woman next to me, and I heard her say, 'I just finished a two-year stretch at Sybil Brand, and I'm horny as hell.' My ears perked up. I watched her use her finger to stir her drink, and then she gets up and walks through the bar. She's scoping out the dudes, checking the lineup." She must've decided to grab the pick of the louche, lay about litter, because, as Ray explained, "She joins this guy at his table, and in about fifteen minutes they leave. Very funny. Just when you think you've seen everything, bam."

"Oh, I bet they bammed. But yikes, just my luck," I complained with sour grapes. "I'd wish I'd been there. I'd show her what a stretch is, nyuck-nyuck. And I bet she wanted to kill two birds with one stone—get laid and maybe score a place to stay for a couple of weeks, or more. By the way, is the economy so bad that we have to kill two birds with one stone? Can't we just kill one bird with one stone?"

"JM, you're so cynical, but you're probably right."

"Well, Raymond, I gotta go make some money. Nice talking with you. Good luck."

16

"Tow Truck" Mark

WHEN I FIRST STARTED playing Lowball a man sat next to me. Obviously, he'd been hitting the Jack hard, and I could smell it on his breath. He huffed and puffed when he sat down as if it was a strenuous task. Most likely he'd gone straight to a bar after work, for he was wearing a tight-fitting suit. He looked for all intents and purposes like a turducken stuffed into a cheap suit. We played a while. He stuffed barbecued chicken wings down as if he were in an eating contest as he said to himself, "Dis brok da mout." In Hawaiian pidgin, This is so good it breaks my mouth. Out of the corner of my eye I saw him staring at me. I thought of being a smart ass. When someone is staring at you in Hawaii, a brah'd say, "I owe you money o' wot?" Thinking better of it, I turned to look at him. He had a very puffy, ruddy face that was very oily. He smiled and said, "Hi. Listen, do you mind if I call you 'Indian?'" [As I alluded to earlier regarding PI, in the seventies, this moniker wasn't as offensive as it is now.] I started laughing. He'd been studying me trying to place my ethnic background. I smiled and replied, "Sure. It's okay."

"I'm Buck," he choked out. "Glad to meet you, Indian."

$$\$\$\$$$

Though not a nickname, people know I prefer being called JM, but from time to time someone would misremember my preference ... or they'll think that they'll be more friendly and call me by my first name. Of course, some want to irritate me or try to upset me by calling me John. Aside from those jerks, it's hilarious when someone gets my first name wrong. For example, I've been hailed incorrectly as Jimmy, Jim, Jack, Juicy—but that's more of an ironic twist—and Johnny. "Johnny" is a natural assumption. I regularly played with a guy called "Tow Truck" Mark, a Russian who was very stout, always with a slight grin and grizzled stubble. But his distinguishing feature was his Russian-like military cap with ear flaps folded up. Like a trapper's hat. Remember "Amarillo Slim's" epigram, "Not all trappers wear fur hats." Let me add a corollary, "Although they might wear pelt underwear." I learned later that his cap was called an Ushanka. Since he drives a tow truck, he uses it to keep warm.

Another indelible trait was his misuse of words. He once told me "There was a flaw in the ointment," and, "I can't watch horror movies before bed. They give me inzombiea." Once when he was eating either an early breakfast or late dinner at the table, he complained about a fly disturbing him and asked the porter, "Get me a fly squatter." His best twist was telling a young dealer they were wise beyond their ears. Kinda makes sense. Smart between their ears—in their head. One more thing. He leaves the acrid smell of cigarettes in his wake.

One of the funniest instances of people misnaming me was Tow Truck calling me Larry. Since Mark was looking right at me when he called me Larry the first time, I answered him. Thereafter, he kept calling me Larry. I always answered, and, thus, perpetuated this mistaken identity.

A fallout of this was another player, May Faire, a Groundlings member, heard me respond to Larry, so she called me Larry for decades. Later, when she learned my correct initials, even though my first initial doesn't start Larry, she said, "My stars, all these years I thought your name was Larry. You always answered me."

17

Negative Turn Arounds

AFTER A LONG, DISMAL night, I dragged myself, like a half-drowned stray, over to Janey's, my girlfriend, and I let myself in. She was in bed, and sleepily said, "Hi, babe. How are you?"

"Sorry to wake you."

"So-kay," she dreamily murmured.

"Go back to sleep."

"No, tell me how you are."

"I had a miserable session. You know my old song and dance. I was up $1100, didn't leave and ended up losing that plus the $1200 I took. I call it a Negative Turn Around. It's like a *futbol* own goal. Or shooting oneself in the foot. It was $2300," I whimpered. "I keep saying when a ritual becomes habitual, you gotta get spiritual and change."

"I'm so sorry, Indian. Is there anything I can do to ease the pain?"

"Just shoot me. No, but thanks for the offer. Right now, I just want to crawl into a cave, pull up a bearskin over my head, and sleep till spring."

Genuinely concerned, Janey commiserated, "Awww."

"Man, when the cards turn, they can go nuclear really fast. Toward the end, they weren't just beating my like arum, but beating me like an ugly, redheaded, left-handed, cross-eyed stepchil."

"How's that?"

"Oh, you know, gingerly. I don't mean to sound unsympathetic to stepchild—I was a foster kid before I was a stepchild. But some at the clubs have kept adding adjectives to the old saw beating me like a stepchild. It's just dark humor. And you know me, I wouldn't think of hitting anyone, let alone a woman or child."

"I know."

Yes, I could relate what it was like being a stepchil'. How'd you feel if you couldn't live with your parent(s), had to change elementary schools every year, were always the new kid in class, and every year lost friends it took a year to make? How'd you react to being commended for eating like a bird—less grub eaten by you meant more parent profits; went to bed hungry; had to deal with the older, creepy son who wanted to *play;* always were second class and shunted? I think I bitterly earned my *stripes* to use sick humor on this subject.

Janey sweetly offered, "Since they beat you up, how about I rub your back?"

"That'd be great."

I firmly feel massages are sometimes better than sex. Phi Beta Kappa, Lisa Kudrow, in *The Opposite of Sex*, expressed it best: "I'd rather have a back rub. It lasts longer and there are no fluids." As Janey firmly massaged, I reflected on this last catastrophic debacle. Like from a crane shot, I watched myself shuffle out of the gambling den like thirty wasted years limping by.

After such a session, to cheer myself up, I used to buy a Baby Ruth candy bar—which I usually don't eat for dietary reasons—at the card room's gift shop. I usually do not eat them for dietary reasons. Then I realized that in some minuscule way this coping mechanism reinforced bad behavior. Why should I treat and or reward myself after losing? Hence, I modified this by *only* treating myself at home after a winning session, *never* after a losing outing. Tellingly, I have the self-control during the week to avoid eating them even though they are always in the cupboard. It is ironic that

I have excellent self-control in the real world, but not in the vibrant, poker realm regarding quitting. Consequently, I really need drastic aversion therapy to avoid, or at least decrease, these costly, pernicious NTAs. I could impose a $1,000 fine on myself. Nah, I already would've incurred a monetary penalty greater than that. I settled on having Janey give me a back rub or other favor when I successfully implement my dubious stop loss system.

About gift shops, interestingly, card and casino shops don't sell gum. I read that the act of chewing reduces cortisol levels and so relieves stress. This somewhat explains comfort eating. Recall Toothpick Dick, described earlier, who always had a pick in his mouth. Poker is nothing if not stressful; hence, some sessions I want to buy gum. However, casinos realize if they sell it, some of their low life, inconsiderate customers will fasten depleted wads under furniture like the card table itself. Did these people grow up in a barn or juvie? Or some rude turd will spit a glob out onto the carpet. Sm-ack, sm-ack, ptui. Then we'd hear op-lop, op-log, op-lop as patrons would walk around with gum on the bottom of their shoes. I beat this gift shop, gum embargo by buying gum outside and putting a pack into my Banana Republic jacket. I never wantonly disposed of it.

$$$

To quit or not to quit: That is the question. Whether it is richer in the wallet to suffer the slings and arrows of outrageous chance and bad beats—as elementary school kids, we learned quitting was bad. Don't be a quitter. A quitter never wins, and a winner never quits. Sage playground and sports advice but applicable to commitments, projects, jobs, duties, etc. However, leaving, quitting a game while ahead is extremely desirable and profoundly important. Paradoxically, as much as I prided myself on having good self-discipline, staying rather than leaving when way ahead, was a failing. More precise, it was an area with vast space for improvement, say 10 parsecs by 10. Optimal leaving a game, for me, is like pulling teeth from a hungry alligator! Furthermore, it's one of the hardest things to do in life, on a level with being married, so I've heard. Extending my hard as being married metaphor, my struggle to quit efficiently was on the upper limit of what I call the Hef Scale, measuring problems with multiple, contiguous wives.

For we procrastinators often the most challenging element of any task is starting it. We don't even reach the embryonic stage. However, pertaining to poker, my hardest chore is stopping. Applying the adage that A quitter never wins, and a winner never quits to poker seems errant by comparing A) Quitting while winning and B) Failing to perform a duty. Comparing A and B is a misapplication. My ultimate goal, my duty, is to leave a winner. That wasn't quitting in the traditional sense of lacking tenacity. The real job of a professional is making good decisions and going home ahead. As noted, Bob Seger's on point: The key is to avoid playing a game too long.

$$$

As Hawaiians say in pidgin, *kay den.* Referencing Caro's discussion of a stop loss system, it advises that when ahead, set a floor, or amount that you're willing to lose back. If that arrives, leave. So far that hasn't worked for me. Stop loss' success rate was sporadic, required both an iron will and a steely discipline, and had two phases. First, I noticed when an opportunity came to set such a stop loss point, I may've been working many hours; thus, I was tired, and discipline was lower than when fresh. Second, more time may have passed with more tiredness, so actually following the plan, quitting, was challenging. Supposedly the brain uses about 20% of the body's energy. In a session I used a great deal of discipline during the card war, made hundreds of decisions, avoided being irritated by players and single hand outcomes. All that was enervating. Keeping willpower shields up at full strength takes Herculean energy. We know what we *should* do, but as we tire, we don't. That's why most of us start a gambling foray with good control and intentions. The rate of self-discipline decay, discipline depletion is different for everyone, and mine is slow; yet eventually it does degrade like a sailor's morals on shore leave.

Maybe the only treatment for stop loss failure is one-eighth testicle castration. Honestly? Yao Ming! That's nuts and is slightly Draconian. Do ya think? How about gentle, synaptic pruning that automatically happens in babies after twelve months? Honestly. Too late for me. This sparked an instantaneous thought in my mind: *I need to aim as many neurons as possible to blast poker Negative Turn Arounds to oblivion.* Isn't inheriting good genes like fate interceding, like the luck of the draw? In any case, I wanted that purifying, but stimulating, feeling of pool chlorine up your nose. But I ramble.

With Nietzsche in mind, to utilize stop loss successfully I need a ℞ for sure, strong medicine that won't kill me. ≠ 💀. You know, Friedrich Nietzsche's famous dictum: "That which does not kill me makes me stronger." He also wrote, "There is always some madness in love. But there also is some reason in madness." Tangentially, there's an urban legend, granted an intellectual urban myth, with public bathroom wall graffiti: God is dead—Nietzsche. Scrawled under that: Nietzsche is dead—God.

In principle, I recalled using stop losses in the stock market, but this idea also could've applied to futures, commodities, et al., and poker. Stock market forecasters, investors and advisors who used technical analysis, rather than fundamental analysis (which I prefer), created a filter system of using stop loss orders.

There're two different styles predicting stock or index prices in the future: A) Technicians using charts of past stock or index performances to try and predict advantageous, profitable times to buy or sell, usually in the short run; while B) Fundamental analysts using a slew of data on the general economy and business data pertaining to the target company projected sales, accounting, industry projections, etc.—to try and find a stock's intrinsic value. Aside: Applying technical analysis seems similar to having the Gambler's Fallacy, aka the Monte Carlo fallacy. Unwitting adherents believe that past, chance events can know or influence or predict future events. When a coin comes up heads 99 times in a row, what's the chance that the 100th toss will be heads? Exactly fifty-fifty. Those with Gambler's Fallacy think otherwise. As the poet, Sumner A Ingmark, wryly rhymed:

Those who think a game's a gift,

Pay the laws of chance short shrift.

Whereas I successfully adopt the idea of using a stop loss in some of my stock picks, paradoxically I haven't been very successful in using it for poker. Some of the failure is caused by structural reasons, i.e., in my poker dystopia ecosystem, I can't place a sell order and have it filled. Thus, I'm not bound to quit by an external force. No, I need enough self-discipline to utilize an approximate JM's Law #1 (... strongly consider leaving). Regarding going home a winner, in a perfect world, I'd be like a robot without an amygdala processing emotion. The dissolution of ego wouldn't be necessary. However, I'm living and, therefore, have what I'll call wetware (brain software) causing emotions. Thus, giving back 10-20% in poker profits is often unpalatable. Note that I disregard the sessions when I plummet steadily into the loss territory. Losing from the git-go was part of the game, and I accept that. All in all, using my QAP (Quitting At Peak) strategy was better than the stop loss strategy.

18

Superstition II and Dealer Whisperers

AS WITH LOWBALL AND High Draw, customers can request a deck change, but now with house dealers, players also can ask the dealer to start with the green rather than brown deck. Later rules mandate a certain color be used during specific half hour periods. You often hear many of the following annoying requests, demands: Scramble the deck; Dealer, give them an extra riffle; Use the brown deck. All this is to change one's luck. Apparently, they haven't heard the incantation, Kiss a duck to change your luck. Recall that Sartre's Existentialism movement hadn't reached Gardenia yet. I jest. I believe it just totally bypassed Gardenia players. These sorts must think: *Well, of course, the fact I'm losing has nothing to do with my play, skill, personality, statistical likelihood of a losing period. It* MUST *be the cards, card chucker, seat, table, casino, moon or sunspot phase, or* El Niño. Therefore, Change the cards, and change them again just to be sure. Even from some of the better educated: Sure, I've heard of the Gambler's Fallacy, but it's just that, a fallacy. *Of course*, the cards and deck remember past events. Dah. [OMG]

Parenthetically, let me comment on poker skills. Just as everyone considers that they have a good sense of humor and they are good drivers, so too regarding their card playing. There are two assertions a typical player will be insulted by and furiously deny: First, that they have other motivations (even subconscious ones) for gambling besides just winning money. Second, they are a bad player.

$$$

Superstition is the interface between faith and dark forces, and it's a laughable, but destructive belief. Superstition's illogical but isn't that its essence. Post 1987, with the legalization of card games like 7 Stud, Razz, Hold 'em, and Omaha, games have up cards in plain view. Those inclined to believe in the supernatural, and even those consorting with the powers of dark magic, these muddle-headed numbskulls now had a new, arcane realm in which to practice. It was as if they'd discovered a new constellation of excuses from which they could find and assign blame. They weren't members of a Cathedral, Temple, or Mosque of Rationality; rather, they were a flock, congregants of a brain lame, storefront church. Perhaps it was called the Sacred Heart Break of Psoriasis. Or the Cathedral of the Cryptic Pregnancy.

Under the religious veil, perhaps I have a savior complex by so vehemently preaching and nagging against superstition. (Random thoughts. Is it better to have a savior or inferiority complex? You know my watchwords: When a ritual becomes habitual become spiritual and change, drop it just as Sarah Palin did that moose. Rituals also sometimes become religion.

I label some of these lame brains, who ask for a dealer's telekinetic, divine intervention with the cards, dealer whisperers. These gamblers sit on the card deliverer's immediate right or left (seats 1, 9 or 10), and, thereby, facilitate whispering to the dealer as to what card(s) s/he wished for. If one has good ears, one might pick up a valuable tell. Eerie.

Possibly, some might sit in 9 to glimpse of the location of a card(s) during the shuffle, box cut, and shuffle cycle. Then, depending upon the cut point, s/he might guess when a card *may* fall. As most shufflers' proficiency improved, this sloppiness was cut. One such dealer whisperer was Curtis, who'd beg the dealer before they spread the three community cards of the flop, "Come on, dealer! Help the little people."

$$$

Curtis was about 45, stocky, about 5' 7" with a Mediterranean complexion. He was so hyperactive and energetic that he probably could charge a Prius in ten minutes by touching its charging port with his tongue. He was like a drop of water on a red-hot skillet. There's a high probability you have an acquaintance who constantly likes to interrupt you. If you haven't chanced upon such a person, count yourself lucky; moreover, if you have a low frustration, tolerance level, count your blessings for somehow avoiding such a character. Curtis was psychologically compelled to butt in, and because of this he acquired the sobriquet Curtis "Interruptus."

Lord have mercy, that man could talk. In *Sea Wolf*, Jack London could have been describing Curtis: "He suffered a constitutional plethora of speech." He could not only finish your sentence, but your paragraph. Okay, okay. You got the idea. He certainly would fail the Marshmallow Experiment on delayed or deferred gratification.

$$\$\$\$$$

Another prayerful, dealer whisperer was Ali, a Pakistani who later became known as "DotCom." Before the dealer would board the flop, Ali would silently mouth something to himself, probably a prayer. As a footnote, "Texas Dolly" Brunson quipped in the *Card Player* that a poker room is like a church wherein some pray and some prey, but everyone wants to get to chip heaven. Tangentially, I divine that people praying think they're using white, not black, magic.

Returning to Ali. After a brief, silently mouthed chant before the turn or river, he would peer over his half-framed eyeglasses, violently slap the table with his palm as if he were smashing a cockroach without having a shoe handy, and shout, "Come on!" (This made him more of a dealer shouter.) If this wasn't a magnitude ten tell, I don't know what was. It was verbal, physical, visceral, and authentic, not an act. He didn't display this every hand, but in the large pots, $1,000 or more. I recorded this on his player profile card; namely, he had a drawing hand; a speculative holding; and didn't have a strong hand yet. Consequently, he had to catch the right card to make a potential winner. Hence, one could deduce if neither a certain suit boarded for a flush, nor a specific numerical card for a straight, he'd lose the hand. You could bet for value or bluff if heads-up.

Additionally, I sometimes observed him spy the turn or river card and sadly, almost imperceptibly, shake his head. Looking at his narrow face, one'd think that he just had found his pet monkey, Bubbles, dead. ☠ . Alert! DEFCON 1. Wham! He check raises any bettor. Then he bets the rest of hand with both barrels blazing, for he's made the *nuts*—a lock, an unbeatable, hand. The nuts is like a wheel in Lowball, immortal. So it goes, not. ≠ ☠. His *act* demonstrates a classic Mike Caro tell—weak is strong. A dolorous sigh means strength. My tag is A sigh is a lie. (BTW, the singular, *nut*, means your daily poker overhead.)

Also, a serious horse bettor, handicapper, Ali most always had his substantial, XKE nose stuck in a racing program when out of a hand which was infrequently, for he loved to gamble and play a myriad of hands. He'd look over his reading glasses and gleefully explain his complex bets—Exactas; Trifectas; Superfectas; Quinellas; Pick 3, 4, 6, and other exotics. During televised races from anywhere in the world, for example, Hong Kong or, of all places, Dubai, he'd excitedly scream at the big screen TV. So, yes, he was both a dealer and a horse shouter. When his horse lost, the casino would hear an ear piercing, "EYEYEEE!" Even to regulars, this scream never got old.

$$$

It was hilarious watching people react to a flop fanned out like caviar crackers ... or cow pies, depending on one's hand. I carefully watched players, and some intentionally would look away from the flop. I surmise they didn't want to give away any reaction. Except, eventually s/he would have to look. However, I noticed Lan didn't look at all, and if he were one of first to act or bet, he would check blind—without looking at the cards. He was somewhat like a pitcher who has just served up a fat meatball. Judging the batter's swing, the ball's trajectory, the speed and sound off the bat, the pitcher guesses it's going yard. He doesn't want to see it; maybe he's superstitious. Other participants sneaked a peak at the flop as if they were trying to look at cleavage without being too obvious (Rude). Hold on. Nowadays it also might be a woman sneaking a peak (Hot).

I speculate about one in nine wear dark sunglasses to deter eye scrutiny. I cite this weird fraction because on average there were one or two people at a nine-handed Hold 'em game shielding their eyes. But some use the visor of a baseball cap to screen. If you want to see an unusual ploy and funny sight, watch tape of Phil Hellmuth after he's gone all in. He's sporting an exceptionally dark pair of glasses and a logoed hat covering 60 percent of his face. But hold on. Then, as he knows he'll be scrutinized, he pulls up his logo-covered jacket hood around any remaining exposed skin leaving only the tip of his nose showing.

Along comes a player who doesn't need anything to hide his eyes, for he's blind! The Floor man escorted a blind man to our table and asked, "If you all agree, this gentleman has to sit in seat 1 or 9 so the dealer can whisper to him what his hole cards are, what flops, turns, rivers, the action from opponents." I was in seat 1, but I agreed to move to the open seat 5. This was my least favorite because I couldn't observe others as easily from an end seat. We all agreed with these conditions, for he seemed very personable and, come on, what a novel experience. After about an hour, he played with skill and was down a little. We got used to the somewhat slower pace, whispering, and his carefully feeling the right bet amount. The dealer kept his bets correct. In one hand there were about three players at the river in a moderately large pot. The first player bet, the second folded, and the blind man asked, "Dealer. Are there three spades on the board?" When the dealer said, "Yes," the man raised. The sole opponent thought a brief time and folded. As the dealer pushed the pot to the blind man, he revealed his cards. He didn't have the flush implied but a certain loser. We burst out laughing. It was such a masterful, good-humored bluff even the loser laughed. What he lacked in sight he more than made up for in psychological skill and *chutzpah*. Any who may have felt a tinge of sorrow for his blindness dropped that fast.

$$$

I admit when I was getting scorched and my arse handed to me, I'd get my prescription shades from my Banana Republic and put them on, too. Remember JM's Law #5 (If there are greater or equal to three players at a table wearing sunglasses, avoid the game if possible.) By donning these like armor, I'd nudge the game tighter.

JM's Law #5 Corollary: If the shade wearers also wear hats and or headphones connected to some type of sound system, fuhgeddaboudit. It probably is rocked up. A rock garden (a tight, conservative game) like this, with four to five pros, has very little action, gambling, risk taking or profitability. They play optimal strategy. It's like a vault of vultures waiting for some prey. As Nicky The Greek might say, "I wouldn't play in dat game with counterfeit money."

Over the decades, these professional players continued employing the low-tech hat and shades; however, the common portable radio, earphones apparatus mutated into flashier and fancier sound systems. These pros make no attempt to hide it. From their cocoon, they must feel it's in their best interest more to be comfortable and immune from as many distractions as possible than to be labeled a pro. Along with shade wearers, a corollary was if there also was one or more who brought her or his own back cushion for the chair and possibly homemade health food, snacks, avoid that game given other choices.

19

How to Make Money

The rite of passage in the US is different from other countries' and from pre-mid-20th century America. Now, for some kids, this journey and quest begins when they leave home for college, especially out of state. I worked in the corporate world post college. This period coincided with an inverse relationship between playing in a game at someone's home (increased) and playing in legal card clubs (decreased). That I don't discuss my default life, time outside the gambling or pinball halls, as much in detail, is a testament where my heart lay.

Eventually, after job changes, my career path resembled the trajectory of the early North Korean ICBMs, bumpy. At last, I landed my dream job as a manager for a chain of clinics. I was the top guy at one facility with about one hundred employees under me. During the probationary period let's say I worked my butt off and sweated like a Cardigan wearing hound; alas, corporate downsizing and being the newest manager punched me out. I was laid off due to circumstances out of my control. Crushed and totally stymied after my last layoff, from the grass is always greener pasture of the corporate world, I vowed never again to have my destiny in another's hands or be subject to circumstances out of my control. Like Nixon saying, "They won't have me to kick around anymore," I felt the same way re the business world milieu. Since the corporate world had demonstrated that it didn't want my talents, I'd leave it and start my own business. The corporate world's response, like the old monopolistic Gardenia card clubs, "Go ahead. See if we care." Maybe this was a blessing, or dildo, in disguise.

Maybe behind every cloud there's a silver dildo, lining. Always having entrepreneurial dreams during college, I promised myself I'd start my own business, and, whenever possible, I wouldn't be subject to circumstances out of my control. I embarked on a research journey to find a venture. Naturally I continued working poker some evenings.

$$\$\$\$$$

A college instructor had informed me of a UCLA extension course on entrepreneurship given by Mr. Scott Castillo whose most important teachings were more general than specific, more philosophic blueprints applicable to any start up or existing business. Controlling value, like owning copyrights or patents, he termed owning a toll booth. Hence, he positioned himself so that buyers could only deal with him—assuring revenue. He also incorporated the concept and theme in *Beau Geste* of altruism or *noblesse oblige* which I have to look up about every ten years. It's the obligation of anyone who's in a better position than others—due, for example, to high office, wealth or celebrity—to act respectably and responsibly. Mr. Interruptus, beautifully summarized it: "Help the little people." Let me add, if I've gone this far in life it's because I've stood on the shoulders of little people.

$$\$\$\$$$

From poker I'd amassed, if that is the proper term, a chunk (or in poker parlance, a *load* or wad) of money to invest. I mostly considered sole proprietorships, for I didn't have enough to buy a franchise or company. And I was cautioned in school to be wary of partnerships, especially, between family and or friends. Later I'd regret disregarding this lesson.

Needless to say, this process of choosing where to invest my nest egg was overwhelming. Like standing at the base of Mount Everest, wanting to climb it wearing sneakers, shorts, and a tee shirt. Although winning at poker gave me an easy-come, easy-go attitude, I still wanted to invest wisely. Is it no wonder I wanted to play, I mean ply, my trade at poker in the evenings? It seemed to be Easy Money and like escaping the real world for fun most of the time.

Eventually, I went to a business expo at the LA Convention Center. One of the hundreds of exhibitors was a company that sold their pinball games and located—placed them. I was positive this would be successful. In college I had a friend, a rodeo cowboy wannabee, who got the administration to allow him to install one pinball game in the student center basement on a trial basis. If the revenue generated and student welfare were mutually satisfactory, he could keep his machine there. It was a roaring success, and that pinball game financed a video game. Eventually he had about twenty machines across the entire back wall. After the university's cut, and once the machine was paid off, the rest was pure, positive cash flow. And the beauty of this type of business is that I wouldn't have to be present to earn money. This fit some of my financial goals and lifestyle as a ramblin', gamblin' kinda guy.

20

Negative Turn Arounds (NTAs)
Are Everywhere

OSTENSIBLY THE EARTH'S MAGNETIC poles reverse from N to S every 250,000 years. But there's a greater chance of that happening than my eliminating self-inflicted NTAs. Oh, how I wished I were like a Samuel Hoffenstein couplet:

The earth is not steadier on its axis

Than you in the matter of prophylaxis.

When I'd slept off the aftereffects of an NTA, in a cave as I told Janey, the alarm clock was like a phone call from the new day. I'd awake from the inertia of deep sleep feeling depressed. My dolorimeter's readings were off the charts. It'd be like slowly, glacially regaining consciousness and feelings after general anesthesia. I often delved into whether I had sub-conscious needs to suffer NTAs. and what were they? Self-punishment? Greed? Absence of love? I needed a universal diagnosis and cure. I needed a cosmic change.

Here's a hypothetical. Obviously one can incur a Negative Turn Around in any investment or financial instrument. But can NTAs occur in other endeavors? Suppose a cheating husband is forgiven. He's been granted a second chance. He attains a state similar to a poker player getting even after being obliterated. If, however, he's discovered cheating again, he has caused an enormous NTA upon himself and family; additionally, he could harm the co-cheaters family.

NTAs are different from losing streaks, although sometimes a nasty NTA starts a losing stretch. That said, no matter how well one is running, winning for some period, eventually and inevitably the cards will turn. Then, in a pit of despair—a Slough of Despair John Bunyan called it—a gambler *can't* understand how things get so bad, so bleak.

A wise friend suggested that I look at these periods like baseball slumps, rather than losing streaks. When they happened, the most frightening realization was this: *Oh, no! I may have to get a real job!* I'm unsure whether Henry Miller played poker socially, but he captured this dread beautifully in *The Tropic of Cancer*. A horse stable worker whose job, mucking feces, can learn to love manure if his earnings, and therefore welfare, depend on it. A 1940s noir movie character, "Lefty," might say, "See, youse guys, even a rummy like dat can getta nudder job. Butta poker player, it's curtains, see."

Essentially, the possibility of having to get legit employment frighteningly chills a full-time poker player; moreover, it's pointless telling the stable worker that their job is disgusting just as telling a gambler that poker playing is deplorable.

During these dark, dismal, slump times, periods like my own Great Depression, it was like an extended NTA hangover discussed above. I'd have major self-doubts, and I'd chastise myself for not undertaking this or that. Why'd I turn down that scholarship? Why'd I self-destruct that relationship? Why did or didn't I change jobs? Am I a self-saboteur? On *ad infinitum*. Part of me, the part earning money from poker, felt as if I were near a black hole's boundary, the event horizon. Soon I, like light, wouldn't be able to escape gambling.

Like everyone, I predict that ruminating like this is an exercise in futility—the guilty pleasure of wallowing in the sweet, poignant, masturbatory warmth of self-pity. Since I treated poker playing as a job, during these low cycles I'd force myself to get it up again and go to *work*. I altered the US Army's, recruiting slogan "It's not just a job, it's an adventure" to "It's not just a misadventure, it's a job."

Still, the greater and longer the slump, the more refractory period I required. Rebounding from a losing streak is similar to recovering from the sad end of an amorous relationship. I hypothesize that the length of recuperation, its half-life, if you will, depended upon the length of each; also, one can snap out of poker losing streaks with one huge win, whereas an affair of the heart takes longer. As a slump treatment, sometimes I'd take off a week—my week being two–three days that I normally played, er, worked. While I sometimes wish I'm a robot when it's time to leave with a satisfactory win, I also wish I'm another being when I slog around in a losing swamp, I mean slump. I wish I could regenerate like a planarian: Those flatworms that can regrow a tail, head, or its entire body. In theory regrowth like this would solve male pattern baldness, too. Have you concluded these planarians have a leg up in survival of the fittest? Yeah. But that's what I need, a transformative, Atkins' Planarian Diet—a Diet of Worms like Martin Luther.

$$$

The next time we were together for dinner, Janey offered this, "Ya know, Indian, when you first sit in a game, why don't you just introduce yourself? Hi, I'm John, but call me JM. They wouldn't have a weapon and power over you."

"Thanks, Sweet Cheeks. That's good. I hadn't thought of that…"

I greatly appreciated that she'd taken time to cogitate on the matter, and it demonstrated love. Yet, I felt by using her idea, there'd be a fly-in-the-ointment or soup, or a bug-up-the ass system. I wanted the anonymity, secrecy, and safety of being unknown to the RAMS. Believe me. You don't want to experience ID theft. In addition, I still felt if opponents were comparing notes, being less well-known was advantageous. I compared card pros discussing my style to baseball pros and scouts comparing notes on a batter's tendencies; therefore, I didn't implement her openness plan.

Contrarily, weakening my theory, regulars remembered JM like a first name, and they could describe me well enough for discussion. And other JMs playing typically used their first name, so I may've drawn more attention. Aside. Some theorize that your name can be utilized like a mantra to remind yourself of the greatness you were born to, and a call to fulfill a mission. Remember Alexander the Great, Genghis Khan, The Hulk. But John Maynard... Nah.

Janey continued, "I also thought about quitting ahead. Can you imagine your win goal like a race with a finish line? You reach that line and leave."

"That's also a good idea. I'll try it. But it all comes down to discipline... It's so ironic. I can set stop-loss, or a trailing stop-loss, orders in the stock market, but not apply that concept to poker. It's like two compounds that are inversely related. By your expression I see that you are wondering what in the heck I'm talking about. Okay. Take clay and glass. Clay is malleable at room temperature, but when you fire it in a kiln, then let it cool, it's hard. It becomes brittle and will shatter. Conversely, glass is hard and brittle at room temperature, but if you heat it to a certain temp, it becomes malleable. It isn't a perfect analogy, because when glass cools down again, it hardens and can shatter."

She asked, "Why are you mentioning this?"

"I'm like clay when I'm playing stocks—flexible; but like glass when it comes time to use the stop-loss system in poker—more fixed by old habits."

$$$

I sauntered through the casino coffee shop, The Déjá Brew, looking for Shah Kwah, but I saw Tony instead. "Hello, Tony. How're you doing?"

"Fine, JM. Come on, sit down with me. Can I get you something to drink?"

"No, thanks. I'll get comp'ed out on the floor when I'm playing."

"You know I told you I was an engineer in aerospace, Raytheon. I do calibrations of instruments—borescopes, oscilloscopes, signal analyzing equipment and the like—generators, lasers and other equipment. Me and my brother and some of our co-workers from his department sit around tossing ideas on how to improve procedures and testing equipment. But believe me, trying to get management on the same page is like trying to herd cats. Or keep a bunch of frogs in a wheel barrel."

"Or herding frogs and keeping cats in a wheel barrel," I added.

"If the company won't take our ideas *or* they'd own the patent, we dream how we're gonna invent something and get rich. And now we've developed something that'll revolutionize calibrating. Problem is if we created it at work, Raytheon owns it and gets all the profits. So, we want to go out on our own with this new idea, but that'll take a lot of money."

I knew what was coming. Like Janey, like me, really like everyone, he wanted to advance his career, economic status.

He asked, "Are you interested in investing with us?"

"Of course, but I have to think it over. Can you give me your business plan and more projected sales, income & expense, you know, the P&L statements?"

"Sure. I'll bring them next week." Putatively Benjamin Franklin opined, "Jump at opportunity as fast as you jump to conclusions." But I was conflicted. On the one side I didn't want to miss a chance—FOMO—to get in on the ground floor of some million-dollar business, but on the other side I didn't want to get burned by investing in an industry about which I knew little.

21

CCC and Horsing Around

THERE WAS A WILD man, a Lowball player named Clyde, aka "Triple C." He went on the wait list as CCC. He wasn't odd or wild in appearance, but in giving a lot of action and making unorthodox plays. He marched to the beat of a different rum. He was a successful stockbroker and usually playing when I got into his game. He'd knock off work around 3–4 p.m., and he had the discipline to quit poker by around 10:00 p.m. since the Big Board opened at 6:30 a.m. our time. Bespectacled with gold-framed, Dior glasses, a ruddy, maculated complexion, dressed in conservative slacks and a starched white shirt, he said in his deep voice, "Hi, 'Jimmers.' Sit right on down." He had the best enunciation in poker—he had the elocution of a voice coach like Lionel Logue. Unlike others who called me John, trying to be irritating, rude, cute, or sometimes forgetful, he meant no harm. Never mind that 'Jimmers' wasn't exactly John or Johnny.

One day I decided to go to work early. It was grueling to fight the rush-hour traffic, but I wanted to investigate the late afternoon action. As was my habit, I greeted Clyde with a stock axiom. "Hey, Triple C. Buy the rumor and sell the news, because there ain't no free lunch."

He rolled his eyes and said, "Great advice, Jimmers. But you bring up a good point. Buy the rumor. If only you had a crystal ball or was clairvoyant. Can you imagine the supreme advantage you'd have in stock picking or cards?"

Often the superstitious card player prayed to be prescient, but to no-good ends. And you wouldn't want to be like Greek mythology's Casandra who was cursed to utter true prophecies, but never to be believed. Also, at the table was Ali, DotCom, who was referenced earlier as one of the players who invoked higher (lower?) forces to get favorable board cards. He wasn't always known as DotCom, but when the Dot-Com, speculative boom and bubble was inflating, especially 1997–2000, he was betting with both hands and pushing money in with his forearms too. Even after the bubble popped (around 2000), bursting like a regular Trojan on an aroused King Kong, he continued investing. Since he was always discussing his stock plays, he eventually earned the DotCom moniker. Ali was such an action junkie that he also played cards and casino games, bet on sports and horses, his unbridled passion.

Carlton teased Ali saying that Ali reminded him of a Rodney Dangerfield story. Doing a gravelly voiced impression, he croaked: "I tell ya I have bad luck. Opening day, the starter's gun killed my horse." 💀.

Unfazed, Ali asked, "Hey, Carlton, you wanna go in with me on tomorrow's trifecta?"

Carlton grinned and said, "Listen. I don't bet on anything with four legs, eats grass, or shits. You may think that I want to stirrup trouble, but I have a piece of advice for you. If you wanna get revenge on the horses, eat horsemeat."

"You know as a vegetarian I can't eat meat."

With a straight face Carlton replied, "I know. It's the wurst."

$$$

After Ali left our game, he moved to an empty table next to us to study the racing forms. A nicely dressed player, who apparently just left work, was at our game. This stranger called for the bet runner. "$400 to win on #11 in the third."

Overhearing this from next table, Ali intercepted the runner and asked her, "Did I hear that bet right? He put *$400* on 11?"

"That's right."

"Is he any good at handicapping?"

"Don't know."

"Hmm. He must know something to bet that much. Give me $200 on 11 in the third. And send Piaget over with a Preakness cocktail."

Meanwhile, to be sociable, I asked the recreational player, "You must like 11. Are you good at betting the ponies?"

"Nah, but I'm *due* to win. I haven't won in a month."

Oh-oh, I thought. *Good luck, Ali.* Some minutes later, after the race, I heard Ali's scream, "EYEYEEE!"

I immediately asked the social player how his horse ran. "Great! He's still running!" Catching Piaget as she dropped off Mr. Interruptus' drink, he said to her, "Let me have a Turf cocktail."

$$\$\$\$$$

Perhaps stretching the truth around the far turn, Ali swore he won betting thoroughbreds. Another time, when there was a lull in the televised races, he was sitting at an empty table constructing his Pick 6s and intricate parleys. "Hey, Ali, may I join you?"

He glanced over his glasses and said, "Sure, I'm ready for the first post." He alternated between looking over the glasses sitting halfway down his nose to see the screens and tilting his head down to read his forms.

"I read that horse racing is dying," I said. (Hollywood Park stopped in 2013.) "The betting population is aging so much, and tracks aren't getting new fans. Is that true?"

"Yeah. I'm one of the young guys, and I'm forty! Hollywood Park used to get 80,000 but now just a few thousand."

Reputedly Amazon founder Jeff Bezos said, "If you want to ensure your demise, fail to evolve."

Ali turned the pages on his racing form and tip sheets. He peered over his half-framed glasses to look at me, and said, "Now look at this horse, Oprah Whinny. She has a rep for zigging and zagging through the pack, but if she has a straight path, she doesn't take it. If she's on the turf cutting in and out, it looks like a lawn mower kicking out chunks of sod, pink flamingos and lawn jockeys. And this one, Karma Lite. Must've been an Arabian champion in its prior life, but now reincarnated as a donkey-horse. Must've banged too many camels."

"How do you know all this, dare I say, horse shit?"

"Oh, good one. I subscribe to all the touts' tip sheets and newsletters. But I admit sometimes I've a hunch, and against my quote, turf accountant, I bet the jockey, not the horse." This is like a stock market strategy of betting on the CEO. "See this jockey, Chris McCarron. Made a great ride once where he knew that the favorite wasn't passed easily. So, he took his mount wide and out of the favorite's view and he just passed the favorite at the wire to win. That's *riding*!"

"That is cool. But let me understand you about tip rags. Using and paying these advisors and swamis for picking winners reminds me of the stock market, newsletter writers. And another thing, Malcolm Forbes supposedly said, It's far more profitable to sell advice than take it. But I'm curious. Except for you, a winning handicapper, can't the regular horse players figure out they can't beat the track or bookie?"

"They eventually realize that."

"So why do they continue going to the track and, you know, horsing around?"

"They're addicted. They can't quit."

Thinking horse bettors could benefit from my theory that when a ritual becomes habitual, you know, it is wise to rethink it, I offered: "Forget status quo, and set a new goal. But can you quit?"

"Sure. Any time. I'm not like them—look at my horse. Come on! Come on three! *Come onnn three!!* EYEYEEE!!"

$$$

As it happened, the Bicycle Club, affectionately known as The Bike, lost its place as the gambling Mecca and became passé. Once the epicenter of poker action, owners and management didn't invest the time, money and effort to maintain its marque name and panache. However, as described about Gardenia, poker emporiums' popularity usually fell as newer places became hot and *the* place to play around LA. That said, one night I thought rather than going to Commerce, I'd make an expedition over to The Bike. You have heard of The Silk Route, MiG Alley and Tornado Alley. I liked to call the road between the Commerce Casino, and California Bell Club, Bicycle Casino the Road of Shattered Dreams.

To paraphrase Carly Simon, I walked into The Bike like I was walking onto a scow, but I didn't immediately see the sign-up board. To recapture the glory days, management often would change the decor and layout. Of course, I believe they made these alterations with unstudied, unprovable logic. It was unfathomable to me that card emporiums, even the usually well-managed Commerce card barn, implemented changes without first getting patrons' input. Or maybe I wasn't privy to it.

Zig-zipping through the construction partitions, and somewhat disoriented, I was scanning The Bike's interior horizon, the area of almost two football fields, looking for the board when I heard the distinctive baritone, "Hey, Jimmers! Over here."

Some players were loyalty to one club. For whatever psychological impetus, they'd continue playing at a gambling haunt which had sunk like a Schindler built U-boats into disfavor. Maybe their staying was due to comfort, a major factor, liking the staff, close proximity, or car-pooling. Triple C and Kelly were fixtures at The Bike. More on Kelly later. Unlike them, I went where the action, meaning profits, was. I was an apostate—not loyal exclusively to one casino—so I defected from The Bike to the new, *in* place. I'm a very loyal friend, but pertaining to casinos, my loyalty is to my bank account.

During a deck change, per a player's request, someone asked Triple C if the market would ever recover. "Sure, it will. From the beginning of the Dow-Jones Industrial Average, it's had huge swings. It ticks up and ticks down, but it always trends upward. Now's the time to buy. When they're cryin' I'm buyin'."

An incredulous player *cried*, "Buy! *Now?* I don't ever want to go back into stocks. If I recoup my money, I'll *never* go back in. Of course, this mirrors poker players saying, if I ever get even, I'll *never* play again.

"Listen," Clyde attempted to persuade this doubting Thomas. "I read a stock writer, Bill Shapiro, who made a great point. He said it's weird, but people will buy socks on sale, but not stocks. Stocks're on sale right now. The Dow-Jones was 1287 in January and now it's 1086. How much is that down, percentage wise, Drew?"

Drew said almost immediately, "Oh, about 15.6 percent."

"Thanks. So, in a way the overall market is selling at a 16 percent discount. Of course, individual stocks are down more or less than that, depending." Later, as he left, he said, "I'll give you my card. Call me, and we'll have lunch or at least talk where the walls don't have ears or noses.

22

JM Tries to Up-Date

I HELPED JANEY GET into dealer's school, and she got a job dealing. She was around a lot of guys hot for her. Eventually, she wanted to have the Talk. Why do so many women want to explode this IED? Another eternal mystery like why men are from Mars and women are from Venus? How do you find the G-spot? Who put the bomp in the bomp ba bomp bah bomp? Almost inevitably she broke up with me because of her poker dealing, work angst, general budget worries, and a desperate desire for marriage. Ultimately, she dealt me a bad hand when she started seeing Saul Offenbach behind my back and eventually married him. It seems that cheating in a monogamous relationship is like stealing in that it's taking trust and love for selfish reasons.

Although very down, looking on the bright side, I felt that Janey wasn't the lucky, future Mrs. JM. Until I met the lucky one, if she existed, I was ensnared, like those cocooned in *Alien3*, in a conundrum. Dating women working in the gambling industry or playing poker had many advantages. They were young and attractive. They understood poker, its elements, its economics, its ups and downs, and dynamics. And since I regularly spent two to three evenings a week at the clubs, the most important advantage was accessibility, easy to meet. Plus, they knew I played poker, so I didn't have to pirouette around the subject of how I earned some money.

Over the months, they'd get to know me and see I was a gentleman, rarely, if ever, losing my temper with inept staff. Like anyone, I could be curt. However, on the flip side of the chip, many didn't have the desirable qualities I wanted in a wife—college educated, classy, middle or upper-middle class family. You might wonder how such a sterling, fetching catch like me, aspires to such a wife? I'm optimism incarnate.

$$$

Cherchez la femme. In "Gold" John Stewart and in "California Girls" the Beach Boys proclaim girls from California are the greatest.

Playing cards, hanging with card players, and being self-employed often precluded socializing in the circles of women whom I wanted to meet. There were the usual dating landmines surrounding my target market's territory; also, I had no passport. What I'm clumsily trying to say is I had limited access to my desired type. My target demographic was further shrunk by my motto I don't smoke, I don't chew, and I don't go with girls who do. Believe me, I strongly identified with "Looking for Love (in all the Wrong Places)" sung by Johnny Lee in *Urban Cowboy.* I also sometimes felt intimidated by the high-powered women I sometimes met at business mixers. Consorting with those types, I felt less like John Travolta in *Urban Cowboy*, and more like Eddie Murphy in a SNL sketch as Buh-Weet (Buck Wheat) singing "Wookin' Pa Nub."

I briefly dated Christine, a medical sales rep. She dressed impeccably, had a face and figure to die for, flawless skin, perfect diction, and the posture of a model. She was striking. On our first d-d-date, I felt as nervous and inept as Dan Quayle at a spelling bee. But my most vivid memories of her are her beautiful face, bonnie complexion, and especially crisply starched blouse, white collar, and cuffs.

$$$

I've mentioned one tectonic strain in the poker terrain, and later I'll describe two more. Likewise, I had a geological upheaval of my own. Notwithstanding my happy, single, swinging bachelor days, sometimes I was as lonesome and cold as a ship's forlorn, baritone foghorn. I now wanted to fulfill my biological imperative, marry, and start a family. Fortunately, I didn't suffer a Cophetua complex—where a person can only sexually desire partners to whom he feels superior. Therefore, I began pursuing college grad women.

How many times have I counseled it's time to reset when that ritual becomes habitual—when the habit turns to an automatic, conditioned-response? Thus, I attempted to modify my regimen. Put another way, I wished to update. I learned of various mixers and dating clubs. One hosting mixers was Successful Corporate Organizing and Rejuvenating Events (SCORE). I attended many of their parties, and sometimes hundreds showed up for these love roulette soirees. Once, the organizers had a slick gimmick for breaking the ice. Women paid a fee at the door and were handed a threaded nut. Men paid and entered, and they were given a red, plastic bolt, for obvious reasons. Phallic or what? A couple whose bolt and nut fit got $50 each. Essentially everyone approached and talked to everyone else. Unlike this ice breaker technique, you, like me, may have experienced the following, usual awkwardness.

"Hi, I'm John."

"Hi, I'm Kate."

"Are you enjoying yourself, Kate?"

"Yes. How about you?"

"Yes. Now that I met you, I'm on top of the world."

"Oh, John, does that line work?"

"Not so much, but this one has better success—Katie, oops, Kate, you have the most alluring, velvety, violet eyes."

"Thanks, dear John. Well, it seems that you're a man who has a way with words."

Showing off I uttered, "Yes, I'm a sesquipedalian."

"Okay, Mr. Smarty Pants. What's that mean?"

"Germanely, it means someone who uses big words."

"Are you a teacher or professor of English?"

"No, Kate."

"And will you at least tell me where you're from?"

"I'm from Funky Town."

"Oh, and you probably lived on Easy Street—"

"That's a great guess. No, I live on Electric Avenue," I interrupted.

"—But I see that I'm not getting anywhere with you, so I'll ask again. What do you do?"

Here's where it gets dicey. I must've had this conversation a hundred times with someone I've just met. I get the overwhelming sensation of *déjà vu* that was weirder than a witch's cosmetics. Naturally I'd discuss my video game business but trying to explain my poker playing to their satisfaction without being written off was like trying to juggle tiny bubbles. It was a Catch-22. If I was totally above board and revealed that I made money by cards, I likely wouldn't get a phone number. But if by chance we dated a while, and then disclosed gambling income and the amount of time spent doing so, she'd feel I wasn't entirely honest. I determined most women, if seeking a committed relationship, preferred men with a stable job and traditional sources of income. A Babbitt if you will. They wanted to understand the work or product or service. I discovered saying, I'm a professional poker player was usually a deal breaker. (Maybe it was my personality or, [gulp], my looks, or double [gulp], my odor.) Thus, I usually hid poker income until later in the dating cycle if it progressed.

I plunged in, "Kate, I own a video games company." *Oh, what the hell,* I thought. "But I also play poker." Sometimes, attempting frivolity to deflect her uncertainty about playing cards, I'd say, "Let-let-let me lay my cards on the table. Another way that I view my poker work is that like Robin Hood, I'm redistributing wealth. But instead of taking from the rich to give to the poor, I'm winning from the lame and giving to the needy—me."

Sure, I can argue with all the facts and figures and a plethora of logic, but when it come to the showdown, most women seem to relegate gamblers to an undesirable population, a caste of pariahs haunting the nether world. Never mind my rational arguments. Gloria Steinem brilliantly quipped, "A woman's total instinct for gambling is satisfied by marriage."

Kate looked at me quizzically as if I were a fascinating but weird, repulsive, sea creature, and said, "That's interesting."

"I also look at playing poker as work, and I'm very serious about it. And I'm good at it. Also, important, I don't gamble on any Las Vegas casino, table games. On neither keno, chuck-a-luck, nor slots. I may've put two or three nickels in a slot in my life, but the *hold* is too great on those games of chance."

"What's the hold, John?"

"It's like the vigorish. That is, the percentage of all bets, the money gambled, that the house keeps. All the money bet, the wagering total, is the *handle*. The house may only give 2 to 40 percent of fair, true odds. Too much detail? Anyway, I don't bet horses or sports, or waste money on lotteries either."

"That's comforting," she said with her tongue firmly planted in her cheek. "If you don't bet horses, then I guess you could say you're not in a stable relationship."

Laughing, I replied, "True." But I soldiered on, although I sensed she was losing interest, "I-I have read about thirty books on poker. Poker's like chess where the best player usually will win. Sure, there's an element of luck involved, but over the long run, the best players will beat the less skilled. He'll win more and lose less with the same cards. And I have ironclad will power. Good discipline. I'm also a lucky guy."

She wondered, "Why? How?"

"It's my hard work and prep. And you know being lucky is all about perception…"

"You remind me of my girlfriend who says she always wins when she goes to Vegas."

"I'm dubious. No disrespect to your girlfriend, but those billion-dollar casinos are funded by one-armed bandits and house edge. I don't see any unprofitable casinos, do you?"[Except for Trump's.]

"No."

"You've heard the saying, You can't beat the house. I firmly believe it. On the other hand, I view poker playing as a contest of skill where the better player should win. A poker author, guru, Mike Caro, always preaches Good players beat bad ones."

"I think you mentioned that in relation to chess. Let me ask, you always win?"

"Of course not. In fact, poker is a special job where at the end of the day (or even month or year) you may have less than when you started. There's an important poker saying that poker is 90 percent skill and 10 percent luck *in the long term*, but the opposite in the *short* term. Surely in one session, short-term luck *may* overwhelm skill by nine to one. I must emphasize *may*. The skilled player can better weather a run of losing hands than the weak player."

"Clever. And how do you define short and long term?"

"Short term would definitely be one hand where luck really resides; however, for my purposes, short run would be about a month and long term would be closer to a year. And short-long term depends upon how often one plays. But also, Blackie Sherrod brilliantly observed, If you bet on a horse, that's gambling. If you bet you can make three spades, that's entertainment. If you bet cotton will go up three points, that's business. See the difference?"

"Kinda. Do ya think you'll *win* over a woman like me with this?"

"Dah. S'pose not. But I never said I was the smartest knife in the drawer."

"You mean, sharpest knife."

I winked and joked, "Whatever." I abashedly asked, "Oh, I'm so sorry, Kate. What kind of work do you do?"

"I'm in the tourism industry promoting and marketing Las Vegas to the world."

"Oops! Apologies for knocking Vegas revenue sources."

"No, I'm kidding. But nice meeting you, John. If you'd played your cards right, I might've given you my number. But, still, thanks for the dialectic discourse."

Maybe I was overselling myself and my card skills, too much hard sell and not enough Soft Cell. Unlike their song, I did not want tainted love but true love. Paraphrasing Shakespeare, I doth protest too much, methinks. I beat myself up thinking, *Way to go, JM, you fumbled. How boring could you be? Why not tell her about your phenomenal dream. You explained yourself but didn't find out much about her.*

23

Taking Stock

ONE TIME I WAS eating at the poker table, and Clyde, Triple C was playing. Naturally I teased him with a stock market axiom, "Everyone looks like a genius in a bull market."

He smiled, looked up as if studying a vision of the Virgin Mary, and replied, "I was trying to recall something that Warren Buffet said, or supposedly said. Something like, When the tide goes out, you know who's swimming nude. This quote's so true that it's profound. The investor, in my case my client, will see who knows his stuff, who knows the facts, has knowledge and the financial acumen to make money for him. Don't judge me as your broker based only on my success in a bull market."

Clyde noticed I put heavy soy sauce on my rice, for I loved it. Another player sitting with us, a very pleasant Chinese immigrant, "SS," an action-seeking, everyday player with an extraordinary square face, also saw me drown my rice. SS said, "Hey, JM. When I was growing up in Guangdong, only the poor used soy sauce. The wealthier people used delicious sauces. So, when I see you drench soy sauce, I remember my poor family."

"Me too," I told SS.

Clyde continued, "When I interviewed for my stockbroker job, they had what was called the IBM test. I heard this later from a friend in personnel. The department manager and or personnel guy'd take you to lunch. If the candidate salted their food before tasting it, they'd reject you outright.

They believed the interviewee was too set in their ways and didn't have an open mind. They wanted to hire someone who tested things and investigated first. I don't know if it was true, but it made sense. When a stock analyst or broker is meeting with corporate officers of a company that he might recommend, having an open mind is critical. You don't want to get schmoozed and blinded by the sales glitter before tasting.

"Thinking back on starting my job as a broker, I'm sorry I haven't done more with my mental gifts. All these decades later."

In this regret, I realized a connection between Clyde and Math Drew in that both felt they underutilized their respective intellectual talents. They were at odds with themselves. Furthermore, his interviewing experience crystalized in my mind, and I had another epiphany. I said, "Interesting, Triple C. I had a friend who interviewed for a commodity trading company. One of the chain of interviews was with a psychologist who asked, 'Mr. Denice, would you say you're closer to San Francisco or Liberia?' to determine his self-awareness and perceptions of the world. I've also heard about stress tests during which interviewers put the candidate in complex, awkward, very uncomfortable situations. They place the interviewee in a no-win position to see how the aspirant responds and thinks on his feet. You know, does the applicant have courage and grace under fire. But I get your point to avoid seasoning before tasting. This is vital, especially for poker, where immediately pigeonholing an unfamiliar opponent, or keeping a known player in a slot, can be dangerous."

$$\$\$\$$$

While playing poker, Clyde didn't conceal that he was a stockbroker, as I might've done. I was very private in the gambling milieu. I surmise he figured he might get new clients from the casino. But once, when The Bike was the hot spot in LA, a local TV camera crew came in for some footage of the players and layout. It was newsworthy because it was extraordinarily busy and attracted actors, sports figures, the famous, and the beautiful. But in this case Clyde didn't want the notoriety. He recoiled and screamed, "Get those cameras out of here!" He didn't want his current or potential clients to see him, although playing poker there was perfectly legal. Maybe he felt a guilt by association with gambling might rub off on him. Or he thought they'd be worried that he was blowing their money.

Just like other business, legal, or medical professionals, Clyde invariably was asked for free advice. The free lunch brigade players asked, "Hey, Triple C., what do you think of Gene BioTronics TechDyne; Infinity, Ltd.; Incorporate, Inc.; De Pot Depot; Reek REIT; Disappearing Inc.; Clothes Call?"

These gamblers almost were compelled to take a flyer, a gamble, a plunge. He did dispense one stock tip: "Be fearful when others are greedy and be greedy when they are fearful."

$$$

And oh, yes, freebie advice. Poker players loved that. Examples of imaginary conversations: "Doc, there's this stabbing pain in my brain. What do you think it is?" Doc thinks, *I wish you'd go away.* Someone asked this one witty doctor what his specialty was, and he answered, "I sell body parts." "Should I use a standard deduction rate or itemize? And what's all this crap about the Alternative Minimum Tax?"

From experience in fielding annoying requests for gratis advice, many keep professions secret. Imagine how distracting being bombarded with questions from ill-informed requestors, and not having complete info? Not to mention the possibility of being liable. It was no win. Some, like Clyde, were okay with talking shop, but I wasn't. Remember the Ferengi Rule of Acquisition #59: "Free advice is seldom cheap."

24

Penny for Your Thoughts

BY THE MID-EIGHTIES, I was playing Lowball at a stratospheric limit, the second highest in the Bicycle Club. After Janey split with me, I was on the rebound. I perpetually flirted with one of the top section's food server, chip runner, Penny. She was gorgeous: Petit, lithe, and very toned from doing that 80's fitness craze, Jazzercise.

Unfortunately, she was dating a Floor man, Salvator Mundi. Although Armenian, not Egyptian, he had the looks and high wattage, dazzling smile of Omar Sharif. What a handsome couple; what a lucky guy. Revealingly, he didn't consider himself lucky to have such a hot girlfriend. As Samuel Butler brilliantly wrote in *The Way of All Flesh*, "Pontifex did not consider himself fortunate, and he who does not consider himself fortunate is unfortunate." For that, and who know what, they broke up about eighteen months after I met her.

I overheard someone she was serving asking, "I'm sure you get hit on all the time, but can I call you?" She charmingly smiled and replied, "Take a number." Oh, yes. Everyone hit on her even when she was with Salvator, but after she was available, I entered the lottery, too, hoping my balls were grabbed.

%%%

I put my odds of dating her at about 1,000:1, definitely a long shot. But I kept asking, and somehow or other, fortune smiled upon me. She mentioned in passing that she was dying to see *Ghostbusters*, so I had a sales pitch: "Let's go see *Ghostbusters* on your day off." Later, since she worked on the casino floor in plain view, she surreptitiously gave me her number inside a napkin. My heartbeat skipped to *allegro*. This was extraordinarily good fortune, and I felt as though I'd won a jackpot, lottery, and *El Gordo* all in one.

In the first blush of lusty, busty, rapturous dating, we also had a fantastic time going out dancing; seeing the West Hollywood, transvestites' musical revues; discussing the gambling scene and gossip.

$$\$\$\$$$

Concomitantly, after I started dating Penny, I had a huge winning streak playing Low. Part of my winning streak's perpetuation meant being satisfied with a moderate win, and not getting greedy. I wanted to spend time with her after she got off, so I just got up without any qualms over shoulda, gouda, woulda, as cheese lovers might say. After winning some Münster pots and departing, I'd never know what might have been, and I didn't care. Also, part of the streak's continuation was I was extraordinarily confident. A winning streak'll do that.

Be assured opponents noticed me quickly leaving with small but reasonable wins—known as booking a win. I tried one night to lure a player over to our table. He was young, about 25, hip, lots of ink, even on his face where the scar met the star—a gold star. He was very live and had lots of cash for he owned a bar, The Dew Drop Inn. Additionally, as usual when he played, he sipped vodka.

"Hey, Ralphie. Why don't you change tables, and come on over and play with us?"

Ralphie teased, "Why would I want to play with you, ah, ah, JM?" His interesting tic when trying to remember something, was snapping his fingers. "If you win $700 you go home." Ouch, but true. Proud of it. While dating Penny, I utilized a strategy called hit and run which was widely discredited by the pros. Recall Caro advocated staying as long as the game is good, profitable. Other pros like Gordon, the player who habitually came after sunset and left before sunrise, wanted to put in the hours like a job; that is, get paid for playing hundreds of hands that would equate to so much per hour in winnings. Ralphie bantered on, "Yeah, and besides you, your table has another one of the toughest players. Trying to win money from you two'd be like me trying to get sex from my wife."

It's said discretion is the better part of valor. Obviously, I believe dildoing is the better part; thus, I threw caution to the wind and retorted, "I never had any trouble ..."

A few hours later, I heard someone at Ralphie's game order a martini, and he cautioned the cocktail waitress to tell the bartender, "You usually add too much vermouth. Tell him to just whisper 'vermouth' across the gin."

Ralphie interjected, "Tell the barkeep to just shut yermooth ... And don't even *look* at the vermouth on the shelf."

25

Richer Clientele

SINCE MOVING TO A higher *Low*ball limit at The Bike, I encountered a richer clientele. Sometimes a high roller was waiting for the biggest game in town. Since there was a waiting list for that game, they might kill time by playing in our lower game, the second highest in the casino. Once this high roller was showing off his watch. "I just bought this Patek Philippe. It cost $5,000." Back then this was the cost of a small sports car.

Both curious and impressed I asked, "May I see it?" As I weighed it in my hand, I admired it saying, "Hmm. Very nice. Hefty. Now by comparison, my watch has a stopwatch function, shows dual time zones, has an alarm feature, and the screen lights up if need be. And it only cost $200. What else does yours do?"

"It just tells time. But it does have a perpetual calendar."

"Sweet!" I teasingly continued. "It's beautiful and *only* $5,000. Did the price include the watch band?"

"I know you're joshing me."

"Well, if it only gives time, let's see if at least it's waterproof." I thought I'd try a Melba cracker variation, and I feigned I was going to drop it into a glass of water.

He looked like he was passing a kidney stone, and he jumped up. "Give me my watch back, fool."

"Sorry, man. I was playing with you."

$$$

Being in top section meant wealthier players and the best waitresses—sharper and more experienced. One was "Düsseldorf" Dora. Witness. A drunk, crazy patron studied her nametag and slurred, "Dora, eh. I'd think with a name like that you'd be prettier."

She didn't miss a beat: "With a face like yours I bet you're ordering dog food."

We all laughed at this burn. Even the drunk laughed. Since this tipsy patron was throwing off money, someone tried to mollify Dora, saying with a laugh, "Forgive him. He's a pig."

The richer patrons included Mr. Interruptus, the dealer whisperer. He stuck his substantial nose in and snorted, "A pig is a pal that'll help your morale." Aside from talking nonstop, which might cause lingual tendinitis in normal folk, Interruptus' most distinguishing, physical feature was his large nose. I'm casting no aspersions or nose-persions. I have a commodious proboscis myself.

My nose:

℧

⌣

People just as easily could've hung the handles of "Durante" (too passé) or Cyranose (too literary) on him. But do you remember the hoods on 1960's Jaguar E-Type series, aka the XKE? Those hoods seemed like the flight deck of an aircraft carrier, going on and on. Since the hood sloped down, you couldn't estimate when the front bumper would smash into a wall or parked car. Mr. Interruptus had a schnoz like that XKE.

Later the inebriated customer ran out of checks and pulled out more money to rebuy; since he did not have checks yet, he played the next hand on credit. After he lost that hand, he called, "I need chips, 'cause I owe this man $200. For God's sake, don't hurry!" Düsseldorf Dora didn't want further confrontations, so she avoided coming over. When a softer-spoken chip runner came to sell him checks, he blurted out, "Give me a thousand in yellows ... Honestly? You want the money first!" He gave her the bills and soon bellowed, "I can't believe it. She's counting the money!"

$$\$\$\$$$

Having interrupted myself, I'll return to Mr. Interruptus' circuit breaking. Conversing with Curtis or trying to talk with someone else while he was within earshot, was challenging. There were more continuity breaks than those annoying wake ups caused by a senior's bladder while they're trying to sleep. Here's an example. Normally every twenty to thirty minutes someone would ask a food server or porter for a bottled water. Once an impatient, parched person shouted, "Janet, bring me a couple of bottled waters and—"

Mr. Interruptus dove in. "Water is the universal solvent because many substances are able to dissolve in it." Later out of the blue he interjected, "A catalyst is an inorganic material that speeds a chemical reaction." He didn't care whether anyone was listening.

The interrupted player wanting water said, "You win. Where the hell was I?"

$$\$\$\$$$

In fairness, I've been accused of having "Restless Tongue Syndrome." I'm somewhat a motor mouth; especially when the stars are aligned just right in two situations. If I'm on a rush, I'm more voluble than normal. If badly stuck early in the morning, after playing all night, and needing pep, I drink coffee. Yao! This lubricates my tongue, ignites like liquid nitrogen, and blasts me off the pad. But I still can't hold a megaphone to Mr. Interruptus.

He surely was a *tour de farce,* randomly inserting, "You know the line, A smile is just a frown turned upside down, then also a *smile* is just a kind of metaphor with an *i* added."

"Interruptus, what in the hell are you babbling about?"

"If you add an '*i*' between the *s* and *m*, you derive 'simile.' Rotund is a curious word. Remove the '*t*' from it, you get a word with the same meaning, round. And founder and flounder can mean nearly the same thing. Cool, huh? And while we're on spelling, JM, how do you spell the adjective from the noun mischief? The adjective I'm wanting you to spell means being harmful or irresponsibly playful, and ending in o-u-s."

"Curtis, if you were a song, you'd be The Who's 'Cobwebs and Strange.' One of the funniest songs ever. Anyway, do you mean m-i-s-c-h-e-i-v-i-o-u-s?"

"Enhhh! Wrong. It's m-i-s-c-h-i-e-v-o-u-s. Speaking of music. What's the favorite folk song of a carpenter with a foot deformity?"

"It's probably easier if I just give up and say I don't know."

"'If I Had a Hammer' ... toe."

Discouraged, I said, "Or a claw hammer, but I wish I could remove one m from your comma so you'd have a coma."

And, since he customarily had to get the last word, he finished, "Yeah. By the way, JM, you also have microcephaly ..."

26

Three Day Weekends

THE JOINT WAS JUMPING like a tangle of cats in a sack soaked in cat-nip and Red Bull. Three-day weekends meant that there would be a lot of players drinking and celebrating. The games would be juicy. JM's Law # 6 states that if there are many players drinking, it can be a spirited game and very profitable. If four or more are buying each other drinks, which is very rare, watch out. Fasten your seat belts! The game could be a bungee jump wearing a jet pack. There probably would be mega-action, lots of reraises, bluffing, and frequent bad beats; i.e., the partying gambler would take unwarranted risks, defy the odds and beat your strong hand. Of course, one had to take the good with the bad. In the long run, these are the types of opponents I longed for; yet, in the short run of one session, players pray their money withstands the onslaught of potential bad beats. "Dad, I'm in a *great* game. Send more money!"

Paradoxically, to me, *some* natives prefer a tight game, for they don't like the huge swings and mega-volatility. These more conservative play-ers don't mind competing with a table full of solid players, for they want a predictable, sedate game. They abhor crazy games, for their emotional makeup afflicts them with *bad beat phobia*. I heard one such player say, "Table change. Get me outta here. I'm playing with a bunch of really des-perate players!" Whereas I find the wild games more profitable and to my liking than solid, conservative games. We all have different emotional needs, buttons and reactions.

"Play happy or don't play at all."

£££

Penny was literally running to take and deliver orders. She was getting a decent aerobic workout without being in a gym. "Sorry, JM. This is the first chance I've had to take your order. What'll you have?"

"Yeah, I can see you're harried out of you mind. Please give me a large orange juice, bottled water, and a veggie pizza."

"Okay. What veggies do you want on it?"

"Oh, surprise me. Just drag a scrapper across the vegetable patch I think the casino has out back." Lowering my voice, I whispered behind the menu, "I hope I can see you tonight."

"We'll see ... if I can still walk and think."

Thirty minutes later, when she came back with my order, a dispute erupted between a regular and a British tourist who, as they say, was on holiday. Playfair, the Brit, had quaffed too many pints. He called out, "Footman. Oh, Footman!" When the Floor man arrived, the tourist said, "I say, ol' chap. The name's Playfair. Reginald Playfair, and we need a bit of arbitration here ..."

Judging by his face, the Floor person was probably thinking, *Just when I thought I'd been called everything, something new.* He smiled and graciously said, "Yes, sir. By the way, my name is Salvator Mundi, and I'm a Floor man, not a footman. Now, what seems to be the problem?"

"Foot, er, Floor man. This knave here says that because my cards touched the, what do you call it—what's the native phrase—the mire, that my hand is dead, and he wins the pot. What the deuce, that's bonkers. He's trying to nick the bloody pot from me. Bugger."

After Salvator the Floor man questioned the dealer and others, he gave the bad news to the tourist. "I'm so sorry, sir, but by the rules your hand is indeed dead once it touches that heap of cards, the *muck*."

"Oh, bollocks! That's a bad show, what. It's true that I've been drinking and am a little squiffy, but that doesn't quite seem cricket. Beastly business, that. You may think that I was born into clover, but I say, ol' chap, I need a chin wag with someone higher up. What."

"I'll get the manager, Reginald."

"Thank you, ol' man." This apparent gourmet then caught the attention of a food server. "Oh, serving wench. Penny, is it? I'd rather like to order some fried aubergine ..."

27

Second Tectonic Shift

I POSITED EARLIER THAT the first tectonic shift in the Southern California poker world occurred when other card clubs opened outside Gardenia. For the populace these new establishments offered competing choices to Gardenia. Thus, there was a ground swell of players migrating, like people from the southern Great Plains to California during the Dust Bowl decade, from Gardenia to other locales. In Gardenia jargon, these players were seeking a strawberry patch (sweet, juicy opponents and games), not a rock pile or rock garden.

Pressure was building for novelty and a game generating more action than Low. It was released with the second paradigm demolition and earthquake leveling of the poker landscape, the legalization of Hold 'em and 7 Card Stud in May 1987. This too was cataclysmic. (Curiously, Pai Gow Poker was legalized under certain restrictions in 1985, but I never played it.) That I never played Pai Gow, Pai Gow Poker, or Pan 9 doesn't mean I was incurious. I saw, however, that you played against the casino which raked or took a fee, cut, of each hand. Since it wasn't beatable, I avoided playing them.

These and other gambling variations were offered in a separate casino section called the Asian Games section. It wasn't named the Oriental Games area, for circa late 1960s that would become PI. In colonial times, the white man called the Far East countries the Orient. Being a word lover, I learned the approximate antonym of Oriental was Occidental.

In the late 1960s to early 1970s ethnic pride was a big movement. I understand the 1960's rationale for African Americans wanting to re-brand a semi-derogatory term, black, and having it evolve to a term of pride. Hence, Negroes preferred being called Black, then African Americans, and now African American or Black (and not *the* Blacks). College kids of Mexican heritage preferred Chicanos. But since not all Spanish speakers don't want to be lumped together, Hispanics, Latinos or Latinx derived.

Transforming *Indian*, a European, colonial term that Columbus mistakenly gave the new world people (thinking he found India) to Native American is understandable. But I wonder why we changed Oriental to Asian or Asian American? Why the term Oriental was offensive? My loose theory was it connoted a stereotype and colonialism. I pondered this until a friend explained that Oriental was given by the ruling class, The Man. "The people of the Far East didn't vote on this. And furthermore, when I hear the word Oriental, I think of an object, like furniture or art, not people."

$$$

Exploring the Asian games section for the first time was like voyaging to an exotic, strange, and wondrous land. Once landed I felt like an anthropologist moving through the milieu. Before the smoking ban, a legion of puffers created a smoky pall, almost obscuring the Asian characters on the walls and the gold and bright red decor far more vibrant than poker sections. Smoking gaspers took the WWII mantra, "Smoke 'em if ya got 'em" and "The smoking lamp is lit" to new levels of toxicity. This ghastly cloud of smoke was the first thing I noticed; furthermore, compared to the poker section, the Asian section had way higher energy with the banging of dice cups and exuberant shouting to encourage luck that assaulted one's ears. Other characteristics included great attention to *feng shui* and a cacophony of languages. Not speaking any of the languages, I assumed the loud exhortations were to the gods, spirits, even to revered ancestors to bring luck and fortune. I half expected to stumble into an opium den.

$$$

Just as Jacks or Better to Open (5 Card Draw, High) was supplanted by Lowball, so Lowball was replaced by Hold 'em as the most current, popular game. During the transitional periods, I bounced between both. Yet, by the mid-1990s I was exclusively plowing Hold 'em fields like the share cropping Joads. "In Divés' Dive," Robert Frost cites drawing five cards in Draw:

> It is late at night and still I am losing.
>
> But still I am steady and unaccusing.
>
> As long as the Declaration guards
>
> My right to be equal in number of cards,
>
> It is nothing to me who runs the Dive.
>
> Let's have a look at another five.

Frost's poem is brilliant; especially, spot on for a player like me who's non-blaming (except toward myself) when losing and equality oriented. Be that as it may, the poem's relevancy applies to draw poker—not to the now more popular Hold 'em. But yo, I'm up for a rhyming challenge with my poker couplets:

> If self-abuse is your aim,
>
> Then poker should be your game.
>
> If risky behavior you wish to embolden,
>
> Then you must try a little Texas Hold 'em.

$$$

Gamblers seek certain effects through gambling. Universally, and instinctively players swear the reason they play is to win money, but sometimes winning money is secondary, and they derive pleasure in other ways. For example, it might fill a void; deliver thrilling jolts like drugs; be a surrogacy for love, sex, emotional connection; inflict self-punishment, etc. Regarding these non-monetary goals, the *type* of poker, any gambling really, is irrelevant. These observations aren't as pertinent to the professionals as they are to recreationalists, dilettantes, and pro wannabees. Generally, average poker players love to take chances, drink, smoke, cuss and sometimes do drugs; for them the more ways to meld these the better. Ascetic, gamblers are not. Most aren't stoics or Spartan. Imagine ancient Rome and Sparta. Will Durant's brilliant insight on stoicism, "A nation is born stoic, and dies epicurean (recall Roman Empire)," could help some players.

$$$

Just as after my college freshman year—when I'd read Yardley's *The Education of a Poker Player*—so in my freshman Gardenia year I read John Fox's *Play Poker, Quit Work, and Sleep till Noon*, learning of it from an ad in *Gambling Times*. What great marketing and the phrase Sleep til Noon was pure nectar, a trap for aspiring poker pro wannabees and the free lunch bunch. I was seduced by the idea of *free* income for life. Likewise, decades later, after Hold 'em became prevalent, I eventually studied and read everything I could about it, and in about a year I became proficient—not expert. Probably you'd never master it, especially no limit, but I constantly studied the nuances. Hold 'em is vastly more complex with decidedly more room for strategy and skill than Lowball. Hold 'em betting's critical to reach Value Town—to milk chips from an opponent.

$$$

You often overhear someone say, "A live one open raised it from spot 3. Next to act, I had A-Q offsuit, and I'd been getting beat up. What should I do?" One heard this or variations constantly. Though fascinating to a card smith, I won't discuss Hold 'em strategies and play of the hands in detail, if at all, for there are scores of fine books on strategy. The strategies herein are general.

With the legalization of Hold 'em and 7 Stud, I had to decide which game to concentrate on. Poker intelligentsia (is there such an animule?) believed the former would be profitable when it was newly spread, legal in a town, but later, 7 Stud generally would be more profitable. Furthermore, comparing Lowball and Hold 'em, the wags and poker columnists predicted that since there's more skill in Hold 'em than Lowball, there'd be less variance in Hold 'em. Years later, I didn't experience this predicted decrease in fluctuations.

Math Drew concurred, saying, "The standard deviation in Hold 'em should be less than Lowball."

Someone looked at Drew as if he were snarling Klingon, "Say it in English."

"Oh, right. I mean there should be less volatility in Hold 'em. Your ups and downs over time should be less."

I previously mentioned that the poker scene sometimes could feel like a carnival. But like a carnival's roller coaster, there were major emotional gyrations up and down.

Arguably, the differences between Lowball and Texas Hold 'em are the inverse of cleaning old vinyl records compared to cleaning a CD. I won't bore you with the differences, but I have more positions on this than the *Kama Sutra*. Like audio sound, was Lowball warmer than Hold 'em? I suppose so, for the Hold 'em *aficionados* were younger, and, therefore, less curmudgeonly.

$$$

Evolving from being a Lowball player to a Hold 'em acolyte, I didn't see or play with Clyde as much as in the past. Still, from time to time I would mosey over to the Low section to say hi; whereas, in its heyday, The Bike's Lowball games were legendary and numerous. Now there might only be one high stake table spread going. While playing Hold 'em, occasionally some unusual hand occurred. For example, a player loses a big pot to a live one (Player L) who got lucky. L had two clubs and only one was on the flop, but he had two over cards. (In other words, L flopped a three flush, meaning that only one of his suits was on the flop. He needed one more on turn *to even make a flush draw*, and river to make a flush.) L took some betting heat and saw the turn card. More betting. Then L wins when the third of his suit rivers. The loser (B for bad bet) who had the top set is crushed and incredulous. B plaintively wails, "What're the odds?"

Next chance, I'd took a break and went to see Math Drew who might be in Clyde's Low game. I found their table, and I solicitously approached.

"... short Bechtel. Then straddle it," Clyde was advising. When Triple C saw me, he smiled and said, "Hey, Jimmers. How's Hold 'em treating you?"

"I'm *holding* my own. Nyuck-nyuck." As usual I repeated investing advice which he already knew, "By the way, Don't fight the tape."

Math Drew was there, and realizing a new dealer was settling into the *box* (dealer's seat) for her *down* (time at this table), he continued a prior conversation with a crossover player like me. "I can figure those odds. Let's see ... the odds of flopping a flush is about 118:1 or 0.8 percent."

Someone at the table teased, "Drew, you probably just memorized those odds."

"No," he disagreed. "I can do them in my head."

"Okay. What're the odds of being dealt pocket aces? Show your work."

"See you multiply the probabilities of receiving each card: 4 divided by 52 times 3 divided by 52 equals 12 over 2,652 equals 220:1... And you know the chances of being dealt two aces is the same as being dealt two deuces, or any pair."

The dealer interrupted us saying in her sweet voice, "Good evening, everyone. Is the button here? Okay, good luck to everyone."

I politely waited until Math Drew was out of a hand, then asked, "How're ya doing, Drew? Let me ask you a favor. Let's say you flop a three flush [you're suited, but only one of it flops]. What're the odds of making a flush?"

Drew turned around to look at me, took about five seconds and replied, "The probability of getting there is about 24:1." Maybe to show off, or maybe to test himself, he revealed, "The turn has to be a club. That's ten divided by forty-seven, times the river chances, nine divided by forty-six. This equals a probability of about .0416. One divided by this number gives you the odds against or 24:1. That's *if* the opponent doesn't make a hand that beats a flush."

"That's awesome. Thanks, Drew." I couldn't wait to get back to my table with this pearl of wisdom and praise him.

"You're welcome. And, hey, JM. Kiss a duck for me."

$$\$\$\$$$

As I noted above, I was a newcomer crossing between Low and Hold 'em, aspiring to be a Hold 'em *maven*; thus, I moved down in limits from very high Lowball to mid-sized Hold 'em limits. My bankroll, working capital needs, potential gains, losses, and swings were about halved. I competed in the lower games of the top section, just above the jackpot games—just higher than games that dropped chips for the jackpot (See Appendix, #1). As a result, I encountered a whole new cast of characters who had some 7 Stud experience and felt they had an advantage playing the newly legalized Hold 'em. Illustrative interaction. A 7 Stud player says to a novice Hold 'em player, "Seat 6, you played that real bad."

Someone notes, "What's worse, this Hold 'em criticism is from a *Stud* player!" Also, some who previously played Lowball at the jackpot games' limits, decided to try Hold 'em and migrated northward, up in limits.

Class, as in caste, isn't usually a concern to poker *aficionados*. Good players are generally respected. Most admired the highest stakes players, the elites. Nevertheless, normally pros look down on recreational players (even though pros derive most of their income from them); whereas the pro is also silently disdain or cautious of the pro wannabees. The wealthy might look askance at the pro while most lack respect for the players in lower limits than themselves. Many view people playing lower limits almost like they are mouth breathers. Oftentimes we see someone, with whom we've done many hours of battle, moving south, a step or two down in limits. We say hi but have compassion for their plight. Everyone knows they can be next. Profanely, "There, but for the grace of God, go I." No one likes degenerates or the obnoxious, be they winners or losers. And realize there's a fine line between the sub reputable and the supra disreputable.

$$\$\$\$$$

I should explain bad beat jackpots. It's comprised of two parts. 1. Until the jackpot is hit, won, money's taken from every pot and added to the pool; I've seen it as high as $90,000. 2. The jackpot is awarded when its threshold, a bad beat, is met; that is, an opponent has a remarkably strong hand but is beaten by an even stronger one. Incidentally, the hand's loser gets the bigger share, let's say 60 percent—depending upon the casino—while the hand winner gets remainder. Thus, in Low, the second-best possible hand, 6, 4, 3, 2, A is beaten by a wheel. In High Draw, Aces-full or better beaten. And later this threshold was applied in Hold 'em.

One such competitor making the perilous migration from Lowball jackpot to Hold 'em games was a large man with curly, scrambled hair which looked as if a small tornado had touched down on top of his large head sitting atop his sloped shoulders. He was usually unshaven (decades before this became fashionable), and his moustache looked like two flying buttresses supporting the base of his bulbous, vein-crosshatched nose. With clothes crumpled, he was slovenly with the carelessness of someone who would vacuum up a ballpoint ... or a small dog. He usually modeled tee shirts, stretched to the splitting point. One read "People keep thinking I care. Weird." Another was one of the funniest I ever saw, "Tijuana" it proudly proclaimed. He was large, gigantic and majestic. He was so large that when he sat his commodious butt on the commode, his can on the can, *it* groaned, and the pipes farted! I'll bet his turds were like constipation, big boys the size of Red Bull cans caused by taking Oxy for a week. Yao! In Yiddish, he had a *tuches un a halb* (literally a backside and a half).

Adding another half—his big pot belly—to total two people, he'd dourly sit at the table hour after hour without stirring. Since he had this ponderous beer keg in front, his pants rode low in back, and one often saw his ass-fault. Would you like to guess this magnificent specimen's nickname? Full credit for "Buffalo" or "Buff"—not the cut, ripped buff. Half-credit for "Wally," short for Walrus. Oh, poker connoisseurs can be cruel! Also, he drank excessively but didn't get sick, for he could *really* hold it. He had an interesting speech tic, too. Often, he'd end a sentence by affectedly saying Kenya's capital, "Nigh-*ROBE*-ay." Why? No one knew. Once we were playing, and he gruffly said, "With all the weirdos out there and freeway shootings, I'm afraid to drive. Nigh-*ROBE*-ay."

Risking raising his ire or getting trampled, I chipped in this burn: "The way you drink, so am I."

$$$

There's a good reason Las Vegas is called Sin City. (Here comes my diatribe again.) While it doesn't have a monopoly on sinners, it has an ultra-materialistic philosophy. "What happens in Vegas, stays in Vegas." What a creative ad campaign to recommend forgetting morals. Delightful. And for God's sake, its own past mayor, Oscar Goodman, was a mob mouthpiece, investigated for illegal influence peddling and a shill to legalize prostitution.

Vegas had allowed Hold 'em years before The Golden State. When California legalized it in 1987, early pioneers from Vegas visited and telegraphed back to the folks in Glitter, not Dry, Gulch: "Come on out. The fields are bountiful. The sheep are ready for frying and the fish are ready for shearing." As the late 1980s continued into the 1990s, the influx increased because the games were so much more juicy, profitable, than in Las Vegas.

Consequently, besides the locals like Buff, another class of players also migrated to our Hold 'em games and sunny pastures of Southern California where we locals didn't have much, if any, experience in Hold 'em. The word got to Texas and especially Vegas that the pickings were good in SoCal after Hold 'em was legalized.

This opportunistic crowd descended almost like locust expecting to chew up the competition; however, some of them couldn't handle or quickly adjust to the *poor* play we manifested. Many of them became neurotic, mumbling shells bleating about constant bad beats. California bad beats were a special class. A gambler gets lucky to catch one to X possible cards on the turn or especially the river to win the hand. If I encountered a stranger from Lost Wages, I'd joke, "Welcome to the game of California-style, You're not gonna like the river, Hold 'em."

In conclusion, you could say the second tectonic shift, legalizing Hold 'em in California, caused a mini earthquake by bringing in players who migrated from afar.

28

Virgil Caine Was His Name

I BEGAN PLAYING WITH one of these recent emigrees, a Texan *hombre* named Virgil "Virge" Caine. Having recently moved from Las Vegas, he was a very skillful Hold 'em player. Everyone liked him, and his predominate traits were his geniality and generosity. He liked to buy others dinner, a drink, make a music CD, or lend a movie. He had a flat top, acute vision, and had a husky, 6' frame. He spoke with a slight accent, but unlike some Southern accents, his soft, manly, Texas drawl was endearing. Please don't get your hackles up, but to some of us hereabouts, a Southern accent just rubbed people the wrong way. Without delving too deeply into a sociological substratum, a Southern twinge hinted at prejudices. Eventually becoming friends, I joked that I could've nicknamed him "Johnny Reb" (obscure reference that "The Night They Drove Ol Dixie Down" was about a Civil War Confederate).

"Well now, don't that beat all," I told him. "I'm prejudiced against a regional speech pattern.

"Shucks," Virge humorously and for effect replied, "Tha's all right, JM. I know what ya mean. I'm from Horsefly, Texas, and we was prejudiced against the people from Preacher's Daughter. So, no offense taken."

I continued, "The best definition of prejudice I ever heard. The dislike of the unlike. But you know, some people use regional patterns like 'y'know' and 'y'all' to engage the other person into replying without expecting a response. Or they *suck teeth*, you know sounds like *tst*, to signal something meaning 'Stand back. I'm thinking.'"

At the same table, we tried to sit next to each other so that we could chat. I recognize, however, that shooting the breeze with someone isn't optimal use of one's time and energy, for it's distracting. Like most successful players, I always try to notice things. It's important, even crucial, to note who's live and who's tight—those who enter pots with junk contrasting those with premium hands only. Who gives action by raising and reraising on the come—speculating, so to speak? Who bluffs? Who's on tilt? Even a normally tough, winning player occasionally can be off their game. Who's usually a losing person but now is winning big, and, therefore, playing preternaturally well, almost unconsciously great?

That said, I liked to be around Virge. It might sound strange, but we didn't mind losing to each other. Granted, one must lose hands and have losing sessions; we just preferred losing to a friend rather than a plick or yak off. Since he was more experienced than me in my inchoateness, early Hold 'em nights, I could discuss strategy with him, and I learned. On his side, he liked to learn vocabulary, history and other things from me.

"What's goin' on, JM? Listen. I heard an interesting word on the radio driving here. Something like a-poth-E-us."

"How were they using it? What was the context?"

"They were talking about the nature of professionalism in sports. What's inside an athlete that makes him great."

"Yeah, I think it's 'apotheosis.' It's like the essence of something. The embodiment."

"Spell it for me—here, give me your pen—and I'll write it down on a napkin."

$$$

Later when Virge was facing a tough call on his opponent, he said to me, "Well, JM, the *chips are down on this hand.*" Then to his adversary, "Okay, you probably got me, but I call." After Virge caught the opponent's bluff, Virge chuckled softly to me and said, "I thought I was being *sandbagged.*" He pulled in a pile of chips and began the joyous task of stacking them.

Hearing these poker idioms, I noted, "I love words and definitions, so those two terms you used have become part of our vernacular."

"Huh?"

"*Chips are down* and *sandbag* are poker terms creeping into everyday usage. They've entered our lexicon, our dictionary of common, acceptable words. Then there's patois, which like an argot, means sort of a specialized language, slang or jargon."

"Yeah. … I fold."

Perhaps a new dealer would sit down in the box, and she'd take a minute to get situated by adjusting the chair, opening her checks tray cover, and scrambling the deck prior to beginning her down. This gave us a chance to try and recall more terms.

Virge recalled, "This dealer's murder. She pronounces her name Tree, so I when I talk to her, I say Ms. Tre. It's a *mystery* why she kills me. Hey, I mentioned *sandbagging*. I wonder where that came from?"

"Yeah, me too. I'll look that up."

He added, "What about *having a poker face.*"

"Good. I brought up geopolitics earlier. You can have a nuclear *showdown*, like the Cuban Missile Crisis, or a showdown with your boss or enemy. At the showdown one lays one's cards on the table. Think Saddam Hussein and his claim he had, and would use, Weapons of Mass Destruction. Threatening to use chemical weapons gave him *bargaining chips*. He *upped* or *raised the ante*—made the stakes bigger—but inevitably had to fold his cards when we *called his bluff.*" As an unknown wit expressed, Remember, that if you tell a lie, don't believe it deceives only the other person.

When another hand was over, Virge fired off a good one: "Saddam wasn't *playing with a full deck.*"

"Nor did he *hold all the cards,*" I added.

"Hey, are you two gonna twitter like some old ladies at a sewing circle or play cards?"

"Sorry, guys. Virge, we'll talk about this later." Opponents can be cruel, especially when they're losing. I blush to admit that I was slowing down the game. You can bust me, for I mentioned earlier I wanted a speedy game to maximize my potential profits. And I hate being rude. In my defense, I am human, err, and I very rarely slow down the game.

$$\$\$\$$

Weeks later I discoed down to the pasteboard, and eventually Virge and I were at the same table.

"Virge, how you running?"

"Not so good. I can't make a hand stand up. They keep running me down." That is, various combatants defied the odds and kept beating Virge's good starting hands.

The Mad Genius of Poker, Mike Caro, writes of complaining at the table as Virge was doing now. Taking liberties, I'll not only paraphrase Caro, but add colorful metaphors. Although it feels good to unburden yourself and vent your pain and anger, don't complain at the table. Maybe you feel better after complaining or maybe you want sympathy, but if you want sympathy see your mom ... or a kind hooker.

Opponents'll pick up on your plight, and like sharp-eyed jackals or crossed-eyed tigers, they'll pounce. They'll know your situation, sense your frame of mind, and certainly will hear it. It's a green felt jungle, and you're the straggling, injured wildebeest. Okay, enough jungle references.

When one gripes about how the cards are running, the poker beasts gain more confidence than ever before against the complainer. Suppose you're heads-up with someone who bluffs *you about* 0–5 percent of the time. However, s/he sees you're off your game, licking your wounds. You're folding when you should call, calling when you should fold, calling when you should bump it up, and calling other's raises when you should fold. You're a basket case. Thus, instead of trying to bluff you 0–5 percent, this astute player tries 20 percent. Since you know s/he essentially never bluffs, you might fold a winner. Assuming you fold the best hand, can you compute how much those extra bluffs might cost? Could be thousands. Additionally, when others see you fold a lot, they might take more shots at you. Like sharks smelling blood, others itch to get into pots with you which increases the number of opponents fighting you every hand. (At least this wasn't a jungle metaphor.)

Try as I might, I couldn't instill this lesson in Virge. It grieved me, but I gave him the benefit of the dildo. Then it occurred to me. Tsunetomo Yamamoto wrote in *Bushido: The Way of the Samurai*: "There are many in the world who are eager to give advice. There are few who feel glad for being given advice. And there are still fewer who follow the given advice." Love the lesson, and I should adopt it. To summarize, I firmly believed Caro's lessons to refrain from complaining at the table. And how can you even imagine something for zilch if you don't learn, rejuvenate, and evolve.

Virge wanted to tell me another example. "You wouldn't believe it. This live one hit a one-outer on me and took down this huge pot, maybe $1,000." A one-outer means his opponent caught the *only* card that could beat Virge's hand. If any other card rivers, Virge wins. "Well, we had a sayin' down to Texas. Sometimes you get, and sometimes you get got."

I bit my tongue. See, one wants to have competitors who don't care about the odds. There only might be one card to make their hand win, but they don't care if they need a miracle. They want to gamble, and tempt destiny, so to speak. Yet, remember, in the long run they cannot beat those odds. Eventually they're going to be losers. The winners are going to get that money. And the house, of course, gets its skin, for winners and losers pay at the same rate. With patience, Virgil would earn his share from this live one and producers.

Maybe patience wasn't his virtue, but I felt concern for him. "I'm sorry, Virge. Hang in there."

He followed with, "Another time, I had pocket aces, and she called two raises before the flop with Q-9 offsuit. She flopped middle pair, kept callin' all the bets, and on the river, she made two pairs and won."

To reiterate, if an opponent calls two bets cold with Q-9 offsuit, what's known as *fromage* in the arcane vernacular of no limit Hold 'em, then more power to her. This wouldn't, however, assuage his pain. Still, if I thought this was a suitable time, I would've told Virge to file it away under a lesson about that player; refocus on the next hand.

Mike Caro wrote in *Professional Poker Plan Three,* Mission 13, "Every time you lose a pot, take several seconds to psyche [*sic*] yourself up and then FORGET completely about the pot you just lost [...] After you lose a hand, get psyched up [to win the next one you play], determined, then forget that hand [...] Nothing must bother you. Repeat it: POKER IS FUN AND LIFE IS FUNNY."

I adopted those lessons and missions. I'd discuss this with Virge later, perhaps while we ate.

$$$

I couldn't wait to share some new knowledge with Virge. "I have this book of word games, and I came across an interesting fact. It seems there're only three words in the English language that have all the vowels, including y in order. Do you want to give it a shot?"

Virge said, "Let me cogitate it."

"You wanna masticate on it a mite." As my Hold 'em skill improved, sometimes I didn't want to play at the same table as Virge, for like Boston, Virge was solid, winning player. But sometimes his was the best or only table. As buds, there still was one thing Virge and I knew for sure: Neither one would bluff the other heads-up. And if I made my hand, one I felt was a sure winner, I might check it, saying, "I made my flush."

Once, when he bet his nut flush on the river, I didn't raise with aces full, the nuts—given the board cards, I had an unbeatable, lock hand. For purists, technically I had the second nuts, for four of a kind beat my aces full; yet, given the action, I had the nuts. He'd done so many solids for me over the years that I just called, showed my hand first (a rarity for me), and said, "Aces-full."

He smiled at me. "I can't beat it. I had the nuts on the turn, but when the river paired, I went from having the nuts to the nut house." Per custom, the winner gives the loser a $5 check. He nodded and said, "Thanks, and thanks for not raising."

I mentioned our non-bluff pact pertained to being heads-up. We never discussed this, but it just evolved over the years. Pacts like this aren't cheating, because, let me emphasize, we play predictably against each other only when no one else is in the pot. However, if there are other contestants, we act in our own best interest. Each plays to optimize their chances of winning the pot and or winning the most. We trusted each other so much that if one asked the other what he had, we took each other's word and didn't have to see the cards. Unless great friends, virtually no one trusts a player's statements; after all, their statement in itself can be a bluff. Obviously if a player's final bet is called, the cards need to be shown. Still, if the winner isn't called, an opponent might ask, "What did you have?"

Responses varied: "You gotta pay to see," "Nothing," "What'd ya think? I had a monster," or "I bluffed you."

I decided that I'd just say, "I don't want to say, and I don't want to lie. Anyway, you might not believe me if I told you the truth." As you might imagine, I virtually never show. Still, I might show it after winning a humongous pot put me way ahead or even, and I knew it was my last hand. Like donating to Gamblers Anonymous this was an act of good will.

Legally anyone could request the Dealer to show the winning hand. If the loser's hand was still live, one could ask to see it, but as noted previously, this is bad form. Did s/he make the correct decision and, thus, save money? Or fold the best hand and lose money? It was an itch that *had* to be scratched. I'm different—most of my itches are over my funny bone. Still, some friendly players tell you the truth, and if someone expresses doubt, the winner voluntarily might show. I suppose this violates my dictum that there ain't no free lunch, but it still is unusual and rather insignificant. As Spock notes about this exception to the no free lunch rule, "Fascinating, Captain," or more pertinently, "Fascinating, Floor person."

$$$

Besides Virge, another tough opponent was Lan, an apex predator, the top of the poker food chain. Occasionally Lan'd show his hand for free when no one called. In the meta-game of poker, he could elevate this revealing to a second or third level. For example, Lan might raise and reraise, bet all the way. He was so aggressive and had such a strong, well-deserved reputation for skill, opponents often folded when he bet the river. Like the pull of the moon, someone'd be compelled to ask Lan, "What did you win with?"

"Me? I had 7-2 X. This is the worst starting hand in Hold 'em. X means offsuit.

"No, way!"

He jovially replied, "If my hand isn't called, I usually only show my hand in two cases. It's a pretty woman, or if I think the person'll lend to me. But I'll show this time." Then for chuckles, he showed exactly 7-2 X. Depending on the cards on the board, these cards demonstrated a total, masterfully executed Melba cracker ploy. His sole opponent in the hand exasperatedly and forlornly mumbled, "I had a pair of sixes. I folded the best hand."

Lan laughed and said, "Oh, that's a shame. Wha-whah."

Everyone laughed because he wasn't malicious. Even the loser(s) in the hand had to smile, but not as much. Making plays is part of the game. He used this meta-strategy of revealing a bluff to add humor and spice to a table, but to instill doubt. As John Vorhaus, an insightful, witty poker writer, quipped on bluffing, "Sometimes ... a good offense is a good pretense." That seed of doubt, kernel of deception, returns big dividends. Therefore, he loved to plant the seed, let it germinate, and then stir up the pot. (Go ahead, accuse me of excessively smooshing metaphors together. I freely admit to being wordy and creating word salads.) To beat a dead horse or cat to its demise, 💀, on getting something for nothing, on the surface it seemed Lan seemed to; however, though he might win a particular hand, many other times he'd get called at the river and discard his hand. No one was sure, but he might have broken even on these plays. Still, he reaped many dividends on subsequent hands when he had the goods.

Besides sometimes showing his hand gratis to plant doubt, Lan's other m.o. was most known as changing gears but also mixing up one's play or zigging and zagging. Obviously, his behavior was for strategic reasons; however, his actions must have fulfilled some inner need, too. I'd say he was a master at veers gears, and opponents never knew what he had. Analogies abound. His style had more layers than a wedding cake at a Mexican triple wedding (PI?). Or imagine soldiers trying to avoid enemy fire by moving hither and thither. The ability to make quick, directional changes obviously has huge evolution and survival benefits. Have you ever tried to swat a fruit fly? Very challenging. That is like trying to catch Lan bluffing *or* make the correct play.

As an advocate for evolving to survive, let me add that likewise humor needs to evolve. As I altered the vaudeville routine above, so I offer this: A plumber is an alchemist who turns lead into gold, transmutes to, an alchemist turns copper and plastic into gold … or Bitcoin. Of course, all that dildos, glitters, isn't gold.

$$$

The following week, Virge greeted me, "Wha's goin' on, JM? I think I got one of the words with the vowels in order. Facetiously. But I couldn't come up with any others."

"Great job! I'll tell you the other two after you've thought more about it."

He shrugged and said, "Nah. I give up, so tell me whenever you want."

"Okay." We left it hanging like a Metamucil-stained, Florida chad.

The following week I saw him standing by the sign up board. "JM, wha's goin' on?"

"Hi, Virge. Hey, since you said you gave up on guessing, I'm gonna reveal the second word. Abstemiously."

"What? … Oh, yeah, English words with all the vowels in order. What's it mean?"

"It's refraining especially in diet or drink; sparingly used or indulged in. The way I like to remember it is that it's from the root to abstain."

He grinned, "Like you should abstemiously bluff."

"Exactly. Or in my case," I *kvetshn*, "minimizing Negative Turn Arounds. I should abstemiously avoid them in the future."

In commiseration, Virge said, "Hey, JM, don't beat yourself up." Then he asked, "What's the third wor—?"

Over the speakers we heard, "Virge, $20 Hold 'em. Seat open."

As he gathered his stuff to leave, I said, "I'll tell you later. See you in the must move game soon. I'll keep my dildos crossed that you have good luck."

29

NTAs and Stop Losses

AFTER HAVING AN INANE spat with Penny, I was really down as I drove over to the Commerce. Recalling author, player Roy West's rule, "Play happy or don't play at all," I was very ambivalent about playing. Still, I decided to work, and not let emotions interfere. There was a chance, 30:1, that things with us would be fine.

"Yo, Virge." I saw him at the cage window. "Did you get 'em or get got?"

"Wha's goin' on, JM? Yeah, I liked the game. They were very generous today. It was like they was throwin' chips at me."

"They were magnanimous, nyuck. Let's go to the coffee shop and talk." Being somewhat blue over Penny, I didn't start blabbing right away as usual. "I may have an answer to the third alphabetical vowels in order word. Ascepticously. The surgeon was very aware of potential infections, so he was *ascepticously* diligent."

"Ennnhhhd. Not a word."

"Damn, shoot me in the foot."

"But, hey, if I shot you in the foot, 'standing pat' would be hard."

He told me about some music and movies, and I listened. Then I said, "I was thinking while I was driving over here. Did you ever notice how many words about sadness begin with d? T here's depression, despair, despondency, disconsolate, dishearten, distraught, downcast. But my favorite, dildoed."

He responded, "You sound like George Carlin riffing on words. But I hadn't noticed all the d words. Hey, Debbie Downer, I suppose you could add down and dejected, and you'd definitely be sad if you were dildoed. Hey, what 'bout doo-doo?"

"Funny, Virge, but that's two words ..."

"Depends how ya spell it."

"True."

30
Dreams of Getting Even

I RAN INTO COWBOY Dan a few months later. "Hey, JM. What's up?"

"Hey, Cowboy. Not much. You know I had this weird dream about you, muscle cars and nuns ... Do you remember your dreams?"

"Whoa. Whoa. First tell me about the dream."

"I forgot a lot, but you and I were playing water polo against a team of nuns, in their habits, they looked like a bouquet of black jellyfish, and suddenly we're stealing muscle cars and shipping them to Cuba for parts."

"Wow! Strange. But, no, I don't dream, let alone remember them."

It always amazes me when people say that they don't dream. Everyone dreams even if they don't recall. Dreams are like a Wi-Fi connection between our conscious and unconscious worlds. Although it's peculiar to humans, dogs must dream. I saw our dog Brandi asleep, but her legs were jerking, and she was moaning. Probably dreaming of chasing a hoodoo hare. People might not recall them, but they occurred.

I described one of my recurring dreams to Cowboy Dan. "I'm out walking around, and I happen upon a grassy area. There're a lot of coins that have fallen out of someone's pocket. I happily pick them up. Found money. It's always coins, not paper money. Dream-wise, I'm an adult, but with a kid's frame of mind." This probably derives from being a poor kid when finding coins was glorious. Or it might mean I think small? "Another recurring dream concerns poker. And May Faire has had it, too. You know you have a winning hand in this gigantic pot, but when you show your hand, it isn't the cards you thought you had, and you lose."

Cowboy yawned. "You know, there's one I remember. I dreamed I was eating a big marshmallow, but when I woke up my pillow was gone. But you know, I was thinking about what you told me a while ago. How it's hard for you to leave when you're off your high point and sometimes lose everything."

"My Negative Turn Arounds."

"Yeah. If they torment you so much, and you concentrate so much on avoiding them, and focus so heavily on counteracting them, you may perpetuate them," he reproved me. "It might be like a wish fulfilling prophecy. Or the power of suggestion."

"Yikes! You're right," I recoiled. I continued, "You know, to my credit, I occasionally enjoy positive turnarounds, and those are extremely rewarding. The way I look at it is if I was down $1,000, and I wondrously claw back to even, it's almost like winning $1,000." Realistically, getting even didn't increase my net worth, but a $1,000 hit would've decreased my worth. D'oh!

Dan made this profound observation on human nature, "Yeah, avoiding a $1,000 loss by getting even somehow feels better than just winning $1,000. Weird."

"You said it. *Feels.* Our emotions are fully engaged when we consider results."

Just as losses yield double the emotional impact of gains, dread yields double the emotional impact of winning. In cognitive biases, this is known as *dread aversion.* This seemingly paradoxical observation of human nature also applies to stock market investing. Albeit those profits and losses usually are thousands of dollars more than poker swings; thus, the pain of market losses is astounding and can be disastrous. It's curious, though. Often gamblers will blame luck for their misfortune, rather than their actions; contrarily, whom could one blame for losing via one's bad investing decisions, huh?

It turns out that Cowboy's *weird* observation sums up people's loss aversion tendency, nor is this peculiar to gamblers. In 1979, Nobel Prize winning economists Daniel Kahneman and Amos Tversky founded prospect theory. It posits that stock investors facing potential gains or losses, choose depending on personal values. For most, the pain of a loss is about twice the strength of pleasure from a comparable gain. This explains a great deal of why people prefer to hold onto their losing stocks rather than sell. Selling and taking loss forces you to admit you made mistake. This theory hit me like a ton of Bricklins. It was human nature to want to avoid this pain. I was happy to be normal, so to speak.

Prospect theory is a branch of Behavioral Finance, a field of finance that proposes psychology-based theories to explain stock market anomalies. Investopedia explains that many long-term historical studies show why sometimes securities markets contradict the efficient market hypothesis, and perfect investor rationality cannot be modeled. Behavioral Finance wants to fill that failure.

$$$

The opposite of an NTA is a positive turnaround (so unusual that no abbreviation is needed). My buddy Shah Kwah once saw me as he was leaving. This is back when we played similar limits, in the same section, before he dropped down after marriage. I told him they were beating me worse than a *rum*, but like an ugly, red-headed, stepchil'. Not that cross-eyed one. He replied, "Well, then they deserve it; unless, they have lazy eye."

"Cruel, Shah." I told him I felt ultra-perseverant, and I vowed to get even.

Eventually the Earth made another rotation, and after about twenty-six hours, if I won the next hand I played, I'd be even. In these cases, I am extremely selective. *If* I'd been as careful in the beginning, I may not have been losing. About then Shah walked by, and he saw me still there. Seeing me with a mass of chips, he assumed I was winning in a new session. When I revealed I'd been there since the previous night, he knew why and complimented me, "JM, you may be an impure Pyongyang half-breed, but you've got a lot of heart!"

Admittedly these big comebacks are an anomaly, but I bailed out numerous times. I, however, didn't study the net results of the rare times that I got more money from home or borrowed only from Virge or Shah. Rephrasing, I didn't analyze if, overall, I came out ahead or behind when I lost my original stake and then got more for an obviously great game. Studying these rare instances didn't seem worth the effort. Or was I lazy?

Concerning my perseverance, indeed, sometimes I had the patience of a mother caring for a sick child. I never gave up, but I often unwisely refused to embrace Mike Caro's advice that "Life is one long, continuous game." Therefore, like many, I just didn't want to have that miserable pain of leaving with a loss. Later I had an *aperçu*. It was astronomically ironic that as much as I took pride in my steely will and my high so-called delayed gratification talent, when losing, I strove to get to even almost at all costs. Hence, I played many marathons.

An aside on marathon sessions. The king marathoner had to be KK, who was a third generation Korean. He played forever sessions in the highest limit Hold 'em games at Hollywood Park. By marathons, I mean he was proud of playing semi-continuously for one to two weeks without leaving. Years later, disastrously, KK lost his business due to paying more attention to gambling. This was at least the third person I personally knew who went bankrupt, so there were most likely many, many more. Perhaps being only half Korean, I was somewhat immune to gambling addiction unlike two Koreans, KK and Dobat—you'll encounter him later.

$$$

Eventually I learned that if I drop down near broke, but scramble back to my starting point, I skirr out of there like a skip tracer or like a bounty hunter's after me. JM's Law #2 (Suppose one's down about 80 percent of one's budget implying a long session. If one has gotten even, eject out of your seat like James Bond and leave running). There were too many times back in the bad old, Gardenial days when I wouldn't leave after getting back to where I started. Big, *big* mistake. That old NTA wind shear would smash me into the tarmac. Sometimes opponents humorously would chide me, "How can you leave this game? It's so juicy."

Of course, I'd say, "When I get even, I go home."

To which the wags would josh, "You didn't come here to get even did you?"

I finally thought of a suitable answer. "No, but I didn't come here to get stuck either."

31

Poker Terms Barge into Polite Society

BEING NOCTURNAL, I USUALLY slip from the shadows like a Ninja and into the clubs to wage a camisado, a night raid. This night I went to the Commerce. Virge was already in the game, and he appeared to be winning. I waited until he folded and said, "Yo, Virge. Looks like you got 'em tonight."

"Wha's goin' on, JM. Yeah, I'm running good."

"May I sweat you?"

Perhaps the etymology of this colorful term, sweating, is from worrying about, or sweating bullets over, the outcome of the hand. It doesn't, however, have to do with either Don't sweat the small dildos.

A sweater, synonymous with a kibitzer, mostly is a fellow player who, for whatever reason, isn't currently playing. Possibly they want to scout the game and or opponents, kill time, eat at the table with a friend, socialize with the player(s), and strategize.

Sometimes, however, the sweater is a spouse, s.o., or non-poker playing friend. It's unique, but the watcher can be a player's offspring; after all, the dildo, apple, doesn't fall far from the tree. Hopefully that person isn't someone who can't see the dildo from the trees. Incidentally, dildo subbing can work into poems also. "I think that I shall never see. A poem lovely as a dildo, tree. "Trees" by Joyce Kilmer who was male! It stands to reason, who's better to appreciate a sad story than a friend who might actually care? The other players at the table certainly don't want to hear of another's tragedy.

Kibitzers always provide moral support and a sympathetic ear. Oh, how players *love* to tell their bad beat stories wherein an opponent plays poorly, beats horrendous odds, and has their prayer answered when they got a miracle card to complete a Hail Mary. Hence, the favored hand gets crushed and loses maybe $1,500. In the World Series of Poker (WSOP), a bad beat might cost millions. Naturally, the number of cards available to cause a bad beat—the number of *outs*—is case specific and ill defined. That is, most consider an opponent hitting one to three outs a bad beat, but, depending on a player's psychological makeup, some whiners might feel losing to an eight to twelve *outer is a bad beat.*

$$\$\$\$$$

Having asked Virge if I could sweat him, he replied, "Pull up a chair." After he folded another hand, he said, "A while ago we talked about poker terms we use in everyday life. I thought of some others. He's a *four flusher* meaning dishonest.

"Yeah, that was used in the old days. Not when I was born," I laughed, "but older. Mississippi river boat times. A four flusher might spread four of his cards, but leave the fifth one, not of same suit, under the others. He'd pretend he had a flush, and quickly try to take the pot. He did things *under the table* and wasn't *above board.*"

Virge finished a hand, and nodded saying, "Interesting. That reminds me of another. He was *dealt a bad hand* at birth, but he *played the cards or hand he was dealt.* Do you know other ones?"

"Sure, but I don't want to distract you."

"You aren't, so go on ahead."

"A four flusher might put in a *stacked deck.* You read all the time about some poor criminal who claims that at birth he has the *deck stacked against him.* Boo-hoo. As if his circumstances justify his murdering spree or kidnaping some child. But returning to the Mississippi River boat days, someone'd play his cards *close to the vest*. He'd look at his cards this way so a four flusher's sneaky eyes couldn't see what he had; he didn't want to carelessly show or *tip his hand*. Nowadays a close to the vest person is a very conservative, circumspect person. (A woman player might want to play her cards close to the chest.) Maybe this conservative type wants to stay in smaller, *penny-ante* games. Some don't want to *ante up*. If he is reckless, he lets the *chips fall where they may*. Of course, a close to the vest player's opposite is a *wild card*. He is like a loose cannon. And that term, I think, comes from the old sailing ships, man of wars, where if a cannon wasn't tightly secured, it could roll around the deck and cause destruction, maiming and death. One definitely didn't want to have one of those—"

"I raise," my friend said, going into battle. Since I was a sweater, he carefully showed me his hand. I keenly watched how he, and his opponents played, their reaction to new board cards and pondered what I'd have done.

After Virge won a hand, as usual, gave me a $5 chip. I said, "Thanks. I'd've played it the same way. Nye pot."

"Yeah, but I was worried when that third club hit the river."

"Yeah, that's another term."

"What?"

"You know, poker terms transferring from poker to our common language," I continued in my monomaniacal way. "Sometimes it *isn't in the cards. Down the river*—way in the future, way far away. Of course, that can just be from people who dwell along any river. But you can *bet your bottom dollar* that I'm glad for you that the *cards fell into place,* and that you won that hand. But how cool is that phrase, bet your bottom dollar? It's the chip that used to be under a stack of chips, and now it's the last one left. You've lost the ones that used to be on top. It seems more valuable, for it's your last chance for redemption and getting even."

"And if *I played my cards right,* I win."

"I saw that. Your strategy and play aren't lost on me; it wasn't *lost in the shuffle*."

"JM, good thing I'm winning. Otherwise, you're talking'd worry a hound dog."

By chance, over the loudspeaker, "JM. Your twenty Hold 'em seat's open."

I caught the Board Person's attention, and I signaled with a twisting fist, "Lock it up! Virge, they just called me, so I'll see you later. Maybe we can get in the same game if it's a good one."

$$\$\$\$$$

"What's goin' on, JM?"

"Hi, Virge. Did you see the President's speech last night? About the war he said, *the buck stops here*. Supposedly, Harry Truman had a sign on his desk saying that. The responsibility lies here, with me. He didn't *pass the buck*."

"Didn't see it. I dunno. But what's a buck mean? It can't be one dollar."

"Good question. I read it was possibly a knife with a buck horn handle placed in front of the current dealer, like the button now. It indicated who dealt and was last to act. Afterward it rotated clockwise to the next dealer."

"Interesting."

"In 1902, Teddy Roosevelt, promised a *square deal*; an honest hand."

"Wait," Virge interrupted. He showed me his junk hand and whispered, "I'm gonna take a flyer on this hand."

After he lost the hand, I commiserated, "You play trash cards and hope for a supernatural flop. You know that's a losing play."

"I know. But I was bored." Enervation had set in, and he reverted into a mesquite-smoked accent, "I git tar'd of sittin' har ..."

I went on. "There're so many poker terms used in negotiating and in politics, local to global. For instance, China has a *strong hand*. Undoubtedly, you've heard *Don't show your cards too early*, the same as don't *tip your hand*. Remember in 5 Card Stud, the best card to have down is an ace, *an ace in the hole*. Therefore, a cheater hides an *ace up his sleeve*. Now, it's someone hiding something that gives him an unfair advantage. Saddam Hussein, by implying he had WMD weapons, felt he had an ace in the hole—or up his sleeve—but the world called his bluff. Everything didn't *come up aces* for him.

"It's usually unwise to *stand pat* rather than adjust to changing world alliances and conditions. And they hung him, so he, or really, they, *cashed in his chips—*"

"You was gonna tell me 'bout sandbaggin'? Before you tell me, let me git some iced tea ta perk up ..."

"Oh, yeah. I finally remembered to look it up. Before I tell you, let me say I didn't think sandbagging applied to bags used to divert water. I guessed its derivation, its etymology, pertained to shortchanging a customer by putting sand into flour bags, for example. Wait. I think that's wrong. Not into flour, for a customer would taste sand soon. Maybe short weighting a bag of wheat which would be ground up into a fine powder. Adding volume of a foreign substance would make the bag heavier, and, thus, cost the same but for less wheat. Kinda like a butcher putting his thumb on the scale."

Virge took all this in and asked, "Yes, but how'd that sandbagging apply to poker sandbagging where the sandbagger pretends to have a weak hand when they have the nuts?"

"You're right. So, let me chip in this research. Har-de-har," I joked. "I wrote down some possibilities. The root of sandbagging has nothing to do with diverting water or bullets. Using sandbagging as a deceptive sport play strategy might relate to a bag or sock filled with sand—a surprisingly tough weapon connecting hard but leaving no mark. Doesn't leave a mark on the mark I might add."

"And how does this apply to poker?"

"As you pointed out, when you mentioned having the lock hand, aka *Brazilian nuts.*" Reading verbatim from my notes from a *Card Player* article, "To sandbag someone came to mean not just to attack them with this weak looking, but surprisingly a strong weapon, but generally to intimate [sic] or otherwise bully someone. However, it finally came to mean what it does today through poker. Slow playing, in which a player with a good hand bets lightly at first to get others to invest more in the pot, reminded players of the harsh surprise of this rough fighting tactic and picked up the nickname—"

"Are you done?"

"Sorry to bother you. Let me buy you dinner. Hey, I'm not sandbagging. I'll actually pay."

"You mean you're not *bluffing,*" he laughingly corrected.

32

Virge's Dallas Days

VIRGE SUGGESTED MANY TIMES in passing that we should have lunch away from the casinos. He was such a good friend I knew he wasn't brushing me off like a Hollywood agent saying to an actor wannabe, "Seriously, let's do lunch." And notice *seriously* often doesn't mean sincerely or honestly? Finally, after about twenty half-hearted efforts, we finally met in San Pedro.

"Wha's goin' on, JM?"

"Mr. Virgil Caine, I'm doing great. We finally met for lunch! Hallelujah. What's good here?" He didn't drink, so I also declined when the waiter asked.

He smiled kindly and asked, "How's poker treating you?"

"Ah, you know, up and down, but I'm ahead this month. How 'bout you?"

"I'm breaking even. These new young hot shots're so aggressive, and the games're getting so tight."

While we ate, he asked, "Did I ever tell you about my misspent youth in Texas, in the Big D? I was a legend. I used to run with a wild bunch of *hombres*. We'd cat around and carouse and drink and chase the skirts. I was a really good pool player and made a fair amount of money. I used ta hang out at the Mule Kick Bar. I used to lemon, and pretended I was a lobster—"

"Wait. What're those things?"

"Sorry, JM. I lemoned, hid my skill, and look like a lobster, a bad player. Anyways, there was a time we was playing and drinking and messing around. We was woofing trying to goad a lobster to play me. Some of the guys started twirling their pool cues like batons. Then 'Mad Dog' decided to toss his up and try to catch it like a baton behind his back like a drum major. He was so drunk he flung it into the ceiling fan instead, and it came spinnin' back like a bank shot. Liked ta killed us. It missed us and knocked a bunch of beer bottles over ... and some weren't empty. Usually, we started fighting.

"When we was in an ornery mood, we'd cozy up to some poor guy just driving through town on the state highway. Poor slob just stopped in to have some food and maybe a soda or beer. So, we'd ask him where he was from and what type of work he did and all. After we was all friendly and such, we'd ask him if he wanted to see a really cool pool trick. We'd put a nickel on the break spot and had him put each hand in the corner pockets. Then one of us'd shoot the cue ball over the nickel. You know it jumps up and hits the man in the forehead. The shooter didn't hit it really hard, but this was really dirty pool. And we got in so many fights, but usually the guy'd just leave 'cause he was outnumbered. If he wasn't too mad, and kinda laughed at himself, we'd buy him a beer. Well, we raised so much ruckus, but we was such good customers they could only bar us for one day.

"Another time, me and my buddies went to Ronnie's funeral. Ronnie was an ornery redneck, and he got in a bar fight over some littl' thang down in Galveston, and he got shot to death."

I interjected, "The bigger they are the harder they dildo."

Smartly he ignored me. "So, we went to his service in the Big D. Everybody's all solemn and sad. We'd been drinkin' mighty hard, and we thought ol' Ronnie wouldn't want everybody all sad and depressed. We thought it was a good idea to lighten things up. I had this duck call in my jacket, and real secret, I pull it out. And when everyone's bowing their heads down during a prayer, I take the biggest breath I ever took in my life and let out a loud QWaaaack!! You'd a thought that it was the Second Coming and the Earth split open. People jumped out of their skins. When the flock realized we were the culprits, it wasn't hard to smell the alcohol on our breaths, and what with our reputations for trouble making, man, they liked to run us out of the church on a rail. We laughed so hard we was cryin.'"

I observed, "So you cried not from sorrow, but maybe from joy in remembering the good times you had with your bud."

"Yeah, tha's right. I sure miss him. When we was in high school, he was still a virgin. I planned to hide him in my closet when my parents were away. I get my girlfriend, that I was screwin', nude and ready to go, he was supposed to sneak out and pretend he was me and get it on with her. Of course, she knew. Boy, she was so pissed she like'd ta killed me. It took me about a month to get her back friendly. Say, I remember when I first started datin' ol' LuraLee. Some of the boys called her 'Lurid Lee.' Well, when we first started dating, I went over to pick her up one night. I knocked on the back screen door, and I heard a voice sayin' come on in. So, I went in, and it was totally dark in the kitchen. I'm feelin' around for the light, but I bumped into the kitchen table. I grabbed an arm and it grabbed me back! I 'bout jumped outta my skin. Her mom was sittin' in the dark because she was blind. She was knittin'. Man, LuraLee! You coulda told me your ma sits in the dark.

"Anyways, the boys and I used to party until like three in the morning, then get up at 5:30 and go hunting. We'd do this maybe 2–3 days in a row. One time we thought it'd be fun to go out to some farm and steal a tractor. So, we park about a hundred yards from a farmhouse. We're real quiet, and we sneak up to this barn. There's this ol' John Deere sitting there. Homer's been drinking, well, all of us'd been, and he trips on a piece of lumber, and he yells, 'Owww!' This wakes up two German Shepherds that start barking like hell, and they start in to chasing us. And we ran like hell. It's a good thing we was far enough away to have a head start, but, man, you never saw four guys hightail it out of there so fast. You'd've thought we were a prison relay team. We got to the car ahead of the dogs, and we thought we was clear, but then we heard a shotgun, *Boom! Boom!* It's a wonder we're still alive."

"Well, I'm certainly glad you're still alive. I'm better for knowing you."

"Well, thanks, JM."

"But go on and tell me more of your hell raising days."

"Yeah, and we'd drag race. We borrowed a sayin' from NASCAR. Drive it like ya stole it. One time we was just cruisin' around on State 21 out to Nacogdoches, causin' trouble, listenin' to Spade Cooley, and we ran into these dudes who thought their cars were so tough. One guy thought he had a real shaker, so we bet $200. He was such a jerk that I really wanted to crush him."

"So besides wanting to win the money, you had manifold other reasons, too."

"Good one, JM. Yeah, I beat him, and he complained that the only reason I won is because he missed third gear. It'd get so hot down home in the summer. It was like an ol' Bessemer in hell. And we'd just sweat everywhere. It was so hot we sometimes wanted ice cold water more than a Lone Star."

I could relate, for I'd been out there. The air is still like the whole world is in suspended animation inside a running microwave. Not the tiniest whisper of a breeze, and you think that the sun's getting closer. The cicadas get animated and startlingly loud with atonal hissing sounds you think you're atop high-tension wires. By their frequency and pitch, they're the only insect that can indicate air temperature. And Virge was right: Ice cold water, shade, or preferably AC, were the top priorities.

Continuing with a smile, he said, "The air was so steaming that you could see the heat rising off the road. We called armadillos Hoover hogs, and we played this game called armadillo slaloming. We'd be driving real fast and trying to avoid the armadillos crossing the road. We'd juke and shake to avoid them, but man, I can't tell you how many times we'd almost got into a ditch."

I said, "I wonder if Thomas Preston got his nickname by driving like that."

"Wha's that now? Thomas who?"

"You know Thomas Preston, more commonly known as 'Armadillo Slim.'"

"You mean *Amarillo* Slim, don't you?"

"Whadda you think?" I wised off. "And Slim famously said, 'Not all armadillo trappers wear beaver hats.' But that was kind of y'all not to run them over by zigging and zagging," I added. "That's why you don't arm-a-dillo. It might shoot at you."

"Tha's just stupid, JM."

"Say, Virge. Is it true that armadillo piss'll cure warts?"

"Nah, tha's jest a rural, not urban, myth."

33

Quote, Movie, Drink Game

ONE AFTERNOON I ROLLED into my video account at Howzit #1. "Howzit, Kaikane?"

"John, eh. Howzit, brah? Or, as I like to say to my Jewish customers, Aloha, oy?"

"It's da kine." I really liked Kaikane, and part of it was we loved movies and liked intellectual and/or trivia games; especially, one I created called Quote, Movie, Drink. One player throws out a movie line, and the other tries to name the film and an appropriate drink for the movie. For example, "Quid pro quo, Clarice. Quid pro quo." The *Silence of the Lambs* and without question the drink is Chianti. Kaikane proffered, "Frankly, my dear. I don't give a damn."

I answered, "That's an easy one. *Gone with the Wind*. The drink has to be a mint julep."

"You know, I think Southern Comfort would suffice, but even more suitable drinks would be the Scarlett O'Hara or Rhett Butler."

We would argue the merits. No score was kept; sometimes a game's just fun. Over the course of playing hearts, cribbage, and especially poker, card games are way more realistic and authentic when played for money. Bridge is \the\ one exception. Social bridge's payoff has ego and intellectual rewards, while duplicate bridge has those plus master's points. I'll add that hearts, bridge and maybe golf also are much more captivating when playing for money.

$$$

Today was smoldering. High humidity … like being near the Gulf of Mexico where Ma Nature gifts the residents a free, though unwanted, steam room. I melted into Howzit #1. When a new customer enters a bar from the sunny outside, s/he noticeably brightens it. Kaikane saw me and haled, "*Eh, Howzit, brah?*"

When my eyes finally adjusted, I got close to him and I cheerfully replied in a low voice, "Pussy—"

Feigning shock, he interrupted and chastised me saying, "Excuse me, sir! This is a respectable establishment."

"No. Listen." Trying to mimic Sean Connery, I huskily said, "Pussy. Pussy Galore. You know, a line for our Quote, Movie, Drink game."

"Oh, of course. That line's from *Goldfinger,* and the drink has to be a Martini."

"Exactly. But shaken, not stirred. Let me add an imaginary drink, Live and Let Rye. I haven't formulated the rules sufficiently to insist a drink can only be used once. So, let's let the rules … ferment." Kaikane started talking with a customer who'd just arrived and said, "Ki, let me get him a MGD …"

$$$

Having finished with the games, I went to the restroom. While Kaikane was signing and storing the coins, he asked, "Can I get you something?"

"A Slippery Nipple," I leered.

He played along and replied, "Well, of course. I'd like one of those myself. Oh, you mean the drink with 2 ounces white Sambuca, 1-ounce Irish cream liqueur and a dash of grenadine."

"But you get my joke. Coke'd be fine. You probably know this, Kaikane. Someone wrote on the rubber dispenser in your restroom, Don't buy this chewing gum. It's terrible."

"*And* it's chewy but flavorless. Hey, I had a flashback to Moloka'i. I'd say about second grade when we had recess, all the boys in my class would go running. We were like a herd of wild Mustangs. Kip was the fastest, and so he was our leader. He'd guide us all around the playground until the bell rang. Sometimes I could get ahead of him, but he was older and had more stamina, so he eventually resumed the lead. He kept leadership."

"Ah, the world of pecking orders. Okay, see you next week ..."

34

Irritants

HAVING MENTIONED SMOKING AS an irritant, some players were overtly obnoxious and blew smoke up people's faces. I encountered all types. Most people, including me, try to get along with everyone. Occasionally, though, one encounters a player whose strategy is to upset his opponents.

One day I was driving westbound on Exposition Boulevard by USC (Fight On!). A railroad right-of-way, about thirty yards wide for sets of two tracks, formed the median on Exposition. I wanted to cross at the rail crossing and U back eastward; however, there was a giant locomotive moving about ten miles an hour coming toward the crossing, gateless gap. I was positive I could safely cross the track ahead of the train. But you better believe that this black monster had my full attention like a Kalashnikov brandishing crazy. I didn't see an approaching car, it being about 1/20th the train size, until the oncoming driver honked at me. I barely saw it. Wow! We perceive the bigger threat to our safety, bankroll, health, ego.

Raj was like that locomotive in being dangerous and *loco*. He was a big threat to one's bankroll and peace. His catchphrase could have been, when in doubt, irritate. Delightful! He was a very aggro, gear-shifting pro who could be extremely abrasive and caustic like a professional wrestling villain. He didn't have IBS, but Aggravating Bowel Syndrome (ABS). Realize, sometimes high stakes poker feels like an alley fight or an MMA cage fight. Consequently, other penies in this annoying class might shout, abusively confront, and certainly demean others. Getting their low pleasures in low places, they'd spew out their rage like an annoyed skunk because they're A) Truly angry with the world or B) They try to put people on tilt. If his motivation is A, perhaps the following will explain their behavior. I heard a pearl of wisdom, almost a koan, that an angry person isn't rude from spite, but because they're hurting. On the coin flipside, if his impetus is B, then their ultimate aim is profit. Yet, offending your *customers*, your opponents, seems counterproductive. It's like throwing the dildo out with the bathwater. Whatever the cause, it's excruciatingly unpleasant to play with such a schmuck, a-hole, or plick. I admit, assholes doth vex me. Saying Raj was blistering and annoying like Sarin is an understatement equal to saying *American Psycho* is a little dark.

$$\$\$\$$$

When the target of Raj's vitriolic taunting, the best countermeasure was to dive for the nearest bunker or foxhole—not retort or interact. Customers complained to the floor personnel about him, but it usually only resulted in a mild warning. If these abusive tantrums continued, he *might* get a slap on the wrist like sitting out a hand or a round.

Club staff and management forbade abusive behavior toward staff, other players and swearing, in theory, but often tolerated customers' bad behavior, up to a point and on a case-by-case basis. But that said, staff could not let it go unchecked for fear of a chain reaction of explosive incivility. Staff wanted to quash abusive, offensive language like a--hole, p-ick, m----- f-----, f--- you, et al. That said, enforcing the rules was always fraught with perils. Nevertheless, floor personnel had to invoke rules of behavior lest the players devolved into savages like the kids in *Lord of the Flies*. Women usually don't use bad language or revert to bad behavior like Raj, for women can employ more effective, sometimes devastating stratagems: Play the sex card, so to speak. An attractive woman has an enormous advantage over interested men by feigning innocence and helplessness, to elicit kinder actions from male opponents. Men might take it easier on her by raising and bluffing her less than a male counterpart.

$$$

The odious Collison was discussed earlier, but I don't think Raj's strategic aim was Collison's main motivation. Collison just had it in for players he *thought* were professionals—he mistook me for one—not everyone. Or Collison was just mean, and being smug, didn't care whom he offended. While Collison tried to irritate opponents who stood up to him and or try to throw off their game, Raj was in another class (used loosely here). Whereas Collison was as bothersome as persistent telemarketers, Raj was more like a bleeding ulcer. Raj was a master chef of stirring the pot and ferociously burning opponents. I felt he declared *jihad*, not just on me but everyone. It seemed he had so much anger that he'd burn down an enemy's home and then return to torch the remnants. He also had a delusional, self-satisfied air of infallibility. He wanted to claw atop the pecking order and have the whip hand at a table—to dominate it. His desire to be the top banana reminds me of elementary school behavior. Not unlike a school yard bully, Raj needed to establish dominance. Not so curiously, he also tried to get any edge available. One Floor man told me, "He always wants the best of it."

Obviously very smart, I suspect he graduated from college with a philosophy degree, majoring in taunt-ology. Seemingly Raj's causing conflicts and creating a tense, unhappy, revenge-filled game is counterproductive and at cross purposes, but who can fathom his motives? Possibly he has a Jungian need to cast and perpetuate a negative first impression. Possibly he strives to throw people off their game. He surely violates JM's Law #4 (The quieter one is the better; unless, one has a need or strategy to be the center of attention and action).

Seemingly, compared to his opponents, he's more immune to counter insults, more used to hostility and more accustomed to being a target. Surely, he seemed bulletproof. If he infuriated someone who told him, "Go piss on yourself," he had the presence of mind, the sang froid to reply, "Urine luck. I just did." Hence, his résumé could describe him as a master manipulator, a prototypical penie who profited financially and subconsciously from his behavior. Still, he might have profited from embracing Caro's truism that a happy game usually is more profitable. People want to gamble more, take more chances, and are less upset to lose if they're having a good time. Raj, in creating an unhappy game, made everyone play more tightly. The fun-loving player might even leave the game. Ultimately, I believe Raj diminished his profits. His strategy was dicey. He created enemies in low places. As I described before, however, venting his anger and being a nemesis may have been more important than winning money. Like some athletes, maybe he played with more focus when angry.

$$$

These obnoxious opponents, consequently, hear various threats; such as, "I'd like to throttle you till your eyes bugged out; I'd like to put you in a sleeper hold that you'd never wake up from; I'm gonna put a tire iron so far up your ass that you can use the other end for a toothpick." These irritated responses are exactly what the jerk off desires. Maybe he likes receiving verbal abuse recalling an abused childhood. Who knows? One week during a very rainy week, someone asked Raj if wanted to go outside and fight. He coolly replied, "No, I'll take a rain check."

One couldn't casually chat, "Hey, I notice that you like to cause fighting and turmoil. Why is that?" What kind of response would one get? "Go f--- yourself," is my guess.

Another time someone told Raj, "You're a real piece of work." Raj calmly and venously retaliated, "Yeah, well you're a real piece of—" Just then a Floor woman swung by, so Raj finished with, "—piece of doodoo."

After many hours on the poker battlefield, I learned to block out background static, chatter, and sometimes loud music from an in-house bar band. Still, filtering out irking, rude people is harder than trying to eat with a beekeeper's outfit on. I guestimate that 90–95 percent of players are decent and courteous, but the remainder—who're galling needlers, maddening, or downright obnoxious—spoil the bonhomie for everyone else. Good guys far outnumbered the bad, but a few penies still can tilt the scale downward to create a hostile, unhappy environment. Everyone's entitled to a bad mood night, but these rude patrons perpetually cause friction and unpleasant maelstroms.

$$\$ \$ \$$$

Sometimes I'm testy when losing. Losing, lack of sleep, and low nourishment also causes low blood sugar, resulting in hanger, the state of being hangry. But in contrast with some, I try to remain even keeled, and being even-tempered was one of my strengths. I was as steady as a Hawaiian TV weather report showing a high of 81°F for the next seven days. I also believe in moderation and *lots* of it. Furthermore, I adopted a live and let live attitude. After all, life is short—as short as my attention span. If someone disses me, I might let it go, provided the speaker's *Liveness Factor* is high. However, if, for example, a player like Collison or Raj asked to see my losing hand, and continued doing so, I'd reciprocate. I dropped neutrality, and it was all out war.

For much of my card playing career, I brooded at great length on snubs and outright, mean spirited digs. Perhaps there's some deficiency of character extending my discomfort. I wish I'd embraced earlier a girlfriend's lesson that holding a grudge is like allowing someone to live rent free in your head. You don't want anyone to have that kind of power over you.

Yes, I held a grudge against those who constantly denigrated me, but eventually I let it go. Sometimes the other party would do likewise, and our differences disappear in time like a fading echo. We don't have to like each other, but we can be civil.

It's believed that Audrey Hepburn (or possibly Dr. Albert Schweitzer) said, "I heard a definition once: Happiness is health and a short memory! I wish I'd invented it, because it's very true."

Forgiving and forgetting are priceless, but I don't want to develop the most virulent form of Alzheimer's, Irish Alzheimer's—only remembering my grudges.

35

Predatory Game

POKER OFTEN IS AN opportunistic, predatory game. I've depicted the venal Collison and the volcanic, vitriolic Raj. Shiko was also a disrespectful, master of manipulation—a master Machiavellian. He could appear friendly and smiling, but I knew better. Like South African Collison, the reptilian part of Shiko's brain was hyper-developed, and he employed his salesmanship like a lethal Katana. He certainly used manipulation against me often enough. If Shiko were an animal, he would definitely be a weasel. Or, I guess, for consistency, a reptile like a snake. Have you read the X-rated Aesop's fable tales of the snake's wife that was sexually unsatisfied because her husband had a reptile dysfunction?

It was very unpleasant playing against these types, archetypes of antagonism, corrosive players who're like feral dingoes. By comparison, I honestly think most would agree that I was more polite than most, and I was exponentially more of a gentleman than these three loathsome louts. But if you asked a few of the morons (not Mormons) who didn't like me, I'm sure that part of that *elite* group would tell you that I wasn't an angel either. I commit infractions like everyone else, but I feel mine are venial.

In poker, like life, there's always friction and someone who doesn't like you, whom you irritate. That's just how it is. I believe if The Buddha were a playyha, he'd annoy someone by the way he sat, wore his robe or hair, always serenely smiled, or imparted wisdom. Parenthetically, wisdom is common sense in an uncommon amount.

Through the grapevine, Kelly, who only played at The Bike, putatively held a PhD in psychology, but he wasn't employed in the field. Correction. He *was* working in the field of psychology; i.e., he was a professional poker player and a very good one. Like Raj and Lan, he had the apex predator status. Bespectacled, balding except for side fenders of greying hair, and sporting a full, well-trimmed grey beard, he certainly looked like a university don. But he acted like a prissy schoolmarm if someone besides the dealer touched the cards. A fastidious nit and sanctimonious table captain, he was also a stickler about playing precisely by the letter of the law and invoking the rules so that everyone followed them or he'd figuratively rap your knuckles.

I had a smidge like this, but I had bigger dildos to fry. He probably played six days a week and was a formidable opponent. However, his dominant characteristics were his airs of superiority and smugness. You know, he farted thunder and crapped lightening.

Another player, a Korean named Changpi Dobak, told me that Kelly had a lot of problems. Dobak had a severe gambling problem, and, consequently, lost his business. For this deckhead to say Kelly had problems showed Kelly's dysfunction.

Kelly was certainly a predator, but of a different stripe than Shiko, Collison and Raj. To the casual observer, Kelly's seemingly gentle demeanor—a bemused, pipe-smoking, leather-elbow-patched professor—belied that. He was more like a silent, slippery python than a flashy cheetah. Kelly was always looking for an edge, and he made no secret of it. Subtly Machiavellian, Kelly would smile and gently talk to the live ones like Dobat. Their relationship wasn't so much symbiotic as parasitic. Kelly always, always maneuvered to sit on the Korean's left side. This was the optimal, strategic position because Kelly acted immediately after Dobat. If the seat behind Dobat wasn't immediately open, once Kelly had earned table seniority, he would swoop to take it. Unlike Kelly (and me), many changed seats to change their luck! Thus, regulars would see the two joined like an ionic bond, one of the strongest molecular bonds. It seemed the height of hypocrisy for Kelly to pretend to be Dobat's friend, when Kelly just was using him as a cat's paw, a dupe.

Kelly's secondary trait was his precise, pedantic use of English. Like an untenured professor, he was a martyr for precision. To wit, he would correct somebody saying, "I could care less."

Kelly'd correct, "That's patently erroneous. If you actually could care less, then there still would be room for being concerned an iota less. *Ipso facto* [by the very nature of the case] you really mean I *couldn't* care less."

Oh, he loved to use big vocabulary, and whenever he could, he'd drop *empirical* here and *prima facie* there. And it'd be *quid pro quo* this and *sine qua non* that. Additionally, he had an astonishing psychological need to be right, *a priori*. Okay, bust me for using *a priori*, for I had some of his presumptive tendencies. Yao Ming!

I made an extensive player profile card on him. (See Appendix, #2)

$$$

You've probably heard that there're three things a person needs in life: A good doctor, an accountant, and a lawyer. Lester, affectionately known as "Loophole" Lester, was a lawyer, but reticent about this. (This was contrary to Clyde who didn't mind having his stock brokering known.) Over months of battling Loophole, a top player, we learned to respect each other's game. Eventually I asked him whom he worked for, and he quickly joked with a well-practiced line, "Dewey, Cheatem & Howe." Later he confided that he was in private practice. He apparently had an eidetic memory that, do you suppose helped in law school which he claimed was a breeze; furthermore, he said he worked his way through law school playing poker in Gardenia. Whew!

One infrequently, if ever, won an argument against him, for not only did he have an incisive mind, but he was also skilled in lawyering. Years later he introduced me to his son whom I asked, "When you were growing up, did you ever win an argument with your dad?"

We were in a $20 Hold 'em game, when a heated dispute blew up over who should win a pot that we weren't in. Without getting into the particulars, the Floor woman was summoned. Since it was a big pot, Lester and I had keenly watched. As disputants presented their cases to the Floor woman, I whispered to Lester, "Well, counselor, who do ya think'll win?" The player guessing he'd lose the pot got more and more apoplectic and talked louder and louder until he was almost screaming. He looked as if he were a cat about to hack up a humongous hairball.

Loophole Lester shared, "JM, you know Oliver Wendell Holmes is supposed to have said, quote, 'If you have the facts on your side, hammer the facts. If you have the law on your side, hammer the law. If you have neither the facts nor the law with you, hammer the table. Unquote.'" [He had a habit of surrounding key words or phrases with quote-unquote for emphasis] And that's exactly what seat two is doing—pounding the table ... But I'm partial to seat 8's case.

"Didn't Holmes also say that lawyers spend an awful lot of time shoveling smoke? And wouldn't it be more efficient to just use air quotes? I'm all about efficiency in case you haven't noticed."

"Oh, I noticed! For one thing, you abhor deck changes. I assume for efficiency... or orneriness."

The decision's upshot was that the apoplectic player lost the pot. Damning the torpedoes, he sneered at the Floor woman, "Oh, great decision. You're a great Floor woman; you should easily win the employee of the month at this dump."

At any rate, this Floor could have been the employee of the month for this fair resolution. But she wasn't as good as the Negotiator's Hall of Famer who handled the following tricky hostage situation. A bank robber held about twenty customers at gun point and threatened to execute one each half hour if his demands for $5 million, a helicopter to the airport, and safe air passage to Cuba, weren't met. After about twenty hours, the bargainer got the robber to accept two Big Macs and a cab to La Guardia.

Kites rise highest against the wind, not with it. Winston Churchill.

36

Quick Draw and Delayed Gratification

SOMETIMES WEREWOLVES ARE *EN vogue* and claw to the forefront. Periodically zombies shuffle to the fore. Sometimes vampires are ascendant and all the rage. However, the vampire I'll discuss is slang for phlebotomist, lab techs who draw blood and perform other venipunctures. Pammie sometimes played higher limits with us when she felt flush, and or had made a big score in her lower limit games. She'd worked about fifteen years drawing blood, doing blood drives, typing and cross matching, etc. She was about forty, beach ball-ish rotund, had thinned reddish hair and the prototypical pink Irish-rose complexion. With a bubbly personality and ready smile, we all enjoyed her presence.

One night, with her tongue lubricated with Baileys, she regaled us with phlebotomy fables.

"A mom brought in her son. He refused to let me draw his blood. His mom was distraught, and she begged him. 'The doctor needs to find out what's wrong,' she explains. So, he asks her what he'll get if he lets me draw blood. She promises him a trip to Toys Я Us. He makes a tough guy face, clenches his jaw, puts his arm stiffly out onto the drawing board, and he looks away ... And he got what he wanted out of his mom."

"How old was he?" I asked.

"Oh, about ten."

"Wow! What a negotiator ... or a manipulator," I suggested. He had an astronomically high Delayed Gratification score. "He probably has his parents around his little finger."

"I feel sorry for them; they've let him gain too much control. He's like kids I've heard about—unless they get their way—they're able to hold their breath until they pass out."

"Pammie, I've got to stick this in. In that vein, it freaks their parents out, and they relent."

She punned, "Needles to say, that's a little venipuncture humor, you're probably right, JM. He had the discipline to hold out until he could get something from his parents."

"He most likely will eventually learn to apply this strategy to teachers, other adults, and, Lord help her, a future wife. Oops, to avoid being Politically Incorrect, I guess I have to say spouse."

I don't know these parents, but they aren't doing him any favors by giving in to his whims. He won't be prepared for the harsh, real world that often wants to drag us down like an Orca at Sea World. How successful would he be if he wanted to avoid an R.I.F., and his best argument to his boss to keep his job was holding his breath till he passed out?

Pammie, playing many hands, eventually got up to use the restroom. When she returned, and waiting for her blind, she continued, "Another time this big guy comes to my drawing station which is visible to the entire waiting room. I do my normal procedure of asking his name and date of birth. He's so nervous he thrusts his arm onto the table and gets this crazed look on his face."

I look over at Pammie comically mimicking his terrified expression with the rigidity of a dental patient about to be drilled without anesthesia.

"So, he slouches down in the chair, locks his head away from me, and starts literally walking his feet up and down the partition wall. Tap-tap-tap; up and down. I quickly finish and say, 'All done.' He gasped, 'What! You're done? I feel so embarrassed ...' What a baby. Everyone in the waiting room saw this, laughs with him and gives him a thumbs up. And I've seen some patients pass out, and it's interesting that mostly it's the men. Once this guy who looked like a pro football player came in, and he brought his buddy for support. He was hyperventilating. He told me, 'I'm not too good with having blood drawn.' Since we only needed one tube and since he had well defined veins—that we call nurses' porn—the needle would be in and out as quickly as possible. Of course, it's the thought rather than the stick that's critical. Afterward, I tape his arm, and he looks at me and says, 'That wasn't so bad.' Then he turns white, and BLAM, slides straight to the floor. We all rush over to see if he's all right. We pick him up which was quite a struggle. He comes to on a bench, and he looks at his buddy and says, 'Nice catch! No wonder you don't start. Why'd I even bring you?

$$\$\$\$$$

As noted, gamblers aren't ascetic or into self-abnegation. No disrespect. Moreover, they want instant gratification, lack self-denial and are self-centered. Mixing these open chain compounds cab result in a dangerous IED. In my experience, I declare Yulu Unwin the winner (loser?) of the shortest, holdout time during a real-world Marshmallow Test, and who'd get the lowest reading on my Gratification Postponement Scale.

One night my waitress put my lemon meringue pie on my tray. Since it was covered with plastic wrap, I saw no immediate need to eat it. Not taking a break in a while, I went to wash my hands and face. I returned fifteen minutes later, but my pie was gone. Whaa? Confused, I asked, "What happened to my pie?" Maybe it disappeared through reverse entanglement?

Sitting next to me, Yulu had seen my unattended pie, and ate it! "You, um, weren't eating it," she lamely defended herself. "I'll get you another one. It's not like, um, they're gonna run out. Oh, and I'll put a cheery cherry on top. Or I'll get you some burnt Jell-O—lime."

I hypothesize this was a subset of Nicky The Greek's Melba cracker trick, although she made a real piece of food disappear. After about thirty minutes, she hadn't replaced it. When I asked her if she was going to, she looked at me like I was as demented as Hannibal Lecter. She repeated that she would. Then she looked at my ring finger. With her acerbic, condescending spite she insulted me saying, "Um, I see that you're not married."

Lovely. What colossal gall. I was flabbergasted by her rebuff because it was none of her beeswax. This harpy most certainly wasn't a shrinking violet, but more of a blooming, wacky-daffy, daffodil. Unlike Helen of Troy, she didn't have a face that launched a thousand ships but a personality that could sink a thousand. What on earth did my being single have to do with her behavior? Forget logic. This was a classic non sequitur. The fact I wasn't married, *or* chose not to wear a ring, was beside the point, and it was no defense for her actions. But as she got personal, I retaliated. "Yulu, you look tense. Why don't you go out and slip into something more comfortable like a coma?" An acquaintance told me later, "That was one of the stranger things I've ever seen in a casino."

Impulse control? That's for losers. Gotta scratch that itch. In her fractured reality, she'd done nothing wrong. Like impulse buying, she saw the pie; she wanted it; she took it for free. What could be better? She subscribed to Erma Bombeck's advice: "Seize the moment. Remember all those women on the 'Titanic' [sic] who waved off the dessert cart." In my dildo format, The proof is in the dildo. In Spoonerism terms, "A lack of pies (A pack of lies)." Oh, and she never replaced my pie—the kitchen was out.

$$$

Due to my foster homes' experience, I developed a phenomenal Marshmallow Experiment coefficient. Thus, I have a strongly formed sense of holding off, while Yulu doesn't. Yay, I win. Foster kids are forced to acquire strong survival skills, maybe a well-developed sense of independence, and a powerful immune system. At least in my case. Many foster children are far better off in foster homes than in a dangerous, familial home. Of course, I'm not implying that being raised in this lamentable situation is a good way to develop these valuable traits. I'm trying to put a positive spin on my childhood.

Aside from being away from my mom, there were downsides like being teased with "You have big ears" or "You're lazy" and receiving faint praise, a subtle behavior modification, which might result in less costs to the foster parents like, "Johnny, it's great that you eat like a bird." Maybe that's reason why in adulthood I eat like a bird, a ravenous vulture that'll eat anything.

Returning to the pie snatcher, as the Church Lady superciliously sneered, "Well, isn't that special." What was the vanishing pie denouement? By the time she tried to order one, they were out. Hilarious if for no other reason than it provided a slice (nyuck) into someone's mind and motivations. Maybe she was a foster kid longer or in worse ones than me.

Sure, I've asked for a piece of someone's food. Recall at my limits, our food is comped. However, the key difference is I always asked. "Hey, Lan. That banana's been sitting on your tray for a few hours. If you don't want it, may I have it?"

"Sure, JM. You really want it?" Before he gave it to me, he faked like a water polo player feigning a shot.

Smiling, I said, "Hey, instead of handing it to me, you look like you're gonna throw it. Whadda I look like, a monkey? Wait. Don't ans—"

"In a word, yes."

37

Stiffy, Jackpots and Lotteries

JUST WHEN I THOUGHT I'd seen everything, even the great pie grab, something unique occurred. A professor of Speech Language Pathology, Daveed Diphthong, was drinking, having fun and blowing off steam at his *must move game*. When a vacancy occurs in the *main game*, by law (casino rules) the most senior player in the *must move game* has to move to it. Thus, Daveed moved to the game where Interruptus, in rare form, was spouting off like a fire hydrant circumcised by a car. He jabbered nonstop and irritated the hell out of people, especially the losers. Like the four-year-olds in the Marshmallow Test, these yammering types cannot defer the gratification of hearing their own voices.

Eventually Daveed got more annoyed than a tree sloth being badgered and hurried. Do you know how hard it is to irritate a sloth? Because Daveed had switched from the must move game, he couldn't move back. After suffering an hour of Interruptus' inane blathering, Daveed proposed, "Mr. Interrup*ter*, if you leave this game, I'll give you $300."

The question on every mind: Does Daveed honestly mean it? Naturally, Mr. Interruptus didn't believe it either, but the professor assured him that he did. Daveed pulled out a substantial roll of hundreds and peeled off three. Mr. Interruptus left our game even though he'd have to wait one hour before he could go back on the board for the $20-40 games. Interruptus' chattering and nattering may have given the impression that he was a fool, but he wasn't. Come on, $300 per hour. Even I didn't make that in the 80s.

$$$

Here's another instance of something unique occurring. A semi-regular was playing next to me when he answered his cell. In my player profiles, I labelled him "Cirrhosis" Chip, for he had a glandular and or liver problem causing extreme jaundice and obesity. Perhaps a symptom of his condition was his liver-colored lips. These lips, bigger than Jagger's, called to mind the WWII canard that "Loose lips sink ships." His could torpedo a fleet. He perpetually had the tense, pained, worried look of a man scurrying to the nearest bathroom. (Been there.) Given his probable discomfort and medical condition, he was very pleasant.

Chip, in a near whisper said, "Her eyes are open, and you don't think she's breathing, well, check and call me back. Why? I'm in the blinds ..." About five minutes later, "Can you touch her and see if she's cold? You can't 'cause you're afraid. Do you want me to come home?" Then, noting that everyone was staring at him, he tells the table, "My wife thinks our dog died." 💀.

I was compelled to josh, "I'll bet her name isn't Skippy but Stiffy."

Chip ignored all this banter and told us, "I just brought the dog home from the vet and paid $500 for her treatment. If she's dead, I want my money back."

Speaking of that, I wonder what the annual cost is for feeding a Great Dane?

Later someone asked me, "Hey, JM. Are you a dog or cat person?"

I kidded, "Neither. I prefer eating fish."

$$$

Resembling a game within a game of poker, pros, always looking for an edge, often joust for better seat positions or request a table switch asap. Incidentally, keeping track of this jockeying is a pain in the *keister* for Floor personnel. While pros have rational reasons to request a table switch, the non pro regulars and recreational contestants *felt* the green *felt* was usually greener on the other table, somewhat like seeking greener pastures. On top of that, the stupidstitious, of course, believed the other table might be luckier, or due to hit the jackpot like an overdue slot. Concerning slots: Henry Carpenter, a character in Hemingway's *To Have and Have Not*, ruefully complains: "Life is the eternal jackpot. I'm playing a machine now that doesn't give jackpots any more [sic]."

It's human nature, especially prevalent in poker players, to want to avoid missing out on something. How many times have I heard the wail of a player who changed games—voluntarily or was moved—only to have his prior table, or *worst*, his vacated seat, hit the jackpot?

Blaming the rule that you must move allows the feeble-minded to combine two pretzel, logic flaws. First, the cards know and can arrange themselves into a jackpot configuration. Second, the table itself can create a singular vortex to create a bad beat, paradoxically a *good* beat—they get prize money. Unaware or disbelieving in the Gambler's Fallacy, they don't comprehend that the seat, table, cards are powerless and without memory. The pretzel logic bunch believe cards remember past events. By extension, they even go so far as to believe the cards know where in the deck they are, when or by which dealer the prize hand will be dealt and to whom. I'm, however, philosophic. I believed one couldn't be in two places at once (unlike the wave-particle duality of electrons in quantum physics). Thus, you have an equal chance of winning a jackpot at the new table versus the vacated one (discounting almost irrelevant transit time and ignoring table's looseness).

Additionally, a player who recently moves from a site that hit the jackpot, has a great bad beat to wallow in and a great bad beat story to torture everyone with for days, if not months. It's not win-win, but lose-win; namely, lose (the prize money), but gain pain and a magnificent, sad story. S/he can add it to their bad beat canon.

Re jackpots, attendant to superstition about a lucky table, some players think a dealer is bad for them and sit out. But wouldn't you want a bad beat? Depends how you define bad beat, I guess. By convoluted reasoning, if this particular dealer was bad luck, then this dealer would somehow prevent the complainer from winning a jackpot.

$$$

Lotteries are akin to jackpots. Fran Lebowitz said, "I've done the calculation and your chances of winning the lottery are identical whether you play or not." I love this epigram from an unknown source: Lotteries are a tax on the stupid. Witness one skaghead who, when asked by a reporter how he'd spend the money, answered, "Hookers and cocaine."

Aside from human wishful thinking, the media shares culpability for perpetuating and increasing interest in lotteries by spreading soft news on jackpot sizes. It utilizes an availability bias to convince players they're more likely to win because officials proudly show a winner, not the host of losers. S/he'll reveal their successful method using Aunt Sadie or the cat's birthday.

With all due respect to lottery players lurking out there, it seems that from time-to-time lottery fever bursts out like Bubonic plague boils. You hear of people spending $5,000—$10,000 on tickets! But if you want to plunge, why not *bet* that money on penny stocks, options, collectible coins, etc. that could hit big? But maybe an investment payoff is too slow. Perhaps lottery players have low impulse control and high instant gratification needs. Combined with a poor Delayed Gratification coefficient, they also succumb to the Gambler's Fallacy superstition. It's hard to turn down such a cocktail.

Hopefuls will drive for hundreds of miles and line up for hours at a store previously selling a big winner. This illustrates a type of cognitive bias called *recency bias* in believing something's more likely to occur again (sale of a winning ticket) because it happened recently. *Surely* the mechanism selecting the random, numbered balls can divine which outlet recently sold a big winner. In a way recency bias is like The Gambler's Fallacy. (Admittedly there's an exception to my anti-lottery screed. See Appendix, #3)

Occasionally, it's newsworthy that a winner misplaces, washes, discards or eats a supposed winning ticket. First, if they don't have it, how can they know it's a winner? Maybe they recorded the number, but then wouldn't you be just as conscientious with the ticket? Second, if you've spent a lot of time buying one and have faith, why wouldn't you safely store it? Incomprehensible. Don't get me wrong. As I've aged, I've lost more than my fair share of things—just not lottery tickets.

$$$

One Saturday afternoon, since May Faire was about to leave her game, I was going take her seat. As she was racking her chips up into about four racks, indicative of a good win, she said, "Hi, Larry." Even though I'd corrected her, after years of habit she still labored under the impression my name was Larry, a misnomer she acquired from Tow Truck. You'll like this game." As she racked up her chips, she said, "I remember you like wine. I went to this wine tasting in Hollywood that some of my improv friends were hosting. Wow. There were a lot of heavy, story lines there. They called it a No Whine Party. The invitation said, 'Wine in a bottle, cask or a box. We don't care. A hundred years old or one day. We don't care. Hold your wine glass any f-ing way you want. We don't care. Just no whining. Oh, and no ABC.'"

"Always Be Closing?" I guessed.

"No. Anything But Chardonnay. Some actors were there. One quoted Stanislavski, 'There are no small parts only small actors.'"

Of course, I thought, *There are no small dildos only small actors.*

She went on, "He told us of an Alexander Wolcott review of a play whose cast he didn't like. He wrote, 'The scenery in the play was beautiful, but the actors got in front of it. *Acting!* as Jon Lovitz and John Lithgow used to say as Master Thespians on SNL.' You know, acting is about the layers. One independent film director explained that he wouldn't film an actor in a stressful, heart-wrenching scene, or nude scene, early in the shoot. He'd defer it towards the end so the actor wouldn't be overwhelmed or emotionally drained. Let the actor feel their way into character.

"After we watched some ancient footage of vaudeville acts, one of the hosts talked about the Marx Brothers' era. You remember them? Groucho, Harpo, Chico and sometimes Zeppo. Sadly, their older uncle, Karl—Karl Marx—didn't make the act. He was kinda rebellious. Anyway, he claimed the Marx Brothers had contemporaries named the Lenin Brothers. Hippo, Zippo, Cheapo, and Lipo."

"He was kidding, right?"

"Can't bluff you," she joked. Having racked her chips securely, I bought a rack from her. She quipped, "Exit all, save Macbeth. Now I exeunt stage left." She gave me a lucky $5 chip. "Good luck. Or as we say in theater, Break a leg, not gas."

38

"Bangkok" and "Mr. Interruptus"

ONE NIGHT I PLAYED with Bangkok. "I can't believe I saw you on the freeway last week." Southern California is home of the high, and oxymoronically *low,* speed chases. It's extremely rare to see someone you know.

He laughed. "You know I'm on the road a lot for business, and you can't believe how many poker players I see every week on the freeways. That reminds me, I saw a bumper sticker today: I love whales with soy sauce."

Man, when Bangkok made some big sales, he'd roll into the casino with a wad of cash that would choke a horse. Tonight, he was flush in multiple senses: In having an alcohol induced sheen, in carrying a roll, and in flushing money out of his system into the poker ecosystem. The likelihood of a winning session increased for everyone at his table. When drinking and in a celebratory mood, he made a few quips when he won a pot; namely, Push the gravy to Davy or Another lock for Bangkok.

$$$

As chance would have it, another surprising encounter with a poker player was seeing Curtis, Mr. Interruptus, getting some lab work. He was about eight people ahead of me in line. Rather than saying hi, with cynicism, but certainly with curiosity, I wanted to see if his abnormal actions at the card table were an act. He read aloud the sign at the head of the line, "Please wait here, have your membership card ready, and no telling dirty jokes."

Wassat? When I got to the sign, I saw that some instructions were covered, so he verbally created his own dirty joke ban. While I was checking in, I turned my back to his seat in the waiting room. He was chatting away to his poor neighbor, so I went to the back without him noticing. Later, while we waited, he was chatting everyone up. When they called his number, he yelled, "Bingo!" What a stitch or what a card. Everyone laughed and looked at this strange man.

He spotted me after having his blood drawn and said hello. "Hey, JM. What brings you here? In the chair I was thinking of this S.A.T. question: Chapter is to The Bible as *surah* is to blank?"

I thought, *What the hell?*

$$$

When I sat in Mr. Interruptus' game a few days later, he was laying down a riff about collective nouns. With a damn the prevailing winds and torpedoes attitude, he just spewed out factoids like a DC-10 dropping Phos-Chek. "You know a group of lions is a pride, but there're some more really vivid, imaginative adjectives. Like, a parliament of owls. You can just see owls huddled together caucusing. A murder of crows is strange. But some of my favorites are an ostentation of peacocks, an exaltation of larks, and a knot of frogs. Do you know what a group of leopards is called?"

Math Drew guessed, "A colony?"

"A colony?" Interruptus was perplexed. "I could see if you guessed *Def*. But why a colony?"

"Haven't you ever heard of a colony of lepers?"

The worm (a skein of worms) had turned. Drew'd pulled a Melba cracker monkeyshine bait and switch trick on Interruptus.

(Attendant to this, I submit that a group of crackers should be called a Melba.) Curtis was as exasperated as we usually were when he inflicted inanities on us, and he said loudly, "Leopards not lepers! Leopards!"

Drew with a slow shrug continued, "Well, just like you, I thought I'd throw out some pointless humor, too."

Without missing a beat, Interruptus replied, "That's what you should do with your humor. Throw it out." To conclude, Interruptus finished, "So a group of leopards is known as a leap. Cool, huh?"

Picking up the scent, I asked him, "By the way, what is a group of chickens called?"

"Dunno. Flock?" he guessed.

"A motion," I said.

"A motion? I don't think so."

"Yeah. Haven't you ever heard of poultry in motion?"

Interruptus feigned barfing. "And you're gonna tell me they drive a Cadillac C-o-o-p de Ville ... But I wonder what a bunch of poker players would be. How 'bout a stack?"

Others suggested. "A whine," and "A bitching."

$$$

Later, whenever I heard a few collective nouns, I always thought of Curtis. Unlike the well-known flock, pod, etc., here are some of mine: Clutch of auto mechanics, clog of plumbers, pile of hoarders, a quiver of cowards, a host of parasites, a concentration of thinkers, a complement of sycophants, a range of ovens. Citing the last example, not all descriptions have to pertain to living things. Someone coined the term a flight of stairs. Had I been first, I might have chosen story or ziggurat of stairs. Or, even though steppes are flat, I'd coin a steppe of stairs which is alliterative. A lot of Christmas trees.

$$$

It was inevitable, since Mr. Interruptus was already in the game I joined, that trivia would zoom around like a rapidly deflating balloon. I thought I'd make a preemptive strike with an original thought that I had while driving over. To block his cutting in, I spit out, "Hey, Curtis, in rock music what is the magic number?"

"Sixty-nine. No, I'd guess the number one because a band's goal is a number one song."

"Good guess, Curtis, but not what I was looking for."

"Hmmm that's trivium I don't know. Gimme a clue."

I was enjoying this. "Okay, it also could be the expiration date for six."

"That's quite a cryptic clue. More of a detour or blind alley than a signpost."

My poser seemed to quiet him down for a while. It was like the Robert Bloch "Wolf in the Fold" episode of *Star Trek* when Spock asked the Enterprise's evil, Redjac-infected computer to compute pi to infinity. This infinite loop distracts Redjac; thereby, the crew can purge it from the ship's computer and regain normal ops.

Similarly, Mr. Interruptus mulled over my puzzler about fifteen minutes when out of a hand. We'd never seen him so exasperated, or silent, and finally he dejectedly said, "Joggin' my noggin' didn't help. I give up."

I mischievously whispered, "Twenty-seven."

"What! Why's that a rock, musical, mystery number?"

"No, rock music's m*agic* number. I'll let you figure that one out." (See Appendix, #4)

$$$

Wanting to give the impression that I'd just come from a *corporate* job, I usually wore a tie—the last, functionless piece of clothing. To protect these often-expensive accouterments, I usually stuffed a napkin into my collar while eating. This was a false tell, and naturally, one shouldn't judge a dildo by its cover.

Have you ever watched a player, usually male, eating while playing in a fast-moving game? Observing this comedy of gastronomical delight is side-splitting (using gut busting was too easy), but also it can be revolting. If he's wolfing down something like fried chicken, and if he's excitedly explaining himself in a dispute, stuff tumbles out or projectiles shoot out of his mouth like volcanic globs. Depending upon his excitement, "I wraith!" might be a veritable shotgun blast of BB-sized ping-ping-bings. Grease accumulates on his face like Joey "Jaws" Chestnut, competitive eating chompion. Jaws currently holds the record for stuffing down sixty-nine dogs in ten minutes during Nathan's Coney Island, Fourth of July, hotdog eating contest. Yummy. Occasionally a gambler feebly attempts to clean up by wiping his fingers on a napkin that quickly becomes saturated. Heaven forbid he sits out a round or two to dine. No, no. He needs action.

Lest one thinks I'm blameless, I've eaten like this too. Once I was struggling to eat this ginormous tostada over my side tray. As much as I hate others doing it, I was slowing down the game. "Sorry, guys. I'm wrestling with this tostada."

Bangkok intoned, "Looks like the tostada's winning."

"I'm not sure, yet. It's a tag team match, and the tostada's partner, The Flying Burrito, is about to do a diving jaw breaker on me."

Nevertheless, I realized wearing a bib might've been iconoclastic, but I didn't give a hoot what people thought. If they thought me a rube or cube, fine. So be it: Rube I am. More deception. While most of the regulars were used to my idiosyncrasies by now, one night a stranger played against me. After playing a while, he commented, "You know, I find it hard to take a guy wearing a bib seriously."

"I'm teething."

The stranger introduced himself, "Hi, I'm Barge Dupree."

"I'm JM. Glad to meet you."

"And, bib boy, I have another rule. Never call a man who's serenely smiling and bets. Confucius said that."

Conjecturing, I answered, "No, I think The Buddha said that. I think Confucius said life isn't a donkey race. But anyway, they had a historic heads-up match. The Buddha didn't stand a chance versus Confucius."

Barge speculated, "How about a heads-up game between Buddha and Sun Tzu?"

I posed, "Better Sun Tzu against Machiavelli, or Napoleon versus General Patton. How about Mohammed versus Jesus? Certainly, people would pay *big* money to see that match up. Not The Rumble in the Jungle, but maybe The Fish Fry in the Sinai."

"No disrespect to my Muslim brothers, but I gotta give that match to Jesus, 'cause He can work miracles with the flop."

This speculating could've gone on *ad infinitum,* for verily, this is how we passed time between hands. *Meh,* anything to beat the monotony.

$$$

One night, Mr. Interruptus and I both quit about the same time, cashed out, and walked to our cars. "So, JM, how'd you do?"

"Oh, I won a little." It's always hard, almost impossible, to be certain how much a player is in—bought in the game—for the session, unless a player is there before and after a player who leaves, and cares enough to keep track. Also, s/he may have bought chips at another game. Some players give an accurate accounting and others don't.

In this case, I reported I'd won some trifling amount, while actually I had a substantial win. However, I obfuscated for two reasons: A) It wasn't any of Interruptus' business and B) I wanted to avoid further confirmation that overall, I was a winning player. We stopped under the lot's halogen light. "How'd you do?" I asked.

I believed he exaggerated when he bragged, "I won about $2,000. A good night. Did I tell you about the time I was with a blind hooker? You really had to hand it to her. She said, 'Oh, baby, you're so big, the biggest I've ever been with.' And I told her, 'You're pulling my leg.'"

I laughed out loud. "*Tres droll.* Those are terrible, but I like them."

"Didyaknow."

By the time we reached my car, I'd already tuned him out. I said goodnight and got in. As I started the engine, he was motioning me to roll down the window. Unbelievably, he wanted to tell me another story. Trying to get rid of him was as difficult as trying to get rid of toenail fungus. But I'm glad I heard him out.

"JM, have you heard of risk intelligence?"

"No."

"Simply it's the ability to estimate probabilities accurately and make educated guesses. But it involves more, like how to work with limited information, cope with an uncertain world, and about knowing yourself and your limitations."

"For example?"

"There're people with high-risk quotients among bridge players, weather forecasters, and expert gamblers. You can only be an expert gambler where there's room for skill like in poker, blackjack, or sports betting. What high risk intelligence people have in common is they're very disciplined and hardworking."

"Interruptus, I'd love to hear more, but I'm exhausted. Gotta go home."

"Okay. I'll tell you next time."

"Please do. See ya." Truly a card. His tongue control had a Marshmallow Experiment rating of zero.

39

The Great Crash of 1929

I RUMMAGED AND EVENTUALLY found Clyde's business card. I went to visit him in his corner office after the Big Board closed. Offering me a Perrier, Clyde opined, "Jimmers, I'm getting worried about the market. During 1987 there was a frenzy of buying and speculating. Do you know who John Kenneth Galbraith is?" (Harvard-trained economist Galbraith satirically noted, "The only function of economic forecasting is to make astrology look respectable.")

"Yeah," I answered.

"Good. I'm reading his *The Great CRASH of 1929*." He grabbed it from his drawer. "This is from introduction's page X, the common denominator of all speculative episodes—that they (the speculators) were predestined by luck, an unbeatable system, divine favor, access to inside information, or exceptional financial acumen, to become rich without work." This is a free lunch bunch of another stripe and era.

Clyde continued, "I see so many similarities between then and now. Back in '29, the people were so optimistic. It may be apocryphal, but J. D. Rockefeller said when his bootblack told him about the stocks he owned, Rockefeller knew it was time to get out and sold most everything and avoided the calamity of the Great Crash."

"Yeah, I've heard that story," I added.

"The public wanted a free ride—great profits without risk. Without risk! No such animule. Then the chickens and vultures came home to roost.

The market crashed on Black Tuesday, and thus began the Stock Market Crash of 1929. Here Keynes wrote, "When the capital development of a country becomes a byproduct of the activities of a casino, the job is likely to be ill-done." Clyde shook his head.

"But does this sound familiar? Today's geniuses create hocus-pocus, sub-prime mortgages, credit-default swaps, and NINJA loans—No Income, No Job, no Assets. Countrywide even called their loan program The Hustle. Just like the twenties, nothing's created in the economy. No problem."

I added, "Speaking of these finance people creating complex monetary instruments, Einstein supposedly posited, Creativity is intelligence having fun. Those creative speculators looked like they weren't motivated by having fun but by greed. And you know Einstein was a genius, relatively speaking."

"Ha-ha. But what you said is true, Jimmers. And you've probably heard the Wall Street canard about greed. Bulls make money. Bears make money. But pigs get slaughtered. That's the short version. The more inclusive, instructional version is Bull markets climb a wall of worry, and bear markets decline on a slippery slope of hope and often terror. Yeah, when the Dow goes straight down, your pants stain dark brown. But remember, pigs get slaughtered.

"We stockbrokers who use fundamental analysis have a description—the market inches higher, climbing what I mentioned before, a Wall of Worry. But I'm extremely worried now. No, I'm scared, that now if there's some bad news, or a few big players or institutional investors bail out, we'll see the same thing."

"You sound terrified."

"Jimmers, I'm scared shirtless."

I had a chance a couple of months later to chat with Clyde—when we weren't battling at the felt. "Hey, Triple C. We know of bull and bear markets. I heard a new anthropomorphic stock market type, the hippo.

A hippo market that is a large, slow-moving animal that generally moves forward at a modest pace but occasionally reacts violently."

40

It Never Rains in SoCal

THERE'RE SAYINGS IN MINNESOTA: "If you don't like the weather now, wait fifteen minutes," and "There's no bad weather, just improper dress." This isn't applicable to Southern California's usually dry and temperate climate nor would it be mistaken for Hawaii's moderate, steady, heavenly weather. Yet sometimes around LA it'd rain buckets, and this week was Olympian. One night I breast stroked into a card emporium during a real gully washer, whopper. To Spoonerize, it was pouring *p*ain and roaring with *r*ain. Is it rain-generated negative ions that allow one to smell that refreshing, unique rain scent?

Inside the gambling hall was dank and musty with a gloomy pall hovering over the tables like a wet wool blanket. Coming in from the darkness and dispiriting storm, invariably a newcomer is asked, "How is it out there?" Or "Is it still raining?" Similarly, did you ever notice that when party A says, "It looks like it's gonna rain," party B invariably replies either. "Great. I just washed my car" or another inanity, "Well, we need it." I confess I've spouted this banality many times. Of course, we need rain! We live in a desert, dah.

Before I put my initials up, the Board woman and chip runner were passing the time. "This weather is weird. Yesterday it was seventy and tonight it's raining buckets."

"Yeah. But when I lived in DC, one day it was eighty with about 90 percent humidity—weather you can wear. The next day it rained. Two days later we had sleet and snow. It was really schizophrenic."

I said to the Board woman, "Excuse me. Please put me up," and threw in, "DC's weather was bi-polar." They looked at me quizzically. Tow Truck, standing and waiting, overheard our conversation and humorously added two malapropisms, "I don't think DC's weather is that indifferent from the rest of the continuous US."

Throughout the flu season one hears a cacophony of sneezing and coughing with a nasal chorus of "I hahb ah damem code."

Occasionally there're weather-related power outages caused by winter storms or toppled power poles resulting from car wrecks or Santa Anas screeching through. At the frequency I play, about once a year a casino's pitched into total darkness. Before backup generators spark to life, it's like a seance with everyone having their fingers on the table, not to levitate it, but to protect their chips.

Pitch blackness happened this evening. Everyone heard Ali's—DotCom's—panicked scream, "EYEYEEE!" Then I thought I'd play a Melba cracker hoodwink on the guys at my table. I picked up some of my chips, noisily tickled and clicked them up and down, and said in a villainous voice, "Making change from the pot."

41

Vegas Immigration

WHILE WAITING FOR A seat, I saw Ralphie, the young bar owner mentioned earlier who chastised me for winning a little and leaving. Whiling away the wait, I found out that he had inherited the bar from his dad who had died of emphysema. It was on Periwinkle Lane in Bellflower. Then I posed, "Why are some beers like women?"

I could tell Ralphie was about to roll his eyes, but instead he said, "I 'spose you'll tell me."

"Some are blonde. Some brunette, and some are redheads. Those are the ones to watch out for."

"Gee. I haven't heard that since high school."

"Sorry. Of course, you hear lots of jokes and probably all the ones beginning with So and so walk into a bar."

He flagged down a cocktail waitress and ordered a Stolichnaya martini dressed traditionally. I asked, "Why Stoli?"

He went to his happy place and smiled, "It just has a pure, clean, neutral taste. It's triple distilled."

"Just give me vodka distilled once. I like a little murkiness, like my thinking. And with respect, wanting it triple distilled seems a little quirky."

"Oh, [snap] that's rich," he teased. "Like you have no quirks. But heaven forbid if your neighbor wants a napkin from your side table or

- 214 -

wants to put some small wrapper on it. You're so territorial that I've seen you go to war over if someone wants to share it."

"You're absolutely right in busting me," I embarrassingly laughed. "Your point has my Sarcasm Sensing Scale banging the top line, off the charts. But your point about being so touchy about people putting things on my tray's true. I'm very particular of others' germs getting on my food."

Ralphie smiled, "I'd say *peculiar*."

The Board called him. He said, "Send [snap-snap-snap] Vermilion with my drink to the top section. Oh [snap]. And I'll save you a tray for you."

$$\$\$\$$$

A sidenote on side trays. Just below elbow height, these wheeled tables hold beverages, ashtray (old days) or a small plate. A larger, slightly taller dinner tray fits over it. I usually have both. The top table both holds my food and conceals the bottom cart which is my *desk* for scribbling player notes and financial records. The top table also obscures my notes and records from prying eyes, impede a player's theft out of curiosity or malice, and prevents stuff from being accidentally discarded by a porter. As Ralphie noted, I'm as territorial about keeping my table as a religious cult messiah is about his fifteenth, teenage wife.

I keep detailed accounting, statistical records on the casino: Day, hours worked, result. Totaling those monthly and yearly numbers, I easily learn dollars per hour, most profitable days to work, results at each club, etc. Moreover, I study NTAs and estimate how much I would be ahead if I eliminate some of them. I felt eliminating all is impossible. Regrettably, I don't sabermetrically utilize this metadata to plot my plus or minus standing hour-by-hour to see if there's an optimal number of hours to work. Neither did I run regression analyses nor correlations to economic cycles, holiday weekends, political party in power, local sports teams' success, moon cycles, etc.

Covert as I try to be, it's humorous that some opponents easily can see what I'm doing. Naturally, some assume I'm studying stocks. This infrequent playa, Peter Kutoff, once asked me, "Does keeping records help?"

"Yes, but I do it as much from having CDO as anything else."

Puzzled, he asked, "What's CDO?"

"Most know it as obsessive-compulsive disorder, OCD. But I insist it's CDO—the letters *must* be in alphabetical order. I have a mild case."

"I don't know about *mild*," he joked. "And I guess CDO is worse than OCD."

I liked his observation. "True. I was severely potty trained by Frau Blücher."

$$$

I thought Peter Kutoff was a tourist from Vegas. Then after seeing him week after week, I figured he'd become a regular. The Vegas migration was great for the immigrants (the successful ones) and SoCal casinos, but then parking became a problem. A semi-black market sprung up to get counterfeit cards to activate the gates. A big flap occurred. I guess it was a parking gate-gate. (Every scandal or possible impropriety now has a gate suffix. Deflate-gate. Really?)

As the Vegas migration continued, one young man, later to become a legend and WSOP $1 million winner in 1996, was a baby-faced, really tall guy who looked like Huck Finn. Nicknaming him after Samuel Clemens' hero was a no brainer, a slam dunk. I was watching "Huck" once when he was playing the LA casino's biggest game located in a raised, High Roller section. The joint was overflowing, so his table was right against the rail, toward the center of the casino and away from the backwall privacy; thus, I could observe and hear. When an opponent called Huck's bluff on the river,

Huck said to his friend, "How could he call me so weak? Doesn't he know I won the World Series?"

He also loved to make proposition bets which are like, but not exactly, bar bets; i.e., the bettors choose an event, negotiate the terms, conditions, amount(s), and if necessary, the odds. Of course, each side feels they have the advantage; otherwise, why bet? So Yosh and Doyle Texas Dolly Brunson bet that Huck couldn't run a marathon in less than six hours. If he did, he won even money. If he finished in less than five hours, he got 2:1. The CC&Rs (Covenants, Conditions, and Restrictions) meant he had to run each lap—no walking to rest—and he had to run on a measured track. Probably unbeknownst to the bettors, Huck had run cross country in high school. Oh, he only won about $25,000 including the side action. This might translate to about $200,000 now. Re betting, Damon Runyon quipped, "The race may not always be to the swift nor the victory to the strong, but that's how you bet." In contrast, I won $30 for doing fifty consecutive pushups. Since I usually do seventy, it was a good proposition bet for me. Thanks, Arniss.

42

NTAs II

AS WAS HIS HABIT, Tow Truck coasted in late one night after his towing company shift. As usual, he reeked of Russian cigarettes. And whenever he came or left, like Lucifer, there was the residual smell of brimstone. (BTW, what's brimstone smell like?) His work boots were unlaced for comfort, and he shuffle-clunked along. He looked messier than a college dorm room, a *male's*. I greeted him to our game with *"Prieviet."* He settled in. Someone asked him why he always came in around two in the morning. Pulling his hat's ear flaps back, he said, "When I get off, I don't dawdle-dally. I come right over here to see the games, try to win a little, eat, and see if there's an indiwidual who owes me money. You know, the leaky wheel gets the soil."

Someone asked, "Who owes you? Maybe I've seen him tonight."

He smiled and said, "I'm ain't gonna say. What're you insimulating, that I'm a tool pigeon?" He ordered breakfast and shared, "I'm a little unsure of eating their food. When I came in from the parking lot, I passed the kitchen out back, and a bunch of rockcoaches scurried all willy-silly through the grease on the asphalt."

And watching him pack food in caused me to cringe, for I had overly sensitive, almost prissy, hygiene eating standards and sensibilities. You see, motor oil and grease always remained on his knuckles, cuticles and under his nails, embedded like double fried, chicken grease after a church picnic. Bless his heart. No matter how diligently he scrubbed, the *shmutz* stained like a cheap tatt. I noticed his thumb was gruesomely swollen, so I asked him, "What happened to your thumb?"

"*Govno.* Slammed it in a car door, and now it's really off-color."

Loophole Lester, who in contrast was perfectly manicured, asked him why he usually left after winning a few hundred.

Mark explained, "I have this Cardoza Line system. When I get ahead some amount, say $400–600, if I lose back some, go below the Cardoza Line, I go."

"Where did you hear of this quote-unquote, financial system strategy? I've never heard of it."

"I think I heard of it from somewheres on the radio about this book, *The Rambling Walk down Wall Street.* It's like the Cardoza Line in baseball when a player's batting average is less than his weight."

Lester, as an attorney, was usually civil, but he couldn't control his amusement. Thus, he snorted out, "You mor—" He caught and stifled his planned, PI banter with this save, "Ah, you need *more* info on this. It's the, quote-unquote, Mendoza Line!"

I interjected, "Lester, it's sort of like Mr. Irreverent. You know the last player taken in the NFL draft."

Lester laughed and corrected me, "You mean Mr. Irrelevant ... Oh, I get it, JM. You said Mr. Irreverent on purpose."

Tow Truck kept repeating Mendoza Line, and this convulsed Lester with more laughter. Almost purple in the face, Lester gasped, "Wait. Stop! I have to take a knee."

"*Govno,*" Tow Truck swore in Russian and, abashed, he pulled his Russian hat over his eyes. "I get it. Mendoza and Cardoza Line aren't cinnamonous. I know you guys are making fun of me, and I make a tapestry of good English, but I want to nip this in the butt." I got a big kick from that Russian.

Lester said to me, "You'll appreciate this. There was a pitcher who loved classical music but ironically hated to hear Bach.

$$$

I plopped into a seat a player was saying, "... So I check raised him, and he went ballistic!" Before the dealer dealt another hand, he asked if I wanted in. I declined since I wanted to get situated.

Virge asked, "Wha's goin' on, JM? How'd you do last night?"

"Oh, God! If you've heard me say this once, you've heard me say it hundreds of times. I blush to say this, but I was up $1,200, but then I went through that and lost another $1,000. Why?"

Why? Sometimes I think I have a Martyr Complex. It is almost like I don't want to leave a winner. Chiding myself, *Profound*, JM. My couplet:

Should I remain?

Could be my bane.

Virge replied, "I've heard players say, 'why didn't I leave?' about a thousand times, but not always from you. Everyone has those downers. Listen, JM, you aren't alone in having difficulty leaving when way up."

Virge had a deal with a great 7 Stud player, Robby. I knew Robby only through Virge, for Robby and I didn't play the same game. They had been friends for a long time. Robby respected and trusted Virge's opinions. Hence, Virge sweated Robby, and when Robby was up a pre-agreed, acceptable goal, Virge'd recommend that Robby leave. Virge earned a percentage of the score—contingent upon Robby cashing out. Virge sat long hours behind Robby, gave support, comfort, and quitting prompts. However, Robby often wouldn't uphold his end and leave; consequently, Virge earned nothing, and Robby often lost a decent score. Numerous times I heard Virge say something like, "I don't care about my earning anything. I sweat him because he's a friend. But yesterday it was brutal. He was down $5,000, got ahead $3,000, but didn't leave. He ended up losing $6,000." I thoroughly detested my NTAs, and I thought mine were bad, but Robby's was $9,000. Amounts are all relative.

A calamity of that magnitude (a loss of $6,000–$9,000) would have depressed me for days, if not weeks. Like many, including me, Robby was monomaniacal in never wanting to leave the casino losing. More important, like me, he found it exceedingly difficult to quit while he was considerably ahead. How many times have I suffered a big NTA, and melodramatically feel like a tragic, Shakespearian hero?

Virge continued, "So last month we had a heart to heart, and I got him to let me decide when he leaves. Last week he was up $6,000, and I made him quit. The next session, he was down $4,000, got even and up $1,500. I made him go. The third time after our reboot, I met him, and he said, 'The deal's off. We're not playing by your rules anymore. Anyway, what are your credentials for advising me?' I tried to lighten his mood, laughed and told him, 'Credentials. I don't have to show you any stinkin' credentials.' Since then, Robby told me he lost $65,000. This was a horrendous losing streak. He didn't just lose it; he gave it away. Gave it away! I told him, 'What in the heck are you doin'? One time you were up $10,000 and didn't quit.' His excuse was he wanted to win $25,000. I told him, 'You're playin' the fool.'

"Now, JM, it's so bad, the regular 7 Stud players call me and ask, 'Is Robby going tonight?' And if I say I don't think so, they don't go in. There's no game."

That's really a bad sign. You've heard the well-quoted aphorism, If you look around the table and don't see the loser, you're it.

Virge continued about Negative Turn Arounds and his wife, Brenda. "Brenda sometimes gives it back, too." Brenda is a cute, petit, light brunette and about 105 pounds of pure energy, pure Hold 'em focus and skill. She's a formidable foe, a lockdown pro who plays in the top limit game (depending), one limit higher than Virge and me. She's very quiet, taciturn at the table, but likes to whisper to her neighbor or Virge about a hand or player. Her métier is stellar hand reading, selective aggression, and Hold 'em knowledge absorbed over decades. If she has a hole in her game, it's playing marathon sessions when stuck.

He told me that if she's losing at one casino, she'll travel to another and try to get even, much to the detriment of her personal life, health, and bankroll. As Virge described in mixed metaphors, "When she's winning, she can take bad beats. They roll off her like water off a duck. But when she's losing, something clicks like a cat in heat or something. She just wants ta grind it out, and we lose a lot when she does this." I love mixed metaphors, so I would've said she's like a fish out of water running off a duck's back.

He noted, "But it's funny about you. You tell me about your Negative Turn Arounds but don't bore me with bad beat stories, like most people."

I agreed. "Yeah, telling bad beat tales of woe doesn't seem to be productive. And I suppose crying to you about Negative Turn Arounds isn't very productive either. It's worse than useless. And in a way, I'm being treacherous to myself twice. By causing, or allowing, the NTA and then rehashing it. But I suppose I tell you because you might create a solution or maybe say something inspiring me to adopt a successful strategy. Or, in thinking out loud, I may stumble onto a cure."

Interesting, I thought. *When I make a sea of excuses for not leaving— like I can beat these clowns and jokers, or I own this game—I'm rationalizing. And rationalizing is opposite that part of Existentialism requiring personal responsibility. I'm not owning up to this behavior or taking blame. What kind of Existentialist is that?*

Virge interrupted my revelry, "We had a sayin' down in Texas. A mule doesn't have to kick you twice to teach a lesson. You've had a hard time learning it, but I hope you find a cure," he commiserated.

"That's a great sayin' Virge." When I leave after such a losing session, I feel like a massive mauler's hit me on the head ... and chest. Maybe I don't need a mule kick, but need to get some aversion therapy, some stun gun fun. Ritual-habitual-spiritual ... you know. Let me make a reversed Nietzschean corollary: That what kills me makes me weaker. "Anyway, tonight my goal is just win back half of what I lost last night. When and if I get to that point, I'll leave faster than a dildo out of hell."

$$$

As Dr. Phil McGraw drawled, "The best predictor of future behaviors is relevant past action." The past is prolog. However, I vacillate between believing I can and cannot defeat my self-destructive, NTA behavior.

On one side, I'm somewhat dubious of conquering, or at least taming, my old *bête noire* nemesis. (As a sidebar, it's abundantly clear that I like to use *bête noire*.) Another metaphor is that to improve my earnings and be happier with myself, I must unravel this Gordian Knot, although I'm knot Alexander the Great. By Newton's First Law, if an object isn't being pushed or pulled by a force, it'll either stay still or move in a straight line at a constant speed. If working a long time, eight hours or more, and ahead a satisfactory amount, when it comes to leaving, sometimes I become paralytically inert. In a word, I'm immobilized by mind-numbing inertia. After hours one just falls into a rhythm, the repetitive, ebb and flow of hands. However, it's invaluable to visualize myself leaving with racks of chips and what projects, work, reading, or fun activities I'd have time for the next day if I kick out. That helps to dynamite me out of my seat. JM, sear that again and again into your DNA and your memory. A Negative Turn Around is an atrocity to your bottom line! You've got to vaporize it.

On the other side, I'm ever optimistic and as hopeful as a Rogaine user that I can slay this bugbear. I don't expect to eliminate these completely, but perhaps at least halve them. I can make incremental improvements; otherwise, I'll have excremental improvements. Maybe I can find a shaman to help me leave when up a decent amount or a guru who could teach me to eject out of my seat and flee like a flea.

$$$

The following week I sat into a game and asked Virge, "How's this game?"

"Oh, it's so-so, but, man, when we go to the must move game, it's *wild*."

"I can see that by some of the live ones already in it. Phan. Lan. But I don't know many of the other people."

Virge continued scouting the game for me between hands. "Yeah, that's because they aren't regulars. They're some people here for a medical convention."

"Yeah. I was talking outside the bar to a woman, Kimberly, attending it."

"When you get in that game, you need a license to fish."

"Are you implying that there's a lot of fish in the game?"

"Actually, more like whales. Did you bring your harpoon?"

"Yes, but I gotta go out to my cab, Ahab."

Virge shared that Lan told him he had a gambling problem.

I was shocked. "Really? I think most people, especially losing players, wouldn't think Lan has a problem, because he's a winning player." I'm thinking maybe Virge meant that Lan wins so much at poker that he blows his profits on non-winnable gambling; such as, betting sports, horses or any casino games. These pursuits have the odds stacked against the players.

Virge, however, had a different view of Lan's gambling problem. "Some winners like Lan want to gamble all the time, every day. They sacrifice their social life, dating, maybe marriage. Or if already married, sacrificing home and family time. They give up exercise and or a healthy lifestyle."

I realized, "In other words, he can't stop, and he feels he must play and be in action ..."

$$\$\$\$$$

The next night, I sat behind Virge and sweated him while I waited for a seat. As was our custom, Virge won a hand and gave me a $5 check. Smirking as usual, Collison told the dealer, "I object to pushing chips."

This rule is rarely invoked, so the dealer wasn't sure Collison was serious and said, "He isn't in the game. You object?"

Collison sneered, "*That's* what I said. Money's going off the table, and I object."

Amused at his pettiness, I replied, "What's the harm, Collison?"

He retorted, "I object to him pushing chips, especially to you."

He was well within his rights, but most players let it go. Of all possible infractions, this was about a 0.5 on a ten-point scale.

Months later there was rough justice loaded with irony. Because there are so many Mo's around, Mo E. uses his last name's initial when he goes on the board. He's a pleasant, middle-aged man of Middle Eastern background. With his stylishly trimmed Van Dyke and kind demeanor, he appears like a professor of Middle Eastern history. He plays almost every late afternoon into evening, and he has a perfect routine for leaving whether up or down. Namely, he drives his girlfriend, whom he calls his wife, to her waitress job at the casino. When she's off, they go home. He once confided to the table, "I'm glad my wife doesn't gamble."

I good naturedly hit him with, "And she's glad you don't gamble, either." He snort of laughed. To his credit he comprehends that life is one long, continuous game. As long as Mo E. plays well and makes good decisions, it doesn't matter in the long run whether he's up or down at her shift's end. Yet, from the perspective of the dismal science, wacky economists observe, In the long run we're all dead.

Mo E. usually played where we were sitting tonight; whereas, Collison normally played elsewhere. Collison seems to despise dealers, the poor working stiffs, who, one might imagine, make most of their income from tokes. Rather than tipping the dealer after winning a hand, as customary, Collison enjoys stiffing a dealer. He even nettles the dealer by ostentatiously placing a typical tip amount in chips to his shirt pocket rather than to the dealer. Why he ruffles one who riffles is beyond comprehension.

Apparently, in the past, Collison insulted Mo E. one too many times, for Mo E. told me this story. "One night I objected to Collison's putting chips into his pocket, taking money off the table. Collison said, 'If I want any shit out of you, I'll squeeze your head.' So, I went to management about this. He was reprimanded and told to refrain from doing this in the future. I haven't seen him here since." This poetic justice was very satisfying, like a good sneeze after an intermittent, nasal tickling.

43

Poker Molls and Dolls

I WAS SPENDING MORE nights at Bobbie's. Her apartment room had tenement walls barely sturdy enough to hang a crucifix. We occasionally still heard the mysterious mumbles of the right neighbor talking to himself: "... *A rows outage us for tune. Or to tickle arms again and see trouble* ..." The words' meanings were just on my brain, blood barrier of recognition. Another trait about thin walls—one can discern neighbors' musical tastes. One really doesn't have a voice in this, for the decibels are thrust into your face, ears, and life like repugnant political ads. The left neighbor liked the punk and new wave group The Modern Lovers. And unlike the right neighbor's indecipherable, low mumbles, we could hear the song's words: "Pablo Picasso was never called an asshole." This refrain echoed T. S. Eliot's "The Love Song of J. Alfred Prufrock": "In the room the women come and go, Talking of Michelangelo." And we heard ghetto caveats like "Snitches end up in ditches." Still, sound travels both ways, and we sent symphonic sounds their way.

Periodically, Bobbie planned to go to Alaska, but I'd try to get her to stay. Eventually, however, her wanderlust pulsed, and she'd go up for six months. Once we went to an eviction party. Seems a curmudgeonly tenant—certainly not the life, but the death, of the party—complained to the landlord and police about loud parties. Afterward, I was giving her a dozen reasons to stay when, once again, eerie words floated in, "... *Socks that flesh and hair too. 'Tis consumption de pout* ... [unintelligible]." (See

Appendix, #5) Ironically, it wasn't long after my buddy's eviction that Bobbie evicted me. After about three years off and on, phitzz, we broke up.

Finally, she decided to move to The Great Northwest perma(frost) nently. The relationship probably wouldn't have worked out anyway. Since she wasn't a roses kind of woman, one can infer she also was unsentimental. Moreover, since she hated clutter, she often left possessions behind when she moved. This seemed like a waste of money. Even though her self-professed value system was "I don't jive about my money," she liked traveling light and getting a fresh start. Conversely, I saved things and was taught during my impoverished childhood to Waste not, want not. A dildo saved is a dildo earned.

$$$

Although after splitting up with Bobbie I was fancy free again, I was in a fatalistic funk. Nevertheless, I'd still drag myself to work. Post breakup, sometimes, if I slid into a losing streak, I'd sink like ... like the *Lusitania* into the freezing depths of despair. I'd be just on the light side of the penumbra of ending it all. Other times a big score would alleviate the sadness and revive me. Hanging with good friends, seeing a great, inspiring movie, or reading a funny or inspirational book would lessen the hurt. But the best cure was starting a relationship with a new woman.

One night I was chatting with Ricardo, a Latino who claimed he had a brown-eyed soul. He looked underaged and was a top-notch pro, incredibly even-keeled, cheerful and usually smiling. No one disliked him, almost impossible in the poker sphere. I was speculating about my chances of dating one attractive, svelte player, Sanja. I wished to discuss it with him.

"Hey, Ricardo."

"*¿Como está, jefe?*"

"*Nada*, Ricardo. What's hef-hay?"

"Spanish for boss, big cheese."

"I like it. *Mira*, I'd like your opinion. I've tried to get Sanja to go out three or four times. Have you had any luck with her? I hear she isn't with anyone."

Ricardo's cynical, but experienced view was, "Women who play poker regularly, aren't interested in sex. It's their third favorite thing. Poker is number one."

"Wait," I wondered. "What's number two?"

"Poker. Poker is one, two and three." A dispassionate pundit might say the same of gambling men.

$$$

Todd was one of Virge's best friends, for they shared a love of poker, movies, and music. He had intermittent melanism, with a Richard Pryor style moustache. Although he was as bald as a cue ball (no, I suppose, as bald as an eight ball), he was very virile, had a charming smile, and manner.

Early one morning, after the bars closed, Todd brought in a friend one night, and they joined our Hold 'em game. "'Short Route' is in the house. How're all you hipsters and funksters doing tonight? This is Sherice. JM, wassup, bizel?"

I replied, "Wassup, Short Route? You know I know that a Backdoor Man means more than what you told that wom—I mean person, that you were talking to last week." Since he was with a new woman, I'd almost put my foot in my mouth about Kimberly; however, I don't know if I recovered in time. "A Backdoor Man's a guy who prowls around and secretly comes in to see a woman who has a boyfriend or husband."

"Word. JM, how you know that?"

"Whaa? Brother, I'm soo street."

"Yeah, Wall Street," he joshed.

I wasn't sure Todd and Sherice were dating, but out of common courtesy, one didn't want to poach the bird. But one didn't know, so, trying to impress Sherice, I said to them, "Since you're a Backdoor Man, in *Even Cowgirls Get the Blues,* Tom Robbins wrote something profound that the only aphrodisiac in the world is strange stuff.

44

A Random Walk

SINCE CLYDE STILL ONLY played at The Bike and didn't gravitate to Hold 'em, I saw him infrequently when I started playing, I mean working, at Hollywood Park Casino. I missed our discussions about the stock market, economy, and life. I remember him telling me once about his jaundiced view of some shenanigans that some new companies used to pump and dump their stocks. "You know what they say about Wall Street investment bankers' IPOs: What they have on the left side of the balance sheet, there's nothing right. And on the right side, there's nothing left." That is, the left side lists Assets while the right side enumerates Total Liabilities and Owners' Equity. Since Assets minus Liabilities = Equity, this cynical pearl states that there is no real value in some of these IPOs.

Hollywood Park assumed its place in the *en vogue* pantheon of Hot New Place to Play about a year after it opened in Inglewood, 1994. Of course, the usual suspects made the scene, but it tapped another demographic—people I'd never seen before—from the west side of LA, Hollywood, San Fernando Valley, and South Bay. Furthermore, because it was around ten minutes from LAX, it drew casual vacation or business travelers.

Brad was one new face in 1995. He was boyishly handsome, had youthful exuberance, and he played fairly high stakes for his age. I'd seen him in neither Gardenia, The Bike, California Bell Club nor Commerce Casino. He probably didn't want to fight crosstown traffic to those locations. But, since he lived in Brentwood, it was a straight shot to Inglewood.

A young lion of investing. I saw him on a local UHF station, KWHY, trying to get clients by touting his investing methods and skill in picking stocks, futures, options. He used technical analysis, thus making him a chartist. (To some, technicians are akin to users of the occult, or equal to those who cast a copy of *I Ching* for advice). Of course, his program segment was intended to get clients. Thus, he appeared on the scene around 1995. He usually didn't discuss business unless someone like me brought up his trade. "Hey, Brad, I saw you on channel KWHY. You're a trader, aren't you? How do you do?"

"Yes. Yes, I am. And I do all right. And that's no bull, heh-heh."

Once the free lunch bunch players learned this, they asked for advice. I'd lost in options, so I was through with them. Obviously, my free lunch bunch term, wanting something for nothing, applies not only to poker players, but to all strata, and some want society and or the government to pay for its subsistence. Trying to get something for nothing is like taking the easy way. Like picking the low hanging dildos. Even hippies understood there was no free lunch and posted on their vans to hitchhikers: Nobody rides for free. Gas, grass, or ass.

$$$

Brad and I became friendly over the months. I met him one day after work at his office near where I lived on the West Side. "Hi, Brad. Thanks for taking the time to meet."

"My pleasure. Can I get you anything? Coffee, tea, water, Blanton's Bourbon?"

He gave me a tour, and we shot the breeze. It was eerie. The stillness was the polar opposite of the hectic trading day. A myriad of monitors showing world markets gave a ghostly light, and their potentially seizure-inducing, flickering screens almost caused vertigo, the kind one gets peering into a chasm before one's first bungee plunge. If you comprehended all the money zipping around in the ether, you'd really be overwhelmed and dizzy.

I mentioned, "Brad, I read this article [later a book] by someone named Burton Malkiel called *A Random Walk Down Wall Street*. It's about his contention that a random walk is a statistical fact that no one can predict future stock behavior, especially in the short run, based upon past history. According to Malkiel, mathematicians call a sequence of numbers produced by chance a random walk with one clear exception regarding the stock market; namely, there's a long term, upward trend in most averages."

Malkiel was notorious in stock market circles for hypothesizing that random walk would allow a blindfolded monkey, throwing darts at the WSJ's stock quotes, could choose stocks with about equal results as professionals—stock analysts, traders, fund managers. He later deeply regretted this simian metaphor. The astute reader will wonder why the monkey has to be blindfolded. To the market advice Don't fight the Fed, we could add the phase, or the monkey.

Not offended, Brad retorted, "Don't believe everything you read. In my case, I only believe what I don't read. Kidding." With his eyes constantly darting up and checking the screens, he went on. "Yeah, I know about Malkiel, but I don't believe it. I agree that sometimes there're statistical illusions, but I've made a lot of money with my methods and skill. I use The Elliot Wave Theory, which is a long-forgotten technique that Robert Prechter resurrected." After asking me to hold on a minute while he wrote an order that was prompted by something he saw in one market, he continued. "I suppose I'm a Contrarian, too, for Elliot Wave was out of favor for a long time. We Contrarians have a philosophic m.o. based upon avoiding the consensus view of stock picking and markets. And since I'm a gambler, I can live with a high beta, that is, high risk, volatility."

I propose that the reason that The Elliot Wave Theory was long forgotten and unused was precisely because it wasn't profitable. If this arcane, technical, charting method made tons of money, every Tom, Dick, and Swami would be using it. But I was loving this dialectical discussion. "I mean no disrespect," I apologized. "Malkiel believes that random walk disproves both technicians *and* fundamentalists who believe that they can outperform the market. And I guess I'm more of an adherent to Sell in May and go away."

Unfazed, he proposed, "But if I took you on as a client, because you're more conservative than most of my clients—even though you play poker—I'd put you in the Growth and Income, asset class. Let me correct myself. You're more conservative than most of my clients, *but* the fact you gamble doesn't reveal that you're an aggressive investor. No, it's the way you play that indicates you're conservative. So, as a client with your emotional makeup, I'd put you in Growth and Income like REITs, dividend paying stocks, and limited partnerships. Your return would come from dividends and yield-oriented securities. You have the potential for high yields and price appreciation, although there's risk, like all investments. I don't remember if I preached this to you in club. Increased complexity like derivatives, doesn't equal less risk. If anything, it's opposite."

"Thanks. I don't like to mix business and pleasure. Let me think about it."

45

Smo-kin, Rock and Mondegreens

OCCASIONALLY A CRITICAL MASS of players, 5–6, is lost, and the game grinds to a halt like an arthritic knee locking up; especially, when certain long-break offenders are in a game at the same time. Some superstitious players leave because "I don't feel right" or "I just had a horrendous bad beat, so I have to walk around." Other itinerant card smiths go *lobbying,* meaning taking a break to stroll around or go on a *treasure hunt*—looking to borrow money. Sometimes a person had a legitimate, understandable reason to leave for the bathroom, important phone call, personal business, fix, or lay down after a heart attack. Speaking of heart attacks, Gardenia lore asserts that once when paramedics were removing a dead patron who had a fatal coronary, 💀, someone at the table called to the Floor man, "Bring us a live one!" A little gallows or foxhole humor never killed anyone, did it? ≠ 💀.

Nevertheless, a common excuse to leave was "This dealer never deals me a winner." This is a self-confirming bias. After the player in question was infected with this scourge of superstition, perhaps the next time this dealer dealt to her or him, s/he played their hands differently, unwisely. And like a wish-fulfilling prophecy, the player lost more often than normal. Toss in selective memory and superstition, it's mind boggling that those games weren't always short.

During the lull I told Loophole Lester, "There's this category of misheard lyrics that're hilarious. They're called mondegreens, and they differ from parodies that are done on purpose. These are some I heard on the radio. I thought it was I've got two chickens to paralyze."

He laughed out loud. "That's great, JM. I get it. It's 'two tickets to paradise.' Eddie Money. You need a hearing aid."

I teased myself, "I took this test in the newspaper about whether you needed a hearing aid. If you got eight or above, you should consult your doctor. I got *twenty-four*! Yao. Yao Ming!" You know, whether I get a hearing aid or not, is addressed by the incomparable Dylan: "The ants're blowin' in the wind." I moved on, "How about 'Hit me with your pet shark?'"

He added, "'On a dark desert highway, Cool Whip in my hair instead.'"

$$$

From time to time the Santa Anas would blow in. The severely low humidity made it drier than a 3,000-year-old mummy's armpit. These devil winds blew in hot-for-action guys. Usually young, fast-talking, square-jawed tumbleweeds came to gamble. Maybe some of these poker transients were soon to be married, recently divorced, scored a big deal, were bequeathed a big inheritance, or were recently given a year to live. That said, "Bronco" was in town, two weeks as it turned out. It seemed he was there every day, for players revealed that he had played the previous day. Also, I made a rare Saturday afternoon play, and he was there. I asked him how he got his nickname, for he didn't seem like a cowboy. He winked and said, "No. my 'Bronco' nickname isn't from rodeo, but from women who've seen me in a Speedo."

Me [spit take].

Coincidentally, he and I had recently seen Jim Carey's 1994 monster hit, *The Mask*. It contained two famous lines that player would apply at appropriate moments. He'd feign bluffing or raising too much and mimic Carey saying, "Ooo, somebody *stop* me!" Or if someone else was on a huge rush and raising too frequently, we'd loudly intone, "*Smo*-kin!" In my Quote, Movie, Drink game, the appropriate drink would be Smoke and Mirrors. Perfect for poker. "I see dead people." Sixth Sense. Zombie.

$$\$\$\$$$

Being a nonsmoker, the toxic, foul-smelling smoke fumes aggravated me and others. When a puffer blew smoke or left his or her butt burning, I invariably got fuming mad. Ironically, even smokers were bothered by secondhand smoke. The upside, as a wise friend postulated, was that smokers were exactly the kind of opponent one wanted—they generally lacked self-discipline. They could be distracted and not totally focused on the game while anticipating their next fix. But outweighing the pluses were the harmful effects of secondhand smoke, and smoking seemed to calm the inhalers.

Be that as it may, until California outlawed smoking in the casinos in 1998, a hazy pall hovered over tables like an inversion layer over Los Angeles during a Stage 2 smog alert. It was horrendously worse in the Asian Games sections, maybe a Stage 3, where puffers used nicotine smoke as their incense, and it surely incensed their nonsmoking neighbors. But no matter the section, smokers had to be conscious that their smoke signals billowing out of their ashtrays bothered nonsmokers, because they'd been asked to extinguish their smokes hundreds of times. With the courtesy of a serial killer, the real butts were chain smokers who semi-obliviously lit one cigarette with the prior one, took a puff, and then placed it in an ashtray.

Without throwing too much shade, if poker is sometimes a self-punishment, surely smoking also can be a self-abasement. Go ahead and kill yourself slowly, but your smoke is a toxic externality. Please keep your bad habits to yourself. But I scold.

$$\$\$\$$$

Virge was sitting alone at an empty table. I joined him. "What's goin' on, JM?"

"Hey, Virge. Not a whole lot. Are you taking a break or are you done?"

"Yeah, I won some, about $500, so I quit. I'm waiting for Brenda. She's in a juicy game and wants to milk it some more."

"Virge, we talked about California's initiative to ban smoking in the casinos. Read my letter to our state senator." When I pulled it from my Banana Republic and handed it to him, he almost choked when he saw its length.

After he finished it, he said, "Great. I hope it passes. You know I don't smoke, but Brenda does, and *even she's* in favor of banning it. She figures she'll smoke less if she has to go outside. She's funny. She thinks if she quits, she'll gain a lot of weight and won't want to be seen in public. I asked her, 'What do you care what others think?'"

"Exactly. I'm sensitive, too, but really, what should we care what others think of us?" I opined.

"You know opinions are like assholes. Everyone has one."

"But you know, Virge, I've always marched to the beat of my own rum, so it's surprising that I fret over others' opinions. It's ironic. And I think irony is ironic." What a wit.

Brenda had an enormous rush tonight. Everyone has big rushes, but she was a master of finessing the hell out of good cards and pushing her rush. Opponents jammed out of her way, and, thus, she could *steal* more pots. She came over, said hi to me, and asked her husband to rack up the *load* she won in the big game. I saw him carry her six racks with a $1,000 chip—more than $7,000—to the window.

$$$

On a break, I walked by the gift shop. Glancing up at the TV, there's a host, actor John Davidson, introducing a man dressed in clothes so loud they screamed Huckster. Dave Del Dotto and Davidson are standing on a beach in Hawaii preaching, "No one ever excused his way to success." Dave, self-proclaimed real estate expert, was selling his course called the Cash Flow System. He further proffered, "Successful people do what unsuccessful people are unwilling to do." Slicker than dolphin sweat. I walked away thinking and dreaming.

Dave was pitching just as Tom Vu did in his infomercial on a yacht. Realize, Tom could rent, not own, the yacht, mansion, and Rolls for his spot, and hire the babes. Update. I don't know where Tom Vu is now, but decades later I've heard and seen new ads from Robert Allen and Dave Del Dotto shilling their expertise through seminars, books, and DVDs.

However, that they were still hustling didn't imbue confidence in their real estate investing methods. If they'd followed their own advice, they'd be "El Chapo" rich. Also, they made tons selling their tapes, programs, and, in Allen's case, having best-selling books.

46

"Mr. Interruptus" and "U.H.M."

POKER IS BOTH MONOTONOUS and action-packed. In our insular environment, like being in a bizarre Biosphere, we continue playing in the normal, wavelike rhythm of shuffling and dealing, shuffling and dealing, and rinse and repeat. Playing the hands and playing the players, the latter sometimes more important than the cards. We vie for pot after pot, and having minutes and hours drain away like air from a slow tire leak. We hear poker's peculiar sounds: The cicada-like clicking of chips also similar to an office floor resounding with mouse-clicking; the humdrum drumming or rattling of chip on chip; the rapid staccato, snapping sounds of shuffled cards: Tic-tic-tic-tic-thunk; the recurring litany of Bet, Raise, Call, Fold, "You win"; the droning background, white noise; gossipy chatter; and the depressing whine of losers and the happy laughter of winners.

I described Kelly earlier as a Bike Casino regular. Like Raj, generally Kelly was unpleasant to play against in part because Kelly was a priggish, hypercritical table captain.

Tonight, Kelly wanted to retaliate for Interruptus' many boring questions. (Sometimes boring questions relieve poker boredom.) Thus, in his typical soft-spoken, rather ingratiating manner, Kelly posed this to Interruptus, "Okay. Let me ask *you* a trivia question for a change. I have a bunch of questions in a queue for you."

"You mean like a queue and A?"

Kelly pondered out loud, "Does it ever stop? Listen, do you know who Lisa Lisa's boyfriend is?" Before Interruptus could think, Kelly said, "Duran Duran. Or I would've accepted Mr. Mister."

Interruptus had a dumbfounded look on his kisser, cocked his head left, and he said, "What? So you want repeating names like Boutros Boutros-Ghali? And do they have to be from cities with stuttering names like Walla Walla?"

$$$

Mr. Interruptus and his prominent proboscis, nosed over to our table to kibitz a little while he waited to get into the game. Standing behind the table, he couldn't help noting, "There're four kinds of people in the world. Those who make it happen, those who watch it happen, those who wonder what happened, and those who ask what the hell happened."

Recall Ms. Yulu Unwin, the unhinged harridan who ate my pie, and who seemed to want her cake and eat it too. She was getting destroyed and in an even more sour mood than usual. She retorted, "And then there's you. A fifth kind of person who, it happens, never shuts up."

Interruptus kept his cool, and with *sang froid* replied, "What the hell just happened?"

Everyone laughed including the dealer and Yulu.

He concluded, "Those who make it happen, the movers and shakers are known as *machers* in Yiddish and in the moving picture biz…"

Per chance, a new dealer was entering the box. The faith-based superstition-ados called her Ms. Fortune. She was dealing a little quickly and sloppily, for she didn't have an accurate System of a Down. Thus, she delivered a card toward Yulu, an Ace, that flipped over. Of course, Yulu, by law, couldn't keep it. This ill omen didn't help Yulu's mood when two

A's flopped. A short while later, Yulu's boyfriend came over. "Hey, babe. How're you doing?"

"This idiot dealer flipped my Ace over, and I'd have flopped trips and won the hand. Good news is, I'm playing with idiots, especially this one in seat eight. It's like a game of dupes. The bad news is I'm stuck three racks [normally one bought in for one rack]. Let's take a break."

After they left, seat two and four were discussing her. Sitting in seat three, I heard their soft analysis. Player two, "She berates seat eight who puts a bad beat on her, and then tells him how to play the hand better."

Seat four, originally from India, concurs under his breath, "Yeah. She's a real *memsahib*. Why would you want to teach bad players to play better? And don't you want bad players in the game who consistently take the worst of it? What a *badmaash, yaar*."

Seat two and I thought that four said bad ass, so we ignored it. Seat two then observed, "Her boyfriend isn't bad looking and seems nice. I think he plays way lower limits, so I don't think he's very knowledgeable about poker. But how could someone go with her?"

Seat four got off a great riposte, "Maybe she's the man."

I almost did another spit take with my Coke. After cleaning up my drool and regaining my composure, I speculated, "Do you know what I think they do for foreplay? He grovels in front of her submissively, licks her boots, and she tells him bad beat stories."

"That's cruel, JM," said Seat two.

My conjecture was, "Not only that, but we know who wears the pants in that family."

"Yes, and who wears the panties," Seat four added.

$$$

Once a waitress got Yulu's order wrong, and normally this isn't noteworthy—all of us have had meal snafus. But remarkably, thirty minutes later, assembled by her food tray were her waitress, Floor woman, food and beverage manager, chef, and the casino manager. She insisted her eggs be prepared, presented, and seasoned with Heinz just so, which was impossible for the kitchen. It was like Nicholson in the cafe in *Five Easy Pieces*. The upshot of this brouhaha was that diplomatic negotiations of the highest order were necessitated, and they resulted in a Solomon-like compromise rivaling SALT. I recall it involved an oven temperature increase, the eggs atop a substitute bed and a seasoning close to Heinz. She quipped that maybe they'd start stocking Heinz. "Heinz sight is 20-20." Peace spread over the top section like a perfect sunny side up. The players at our table happily resumed a quiet and full table—she wanted to be dealt out during her forty-minute-long parley.

This is a prime example why I nicknamed her "U.H.M." (Stop if you want to guess). A couple of players guessed what the last two letters meant. Without humility, I believe these initials perfectly captured her: Ultra High Maintenance.

Luck smiled, or maybe sneered upon me, and I had the pleasure of playing against Yulu weeks later. Perhaps her EQ needed polishing, but she was a very worthy adversary and very intelligent—passing the California Bar exam. When I told her that I'd given her the nickname U.H.M., and did she want to know what it stood for, she declined. She knew it'd probably be unflattering.

$$$

Like the Bay of Fundy tides, one player left and another rolled in. "Short Route's in the house," Todd announced. Then he greeted me, "JM, what's shakin', your bacon? Hey, JM. You often said that there ain't no free meal.

Then how can you bluff? If you win a pot by bluffing isn't that getting something for nothing?"

Like a flip-flopping politician, I hate it when someone uses my own words against me. "I-I ... Listen, Todd. Pulling off a successful bluff in limit is rare. Mathematically the opponent only has to call, let's say $40, to win a pot containing $300–$600. Hold on. I see a logic flaw. Just now I commented on the *caller* who calls a small fraction of the pot size. A bluffer's failure doesn't address your point. I don't think a bluffer is getting something for nothing, for he's gotta take a big risk. Also, a successful bluff might result from a big-time investment—years of study, learning the right conditions, and observations of a potential victim. But mainly I feel that unless you're a great player, most will be *net losers* on their bluffs."

"Yeah, I suppose" Todd muttered. "Point is you're trying to get something for nothing. And occasionally you're going to bluff and win that $600 pot."

I expounded further. "I feel that bluffing is similar to an advertising budget. If you never bluff, opponents'll always have an easy fold when you bet. Unless they have a strong hand. They won't pay you off when you want. Bluffs insert some uncertainty in their minds."

"Right on," he conceded.

"In the long run, maybe the pots you win by bluffing aren't free but are a calculated risk and cost of business."

Todd raised a valid point remarking, "Successfully bluffing also depends upon your skill, and the opponent's skill, or lack of it. Sometimes it's easier to bluff a strong player."

"Certainly. Anyway, I don't know if I've refuted your contention that I'm wrong to say There ain't no free lunch, at least applied to bluffin—"

"Oh, my stars," May Faire pleaded. "I don't care! Can't you guys see I'm losing big time and only have microchips? Be quiet and let me get even. If I ever get even, I'll never play again.

Todd and I laughed. Todd concluded, "Lesgo, bizel. Keep steppin' on."

47

The Free Lunch Bunch

TONIGHT, THERE WERE FIVE players away from the table, so the remainder wouldn't take the blind. Without an acceptable quorum, the game temporarily sputtered to a halt.

May Faire broached the free lunch bunch idea, a subject that I've flailed in excruciating detail. "JM. I was contemplating your mantra that there isn't a free lunch. What about when I park in Hollywood at a free spot posted two hours, and I go over two hours? I save money by not parking in a pay lot. Isn't that… no. I'll answer my own question. If they mark my tire, and I get a ticket, that parking wasn't free. In fact, all the times that I've saved money by gambling that I wouldn't go over time, all that money over a year Is wiped out by one ticket. And the stress of worrying about it and returning to look on my windshield with a lottery player's anticipation, it isn't worth it. And sometimes you pull into a spot that has extra time on a meter, but that's trivial." May added, "How about free food samples at the grocery store? Halloween candy? Coupons?"

I answered, "Trifling, but I'll grant you Halloween candy, unless you hand out candy, then it's breakeven at best. And a coupon price must *actually* be less than the regular price. Sometimes stores bait and switch."

"How about duplicating friends' records, cassettes, DVDs?"

"That's like sharing your Netflix password, you owe them favors in return."

She broached, "TV?"

I replied, "Commercials." Granted, some items, services appear to be free, for example, free Wi-Fi at coffee shops, free cigarette samples or drug hits; however, according to Professor Richard B. McKenzie in *Why Popcorn Costs So Much at the Movies*, customers pay indirectly through higher-priced coffee, becoming addicted, respectively. I remember clever promotions that gave a free play in a new style game in CA, or one free pull, spin, entry as part of a Vegas vacation package. Seems like a hit of something addictive, gambling.

May had a brainstorm. "But what about people who collect recyclables for money? Aren't they getting something for nothing?"

"Well, I don't think they're in the free lunch bunch. Think about it, May. They work extremely hard, often in extreme weather." I thought of and altered the adage, *Red dildo at night, sailors' delight; red dildo in the morning, sailors take warning.* "To me, they work harder than most people and below minimum wage. In filthy conditions, with no benefits. No, I wouldn't say that they're getting a free pass."

As I had compassion for the homeless, my heart went out to these poor souls. Some came from US or foreign poverty with few educational or job opportunities. Some lacked occupational training or were laid off. Some suffered mental shortcomings.

May joked, "At least the recycling brigade sets their own hours and work in fresh air. Sign me up." She wasn't being callous or mean but trying to be facetious.

Brad, who'd been using this down time to look at the *WSJ*, heard snippets of our conversation and asked, "Why are you talking about scavengers? Wait a minute!" He saw one of our MINAs (missing-in-non-action) players surreptitiously returning to our table to see if the game had resumed. "Hey, seat one. Are you going to take your blind so we can get the game going again?" Seat one sheepishly shook his head no and quickly scurried away to continue lobbying. We knew he avoided playing short-handed like it was visiting Ebola territory. Brad shouted after him, "Come on. You'll make it five handed."

Disregarding that, I picked up the thread, "Brad, to answer your question about scavengers, May and I've been having this on-going debate. I claim that there ain't no free lunch, getting something for nothing. May contends there are, or tries to find, exceptions to the rule. She brought up recycling scavengers."

Brad folded up his *WSJ*. "Hmm. For the most part I agree, JM." With his usual self-deprecating wit, Brad added, "And I know some people think stockbrokers are swindling scavengers and greedy, too. Warren Buffet, 'The Oracle of Omaha,' reputedly said of investing in companies, Buy beer; sell greed. Truth be told, probably about 80 percent of private stockbrokers lose money for their clients—not me, though. But there's an interesting portfolio strategy as close to a free meal ticket that I know of. By adding a mix of foreign stocks, or better, international stock mutual funds, you can increase the average return while reducing the portfolio's risk. At least that's the theory. For example, I might add some EAFE stocks to my portfolio—"

May and I simultaneously tried to stop him. She asked, "Ee-fah who now?"

"Sorry. E-A-F-E stands for stocks of companies based in Europe, Australia, and the Far East. When the US is in a down cycle, the EAFE stocks do better than American stocks. And vice versa. They add good returns to my portfolio."

I summarized, "It seems like a no brainer. I get better returns with less risk by adding a mixture of foreign stocks with my US stocks than if I just had all US *or* all foreign stocks."

"Right," Brad nodded.

Even though I hadn't played with Boston Donny in a long time, for he apparently had other business ventures simmering, he was here tonight. He'd listened, wisely and quietly absorbing all this, and he finally spoke up. "I read ahr heahd somewhah that ah S&P 500 lahge-capitahl mutural fund, a passive inderx fund, retahned about one and a half pahcent annually bettah than yawr actively managed lahge-cap, mutural funds. This was ovah twenty-five yers; 1975 toah 2005. That tells the whole stahry!"

Totally agreeing with Boston, I facetiously added, "But you know the universal, boilerplate disclaimers and caveats, Past performance cannot guarantee future results."

"Boston" quipped, "Sawtah like ah No Limit Hold 'em hands."

Brad added, "I just had an idea disproving your belief that you can't get something for nothing. What about squatters?"

I countered, "Sure they live rent free, but it's stealing and stealing's always something for nothing. *But* it's illegal."

May interjected, "You boys lost me at Ee-fah stocks, but I just saw the cocktail waitress go by. How about cocktail coasters? They're free."

Brad answered for me, as if we were on the same page, "No, the drink on top the coaster makes your liver pay. You could say, Your liver is a giver."

Boston perked up and said, "Hey, look ovah therah!"

Eventually seat two returned and sat down. Brad asked him, "Where were you for so long? The game stopped."

"I was in the bathroom."

Brad teased, "Number one and or two?"

Seat two replied, "Maybe neither. Maybe number three. Throwing up."

"Yuck. Whatever number, did you wash your hands?"

"No. I like to share."

Brad impishly bragged, "You know, my girlfriend lives with me, and she says when I pee, I swing it around like a lariat." He demonstrates as if he's swinging the end of a hose. "She complains she has to clean it up."

May interjected, "Maybe it's just me, but if a man can do that, I think he's kinda lucky. This was so unexpected that everyone roared.

As it happened, a player named Phan was hiding at a distant, empty table. Seeing seat two return and sit down, Phan also returned, sat down and the game resumed. Phan was about forty, five foot seven, super active, and usually pleasant unless, like most, he felt wronged. I labeled him "Ticcing" Phan on my player profile card, for he had a severe tic, crick in his neck. He'd quickly flick his head left and right, snap it forward and back, to try and crack it. But his most defining idiosyncrasy was pounding his neck's cervical region with a chip rack. Hard tap-tap-tap-tap. He also cleaned his ears with a straightened paper clip. Scritch-scritch-scritch. Tap-tap-tap. Phan had more tics than hairpins in an MRI chamber. He desperately needed medical attention. While most bragged, including me, about how expensive our cars, clothes, jewelry or watches were, he was proud that his watch cost $9 and was five years old.

Not speaking English very well, he usually kept quiet. He also had an extreme Vietnamese accent and knew it; therefore, he good-naturedly put up with our teasing. "Phan, you need a peach therapist."

"I know I don't peak Englick too good."

One time a cocktail waitress swiveled by, and he told us, "I lyk small on top. She too volumptuous ... I lye saddle."

When a player essentially doubles the stakes in a hand by posting chips in the pot, voluntarily raising, without looking at their cards, s/he *live straddles*. This is different than the blinds that are mandatory. Often the straddler, usually an action player, might play a hand they normally wouldn't because they already have money in. They suck themselves in. Phan definitely was the opposite of too tie (tight)—really lye (live). Straddling jacked up the game, and we loved his action and personality.

$$$

Most all loved live, loose, action players. I chanced to play with another extremely live one like Phan. From time to time, CC, whom I nicknamed

"Caribbean Charlie," would arrive and pump up the game like when Bangkok stumbled into The Bike flush with proceeds from a big deal. Due to the popularity of 2003's *Jerry Maguire*, CC would shout, "Show me the money!" when he arrived. CC enjoyed throwing his money around, making it rain, and he loved to gamble even more than his Travellers One Barrel Rum—and that's saying something. He was extremely affable, tall, very lean, had a broad face with a perpetual smile. He was dark-skinned, not Black, for he hailed from Belize. Moreover, he was born in Jamaica.

He possessed two other unique characteristics. First, he had an incredible ability to hold his liquor. He seemed like a very seasoned, Saharan camel with the astounding bladder capacity of the *Hindenburg*. 💀. I vow that I saw him drink about seven beers, two or three One Barrel Rums by Travellers, and two espressos without going to the bathroom. In essence, what a constitution. Personally, after two brewskis, regardless of my position, I'd have to go to the bathroom to make my bladder gladder. After three, I'd have to sprint to the bathroom, or I'd burst like a water balloon being filled by a 3-inch attack fire hose. Second, when he'd been playing and, thus, drinking for a few hours, he spoke with an even more relaxed Jamaican patois with an accent that was almost undecipherable to an untrained ear. He had a penchant and joy in massaging the language. Like Cockney rhyming slang, he called cocktails ox tails. While joking and imbibing, to indicate that he was raising, he snapped out, "Razor Ruddock." The reason CC used heavyweight Donovan Ruddock's nickname, Razor, to show he was raising was obvious, for it sounded like raise.

Assuming one heard CC's words correctly and could decipher his rum hijacked, semi-slurred patois, still the meaning was jumbled. I defy you to decipher this adage, my favorite: "Lika downin' manh clotcha stross. It meant "Like a drowning man clutches for straws."

How do I know these are his words? I smiled along with him, and I just asked him. Still, his meaning wasn't entirely comprehensible. Now, if he'd said, "Dat lika stross data broka camel's back," I could've deduced. I'd twist another straw related saying to: I drew the short dildo.

He had another proverb: "Remember same knife that stick the sheep stick the goat, too." Whaa? This may have been Santeria, but who knows? Someone quipped, "Translator to table four."

Equally, once CC was discussing a hand in progress with his friend sitting behind him; whereupon someone irritated by this game's plunge from logical to maniacal, someone on tilt, cited the rule English only and asked Caribbean Charlie, "Please speak English."

CC laughingly replied, "We are!"

On went his drinking, frequently calling out Ox tails, chuckling, bantering. Clarification: When CC was drinking and cutting a hurricane swath, it wasn't so much strategic, staid, rational poker as it was really Gambling. The captain has turned on the fasten seat belt sign and prepared for turbulent weather. The variance and fluctuations were ginormous. These swings were like Triple Witching Hours on Wall Street. CC raised almost every hand. Affecting a CHP attitude, I teased him saying, "Sir, you have exceeded your limit on raises per round."

He paused and devilishly stared at me. Then playfully and frowning fake offence, he looked back at the other players, and he shouted, "Razor Ruddock!" He was a wild card all right.

I was grateful for the many times I got even or scored big wins when he sailed into our game. Still, even if one has the best of it in the long run, in the short run of a few hours, one can go broke. (In the long run, a losing streak could last weeks or months.) Others, however, were puling nits who hated the absurd action and variance CC, this proxy of all bad beats, brought. He might get phenomenally lucky on a few hands.

Remember the disheveled, bison-like player, Buff? His fashion sense wasn't so much eclectic as neglectic. He stuffed his unchiseled chest into a tee reading, "Your ridiculous opinion has been noted." After CC bad beat

Buff in a big pot, Buff got steamed and sneered, "Nigh-*ROBE*-ay! What in the hell were you doing in the pot?"

CC replied, "Well, I had three outs."

Buff replied, "Yeah, but two of them were the exits."

Or people would scratch their heads and say to CC, "You didn't have anything on the flop—no pair, no draw—and you took one off." (*Floating* is staying for a bet or two to see if the turn gives him a draw. Wanting to go from zero to hero.)

Paraphrasing *Card Player* columnist, Andy Glazer, A good fisher neither wants to scare away the fish, nor teach the carp how to avoid the hook. Still and all, I firmly believe the loser of a hand should be pleasant to the live one. JM's Law #8 (Be courteous as possible and nice to the live ones.) S/he should utilize the stock statement, "Nye hand, sir, miss." I laughed and said that to Caribbean Charlie many times. I didn't begrudge him taking the worst of it, having little tactical advantage, and occasionally besting me in a hand. That's poker and life.

There was another combatant at the table who took the bad beats and swings in stride. After enduring a particularly bad beat when he started with pocket rockets (two A's), he said, "CC, it's okay that you beat me with J-6 offsuit. Nye hand. I came here voluntarily."

I jumped in, "Yeah, but I'm different. Sadly, Hollywood Park Casino's poker police know where I live. They came to my place and threatened me with a gun to my head. They said that I must go and gamble."

CC smiled affably at the player who had his pocket A's cracked and philosophically noted, "Jah provides da bread."

$$$

Drinking, laughing, playing, and Razoring continued. Toss in singing. CC would order a drink for a friend or two who were sweating him. They were his Caribbean chums, and they weren't supporting him so much as riding the free lunch bunch gravy train for free food and drink.

One of them saw a cocktail waitress named Indigo glide by like a summer, billowing cumulus floating over the Gulf, and he started singing "Caribbean Queen."

I asked, "Who sang that?" [Billy Ocean]

CC cryptically answered, "Luke' ric-card' em-bah ah mu' tay…" He slammed a stack of chips onto the table, shouting, "Razor Ruddick!"

48

A Question of Unanswerables

NORMALLY, AFTER I PUT my initials on the board, I try to talk to someone who has just left the game or who's getting up for a break. Barring that, I watch the action from a respectable distance. Tonight, I saw Ricardo get up. I asked him if was leaving his game. He said no, he was going out to smoke some weed. I walked with him. As with most poker buds, I love to discuss poker craft. I'd ask him, or Virge, about a hand I'd played, and what would they've done. After describing the situation, player(s) involved, way the betting unfolded on all the rounds, size of the pot, my image, table's vibe, other intangibles, etc., in the spur of the moment Ricardo'd invariably derive a plan that I may have thought about for many minutes, if not an hour. He'd quickly say, "*Jefe*, here's what I'd do. I'd bet right out, for if I go for a check raise, the opponent may check, and I probably lose one sure bet." Whereas, Virge and I sometimes disagreed, I felt Ricardo always came up with the optimal play.

Hold 'em players often ask, What does *The Book* say? Seems Ricardo could've authored, or at least co-authored, *The Book*. I suppose that since *it*'s myth, he'd be a ghostwriter. But the majority of the clueless adhered to other fictional, humorous scribbles such as *Any Two Will Do* and its sequel, *One Out Is Enough*.

Back inside on watch, I spied Mo E. leaving with a truck load of checks. He had so many chips that I approached and asked him if I could help him. "Good evening, Mo, do you need a hand?"

As I helped him rack up, some poor victim of his magnificent rush asked him, "Mo, do you give lessons?"

He replied, "Of course."

"How much?"

"They're free."

"You give poker lessons for free? At the rate you won today, you could charge $100 per hour."

"Oh, I get paid in a different way."

"How's that, Mo?"

"I teach the wrong stuff." Another wounded victim, who'd hemorrhaged chips, said, "You had a hellofa rush, but you gave me a hellofa rash."

As Mo E. pulled away from the table like an overloaded barge, I asked, "Obviously the game was great for you, but how was it to play?"

"That game was so soft, but also hard. There're some weak players, but they'll chase your strong hands down and try to beat you on the river. That's why I was lucky—they chased but didn't catch me. You can raise and raise before the flop, but they won't fold. The only way to get them out is to shoot them."

"Juicy. So maybe shoot them twice to be sure."

"No, JM. Seat nine would throw chips in as he fell to the floor."

I laughed. "Thanks for the input. The game'll probably change by the time I get in, but maybe nine will still be there." I didn't consider this sour grapes, for I chose to play evenings, not afternoons; hence, I accepted the texture of a game that I got.

Along with seat nine, Paul Pimpus was in the game. He was employed by another poker emporium, rose through the ranks and became a Dealer Coordinator (DC). Some DCs, like many regular dealers, enjoyed playing poker. With all due respect, dealers usually played lower limits than me. Paul was playing $20 Hold 'em with us tonight and was somewhat buzzed.

He loved to talk in different accents, and tonight he had a brogue. "Aye ah-doun't think ya 'av anytheeng. So, Aye'm gonna raise you, laddie." After he won the hand, he said, "Thank ye, laddie, for the bonnie pot o' gold. But that's not how ta bluff, is it now?"

Other players got into the Irish spirit(s), and somehow, we got on the subject of leprechauns and shillelaghs. Someone was inspired to pose this: "On land, what would be more dangerous, a leprechaun or a shark?" He and Ricardo decided that a leprechaun would be the most dangerous, on land. I voted, however, for the shark. Even though land isn't its natural habitat, leprechauns are mythical. Between hands, Paul concocted a game within our poker game of questions never before asked. To wit: What's tastier, kimchee or Existentialism? By the way, kimchee is like Vishnu by way of being a world destroyer. What's more cheerful, a dildo or a dangling participle? (Don't bite off more than you can dildo.) Who plays *futbol* better, midfielder David Beckham or the Manchester Unified Field Theory? Who is the handsomest among Keith Richards, Tom Petty, Ric Ocasek, or Lyle Lovett? (Trick question). Does time run backwards faster in *Star Trek's* "City on the Edge of Tomorrow" or in counting time in either BC or BCE? Who's a better reggae musician, a quark or IBM's Watson?

$$$

A week later Ricardo asked me, "*¿Cómo estás, jefe?* You know I think you're a gambllero-a gambler and *caballero*. Hey, remember last week when we were discussing questions never asked before?"

To be funny I answered, "*Qui, señor.*"

"I thought of a serious question. Unless forced, why do people living in a dictatorship or totalitarian regime bother to vote? But a while ago, I read this book by Heimberg & Gomberg called *Would You Rather?* I think Paul, the DC, may've borrowed the concept from that book. It poses dilemmas such as the following. Would you rather fight Mike Tyson or talk like him? Have your head explode or implode? Watch porn with your parents or watch porno of you parents?"

Home players remember, there's no right answer. In another parlor game, "If you could have one power, what would it be?" Mensan Andrew Krause wrote, "The power to lay and collect taxes."

Ricardo teasingly asked, "JM. In a similar vein, if you could be any superhero, who'd you be? I know I'd pick Superman because of his strength and ability to fly, etc. Who'd you pick? Superwoman?"

"Me. No, I'd want to be Super Fly 'cause he's so cool and turned the table on the Man."

Subsequently, Virge ribbed, "Hey, JM. I've got one of those never asked questions. JM, you've bought the last two rounds. Can I buy this one?"

Everyone laughed. Exaggeratedly wincing and doing a double take, I replied "Whaa? I'm-I'm trying to quit and don't want to be a problem drinker."

Ricardo chimed, "Henny Youngman says a problem drinker is someone who never buys."

Virge was enjoying this. "That's JM." After the chuckles subsided, he asked, "Hey. I've been meaning to ask you. What's the third English word with all the vowels in order?"

"Yeah, I remember saying I'd tell you if you gave up and—" I looked down at my new hand I saw two A's. "Excuse me, Virge. I reraise!"

Another player, Schaeffer Screwell, joined us. He had recently immigrated from Las Vegas. We started debating the dealers' competency here, Hollywood Park versus Commerce Casino's dealers. The standard HPH (hands per hour) was about 34–35 depending on loose or tight action and players' alacrity; accordingly, big, multi-way pots having a great deal of raising, betting. Decision points among many players took longer to complete than pots in a tight, rockish game with only two combatants. Four voted for Hollywood Park's dealer proficiency, and three for the card warehouse,

Commerce. The remainder wisely abstained. Schaeffer Screwell presented his case. "The dealers at Commerce average about eighty years old. They get out about ten hands an hour and make a lot of errors."

If a dealer misdeals or otherwise errs, a Floor person has to rectify it and obviously these errors take time to correct.

Someone pertinently asked, "Schaeffer, have you played at both places equally?"

"Yes, about the same number of months. But I noticed something else. The difference between dealers in Vegas and LA is that LA dealers think they're good players." Ouch!

Paul Pimpus almost choked back his Beefeater 24 and tonic.

Schaeffer, in a conciliatory tone, asked Paul Pimpus, "Sorry. You a dealer?"

"No, but a lot of my friends are."

49

Third Tectonic Shift and Superstition III

TO RECAPITULATE, IF THE first geologic inflection point in the poker landscape was casinos opening outside Gardenia, then the second upheaval, the beginning of a new geological age, was California's legalization of non-draw poker. Eventually, when clubs began offering no limit Hold 'em (NLH), what Doyle Brunson called "The Cadillac" of poker games, there were almost imperceptible squiggles on a chart foretelling increased seismic activity in Poker World. As a result, the third geological thrust combined the increasing popularity of NLH with NLH tournaments.

Continuing the metaphor, the fault lines of tournament play, already existed for many years; however, mostly they were limit structure. This transition to NLH-style competitions was like a slow slip earthquake, not a violent magnitude 8.0, if you get my continental drift.

While there isn't an exact date for this shift to NLH tourneys, a milestone might be 2003. Prior to 2003, surface conditions and pressures had been building for new poker dynamics, a different style of play, no limit. The 1998 movie *Rounders* also boosted interest in NLH, as did the advent of online gambling around the same time. Poker websites also increasingly pumped advertising money into TV ads encouraging online gambling and emphasizing a no limit format. In its own right online gambling was like a blind thrust earthquake resulting in a minor, tech-tronic shift. Still, many onsite players preferred live interplay and doubted web security. More about Russ Hamilton's scandalous story later. Assuredly, playing online was convenient; namely, one didn't have to clean up, dress, commute, and wait for a suitable game, but rather just sit at the 'puter and perhaps play one to ten games at once.

Two events transpired in 2003 that made it a watershed year. First, cable's Travel Channel started televising its World Poker Tour (WPT) tournaments that focused attention on no limit Hold 'em. Second, Tennessean Chris Moneymaker parlayed a $39 online, satellite entry into $2.5 million when he won the 2003 World Series of Poker (WSOP). A non-pro winning the WSOP resulted in the Moneymaker Effect. It absolutely gave hope to every player in the world. Las Vegas' annual WSOP became the epicenter of the shift, a new locust. I dreamt of producing *World Series of Poker: The Musical.*

Thereafter, casinos started offering more NLH both in tournament and cash, ring game formats. In other words, limit games were no longer the only game in town. Unlike the first two historic changes, this third one evolved over years following 2003. Which two formats—limit or NLH—will be the pretender or the contender? *Or* will another GMO arise?

In Frank Herbert's *Dune* Princess Irulan says, "If history teaches us anything, it is simply this: Every revolution carries within it the seeds of its own destruction." This echoes Karl Marx: "Capitalism contains the seeds of its own destruction." Paraphrasing Marx, in the capitalists' chase for ever higher profits, they shed workers for machines. The higher return on capital means that the share of profits rises, the share of wages falls, and soon the mass of the population isn't earning enough to buy the goods capitalism produces. My footnote. The Darwinian concept of survival of the fittest is crucial to capitalism.

Three side pots. 1. NLH rewards, demands gear shifting and aggressiveness. Aggressiveness good; timidity bad. By utilizing *carpe diem,* our boldness might win a pot. (But *carpe dildo* wasn't so good in most cases.) Playing NLH is similar to a tactician or general going to war—s/he has to have an objective and understand the enemy, its goals, needs, and methods.

Getting inside an opponent's head, prior to poker battle is like Sun Tzu's *The Art of War*, and it's exponentially more pertinent to NLH than Limit games. 2. In-person, big buy-in NLH tourneys don't have NTAs, but your competition is stronger. Incidentally, ultimately the winner had no bad beats. Think about it. 3. NLH cash or ring games are somewhat boring with a lot of downtime while a group of sharks and figurants loll around, waiting for a monster hand and flop.

Paralleling the three poker inflection points, career had three phases: Jacks or Better to Open (high draw); Lowball; Hold 'em. I envision my journey like dissolute, dissipated Tom Rakewell in William Hogarth's allegorical paintings *The Rake's Progress*.

$$$

Just as having professional dealers created new opportunities for players to invoke stupidstitions, likewise Hold 'em's rise created the use of a new type of lucky charm. I mentioned earlier that before Lowball's subduction under Hold 'em, some gamblers kept all sorts of lucky objects on the table. In hindsight, am I having a crisis of faith in demeaning superstition? No, I don't mean I now believe in superstitions, but I mean I'm less likely to denigrate it. In all fairness I grant that there could be a placebo effect for the stupidstitious, i.e., they might be calmer, more focused, better disciplined—all in all play better—which would hurt my profits. But how do the following actions help avoid bad luck? If you spill salt from a shaker, you have to throw some over your left shoulder. One of the weirder superstitions is don't light three cigarettes with one match. WTF? Don't open an umbrella indoors or bad luck will rain down. What about in a tent? A sub. OMG.

As I had once advised Virge to avoid complaining at the table, he coached me, "JM, why're you complaining about illogical and superstitious people? They're exactly the kind you want. You should be able to take money off them."

I think I've flayed my superstition distain to the point of exhaustion, and I barely have strength for one more. I repeat: Superstition bad; logic good. Moreover, I wonder if it can ever be beneficial? Witness when Hawaiian guides and docents say, "We ask that you not take any volcanic rock, sand or coral home for souvenirs. If every one of the millions of tourists took home a piece of our islands, there wouldn't be any more Hawaii. Plus, it's bad luck. Every year we get one of these souvenirs mailed back with a note, 'Since I took this, I've had nothing but bad luck.'"

In this case, superstition has a positive effect. I hope my recitation hasn't been as tedious as someone describing their *absorbing* dream and by miming.

$$$

With Hold 'em's domination, card toppers became *de rigeur*. For you non-players, one's Hold 'em hand is two cards which, if left unguarded, can be fouled by other cards intermingling. Or a dealer, assuming that the loose cards are discards, could scoop them into the muck, and, thereby, kill that hand. ☠. To prevent this, and to free a hand for betting, eating, etc., one legally can place a weighted object, a topper, on their cards.

Just as during the pre-Hold 'em days when players kept all manner of lucky, ceremonial trinkets on the table to channel good luck, now they move these talismans atop their cards. You see all types and sizes of pyramids made of most alloys known to man. Toy superheroes are favored—The Hulk, Superman, Batman, but strangely, not The Invisible Man. I saw a devil once or twice. (The devil's in the dildos). Whether or not gambling's a sin, I'll leave that verdict to philosophers or theologians. That said, the most paradoxical card protectors are the multitude of religious-themed ones which reside in the realm of religious icons and quasi-holy relics. I've seen plastic-enclosed, golf-ball-sized globs with Jesus or Mary inside. Some patrons, as a matter of faith, *believe* they possessed either a bone fragment from Christ himself, a splinter of the cross, or, let me profanely add, at least a toothpick from the Last Supper. I theorize that utilizing these relics can be considered white magic, not black. Encased pictures of one's kids are popular. (A picture's worth a thousand words, or three thousand in my case. And while experts say brevity is the soul of wit, brevity isn't in my usable vocabulary.)

Probably the most common fetishes are in the coin, medallion, chip family: Heavy chips from a website or other gambling hall specifically designed for protecting one's cards, commemorative coins or chips from all over the world, and US silver or gold coins sometimes encased in plastic. One gambler went so far as to make a little urn-like can inscribed with this message: "Ashes of opponents who try to outplay me."

The most intriguing, Zen-ish topper is, ironically, a top-like, silver-dollar-sized spinner. Some of these totems are fairly heavy with a casino or website advertisement on top. The obverse side has a bearing in the center that allows it to spin. Some even have knurled edges for a better spinning grip. One customarily spins it just before the flop, but I'm at a loss to explain why. Naturally, from boredom and or tension, one can whirl it anytime. I believe rather than spinning it, the moment(s) can be better spent planning what one'll do in certain situations: Consider the habits of those in the pot, calculate odds on drawing hands, etc.

However, I speculated that by carrying my own card cap might mark me as a regular or even a pro. Am I being stupidstitious? No. Hence, I used a stack of chips to hold my two cards, and by doing so, a dealer never fouled my hand. I've only killed, ☠, my own Hold 'em hand once or twice in decades because of inattention and or exhaustion. *C'est la guerre.*

$$\$\$\$$$

Let me bundle two scattered subjects mentioned above. A dealer is a professional, and as such, some are better than others. Far be it from me to cast half ass-persions, for I'm not error-free. Drowsiness, caused by boredom holds sways over players and dealers. But when a dealer kills a player's hand by scooping it into the discards, it's usually because of carelessness and or lack of attention. Here's another example of dealer boredom. Countless times I've seen a new dealer enter our Hold 'em game having just left dealing a 7 Stud game. On autopilot, they correctly deal two cards to players, but then deal a third face up. They saw but didn't *see* two blinds and no antes, huge clues for what to deal. They'd quickly realize that this was a misdeal when players said stop. Another instance of unprofessionalism, Ms. Fortune, to relieve ennui, sometimes started dealing a few cards to the right, counterclockwise. She'd quickly correct it with a laugh, but if one's losing, one didn't want dealer mischief and misdeals that wasted precious time. Remember that regarding deck changes and slow drivers, I conceitedly feel my time is vastly more valuable than theirs (LOL). Yet, it's certain in this relationship that the customers' time is more precious than a dealer's.

50

Pickup Lines and Janelle

EVEN THOUGH MY BUDDY Shah Kwah was married now, he agreed to act as my wingman and go to a party hosted by SCORE (Successful Corporate Organizing and Rejuvenating Events). How ironic that he was my wingman, and we used to compete playing Biplanes. "How's married life, Shah? Did you have to beg to get a free night out?"

"No, JM. I'm the main bread winner, so I have some bargaining chips. I told you a while back I didn't want to play higher limits, so that I wouldn't get stuck too much and want to play late. Also, I don't want to go out too much without my wife."

"Yeah, you don't want to get divorced. I heard a funny line last night on 'NYPD Blue.' Andy Sipowicz says, 'Marriage is like trying to haul a grand piano up to the eighth floor. If that rope breaks, you'd better run like hell.'"

"Katherine Hepburn said, 'Sometimes I wonder if men and women really suit each other. Perhaps they should live next door and just visit now and then.'"

I see various stages of a marriage; it transmutes. Early, when the couple is deeply in love, it's almost like infatuation like the euphoria of drugs. In fact, this stage is like being in a dopamine-induced euphoria. In this phase one spouse might fear death, as normal, but dreads the beloved dying first, 💀, maybe while flying. I'm compelled to point out that in early aviation, they said any landing you could walk away from was a good one; likewise, any dildoing you can walk away from is a good one.

I was trying to imbibe moderately to keep my wits about me. I boldly told Shah, "All right. I'm going to make a strafing run. Wish me luck."

"Technically you're making a reconnaissance sortie, but I'm gonna enjoy watching them shooting you down ... just like I did in Biplanes," he chuckled with a dancing gleam in his eyes and slight, customary seated pogoing.

I reconnoitered over to a lovely, and I tried, tried I tell ya, to open with icebreakers tailored to my target. I knew but *didn't* try the following cheesy pickup lines: Did you fall from the sky, because I think heaven's missing an angel? Are you from Tennessee, because you're the only ten I see? Do you want some raisons? No, then how about a date? (Take it from me, these don't work.) Another corny line I'd never had the nerve to try was a so-called *Bad "Papa" Hemingway line* from Woody Allen's *Midnight in Paris*; namely, "Have you ever shot a charging lion?" You'd really have to have huge stones (or just not care anymore) to blurt out the following line. Imagine this exchange. Man, "You know what would look good on your ears? Your knees." She'd be forgiven for rejoining, "You know what would taste good in your mouth?" Man, "I have a guess, but I'm afraid to say it." Woman, "Your foot." Man, "Not my guess."

No, I wanted to create custom-made openers. "It's really cool. Your dress matches your eyes." "Hi, I'm John. What's your sig—I mean what's your signature line?" By looking at these openings, we have one view. But looking at the end game—did I get a true, honest phone number—depicts a different picture. I learned that women generally don't want to hurt a guy's feelings. Some developed stock answers for guys they weren't inter-ested in. "Oh, I'm just so busy I don't have time." Yeah, right. But if a Brad Pitt or Chris Hemsworth, or whomever rocked their world, asked, they'd feign reluctance, but that number'd be in her phone, blouse or pants very quickly. (BTW, the three Hemsworth boys replaced the four Baldwin bros on the handsome scale.)

Another diplomatic deflection regularly heard was, "I'm *flattered*, but I can't because ..." This one must be imbedded in a chip in baby girls at birth. Or "I'm sort of dating someone now." Sorta? Whaa? You cannot make up your mind? "I don't give out my phone number, but if you'll give me your number I'll call." I am racking my brain as I tickle the keyboard to recall if any woman ever called back. Nope. Or "Let me think about going out with you," and then she disappears like a magician's assistant.

These seem disingenuous. Bless their hearts, thanks for the consideration. And call me goofy, but I don't mind honesty. I'd rather hear, "No, thank you," not some stock fabrication. If you aren't interested, I'll understand, accept, and survive. This isn't my first rejection rodeo or being bucked. We're adults here in the singles' jungle, out to meet people, so rejection goes with colonialism.

Despite this diatribe, there're a few mild, acceptable denials that don't bruise my fragile, male ego. "That's sweet, but I'm not interested." Okay, that's clear and short. Because I like younger women, one of the best, most tactful, rebuff is, without doubt, "That's flattering, but I'd like to date someone closer to my own age." I generously offer you ladies these more humorous declines, "... Someone with perhaps a little less life experience," or "Someone closer to my looks ranking." Ouch. Goofy out.

In contrast, women have it easy breaking the ice. She just has to insert phrases into her conversation like, "Till your brains fall out" or "Can I stir your drink... with my tongue?" I'm obviously joking, but all women have to do is show interest, and "a wop bam boom."

$$$

I told Shah that I had a friend, Brody, whose jam was picking up strippers in their club. He swore he was successful by asking them out in the following way.

Pick up artiste Brody, "How about having breakfast with me. What's the worse than can happen, they burn your scrambled eggs?"

Stripper Candide, "I'm tired of your always coming on to me. Suppose I call the bouncer, and Mace Fragg pounds on you till you're scrambled?"

Brody, "That's okay. What's the worst that can happen, I die and go see baby Jesus?"

Candide, "Believe it or not, I'm a Jehovah's Witness ... Not practicing."

"Well, if you won't go out, how about your girlfriend. I think her name's Lourdes. I hear one of her lap dances'll cure your ills. Do you think she'd have breakfast with me?"

Continuing to Shah I recalled, "Brody bragged once, 'Yeah, I used to date this belly dancer, but I had to break up.' So, I innocently asked, 'Why?' He says, 'It was quite a grind ... I couldn't stomach it anymore.' He also told me once, 'I swear I've seen that Vietnamese stripper before somewhere.' It seemed her name was, was, ah. Dae. Yeah, Dae Ja-Vu."

"JM, that's terrible!" Shaw cried.

Undeterred, I continued to Shah, "It wasn't me that said that. You know, I love Dae Ja-Vu's name. Hey, do people with great memories have more or less *déjà vu*?"

$$$

Despite my fumbling, lame arsenal of openings, I did meet Janelle who worked for a medical device manufacturer. She seemed open to my humor and my looks weren't displeasing or at least not revolting. She appeared to have an open, and not judging a book by its cover attitude, which I needed. These promising traits meshed with her attractiveness. Lithe, tall, blonde, with divine facial features. She looked athletic, too. Even at this soiree where dressy was suggested, she classed up the place. Just my type for a long-term relationship. Clarification. It was one thing for a squeeze to look nice and be sexually available, but I had incredibly high standards for someone I might marry. I hear the female readers, those still left, exclaiming, "You men!"

I boldly approached this stunning creature. "Hi, I'm John Maynard. I was watching you dance, and your lustrous hair was flowing as if it were waltzing. To whom am I having the pleasure of addressing?"

"Hi, John. I've never heard that one before. I'm Janelle Châteauneuf."

"Janelle Shat-oh-who-now?"

"Château-*neuf*, like the ninth castle, chateau."

"Oh, I get it. Would you like a glass of wine?"

She replied, "Who wouldn't?"

After I got the wine of her choice, Pinot Noir, (Ironically not Chateauneuf-du-Pape) I went on, "And, your Royal Highness, are you in the wine industry?"

"*Quell droll.* No, but nice of you to ask. I'm a medical devices manager. I go around the country to hospitals, research centers, medical device manufacturers, biopharmaceutical developers, nursing homes, and so forth, to try improving our existing products or develop new ones."

"Cool." I gushed, "You get to travel, which I love to do. You're on the company's dime. And I'll bet it never gets boring."

"Oh, the traveling can get old, but, no, the work doesn't get boring. And occasionally I, or we, have an ah-ha moment when we think of a new product. It's very rewarding and exciting."

"Wonderful. Do you ever see a product or improvement that you'd want to make yourself? To patent and make for a company you'd own?"

"I've thought of it, but I'm under contract to the corporation, and they'd own the rights."

"The reason I asked is that I have entrepreneurial aspirations. I'm always looking for that million-dollar idea."

"Cool. What do you do now?"

"Oh, I'm not defined by my work," I joked. Seeing this answer was unsatisfactory, I proffered, "I love work. It's enthralling, and I can watch it for hours."

With my apparent evasiveness, she seemed a little wary as though she was considering poking some weird-looking, dormant creature. "I didn't mean to pry, but you asked me about my work. I asked about yours to get to know you, and not hog the conversation."

"Sorry. I was trying to be philosophic and funny. I guess I didn't succeed. I own a company that puts out video games."

"You mean like designs and sells them?"

"No. Perhaps I used a poor choice of words. My company places video and pinball games in our accounts. Pizza parlors, convenience stores, bars, restaurants with waiting areas, etc. And by the way," I quickly mumbled, "Imakemoneyplayinpoker."

"I see. I'm not really sure what you said at the end, but that wasn't so hard opening up was it?" She suggested, "Hey, do you want to dance?"

While we freestyle danced for about fifteen minutes, On the floor she was gracefully swaying and thinking. *He's quite intelligent and has a good sense of humor. I like his looks, and he seems to be a gentleman. But I wonder about his work, and he has some moves on the floor. I wonder if that carries over. What'll say if he asks me out? Will he? Well, since I'm not seeing anyone now after Baptiste, I'd give him a chance ...*

She shouted, "It's so hot out here."

"Wanna to sit down?"

She paused. "Wait! This is such a fantastic song."

Following my lead, she ruminated. *Yeah, Jean-Baptiste. He ends up being a light pusher, and now I might date someone who does something playing poker. I seem to have a penchant for bad boys or dangerous boys. Certainly non-traditional.*

Back at her seat where it was quieter, I said, "That was fun doing the swing. Did you ever notice when couples are dancing West or East Coast Swing, or the Lindy, they're usually smiling. You can't always say that about hip-hop dancing."

"Good point."

I plunged. "You spoke of opening up about myself. Speaking of openings, I see an opening here to ask if I may get your number."

"Sure. I'd like that."

I thought, *Nye!* She was like a Woody Allen heroine in smarts, looks and style. Just my type.

$$\$\$\$$$

"Hi, Janelle. It's JM, you know, John. How are you?"

"I'm quite busy right now, so I can't talk long."

"I wondered if you're in town this weekend, you wanna see a movie Saturday?"

"Who wouldn't? Yeah, I'm in town."

I suggested seeing the porn version of *Kill Bill Volume 1*, *Drill Bill*, or regular porn, *The Hung and the Restless*. She knew I was jesting.

She said, *"Oh, ha-ha. But let's touch bases later in the week."*

$$\$\$\$$$

Waiting in line for *Kill Bill Volume 1*, Janelle revealed, "I was out on the road in Kansas City, and one of the nurses complained that the cockroach traps that they'd been using weren't working anymore. Of course, this isn't our line of products, but I looked into it anyway. It seems that cockroaches have evolved to dislike the fructose corn syrup taste of the old trap bait. They actually jump away from it as if they're being shocked."

"That's interesting," I nodded. "Back in college, I lived in a little, 600-square-foot cottage. I usually didn't have cockroaches, but I saw one. So, I bought one of those Roach Motels. You know, 'They check in but never check out.'"

"Yeah, good tag line."

"I was very satisfied with their product, because about a week later I checked the trap, and there was an adult cockroach with about six babies trailing behind her in a line. Obviously, she'd given birth, and the babies got stuck too."

Janelle answered, "Awww. That must've been some sight. But about cockroaches evolving to hate a bait's taste, let me add survival of the fittest. A few years ago, I went to Club Med in Playa Blanca, Mexico. The red ants on the bathroom tiles skittered about at about three times the speed of a US ant. I figured that over generations, thousands of GMs, staff, and vacationers squashed the slower red ants. The sprinter gene was passed on and on while the ants with plodder genes died off." In this case the race went to the swift, not the slow and steady. This adaptation fully demonstrated the survival of the fittest theory. This is opposite to the trite saying, Slow and steady wins the dildo.

After our minds were blown by *Kill Bill: Volume I*, we discussed, dissected, okay, did a postmortem on, it. She told me about this great Russian filmmaker, Andrei Tarkovsky, who believed that what draws us to film is the gift of time: "Time lost or spent or not yet had."

51

Hypnotic

AT ONE OF MY video accounts, the Dew Drop Inn, the bartender, Pratt, greeted me heartily. "Hey, John. What's the word, thunderbird?"

"Mums."

"Mumm Champagne?"

I proudly said, "No. mum's the word. I finally came up with a reply to your rhyming greetings. Anyway, I'm just here to make my rounds and collect the *gelt* and split it." After I checked and cleaned the machines, counted the money, recorded the digit counter tally, and compared it to the previous number, I gave him his split. He signed for it and gave me a Coke. "Pretty slow this afternoon," I alertly noted.

"Yeah, like always. It'll pick up in a few hours when the guys who quit early pull in," he observed.

"When's happy hour?"

He pointed to his temple and said, "In here it never ends. You know I had an interesting experience last night. My wife, Stella, has a girlfriend, Gina, who practices hypnosis. My wife's been after me to let Gina come over and hypnotize me to cut down on smoking. So, I went along, and it was fantastic."

I perked up—you might say I wasn't mesmerized—because I've always wondered about hypnotism's authenticity and value. I know post-hypnotic suggestions are commands given to a person under hypnosis that s/he acts on when awake and they won't do anything against their morals. These commands help people achieve goals such as stopping an addiction or other unwanted behavior. I was intrigued if Gina could help me minimize Negative Turn Arounds.

But do posthypnotic suggestions work? I've seen people on TV clucking like chickens, going rigid as a door between two chairs, or slapping their knee when the hypnotist gave a specific cue. One golfer had the yips, and so he got professional hypnosis therapy. The therapist planted a posthypnotic suggestion that before the client putted, or when he was in a very stressful spot, he pull his ear lobe. After further appointments, the hypnotist asked the golfer how his putting was going. The golfer said his putting was steadier, but he couldn't understand why his left ear lobe was so sore.

"So, what happened?" I asked Pratt.

"In some ways it was like in the movies—let me get this guy a beer. Anyway, the room was supposed to be dim, quiet, and at a comfortable temperature. Gina told us that everyone could be hypnotized so long as they felt safe, trusted the hypnotist, and weren't schizophrenic, mentally disabled or sociopathic. And, ahem, more intelligent people were more receptive. Sooo—do you have the time to hear this?"

I encouraged him. "Yeah, so long as it doesn't interfere with your work."

"No problem. I recline in a comfy chair, and she has me close my eyes and breathe deeply for about a minute. She tells me, 'Slowly breathe in through your nose and out through your mouth. Breathe in peace and happiness. Exhale tension and cares. In and out.' She guides me into a world that takes me deeper and deeper. It was a happy place. But eventually she said, 'Now, I'm going to count to ten and when you get to ten, you'll be fully awake and totally refreshed as if you had a good night's sleep and you'll be happy and optimistic.' I didn't want to leave." With a serene smile after reliving the session, he said, "You might think it was weird, but it wasn't. It was great, John. It was one of the best experiences of my life."

"Yeah. I can see why. You know me, Pratt. I just realized that it's weird and ironic that the word weird has the e before the i, and not a letter c to be found. But to the issue of your problem, smoking, we all have problems. I wonder if hypnosis would help me with one of mine. You know that I play poker some evenings, so I have a problem with getting my butt out of the chair when I am ahead a good amount. Also, maybe hypnosis would help me connect with, find, and hold a girlfriend. So do you think you could get Gina's contact information, and I'll call her?"

"Yeah, will do. I suppose I could vouch for you. It's about the time people start piling in, so I better stop yakking. Thanks for coming in and for the money."

52

Wine and Janelle's Party

JANELLE POSSESSED A HIGH deferred gratification score; consequently, regarding our blooming relationship, she was as cautious as a Pinot Noir bud tentatively peeking out at the weather, deciding whether or not to bloom. Notoriously sensitive and hard to grow, Pinot has notes of black cherry and spice. Janelle had a light body, sinuous wine legs, with beautiful floral, herb flavors that linger on the long finish. Ah, *oui*. That described Janelle.

I was waiting in the restaurant she'd picked, The Velvet Porcupine, an ironic name and apropos to our relationship's pace which was like the porcupine's mating ritual; to wit, there's a great deal of sniffing, circling, and studying before proceeding cautiously. Janelle hustled in and apologized, "Hi, JM. Sorry I'm late."

"Not a problem."

She explained, "CHP pulled over a car to give a ticket. Now everyone has to slow down and rubberneck and see the poor slob that got busted. We've all been there, and we feel sorry for the poor guy."

"Yeah, we've all gotten tickets. But I'm really amazed and perplexed at people who say they've never been ticketed. How painfully slow and carefully they must drive. I can't comprehend driving that way all your life. You know, I vowed after waiting one to two hours in line during boot camp that I'd never complain about waiting in lines again. We had to stand in the merciless summer heat and oppressive humidity, but fortunately at parade rest not at attention. And we couldn't talk. Brutal. After that I always have something to read, like now."

As she got settled at the table, she exhaled and relaxed a little. "Doesn't it always seem to be when we're in a hurry? I suppose that's selective memory. Speaking of traffic snafus. One time on a dry, clear summer day, everyone's inching along expecting to see the CHP with a car on the shoulder, a fire or a wreck. As I get to a spot, ground zero you could say, there's a bunch of tissue paper floating and swirling in the air. Once we clear this flock of tissue paper, traffic speeds up to normal. These idiots were slowing to a crawl to avoid the chance of hitting toilet paper. Ignoramuses! God help us if it had been the more dangerous strands of triple-ply. Cretins. And traffic engineers have found that drivers have a natural reaction and tendency to slow down going uphill. Every day there's a bottleneck at the same place when drivers fail to maintain highway speed. Caltrans really ought to put signs reading Accelerate to maintain speed uphill. Drivers are morons."

"I agree totally, Janelle. Everybody else is a horrendous driver! But how do *you* deal with infernal, *fakakta* traffic backups?"

She joked, "I just lay on the horn."

She returned to timeliness, "I really try to be on time. One of my girlfriends has a master's in social work, and she gave me some MSW humor about punctuality. You can tell someone's personality by these. Somebody who's always late is aggressive. Someone perpetually early is anxious. And someone right on time is anal."

"That's hilarious. I never thought of it like that. Oh, no! I know right where I fit or sit."

"You're the last type, no disrespect."

"Ouch, you nailed me."

Inspecting the wine list, I noted, "Here's a wine label, L'Hermitage, that implies that it's made in a hermitage. Interesting. If a hermit lives in a hermitage; a rector in a rectory, a vicar in a vicarage, a parson in a parsonage, where would an asshole live? A hemorrhoidage? A rectorium? Wherever they lived, it'd rectum."

Half seriously she replied, "How sophomoric. No, below high school. More like elementary school. And you're being both profane and impolite discussing this before dinner. And I suppose you'd say skanks'd seek sanctuary in a skankuary."

We ordered wine and dinner. Janelle grinned and said, "I told you about my girlfriend in the beverage slash wine industry. After she sips her wine, she'll say, 'Not a vintage year, but a wet year with a rich harvest.' She'll swirl and carefully examine it and say, 'Wonderful, aromatic bouquet, deep color, nice fingers.' After she sips it noisily, she'll say something like, 'Acidity, with a hint of leather and earth notes. Complex finish.' She'll say stuff like 'Cherish your saliva.' It's better too much than too little."

"Yes, you've talked about her before, but what's her name?"

"Oh, sorry. Sherri. We were out last night."

My insecurity slash jealousy meter's needle jolted up about five-fold. I tried to be cool, and I did my best nonchalantly to ask, "Were you clubbing or just eating?"

"No, we went out to eat, and catch up. Anyway, she tells me how snobby the people are in the beverage industry. They'll say, 'Well, of course chain Hotel X has crappy product. They don't order ours.' So, we ordered *off the list.* You'll like this. One restaurant had a Chardonnay named, Berry White."

As our relationship was in the nascent stages, and being somewhat insecure around eligible, attractive women, I was relieved she wasn't at a night club. I knew she loved to dance. I suppose being indifferent to the non-eligible females who didn't match my ideal, high standards gave me a shield against emotional harm. Ironic is it not? To be confident, if not cocky, around some women and intimidated by another group.

Plowing ahead, I mentioned, "My buddy, Dr. Bahr, used to sip his wine and tilt his nose up and nasally say, 'This wine is pretentious and needs a good spanking.'"

"Clever."

Joel Stein in the *Los Angeles Times*, wrote, "When wine drinkers tell me they taste notes of cherries, tobacco and rose petals, usually all I can detect is a whole lot of jackass. I miss the days when we made fun of wine snobs for saying that a wine was 'ingratiating without being obsequious.'" Forgive my presumptuousness, but perhaps Joel could've improved detecting a whole lot of jackass by suggesting "I smell a whole lot of bullshit." Stein in turn then cited Gary Vaynerchuk who said, "I referred to [a] wine as the movie *Platoon*: Awesome beginning; terrible finish." *Mon Deux.*

"Janelle, do you want to try a piece of my salmon?"

"Who wouldn't?"

$$$

Janelle had a New Year's Eve party where I met most of her friends. There was Lillian who explained, "I'm a Pharmaceutical Sales Rep. There're only about 90,000 of us in the US. I met Janelle when we both worked at a Rochester hospital."

To show off I asked, "Rochester, New York or Minnesota, where the Mayo Clinic is?"

"You're right," Lillian replied. "It's homonymous, ambiguous if you will. No, Rochester, New York. She was investigating clinical and product ideas, and I was educating doctors and nurses about our product line, clinical trials and so forth. We became friends. Now I bump into her by chance, about three to four times a year, when we're both out in the field. Mmmm. You've got to try this canapé. Its spread just hits the bliss spot."

"I can guess, but what's the actual definition?"

"Yeah, you probably guessed it. Experimental psychologists who work for the processed food industry constantly search for the ingredients and mixture to deliver bliss to their product and increase sales."

Lillian introduced me to Dr. Ashram, from Kenya who, with her husband, Dr. Uhuru, knew Janelle from a local hospital.

"Dr. Ashram, I'd like you to meet JM. He's Janelle's boyfriend."

"You're a lucky guy. Nice to meet you, JM. Are you a doctor?"

"N-no. I wanted to be though."

"What happened?"

I used a bit from a comedian whose name escapes me, "You know if you dig up bones in an ancient land, you're an archaeologist or paleontologist. But it you do it in the US you're a grave robber. Big difference. That reminds me, I just saw Spielberg's new movie, *Thoracic Park*."

Dr. Ashram studied me and said, "So JM. Do you use comedy PRN to evade answering?"

"I don't know that term. What's NPR?" I asked.

She corrected me, "*PRN* is Latin for *pro re nata*—medical abbreviation for whenever necessary."

And Lillian didn't let me off the hook. She wanted to learn more about me for Janelle's sake, and added, "But I didn't hear your reason for not entering medicine." She laughed.

I shrugged and said, "It's a long story, like my life story." My feeble, febrile deflection got me out of explaining for a while.

Still, Dr. Ashram was on the case and determined to diagnose me.

Peering over her glasses at me with a clinical air, as though I was some blotchy, wheezing patient, she asked, "If you aren't a doctor, what do you do?"

Trying to wiggle out of answering would be futile, for she was very persistent and determined to pin me down, one might say vivisect me, regarding my work. I finally told her I had a company providing video games and confessed that I also earned money playing poker.

"So, in a way you *are* in medicine, a card-iologist."

"Really funny, Dr. Ashram. You might say I'm working in the poker MBA"

"You mean Master of Business Administration?"

"No, poker's MBA—Main Battle Area, the casino." Trying to exude as much confidence as possible, I was somewhat cowed by all the brain and financial earning power present. Like my insecurities around high powered women, I suppose I was intimidated by all the mainstream success there. However, as weird as it seems, sometimes traditional employees envied me for my maverick, devil may care, independence and lifestyle.

Dr. Ashram asked me, "Do you see that doctor over by the balcony?"

There were a half a dozen guests in a cluster like nodding mushrooms. "Which doctor?"

"Some think he's a *witch* doctor, but really, he's a psychiatrist. He loves the psychology of poker." Dr Ashram yelled over, "Hey, Walt! This guy presents as a professional poker player!"

I was mortified that everyone could hear that! Regaining my fractured composure, I said, "Poker's kind of my part-time job." Then I conjectured that, "Maybe you think my lifestyle is exciting, but 'The grass is always greener on the other side of the fence. But compared to the neighbor's landscaping, yours could be deciduous.'"

Walt came in at the very end of my thought, and so he only heard deciduous. He injected, "Oh, I love his rapping. So, JM, you play poker professionally. Do you also gamble on horses or bet sports?"

With a lowered voice I said, "When I was a young man, a friend took me to the track. He gave me a horse, and I bet $2. I vowed to myself if I won, I'd keep betting the profits. But if I lost, I'd never bet again, and I haven't. I did the same with wagering on football. I lost $100 on a team that was a lock to beat the spread. I've never bet again ..."

Walt asked, "How'd you get into your poker, ah, career?"

"When I was a young man, I wanted to get into lingerie. Then I considered being a cemetery director. Desirable because you're above everybody and no one talks back. Also, very little turnover."

Walt indulged me and patiently nodded, "Ha-ha. And people are dying to get into cemeteries."

We chatted with his co-workers, and Dr. Walt obviously was exaggerating, saying, "JM, do you know what a refractory period is? No? Well, it's the time it takes for a man after cumming to sexually reload, so to speak. Mine is about ten seconds," and his friends groaned. "Yeah, and my girlfriend says [in falsetto], *Oooh*, Walt, not again… and so soon."

Someone goaded him on. "Walt, tell JM how virile you are."

"Thanks. Just one of my sperm, on a crutch, could get a woman pregnant."

Lillian sighed and ruefully said, "I've heard these a hundred times."

JM commented, "I'd put your short refractory time in a hyperbolic chamber."

"You mean a hyper*baric* chamber."

"No. A hyperbolic chamber to pressurize exaggerations. That is, hyperboles."

To humor Walt, Lillian fed him a straight line, "Walt. I'm sure JM would like to know where'd you attend med school?"

"It was an IV League school. Rim shot!"

She whispered, "A hundred times," excused herself, and then she circulated onto the next eddy in the party. I continued listening to the shop talk and milled around. Eventually spying Janelle and Lillian gracing a conversation stand, I joined. They were discussing how doctors chose their respective specialties. "... Dermatology because it's mostly medicine but part *art*. Besides I work on the whole body, not just a limited area. We have a saying; 'Abscess makes the heart grow fonder.'"

Another said, "During my rotation I worked the ER. Man, I loved the excitement, adrenaline, having to make quick, accurate life or death decisions. Interestingly, the most crucial thing in the ER is time—to get info, diagnose and treat."

"I was sure that I wanted to be a surgeon, but after that rotation my third year, I was exhausted. I couldn't handle the gore, but mostly it was standing in the operating theater all day. And the mental stress. They say a good surgeon knows when to cut, but a great one knows when not to cut. I didn't think I had it."

When one said, "I considered Proctology," his friend teased saying, "By the way, your Proctologist called, and he found your head."

I whispered to Janelle, "Proctologist are curious if everything's gonna come out right. It's right up their alley."

Another doctor continued, "Oncology. I just couldn't handle so many ARTs."

I shot a quizzical look at Lillian who whispered, "ART. Approaching Room Temperature—death. [☠.] And they're discussing how they chose their specialty from approximately thirty-eight. Cardiologists enter their field because they have a lot of heart. Dermatologists are very rash. OB-GYN often labor under false miss-conceptions. Proctologists are curious if everything's gonna come out right. It's right up their alley. But you get the idea."

I whispered back, "By the way, their favorite movie is *Public Enema Number 1*. A group of them is called a pile. And I just made up this too, What's an Optometrist's theme song?"

Lillian patiently shook her head, "Tell me."

"It's Foreigner's 'Double Vision.' Or Johnny Nash's 'I Can See Clearly Now.' … But I get it. Urologists get pissed off easily."

Dr. Walt continued, "I heard you say Urologist, JM. You know what they call a group of urologists? A stream—"

I said, "Or a drip *or* hold."

"I'm glad you brought up the penile area. I had a friend who went into psychiatry when he learned of this mental illness, a delusional disorder called koro—"

When he wasn't looking, I whispered to Lillian, "Excuse us, Lillian" and we left. Janelle and I found a quiet tide pool where I observed, "You know Dr. Walt is jealous that I can set my own schedule and work for myself. This is The Grass is Always Greener syndrome. I mentioned more of my experiences with poker guys having heaps of sour grapes attitude."

She made a connection, said, "Yeah, sour grapes is like crying over spilled milk. And it's interesting. My English friends say, 'Grieving over *spilt* milk.'"

"Yeah, that's interesting. A word game I like is to combine two homilies into one. It's no use crying over spilled milk that's under the bridge. But that isn't as bad as 'Being dead in the water in the Shit Creek without a paddle and escaping, but you aren't out of the woodwork yet.' Make hay while the sun shines becomes 'Make hay and stick it where the sun don't shine.' How about, 'Having icing on your cake and eating it, too.'"

Ignoring these, she noted, "I think the better proverb is That's water over the dam rather than Water under the bridge. But another way of looking at The grass is always greener is The enemy of good is wanting something better which is about the same as If it ain't broke, don't fix it. Is it just me, but people in pain say, I wouldn't wish this on my worst enemy. But wouldn't you like to see your worst enemy suffer?"

"Yes! I'd want my poker foes suffer, make them cry and whine, and become Chip-a-Waaahs."

She semi-shouted, "Lillian, come help me and make it stop!"

Embarrassingly, too much champagne had pushed me over living on the edge.

53
Janelle

JANELLE AND I LEFT the Stones' concert and its 110 decibels, sound boarding torture, and my head was throbbing like a teenage boy's ... appetite. By the way, they took their name from the saying, A rolling stone gathers no moss. You know I prefer "A rolling dildo gathers no moss."

I loped into her apartment which displayed her classy sense of style with the colors all integrated, the accents flawless. The Mary Cassatt, John Singer Sargent, Winslow Homer, and Andrew Wyeth prints were superlative. The lighting and color scheme were vibrant; yet, overall, her digs were soothing. Yes, a well-educated, classy woman for me. I deposited my stuff, and I gave her a big smooch and pat on her firm rear. Her Chanel was sublime. I asked, "Do you want some Pinot?"

"Who wouldn't?"

Janelle returned and poured two glasses. "How was poker, ah, work last night?"

"I did well."

"*Vous pouvez vous estimer heureux.* You can consider yourself lucky."

"Do you want to hear about work?"

"Who wouldn't?"

"I went on this huge rush that I so richly deserve," I said with tongue in cheek. I guess that makes me cheeky. "It was of Biblical proportions. I was unconscious, making money hands over dildos, and in a zone. I like to describe a rush like tonight's as I was smoking the felt; that is, I was pushing in chips to bet, and dragging so many pots so fast, that the friction was almost igniting the felt. I think it may've been the first time I ever won ten hands in a row. Since it was so wonderfully unique, I didn't want to lose a hand and spoil a great story, I just got up and left." I applied part of JM's Law #1: Quitting At Peak (QAP).

"Then I went over and told Virge, I suppose bragged, about this incredible rush including making a bluff and catching one. I expounded that it isn't a win unless you cash out. For, as the clichés teach, 'You really can't count your dildos until they hatch,' and 'There's many a slip between the dildo, and lip. Virge congratulated me on my fast score and was very happy for me."

"Yeah, I am too," Janelle yawned.

About prematurely assuming one will or has booked a win can be dangerous. (Incidentally, prematurely assuming is better than prematurely ejaculating. Or so I've heard.) Once, I won $1,500 and walked out the door. Normally, I had booked a win. But one night, this happened, fortunately only once in my life. As I walked to my car, I saw this really live one park near me. He was so live that I knew he'd throw off money. I went back in to get in his game! What I thought was good luck turned into a disastrous NTA. Randomly, a kind of bad luck, I left, and he arrived at the same time, and both found spaces nearby. I suppose it was bad luck; yet I still own the NTA result that was caused by my greed.

Swirling my wine and still energized with my big, splendid score, I continued regaling Janelle. "Then Virge told me some more of his wild days as a young man in the Dallas area. He told me about a time he and his buds took a Whoopie Cushion to church. When the pastor told everyone to sit down, this buddy, Royce, plopped down hard on the Whoopie Cushion. *Blaaappp!* He said everyone was looking stunned, and his gang all tried to keep from laughing, but they couldn't hold it. Tears were coming out of Royce's eyes. Another time they were driving around and drinking Lone

Star per usual. Virge's friend Lou Pastafazool was sitting in his car on the side of the road when they drove near. Lou had eyes like a hawk, and he saw Virge's group coming from far off. Lou knew that there was a cop on a motorcycle waiting to catch speeders. So, he waved to warn them, but he forgot he was holding his beer bottle. When they slowed down and pulled over, he told them about the speed trap. They yelled at him, 'Are you crazy, Lou? Put the bottle down.' Virge had some good times," I concluded.

Ever patient, Janelle said, "Good times. Like Virge I'm happy you won. Is that why you left *la maison du jeux* early?"

"L. Mason the Jew?"

She explained, "Sorry. *La Maison du jeux*—the house of the games—the casino?" This is much classier than card barn or gambling joint.

"Oh, right. *Maison,* house; du, of the; *jeux,* games. You bet I left early. I may've mentioned Todd, who goes by Short Route, the ex-football player who is a real Don Juan. This Lothario has that *je ne sais quoi.* Anyway, his motto is I've got to bed them all."

"Oh, yeah, I remember. Men!"

"Yeah," I agreed. "We just want to squirt our testosterone around. Anyway, he came in last night with this new woman. She really wanted to play, but she was so drunk or stoned or both that she was slurring, knocking her chips all over, and couldn't follow the action. He sat behind her, but I'm really surprised he let her play. He said later that he couldn't convince her to stay home and save her money. But the funniest thing was while she was impeccably dressed, she apparently tried to reapply her warpaint after apparently fooling around. I mention she was impeccably attired, because it showed her fastidiousness. She had light rouge on her cheeks, but also randomly on her nose and upper lip. Her lipstick was in the general area of her mouth and had hints of Heath Ledger's face in Joker in *The Dark Knight.*

"They called her for a higher limit game. She obviously was wealthy, and she brought thousands to gamble with. After they left our game, someone at the table observed, 'It looks like she's been ridden hard, and put to bed wet. Yao Ming.'"

"Poor girl," Janelle empathized. "How could this guy—what's his name, Todd—put her in such a position? So, what if he bedded her, couldn't he keep her at home? Couldn't he entertain her without her losing a lot?"

"I can't fathom his reasons. Maybe it was her first rodeo. In his defense, he stayed with her rather than letting her drive alone to *la maison des cartes*. Maybe he's guilty of getting her wasted. But I'll bet you're sorry you said you wanted to hear about work—"

From the kitchen Janelle was shouted, "Babe! 'Springer's' on." It was our guilty pleasure at night to watch Jerry "Salacious" 'Springer.' I speculate that perhaps the audience feels better about themselves after seeing how desperate, sick, and disgusting some peoples' lives are. We're forewarned that these shows are akin to scripted pro wrestling and some dating shows; therefore, these guest outliers often seem too bizarre to be real but were actors. Moreover, it's human nature to watch train and car wrecks or auto racing expecting a pileup. As Michael Moore in *Bowling for Columbine* notes about news programming, "If it bleeds, it leads."

Ladies and gentlemen of the jury, I mention this is a guilty pleasure for two high class people. "Look. There's a three-hundred-pound domina-trix flaying this wimpy guy."

"Let's eat. You don't have to watch."

"You're wrong. I have to watch. My hands are tied."

"Honey, look! There's a thirty-year-old man who likes to wear dia-pers! He has a pacifier, baby bonnet, nipple rings and his twenty-year-old, anorexic girlfriend changes him. Yuck. That's sick."

"He's got some weird fetishes."

"Yeah, but aren't fetishes abnormal by definition?"

The audience is howling rabidly, "Jerry! Jerry! Jerry!" Get a life. Oh, wait. I'm watching, too! *"On our next show, why teen pregnancy rates drop after age nineteen.*" [Think about it]. Oh, by the way, we made sure that we tightly drew the curtains, window not wine curtains.

$$$

"And how was work today?" I asked Janelle.

"Work's okay, but I'd rather tell you about last night. I went to traffic court for the ticket I told you about to try and get traffic school. So, I'm already harried after work, but when I walk into the basement court room, there're about two hundred people there. I think Oh-my-God! I'll be here forever. The judge has a mic apparatus on his chest and asks everyone to put everything away, stop talking, and give him their undivided attention. He gives us a quick spiel saying if we all work together, we'll get out quickly. When he calls our name, he wants us to line up in front of the bailiff's desk. He'll ask each one their names and what do they want to plead. Later he sees a man reading the newspaper. He raises his voice, and pointing to the culprit, says, 'Bailiff, take that guy with the paper back to lockup.' That not only got the miscreant's attention, it got our undivided attention! We're all stunned as the Bailiff escorts the man back behind locked doors. You'd better believe, everyone in the room sat bolt upright, put down anything left on their laps, and there was complete silence."

I laughed and shook my head in amazement. "That's unbelievable. Scary. In the old days he would have been called a hanging judge. Did you ever find out if the man was held in contempt or what happened to him?"

"Fortunately, the Bailiff brought him back about thirty minutes later. Whew. I'll bet from then on he obeyed traffic laws religiously."

"You know. If I'm ever on trial, I'd want a jury of my wharves, not piers ..."

I could barely hear her groan, for the club's MC came on stage. He did a baritone Dangerfield riff, "Ooo. I tellya, I went to a tough high school. It was so tough our school newspaper had an obituary column."

$$$

Janelle's father was an orthopedist who invested most of his money in shopping mall developments. He perpetually complained to his kids about the vacancy rates and losing money. Or worse, he worried about bankruptcy during economic downturns. Therefore, Janelle had a massive aversion to financial instability. Still, like an ionic bond, she was paradoxically repelled by, and attracted to, men who were risk takers. After all, in a way her dad was a gambler. Aren't we all?

Eventually Janelle arrived at a funk in the road. To the left she could end our affair. To the right she could continue onward, although she foresaw a potential dead-end. Presumably she was savvy enough to avoid giving me an ultomato, as Groucho called it, to rejoin the corporate world. She knew better. Finally, we negotiated if I shunned a corporate job, I'd find another business endeavor. Still, we were at an impasse similar to a chess game, although a better analogy is *zugzwang* meaning a compulsion to move and a one-sided *zugzwang* is a squeeze.

Still, I wanted to keep Janelle as another type of squeeze, a main squeeze, and marry her. However, mainly I didn't want to make a move. I liked the status quo in our relationship, my lifestyle, and I wasn't compelled to want to change. We both had high standards, and hers included a partner who had job security and or steady income. If I gave in, perhaps she would respect me less. Who can decipher the feminine mind?

54

Female Sphex Wasp

I PLANNED TO DO my video rounds and then do some research on new business ideas at the college library which stayed open late. I ran into Chuck Fibonacci. As a business major he had an epiphany when he found his true religion, computer programming. Rather than doing course work, he was legendary for developing a poker program and going sleepless for days. JM's Law #10 pertaining to bare metal restored for computer programming: Long programming sessions and a good night's sleep don't meld. During his programming binges he was renowned for subsisting on Cokes and Mars Bars (an appropriate choice) which caused him to appear like a Biafran refuge, an anorexic Biafran at that. He hadn't changed much in twenty-five years or so with his rumpled clothes, tie-dyed tee, and sandy, disheveled, tousled hair. Library rules permitting, he would've been barefoot. A true anachronism. His gaunt face also accentuated his grey, Goyaesque eyes that still stared at you with laser intensity. "Chuck. Chuck Fibonacci. How the heck have you been?"

"John Maynard. Far out! What a trip to see you here."

I asked, "What're you doing now?"

"I'm still working on my PhD in computer science, but my real job is being a financial advisor." He paused. "I can tell by the way you're looking at me that you can't see me instilling trust the way I'm dressed. But I clean up nicely. I had an interesting conversation today with a client of mine.

He's rich but wants more return. He'd read about these floating bonds that purportedly gave much greater interest, but drastically reduced the risk."

"I'd like that, too. Where do I sign up?" Of course, I was joking about using him as a financial advisor. As previously noted, I didn't want to do financial business with anyone either in the poker demimonde or real world.

"That's the thing, John. There's no such animal that will give greater returns for less risk. I'm sure you know that. You can get greater than average returns, but you have to assume greater risk. Or you can gain safety of principle but you'll sacrifice some return. JM, do you know what a *ganef* is?"

"Yiddish for crook."

"Right. Some *ganefs* put their heads together and create certain investment instruments that make claims of higher returns with less risk. They know they can sell these things to some people. Look at mortgage-backed securities. They supposedly had underlying assets, *solid* real estate mortgages, that would insure the mortgage-backed security. They hoodwinked the bond and stock rating agencies like Moody's, Finch, S & P, and they got triple A ratings. No one understood these things. Then these securities got bundled together and sold to other entities like pension funds, other banks' portfolios, wealthy investors, international corporations, and hedge funds. When real estate values tanked, so did these safe investments. You know it crashed the market; bankrupted banks and mortgage companies. On and on. So, like my client, people, including sophisticated businesspeople, wanted to have the best of both worlds. Wanted to dance but not pay the piper."

I thought, *Bingo! They want a free dildo and eat it too.*

He asked me, "How about you? What are you doing these days?"

"I have a company installing and servicing video games." As usual, I didn't mention that I played a lot of poker which I considered my side hustle. It was just simpler not having to justify myself. Earnings from *gambling* were still disdained in some circles.

"Too cool! Let's get together and chase some *wahines* ..."

$$$

Janelle and I phitzzed some ways back. 💀. Why? Same old song and dildo. I'd experienced with prior girlfriends. Because poker is gambling. My NTAs. Not having a corporate or steady job. My life had no security. Trust. I kept weird hours and was too emotionally closed off. I noted I'd had a dysfunctional life in foster homes, had to develop a strong self-survival instinct as a kid, and I learned to keep my feelings hidden deep. Janelle was a fantastic girlfriend, but I guess I blew it.

As part of my emotional equation, I often delve into whether I have subconscious needs for any of the following: Suffer NTAs. Paralleling this, have subterranean, psychological needs to have relationships end sadly. Fear commitment or true love, or is it predetermined that I never find true love? Do I want total freedom and independence more than love? I seem unable to salvage the relationship wrecks that are my life. Do I pine to self-punish, self-sabotage, shoot myself in the dildo, as the case may be, and believe that I deserve a trip to Tartarus? Shrink needed at JM's table of life.

"Life is a comedy to those who think, a tragedy to those who feel."— Jean Racine.

After Janelle's breakup, as one might guess, my spirits were tumbling down faster than the snow globe in *Citizen Kane*. "Rosebud." You've heard of the arc of history. Surely, the arc of my dating history was not a smooth, curved line. Its staccato timing was as irregular as a high-strung Pomeranian's incessant yapping at shadows or flapping. Not discouraged, about two months later Fibonacci and I agreed to attend a SCORE function. Later, while driving, we listened to an oldies station when Mark Dinning's 1960, morbid "Teen Angel" played. Wiping away a faux tear, Fibonacci said, "Cosmic! That's so macabre."

"Yeah. It's so gruesome that it's hilarious, but no more gruesome than what's gonna happen to you inside the club. As your wingman, I'm going to laugh watching you get Biplaned," I teased.

"What's that?" he asked.

"Oh, it's when a woman shoots down a man who's trying to pick her up."

He slipped into the 70s, "Right onnn."

I recalled Bobbie, the Alaskan woman with a high Marshmallow Test score. "You know, I just thought of this woman I knew back in my old Gardenia days, Bobbie. When she'd go night clubbing, she wouldn't take any money. She'd use her wiles to get everything paid for by men, and sometimes by other women."

A Burning Man *burnerd* would label her a Sparkle Pony. "They'd hit on her, buy her food and drinks, but if she wasn't interested, she'd give them a fake phone number, like the LAPD's." She told this to me without any shame. But it's so rude and inconsiderate to the drink buyer who probably just wanted to date her. I guess she thought, *I'll drink your drinks, but I don't want to see you ever again.* This behavior doesn't further honest human connecting or advance detente in the battle of the sexes. Similarly, I heard of despicable people, probably racists, long after WWII and Korean War who ran up big bills at Japanese or Korean restaurants and claimed they forgot their wallet. They didn't see Asian people as human.

Fibonacci was quiet for a while, then posited, "If that's her groove, she's exposing herself to an enfilade of Karmic crossfire, and she'll eventually be bitch slapped by the 'What goes around comes around hand.' Ya know, karma never sleeps."

"Man, I hope we don't meet that type tonight."

"I totally agree." After a while Fibonacci said, "I read this fascinating article about the female Sphex wasp."

"Never heard of them." I, who had taken a lot of biology classes, confessed.

"Barry Goldman wrote an editorial pointing out that we can't fix our political problems doing the same old things that haven't worked in the past. He cites behavioral scientists studying the female Sphex who stings and paralyzes a cricket; she drags it to a suitable hole in a tree; and she lays her eggs on the cricket. Thus, the babies will have food when they hatch."

"Sounds reasonable, and nature instilled survival lessons in the mom."

Fibonacci concurred. "Yes, survival of the fittest-type behavior. But the interesting thing is that before the wasp puts the cricket into a hole, she first goes in to examine it, probably as a precaution. While she's inside, the entomologists moved the paralyzed cricket away from the hole. When the mama wasp exits, she looks for the cricket."

I commented, "She'd probably think, 'I coulda swore I put it right here.'"

"Right. So, she goes and finds the moved cricket, and drags it back to the hole. But now, even though she's already checked the hole, she goes back in to recheck it. She has an internal rule mandating that she does this procedure over and over. In fact, the scientists moved the cricket forty times, and the Sphex did the same thing every time. It was funny. The scientists gave up doing the experiment before the Sphex. Goldman's point was that humans have this 'Sphexishness' internal rule whereby we continue to repeat senseless behaviors. Witness the hopeless war on drugs. Faraway, futile, foreign fights. Rational gun control. We continue to avoid acting. It's stupid not to have background checks for gun buyers and not to outlaw manufacturing and selling of military type assault weapons and high-capacity clips. And we think the gun industry, any industry really, can regulate themselves, and—"

A light bulb went on in my head, dimly, though, and I interrupted. "I have a saying about this Sphex waspish behavior. When a ritual becomes habitual, it's time to get spiritual and kick out—to change this behavior and to evolve. You've really got my attention with humans repeating inane actions. I have strong interest in two particular categories. One, Wall Street and bank self-regulation. And two, I have this self-defeating reaction that I call incurring a Negative Turn Around."

"What's that?"

I explained, "In short, while playing poker, sometimes I don't optimally quit a game. In a way, I'm like the wasp in repeatedly going into the Negative Turn Around hole, over and over on *ad infinitum*. I have to evolve, undergo metamorphosis. I'm proud of that analogy, Chuck. Like an insect, I need to metamorphosize to defeat this destructive behavior. And the side effects of these Negative Turn Arounds are like having nausea during sex."

He blurted, "Bummer. That reminds me of a condition I read about. Dyspareunia. That's when a woman has painful intercourse."

"That's grim!"

"For both partners. Anyway. To be continued. Looks like we're here. Let's go hunting."

"But not for crickets, unless there's a woman in there called Cricket."

"How about for White Anglo-Saxon Protestants?"

"I ain't partial ... Oh, I get it. WASPS. The Sphex wasp connection."

No discussion of wasps can be finalized unless we hear from Ogden Nash:

The wasp and all his numerous family

I look upon as a major calamity.

He throws open his nest with prodigality,

But I distrust his waspitality.

I bucked up my courage as I entered the stag-nation, and I muttered Stuart Smalley's self-affirmation, "I'm good enough. I'm smart enough.

And doggone it, people like me." I wondered if I had the nerve to use one of Fibonacci's pickup lines. "We haven't been introduced. I'm Mr. Right."

55

JM Gazes Back from a Dead-End

AS TIME WENT ON, I parlayed my first video games into newer games, added accounts, but I was still devoting considerable time and effort to my part time job, avocation—poker. There were two sweet attributes of video games. First, they were out there working their little CPU hearts out for me without my presence. I could play poker while, like Pac-Man, my machines gobbled quarters. Second, the old videos financed newer ones. As the old ones earned enough to pay their cost, eventually, I owned them free and clear. Henceforth, the cash flow, besides location3, was all positive like the Holy Grail of real estate investing. I put excess savings into stocks, options, gold. Yet, with stocks, I finally concluded that I couldn't beat the Big Boys and Girls of Wall Street, the biggest casino in the universe—check that, solar system. However, at the time I hadn't embraced what Burton Malkiel proved in his book, *A Random Walk Down Wall Street*; specifically, to buy and hold low cost, broad based, equity and bond index funds rather than individual stocks, bonds or mutual funds.

$$$

Back, way back, when my hair was black and my eyes were clear, there was an endless horizon of possibilities. Thinking back now is bittersweet. The Japanese beautifully express it as *setsunai*—concurrently happy and sad, wistful. In middle age, my scalp's clear and my eyes are black (bags).

Add that my eyes are jaundiced from high cholesterol, and one observes a wheezing husk of my jolly, youthful self.

In good conscience, even though I'm preachy, I could not avow that everything you want is on the other side of fear. I had a supertanker-load of fear. I didn't want to be one of those who spout off about creating the next big thing—a big plan, score, or idea—to deliver fame, fortune and happiness. Talk is cheap except when weak, spineless politicians do it in Congress. "So, the tongue is a little member and boasts of great things."—James 3:5. I didn't want to have the 'All hat, no cattle' affectation, or what the Brits call 'All mouth and no trousers.' I wanted my actions to speak louder than words.

Don't misunderstand me: I deny thinking I'm superior (although I probably am. LMFAO). Sadly, regarding my unfulfilled writing fantasy, I am one of these mournful, sorrowful wraiths, specters. "A poor player who struts his hour upon the stage, and then is heard no more." Place me among this countless, curious, craven clique who've let their dreams disappear like a vape cloud. Thus, I listlessly plodded along in life, maybe along Myrtle Avenue, punching the clock so to speak, shuffling like a half-alive automaton. Grinding out a living wage for bread. For some years after college, I tried to claw up the corporate, Jacob's ladder.

Woody Allen wrote, "If you want to make God laugh, tell him about your plans." Over the decades at the felt, I heard so many others' dreams and plans. "I'm gonna buy repo'ed cars at California and IRS auctions. Fix 'em up and sell 'em at a lot that I'll open."

"My brother started a used bookstore. I can still see the floor to ceiling shelves full of all these hard cover books. All the assorted colors like a rainbow, but with muted, faded colors. He mostly bought hard backs, but he had a small section of paperbacks that prospective sellers would just give him to get rid of them. But the most memorable thing was that stale, musty smell and the dust getting in your nose. I used to help him sort and alphabetize. He bought thousands of books for pennies and sold them for dollars. His profit margin was over 300 percent! That's not on each book, but store wide. That's what I want to do. Do you want to go in with me?"

"I have an idea for a Chinese restaurant with a Hard Rock-type vibe where we'll have local rock-and-roll bands play. I'll call it Wok and Woll. You wanna come in?"

One dreamer mentioned investing in a concrete dirigibles startup. For you from the late 60s generation, these dirigibles weren't going to be Led Zeppelins but something more tangible. You guessed it, Concrete Zeppelins. If they ever got his project off the ground, he would've cemented his place in aviation history (nyuck).

Various bigger thinkers, with more monetary and smarts wherewithal, expounded on investing following. Diamonds. Collectibles like vintage or limited production US cars, Chinese ceramics, investment grade stamps or coins (especially US). Although they couldn't afford Old Masters or famous artists, perhaps they could discover new artists or find a steal at garage sales. "You know fine art has a store of value."

"I'm gonna learn about. Arbitraging; trading in futures contracts, colloquially, futures (like crude oil, natural gas, corn, wheat, gold, silver, and my favorite, pork bellies, etc.; playing futures in financial instruments (like currency, bonds, and stocks) and in intangibles (like stock indexes and interest rates); buying or writing puts and calls; shorting stocks (a sell high, buy low variation of buy low, sell high); stock and bond swaps; buying mortgages and trust deeds; now, cryptocurrency.

"I'm going to find and join syndications buying raw or farmland. Thousands of us put money together, and we give it to the syndicator." And of course, during the late 1990s, stock market day traders were legion. I read the average day trader lasted about six months. Something new was always becoming trendy. Sometimes, though, 'The trend is not your friend.'"

"I'm going to figure out what to do with the millions of tons of rice husks that are the waste product of processing rice. The rice industry has to pay to remove and trash it. They'll pay you to haul it away, so if I can invent a use for it, I'll be rich."

With all due respect, many of these ideas were more entremanure than entrepreneur. Naturally, I must spin into Nothing dildoed, nothing gained.

Then there was the hoi polloi with high hopes in his or her gambling systems; for instance, people who devised horse and sports book betting methods. I had one friend who swore that he always won at keno when he went to Vegas. This seemingly very smart accountant said, "Here's my system. I keep track during the day of what numbers have been called. When I analyze that certain numbers haven't been hit in a while, I bet on those numbers." I couldn't believe his logic, or to me, lack of logic. I felt he suffered from confirmation bias, an unconscious tendency to filter info according to one's worldview. A person gravitates toward evidence that supports a certain idea(s) that fits with that person's preconceptions but ignores contradictory info. It's very similar to selective memory. Moreover, according to Behavioral Finance, confirmation bias narrowly applies to stock market investors who seem to remember their winners and attribute that to their skill. On the contrary, they rationalize and attribute losses to unusual, external factors.

It's no wonder my buddy swore that he won at keno. Telling him he possessed major Gambler's Fallacy thinking, he philosophically replied, "The past is a prologue." Yes, maybe in history, science, art, politics, personality, etc., but *not* in randomness.

My keno-playing buddy was an example of selective memory and hindsight bias. As George Augustus Sala noted, "A gambler with a system must be, to a greater or lesser extent, insane." As Shah Kwah noted, "If you have a system for beating Vegas, they'll send a stretch limo, not Gurney, for you. Just bring lots of Benjamins."

$$$

I want to touch on this. Poet Sumner A. Ingmark theorized, "Science gets leery, When gamblers talk theory." Gamblers are notorious for deciding based upon the Gambler's Fallacy. It's such an important concept that I'll summarize again. It's the tendency to think that future probabilities are altered by past events, when really the chances are unchanged. The fallacy arises from an erroneous conceptualization of the law of large numbers. For example, I've flipped heads ninety-nine times with this coin, so the chance of tails on the 100th flip is much greater than heads. This assumes an honest, fair coin. Similarly, they believe that balls (of roulette and keno), dice, or cards remember what occurred previously. These do not; they *cannot!* Point of clarification: Blackjack's a special case, the only casino game that is a non-independent outcome game. Theoretically, blackjack is (or used to be) beatable using perfectly implemented Revere's or Thorpe's counting systems. As I've hammered *ad nauseam*, about the Gambler's Fallacy, the cards in the shoe don't remember what occurred during the last shuffle; however, an error-free card counter can use the past, the count, to swing their odds from negative to slightly positive. Hence, if you were a perfect counting machine, had sufficient financial backing (a bankroll equal to the casino's), and were flawless in instituting the authors' strategies, you could beat blackjack. But guess what would happen if you did? The casino'd bar you... or worse. Vegas' ethos. Be-autiful!

Shah Kwah was a brilliant card counter, and early in our friendship we took a road trip to Lost Wages. A pit boss told him, "We know you're a counter, so we'll let you get even, but then you have to leave." How magnanimous. Hence, I ask you, "Is this a successful system?"

$$$

There was one hopeful who vowed, "I want to make a lotta money in the stock market. If I achieve that, and once I take care of my family and myself, I'll enter politics. I'd love to be President and do good things for America."

This poor, naive, deluded soul was I! I forgive myself, for it's easy to be idealistic when one doesn't have world experience.

As described, there were an armada of ill-fated, doomed fantasies. I was certain of one thing: Trying to make a living by gambling was a boneyard of dreams. Surely a dead-end. 💀. After poking fun at those people, disillusionment nipped at my heels like a possessive, hyper Shih Tzu. When I was despairing over bad luck in love, career and or cards, self-doubting myself and poker playing, when I whined to close friends that I wanted to write someday, I too was one of the forlorn. Again, I have babbled enough.

56

Showdown

ULTIMATELY ALL MY FUNDS were invested in the calibration venture with Tony, his brothers, and other investors. When Tony asked me to invest in his startup, he espoused, "You gotta have skin in the game to focus one's attention and efforts in the new enterprise." In my proverbial style, put your dildo where your mouth is. Initially our business made money, but now it was losing at an increasing rate. We had many conflicting ideas about how to save ourselves. As the former CEO of RJR-Nabisco, Ross Johnson, used to say, "Did you ever try steering a motorboat from water skis?"

Now it was too late to find a white knight. My partners were true believers that things would turn around if we just kept the faith. "If we can ride out the storm, stay the course, we'll be fine." Naturally, this required more capital. Tony and his family found another investor, and, thereby, we bought more time. This reprieve gave us another opportunity to stay solvent, hopefully expand, or, at a minimum, pay our loans back. One rarely gets a second chance. Hoping for a do over in life is like being in a prison yard and expecting compassion from prison guards. So, I've heard. But I've had my share of mulligans.

Eventually, once again the Flying Fickle Finger of Fate jabbed us, and the economy worsened. Because of that and belt tightening in our market, the company began to Biplane downward again. The partners wanted more cash infusions from each of us. We're all aware of the typical flight or fight reactions, but I experienced another, lesser-known reaction. Like analysis paralysis—comparing and despairing—I froze. (In a crisis, about 80 percent freeze; 10 percent panic and scream; and 10 percent are proactive and take charge.) I couldn't decide, and I just kept hitting snooze. I was massively conflicted between two alternative strategies. First, being ever optimistic, I believed the adage that behind every dark cloud there's a silver lining. (But if you're pessimistic, Behind every silver lining, there's a dark cloud, or a silver dildo.) Thus, I hoped that economic conditions would improve—in US history they always had. Second, a contrary worldview espouses, Don't throw good dildos after bad. Act in haste; repent in leisure. Damn! Damned if you do; dildoed if you don't. What a conundrum. Was I ambivalent? Yes ... and no. My couplet drawn from poker encapsulates this dilemma:

> Question is, should I remain
>
> Or stay and risk a Biplane?

I couldn't wait until all the frickin'-nomics information was known, or until the last card was dealt. In addition, this situation was almost identical to when I was getting killed in a poker session. One'd almost rather plunge further and further down and risk *auguring* into the desert floor (Tom Wolfe in *The Right Stuff*) with the hopes of pulling out of a nosedive. So rather than jettison one's losses and bail out, one gambled on a three outer, a long shot. To cite Caro, I'd crossed my threshold of pain. Crossing this Rubicon in poker usually means way more losses; crossing it in life can lead to self-destruction.

$$\$\$\$$$

I didn't create options in case of failure. Failing to plan is planning to fail. Perhaps I should've set a stop-loss amount for our venture; however, what would lead you to believe that I'd utilize this astute strategy when I'd had spotty results with it in poker and the stock market? Shoulda, coulda, woulda. Concerning a final decision to try and sell my interest to the others for whatever I could recoup or stay the course. It was like a Hobson's choice. I kept kicking the can down the road; rather, I was booting a live grenade down the barracks floor. (That is a whole platoon of mixed metaphors.) I didn't heed the advice, Never put off until tomorrow what you can dildo, do, today. Naturally, this is riff on procrastinator's motto, Never do today what you can put off till tomorrow.

Eventually I shook off indecision, took out a second and eventually a third home mortgage. Regarding my total, annual income, it radically bounced around like what Melville described in *Moby Dick* as a Nantucket sleigh ride. Sometimes I got violently whaled on. Consequently, a NINJA loan—remember, No Income, No Job, no Assets—was exactly what I needed, and they were extraordinarily easy to come by.

Roughly 95 percent of new businesses fail. But meanwhile everyone who invested in Tony's company missed the Cheyne-Stokes, death throes' signs of our venture. Be that as it may, as the years passed, the economy's trajectory trended farther and farther downward. Like the turn of a card, business fortunes could depend upon trends and conditions. Like all cycles, the economy would improve somewhat, and we'd get a glimmer of hope. In stock market speak, there'd be a *dead cat bounce* which is a small, brief recovery in the price of a declining stock so called because even a dead cat will bounce if it falls far enough. Vonnegut's Tralfamadorians would say "So it goes." 💀.

I was in incredibly bad shape and at the precipice. With cerebral astigmatism, here's where I stood, or more accurately, lay: Maxed out on all my credit cards and had big debts to creditors and friends. I had pathetically and feebly approached Ahmed, Virge and his wife, my video accounts' owners, and other acquaintances. It was so true what Ambrose Bierce penned: "An acquaintance is a person whom we know well enough to borrow from but not well enough to lend to." However, most depressingly and embarrassingly I went hat in hand to my ex, Janelle. And her family. I was underwater on my home and had a crushing balloon payment coming due in six months. I needed a stroke of luck, a miracle or divine intervention to survive. Would fortune favor the bold? Or would fortune dildo the bold? I was almost thinking I needed to kiss a flock of ducks, but not seagulls.

$$$

Many look back and ask what might have been. Cole Porter's "Begin the Beguine" brilliantly summed this: "And now when I hear people curse the chance that was wasted, I know but too well what they mean." Also, John Greenleaf Whittier's *Maud Muller* sublimely expressed:

And pity us all

Who vainly the dreams of youth recall,

For of all sad words of tongue or pen

The saddest are these: "It might have been!"

However, I don't. As paradoxically pleasurable as it is to sink into the poor me mire and wallow there, I didn't want to revel in the luxuriant, soft pain of self-pity and sorrow. This is medically known as algedonic that's characterized by pain and especially associated with pleasure. Reliving bad beats is a relevant example. Søren Kierkegaard writes in *Sickness unto Death*: "Ah, demoniac madness! He rages most of all at the thought that eternity might get it into its [The Helper's] head to take his misery from him!"

Here are some homilies to portray my situation. I made my bed, and I have to sleep in it and take my medicine. Correspondingly, I placed my bet. The ball was sent inexorably spinning like a dildo in motion.

Although Camus, ever jocular, wrote "There is no fate that cannot be surmounted by scorn," now the outcome was out of my hands and in the hand of inscrutable Fate. Ironically, was it my fate not to believe in it? I jest. The cards were dealt; I played the hand I was dealt in life; I'll reap what I dildo; the die was cast; and I cast my dildo to the wind. That's okay. As an Existentialist, I accept total accountability. The *Why me* affliction is just as equally countered by a force, *Why not you, citizen?* Besides, one cannot change the past. That's the way the dildo crumbles. Instead of *déjà vu*—that in some ways is a time machine—I wished I had what I'll call *futur vu* (probably improper French), the ability to see the future. Clairvoyance. What would happen to me?

→ (back to present)

Alas, that's why I sold much of my liquid assets and stuff, begged, borrowed, sold percentages of my possible payout, and scraped together enough money to enter this big buy in poker tournament. I went all in. This was for all the didoes, marbles. That's where I am now, awaiting fate's knock. My blind destiny is in the hands of my opponent. Due to the top-heavy tournament payout structure, I must win the tourney to save my home, for second place prize money isn't enough. My mouth feels like I'd chewed acid-soaked sandpaper leaving the palpable, dry-sour taste of terror. My heartrate skyrockets, and I think that I can hear my pulse. I try to breathe deeply, but as normally as possible, to mask possible tells. *Think confident thoughts and send out those strong hand vibes ...*

Ms. Fortune, the dealer, gathers my tournament checks, and she repeats, "He's all in."

My worthy opponent, J. O., shrewdly asks, "What's the count, dealer?" This buys J. O. more time to decide.

After about a minute, Ms. Fortune says, "About $14 million, give or take."

My adversary goes into the (think) tank, analyzing the data: Calculating my range of starting hands; each step of the betting rounds; my betting and reactions to her actions; the percentage that I might be bluffing since there was a draw on the board; what I may think she reads;

and how I think she will respond. I hope, no, I pray my bet isn't called. If my enemy calls, I'll lose the championship, but more importantly the first-place money. I *must* think happy thoughts. Exude confidence or, at worst, indifference. Hold on. Is indifference a tell?

I desperately try to remain calm, Zen-like despite cat calls and zingers from the audience in the gallery. Although not of one mind, the observers are similar to a Greek chorus. They wail out exhortations and admonitions such as: "Beat the plick, J. O."

"Shut up, you yak-off."

"I'm for MOOL boy."

"You a penie," followed by laughter like the polite tittering at a funeral. "Come on, Jimmers."

I avoid acknowledging my detractors or supporters. I almost get the fantods. I concentrate fully to keep from smiling. I can hear the blood thrumming in my ear drums; I feel my heart pounding like a bass guitar.

The tournament director, Tonopah Tony, the dismal, saturnine-out-look Floor man from my Gardenia days, politely asks the crowd to refrain from shouting or encouraging their horse. "Please ladies and gentlemen—"

Someone shouts out, "Nigh-*ROBE*-ay!" Everyone laughs.

Tony, like a long-suffering sub teacher, smiles and continues, "Please. No taunting or yelling. Otherwise, security will escort you out. And they can, and probably will, be rough." He wants the gallery to be still. Still is where I am. I pray, *really* pray. *Please make her fold. I'll cash this tourney win, pay my debts and never play again!*

$$\$ \$ \$$$

Wait!!! J. O. is standing up, and it looks like she's going to announce her decision. Oh, God, *please* let my attempted Melba cracker masterstroke work and make her fold.

Whilst her calling or folding decision is mostly monetary for J. O., it's momentous for me. She contemplates. *I don't think he's bluffing me … But he may've tried to get into my head and know that I'd think that … So, he may be counting on my folding … So … I guess I should do opposite …* She exhales a long sigh [whewww] and says with resignation, "I don't think you'd Melba cracker me, Indian, but I call."

A queasy wave of seasickness nausea comes over me, and all my tension evaporates like my hopeless wishes. The Tournament Director announces to the crowd, "J. O., Mrs. Janey Offenbach, calls."

Since J. O. and I have about the same amount of chips, this hand's winner almost certainly wins the tournament. Like awaiting a capital verdict, she asks, "What you got?"

"Yao. Yao Ming! I—I-aye-yai-yai got *nada* …" By rule the dealer turns both our hands up. I numbly and despondently watch my chips along with my dreams of salvation being shoved toward JO. "Coc-coc-cocktails! I need a double Drambuie. And make it arseniously!!"

One of my backers lets out, "EYEYEEE!"

EPILOGUE

THIS BEGAN WITH A parable: There ain't no free lunch. To anyone thinking of making an easy living in high-risk professions like short-term, especially day, trading (in commodities, stocks, options, or whatever); real estate speculating (flipping); and cryptocurrencies' speculating though profits may be hacked. Let this morality play about JM's journey and swan song be a cautionary tale. I thought winning money at poker was like getting something for nothing. However, that lifestyle exacted an incredibly high cost; that is, spending massive energy, focus and hours gambling interfered with a career, productive achievements, successfully forming relationships and or causing their doom too soon. ☠. All that exploring and hoping to get free money, free rides and a free lunch doomed me. It's impossible to get something for nothing, and choices have costs. *Now* I tell me!

Try to foresee and avoid dead-end choices and paths, especially if they have lots of cavernous potholes, but be at peace with your unalterable choices. Embrace the koan, "Let her go," which is like forgive and forget. Forgiveness is one of the most potent and valuable acts you can do for yourself. Believing superstition, fate and the grass is always greener on the other side are useless, actually harmful by blaming outside influences instead of commanding your own destiny.

When life hands you *wrathful*, sour grapes, make grape juice. Don't drink while intoxicated; don't smoke while immolated; avoid drugs; mask up and wash your hands; stay in school. Life can be like a game, so play your best. And before playing, stretch your body not the truth.

In some situations, life can seem to flit by like the blink of an eye. I say life at the end can seem like time roaring out of a mind shaft. If so, who can dispute that our hero, John Maynard, JM, may have relived his past in minutes? For those criticizing the lack of a plot, I don't need no stinkin' plot. I plan to be cremated.

This allegorical book's messages, depicted by JM's crash, may be weakened by this: In real life I finally learned to quit ahead, for I quit playing; also, by definition, I quit at peak and transcended poker.

Afterword on Wasting One's Gifts

Like "Math" Drew and Clyde, I too regret not utilizing whatever talents I was born with. Don't we all wish we'd done more in life? When my corporate career seemed to be stalled, I'd become totally disillusioned. Or as I worked more poker hours and that lifestyle was in the tank, I'd sing to myself the Platters' tune "Smokes in Your Eyes." And since I have a tin ear, when I sing it rings hollow:

> They asked me how I knew
>
> My career was through ...
>
> Oh. Oh. When the gorgeous pot dies, (☠.)
>
> You must realize,
>
> Smoke tears up your eyes.

When things were bleak, I'd fantasize about writing a book. I don't recall when I developed writing aspirations (or asphyxiations) but stalling and avoiding writing one haunted me like a ghostly, pathological stalker. There were some major impediments to achieving this dream.

1. Biggest blockades reside in the amygdala, an almond-shaped mass of gray matter that's the center of emotions, and they involve anxiety caused by anticipation of some imagined event or experience; the unknown; possible disappointment with success. In an almond nutshell, anxiety attached to an expectation. I understood that we create our own realities. More succinctly, the block was FEAR: Future Events (variation, False Evidence) Appearing Real. Fear of a bad outcome, failure, rejection. Similarly, worry

is a waste of imagination. I encountered the soul sapping terror that if I ever wrote something, it wouldn't be good enough to be published. We can live our lives looking through the windshield or rear window.

2. Another hindrance was that this project felt overwhelming, gargantuan, ginormous, Herculean and humongous. Big assed. Writing a book seemed like wanting to climb Mt. Everest: Insurmountable, a perfect adjective. I envisioned all the preparation beforehand, the time and energy of planning, and the mountain range of costs. Moreover, I had to get in country, climb to the base camp, spend two+ months acclimating, etc. Considering and foreseeing all the potential difficulties, not the least of which was just breathing, I then realized that there was no certainty of successfully summiting. Additionally, this assumes that one has the health, time, and money. It's impossible! I thought. I failed to embrace Confucius" writing that a journey of a thousand miles begins with the first step.

3. The last hurdle, a kind of writer's block—blocking me like a forty-ton boulder on Glacier National Park's Going to the Sun Highway— found me comparing myself to others. Forget about past greats like Shakespeare, Milton, Poe, Melville. I read modern authors like Thomas Pynchon, Tom Wolfe, Jonathan Franzen, Neal Stephenson, David Foster Wallace, et al.; thus, I despaired of even considering myself in their company, or readers whispering my name in the same breath.

This passage from Henry Miller's *Tropic of Capricorn* captures Miller's brilliance:

> But I saw a street called Myrtle Avenue, which runs from Borough Hall to Fresh Pond Road, and down this street no saint ever walked... down this street no miracle ever passed, nor any poet, not any species of human genius, nor did any flower ever grow there, nor did the sun strike it squarely, nor did the rain ever wash it... Dear reader you must see Myrtle Avenue before you die, if only to realize how far into the future

Dante saw. You must believe me that on the street, neither in the houses which line it, not the cobblestones which pave it, not the elevated structure which cuts it atwain, neither in any creature that bears a name and lives therein, neither in any animal, bird or insect passing through it to slaughter or already slaughtered, is there hope of "lubet," "sublimate" or "abominate." It is a street not of sorrow, for sorrow would be human and recognizable, but of sheer emptiness: it is emptier than the most extinct volcano, emptier than a vacuum, emptier than the word God in the mouth of an unbeliever.

This passage called to mind Gardenia's mean streets early in the morning. And when low, it embodied the emptiness I felt. I inhabited Myrtle Avenue, and I subsisted in the inevitable eyesore, tear down house that every neighborhood has. Not even dark matter surrounded me in my vacuum. After trying to absorb Miller's writing, I further lamented ever being worthy. Countless wannabees, dilettantes, and even beat writers, teachers, and professors already employed writing, pined to be published writers. How was I different? What the hell. To write that good (I know improper, lol)? Gimme a break. I might be delusional.

APPENDIX

*1, chapter 27

Alan Krigman. Source: http://krigman.casinocitytimes.com/ 12.16.2001. You can determine the seed for a progressive jackpot from the amount reset after a hit. But the important elements, the piece of what's wagered that's added to the jackpot and the chance of winning part or all of the total, are ordinarily kept secret. You can even find the crossover where the casino makes more than the winning player. The results help show why gambling halls are rarely confused with charitable trusts.

*2, chapter 35

The following isn't my complete, ten-page, profile card on Kelly, but for visualization. Abbreviations" explanations in brackets. Physical description at top was to help me remember, in early interactions, a non-regular player or someone whose name I forgot:

BC [Bicycle Club] $75-150 RBL [↑ <raise> blind Lowball—the 1st and 2nd must ↑. 1989-96] Kelly, KO Bald center Usu. [usually] gold glasses; grey beard. Quiet, cerebral

Very tight. No on-the-come action. Mixes Level I & II [Level I is action opposite to reality—weak is strong. Level II is act = truth. II is = changing gears], so pl. [play] him like he's a computer using g [game] theory.

Highly unlikely he'd b [bluff] me, for he knows I'll call weak. Also, rarely b.s. others either. On other h. [hand], he's seen me b & caught me enuf that refrain from b'ing him. Don't give him more $.

TELL: When bet sloppily, had 6 low [very strong Low h] Tilt very rare

*3, chapter 37

Circa 1984-2010 two groups beat MI and MA lotteries for at least $7.75 million by hard, analytic work finding and exploiting a flaw in the roll-down feature, but that's another book. One retired math whiz said, "It was like free money." https://highline.huffingtonpost.com/articles/en/lotto-winners/#nws=mcnewsletter. This is part of the free lunch bunch's desire.

*4, chapter 38

Earliest to latest, singers or cultural icons who died at twenty-seven years old: James Dean, Brian Jones, Jimi Hendrix, Janis Joplin, Jim Morrison, Kurt Cobain. Amy Winehouse is from a more recent generation.

*5, chapter 43

Muffled neighbor is actor practicing Hamlet's soliloquy, undisputedly the most famous in English literature:

> To be, or not to be—that is the question:
>
> Whether 'tis nobler in the mind to suffer
>
> The slings and arrows of outrageous fortune
>
> Or to take arms against a sea of troubles
>
> And by opposing end them. To die, to sleep—
>
> No more—and by a sleep to say we end
>
> The heartache, and the thousand natural shocks
>
> That flesh is heir to. 'Tis a consummation
>
> Devoutly to be wished. To die, to sleep—
>
> To sleep—perchance to dream: ay, there's the rub,
>
> For in that sleep of death what dreams may come.

ABOUT THE AUTHOR

Bruce "Mr. Mellow" Brown grew up in ... shall we just say he grew up. He proudly served our country during the Vietnam era for four years as a Corpsman in the Navy where every day was a holiday and every meal a feast. Then he got his BA in Economics and earned a fellowship to, and graduated from, USC's MBA program. For a while, poker was his sole source of income, even working a few months as a cardroom, shill-like prop or "host;" however, mostly he worked in the stuff shirt and tie economy. Eventually, he started his own businesses—a video company and ended in real estate. Throughout his life he competed playing poker a few times a week at night, and he had forty-one years of profitably playing poker, what he viewed as a side hustle. He's played against a blind man, a one-legged woman, Dr. Jerry Buss and Maverick, Bart (TV's Jack Kelly), not Pete Mitchell (Tom Cruise).

His other jobs were human test subject, strawberry farm roadside sales, park maintenance worker, helping owners with SBA loan applications, health center consultant and chief administrator for a medical center. Checkered or what?

The author strongly wanted to share his life lessons that he learned from observing the gambling milieu regarding lifestyle, high risk jobs and investing. In essence, the pros and big cons of gambling. Altruistically he hopes to save some reader's the anguish of turning like a Jedi to the dark side of gambling.

Happily divorced, his marriage produced two fine young men who by job diaspora are beyond their childhood home in Manhattan Beach, CA.